# DARK TWAIN

A Compendium of

# ODDITIES,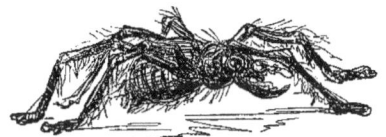

# NIGHTMARES

# & WONDERMENTS

Compiled and Edited by Stephen H. Provost

# MARK TWAIN

©2025 Stephen H. Provost
Dragon Crown Books 2025
All rights reserved.
ISBN: 978-1-949971-77-4

"MARK TWAIN"

*"Every one is a moon, and has a dark side which he never shows to anybody."*

*Mark Twain*

Pudd'nhead Wilson's New Calendar

# MARK TWAIN

# Contents

# Prefatory.

Mark Twain was a complex man; one need look no further than his two names to ascertain this. His birth name, Samuel Langhorne Clemens, is the sort of name one might imagine for a Southern plantation owner. His chosen *nom de plum*, on the other hand, was rough and straight to the point: the kind that one might expect of a dockworker or someone you'd meet in a saloon.

Twain did, in fact, spend much of his time at drinking establishments during his youth, and one story even suggests he discovered his name there: He would ask the barkeep to run a tab on a chalkboard, with the second mark being the "mark twain."

Twain himself asserted that the name was inspired by his time on Mississippi riverboat, where he would "mark twain" when calling out depths. There is, however, at least one hole in this explanation: concerning his statement that he took the name from another writer who had died and was no longer using it. A look at the calendar, however, betrays that Clemens began calling himself "Mark Twain" a year before the other man died!

Twain was, of course, known to bend the truth—or invent it—on numerous occasions. It was in his makeup as a storyteller to do so. He had a love-hate relationship with the truth.

"If I tell you the truth, you don't have to remember a thing," he asserted.

But while he extolled the virtue of truth, he doubted its efficacy. Lies, he suggested, were far more effective.

"I never could tell a lie that anyone would doubt," he once lamented, "nor a truth that anybody would believe."

Twain wrote both fiction and factual narratives, but much of his work straddled the line between them. More interesting still is the way he wove fact and fancy together, beginning with his time as a journalist for the *Territorial Enterprise* in Virginia City, Nevada. He wrote factual accounts, but sometimes embellished them for the sake of readability, and these appeared alongside works of pure imagination designed to entertain and, on occasion, convey some moral via satire.

As an author, he told stories that were demonstrably true, yet even more unbelievable (and on occasion horrific) than anything in the adventures of Tom Saywer or that Connecticut Yankee.

Was Twain a horror writer?

Perhaps not by today's standards. He did not write stories for the purpose of titillating his readers with shock and gore. He was, however, a *dark* writer, inviting his audience to pull back the curtain on their own fears and foibles, and to confront the hard truths of the world we live in. He wrote of ghosts and regrets, of death and devils, of nature's harsh rebukes and mankind's terrible cruelty. There was a price to be paid for folly, greed, bullying, and wantonness, but that price was not the same for everyone and, and there were those who fiendishly forced their own debt upon others.

This is the stuff of horror.

Twain would have certainly been unimpressed with jump scares at modern horror movies. Momentary horror was nothing to him compared with terror cruelly stretched out all the way from one end of a person's life to another. A flash of fright paled next to a prolonged state of torture.

As he wrote of the French Revolution:

"There were two 'Reigns of Terror,' if we would but remember it and consider it: the one wrought murder in hot passion, the other in heartless cold blood. The one lasted mere months, the other had lasted a thousand years. The one inflicted death upon ten thousand persons, the other upon a hundred millions. But our shudders are all for the 'horrors' of the minor Terror, the momentary Terror, so to speak; whereas, what is the horror of swift death by the axe, compared with lifelong death from hunger, cold, insult, cruelty, and heartbreak?

"What is swift death by lightning compared with death by slow fire at the stake? A city cemetery could contain the coffins filled by that brief Terror which we have all been so diligently taught to shiver at and mourn over; but all France could hardly contain the coffins filled by that older and real Terror—that unspeakably bitter and awful Terror which none of us has been taught to see in its vastness or pity as it deserves."

Twain demanded that we take such a view. But he also recognized that the ramifications of doing so were so terrifying that they couldn't simply be laid bare without a spoonful of sugar to help ease the way for his medicine. He frequently couched his horrors in dark and biting humor—so successfully that he was known first and foremost for his wit. The "joshing" intended to soften the blow. Twain (whose first pen name was actually "Josh") knew well that humor is not born out of laughter, but of sorrow. Once the laughter is stripped away, all one is left with are stark and chilling truths:

- We are at the mercy of the natural world—and the scoundrel.
- Death awaits us all, and before we get there, if we're lucky, we become diseased, enfeebled, forgetful, and forced to face the fact that we can no longer do the things that once came so naturally.
- The loss we suffer when we lose a loved one can test our endurance just as surely as a medieval torture session.
- We do not know what awaits us beyond the grave, and in our fear of this unknown, we mortgage our souls to con men who pretended to know the truth:

"In religion and politics people's beliefs and convictions are in almost every case gotten at second-hand, and without examination, from authorities who have not themselves examined the questions at issue but have taken them at second-hand from other non-examiners, whose opinions about them were not worth a brass farthing."

Those who dare to think for themselves find themselves imprisoned in a world dominated by two other classes of people: The willfully ignorant who make up stories to support their own ambitions, and the willfully ignorant who believe these stories—to their own disadvantage—to appease their own laziness and insecurities.

Twain himself was insecure, as is clear from his own musings. He loved receiving affirmation, but he did not regard himself as brilliant. "My works," he stated, "are like water. The works of the great geniuses are like wine. But everyone drinks water."

Twain used horror as provocation. The most famous, and gruesome example of true horror in his catalogue might well be his fictional account of a bloody massacre in Empire City, Nevada. It was meant to lay bare financial shenanigans of the San Francisco Water Company, but he was so effective in setting forth a chilling story that most people who read it didn't even get to the punchline: the moral of the story.

Twain expressed sympathy for the devil long before the Rolling Stones made it fashionable. He said he'd rather laugh with his friends in hell than cry with heaven-bound hypocrites, foreshadowing Billy Joel's hit song "Only the Good Die Young." It was the kind of statement of which Twain would have approved.

He felt sorry for ghosts, and for skeletons forced to leave their graves because the living had neglected them so badly they were no longer habitable. Animal cruelty was answered with nature's wrath in his fiction. Yet he recognized that the truth was often more terrifying than anything he could cull from his fertile imagination: "Truth is stranger than fiction," he said, "but it is because fiction is obliged to stick to possibilities. Truth isn't."

**My own interest in Twain** began in earnest when my wife, Sharon, suggested that I write a book about him to coincide with Mark Twain Days here in Carson City and Virginia City, Nevada. It resulted in the book *Mark Twain's Nevada*, which was followed by further titles touching on his life: *The Comstock Chronicles* and the children's book *The Adventures of Mark Twain in Nevada*.

The more I read about and by Twain, the more my interest grew to become admiration—and fascination. I felt a certain kinship with the man who worked as a journalist before becoming an author, as I have, and who took joy in—and inspiration from—his many travels.

"Travel," he wrote in his *Innocents Abroad*, "is fatal to prejudice, bigotry, and narrow-mindedness, and many of our people need it sorely on these accounts. Broad, wholesome, charitable views of men and things cannot be acquired by vegetating in one little corner of the earth all one's lifetime."

I heartily concur.

Like most authors, Twain delighted in proposing answers to "what if" questions.

What if you could ride on a comet?

What if someone had a sense of smell like a bloodhound?

What if we lived in a world trapped under a microscope?

Taking a cue from Twain himself, I started wondering how the man would have reacted in situations beyond the normal plane of our existence, and I began inserting him as a character into works of historical fiction. Alternative histories. It began with my short story "Messenger Boy," in which I imagined what it would have been like if Twain had returned to Nevada in the early 20th century and crossed paths with a young bicycle delivery boy named Jim Casey in Goldfield on the occasion of a lightweight championship fight between Joe Gans and Battling Nelson. The fight, and Casey's presence in Goldfield at the time, were matters of historical record; Twain was never there, which is the point at which the history became alternative. (Casey would leave Goldfield for Seattle, where he founded the company that became United Parcel Service.)

I later included Twain as an important character in two

novels. *Meteor Ridge* asked what happened to all those famous people who have vanished without a trace, and what would happen if they were given the chance to live forever—as long as they remained within the strict confines of a single valley. In *Evermore: Dark Soulmates*, written with Sharon, I ask what might have happened if Twain had interviewed Julia Bulette's killer before his execution (which Twain covered for the *Chicago Republican*), and found there was something unusual about both the murderer and his victim.

This present work is another departure: It's a collection of Twain's own writings that delve into the dark side of his creative muse. I took great care in choosing and compiling these stories, which are in the public domain, from a variety of sources, including factual accounts and tall tales from his book on travels on the Western frontier (especially Nevada, as related in his book *Roughing It*).

Twain left unfinished some stories I have chosen for inclusion here, and I have done my best to render them suitably satisfying. In one case, that of "Schoolhouse Hill," I supplied a conclusion of my own, not presuming to write "as" Twain, but instead inventing a character of my own to create the exposition I felt was needed to make the story feel complete. From my own familiarity with Twain's work, I feel confident that it wraps things up in a way consistent with the foregoing narrative—and with his other writings.

Another unfinished Twain story, "The Great Dark," exists in the form of an unfinished novel. I condensed the story somewhat to fit within the format of a short-story collection and provided some information at the end of the story explaining how Twain had intended to finish it, based on his notes.

Other editorial changes consist mostly of minor updates in

punctuation and spelling, though I have shortened a couple of his longer works. I also have, on occasion, removed or greatly curtailed (and softened) sections containing racial or ethnic stereotypes that are likely to offend modern readers. None of the text I excised was essential to any of the stories, and I would prefer readers not to get waylaid from enjoying the writer's genius by outdated/offensive wording.

I have chosen a variety of stories, addressing such themes as clairvoyance, superhuman abilities, tragedies, the paranormal, the wrath of nature, and philosophical debates with the devil (and his son). I have also included poetry alongside the fiction and Twain's firsthand experiences, in the same manner as I did with my own *Nightmare's Eve* collection.

There is more to Mark Twain than meets the eye, and exploring his dark side can be both sobering and unnerving. I hope you enjoy "Dark Twain."

*—Stephen H. Provost*
*Oct. 2, 2025*

# Death in the Moonlight

In our house, there was a sort of family prejudice against going fishing if you hadn't permission. But it would frequently be bad judgment to ask. So I went fishing secretly, as it were— way up the Mississippi. It was an exquisitely happy trip, I recall, with a very pleasant sensation.

Well, while I was away there was a tragedy in our town. A stranger, stopping over on his way East from California; was stabbed to death in an unseemly brawl.

Now, my father was justice of the peace, and because he was justice of the peace he was coroner; and since he was coroner he was also constable; and being constable he was sheriff; and out of consideration for his holding the office of sheriff he was likewise county clerk and a dozen other officials I don't think of just this minute.

I thought he had power of life or death, only he didn't use it over other boys. He was sort of an austere man. Somehow I didn't like being round him when I'd done anything he disapproved of. So that's the reason I wasn't often around.

Well, when this gentleman got knifed, they communicated with the proper authority, the coroner, and they laid the corpse out in the coroner's office—our front sitting-room—in preparation for the inquest the next morning.

About 9 or 10 o'clock I got back from fishing. It was a little too late for me to be received by my folks, so I took my shoes off and slipped noiselessly up the back way to the sitting-room. I was very tired, and I didn't wish to disturb my people. So I groped my way to the sofa and lay down.

Now, I didn't know anything of what had happened during my absence. But I was sort of nervous on my own account— afraid of being caught, and rather dubious about the morning affair. And I had been lying there a few moments when my eyes gradually got used to the darkness, and I became aware of something on the other side of the room.

It was something foreign to the apartment. It had an uncanny appearance. And I sat up looking very hard, and wondering what in heaven this long, formless, vicious-looking thing might be.

First I thought I'd go and see. Then I thought, "Never mind that."

Mind you, I had no cowardly sensations whatever, but it didn't seem exactly prudent to investigate. But I somehow couldn't keep my eyes off the thing. And the more I looked at it, the more disagreeably it grew on me. But I was resolved to play the man. So I decided to turn over and count a hundred, and let the patch of moonlight creep up and show me what the dickens it was.

I turned over and tried to count, but I couldn't keep my mind on it. I kept thinking of that gruesome mass. I was losing count all the time, and going back and beginning over again. Oh no; I wasn't frightened—just annoyed. But by the time I'd gotten to the century mark, I turned cautiously over and opened my eyes with great fortitude.

The moonlight revealed to me a marble-white human hand. Well, maybe I wasn't embarrassed! But then that changed to a creepy feeling again, and I thought I'd try the counting again. I don't know how many hours or weeks it was that I lay there counting hard. But the moonlight crept up that white arm, and it showed me a lead face and a terrible wound over the heart.

I could scarcely say that I was terror-stricken or anything like that. But somehow his eyes interested me so that I went right out of the window. I didn't need the sash. But it seemed easier to take it than leave it behind.

Now, let that teach you a lesson—I don't know just what it is. But at seventy years old, I find that memory of peculiar value to me. I have been unconsciously guided by it all these years. Things that seemed pigeonholed and remote are a perpetual influence. Yes, you're taught in so many ways. And you're so felicitously taught when you don't know it.

*"Death in the Moonlight" (title supplied by the editor) is an excerpt from Mark Twain's speech titled "Morals and Memory," delivered on March 7, 1906, at Columbia University.*

# The Mysterious Stranger

Marget announced a party, and invited forty people.

The guests arrived at noon and filled the place. Father Adolf followed; also, after a little, the astrologer, without invitation.

All the house made room for him; Marget politely seated him; Ursula ordered Gottfried to bring a special table for him. Then she decked it and furnished it, and asked for his orders.

"Bring me what you will," he said.

The two servants brought supplies from the pantry, together with white wine and red—a bottle of each. The astrologer, who very likely had never seen such delicacies before, poured out a beaker of red wine, drank it off, poured another, then began to eat with a grand appetite.

I was not expecting Satan, but now he came in—I knew it by the feel, though people were in the way and I could not see him. I heard him apologizing for intruding; and he was going away, but Marget urged him to stay, and he thanked her and stayed.

She brought him along, introducing him to the girls, and to Meidling, and to some of the elders; and there was quite a rustle of whispers:

"It's the young stranger we hear so much about and can't get sight of, he is away so much."

"Dear, dear, but he is beautiful—what is his name?"

"Philip Traum."

"Ah, it fits him!" (You see, "Traum" is German for "Dream.")

"What does he do?"

"Studying for the ministry, they say."

"His face is his fortune—he'll be a cardinal someday."

"Where is his home?"

"Away down somewhere in the tropics, they say he has a rich uncle down there." And so on.

He made his way at once; everybody was anxious to know him and talk with him. Everybody noticed how cool and fresh it was, all of a sudden, and wondered at it, for they could see that the sun was beating down the same as before, outside, and the sky was clear of clouds, but no one guessed the reason, of course.

The astrologer had drunk his second beaker; he poured out a third. He set the bottle down, and by accident overturned it. He seized it before much was spilled, and held it up to the light, saying, "What a pity—it is royal wine." Then his face lighted with joy or triumph, or something, and he said, "Quick! Bring a bowl."

It was brought—a four-quart one. He took up that two-pint bottle and began to pour; went on pouring, the red liquor gurgling and gushing into the white bowl and rising higher and higher up its sides, everybody staring and holding their breath—and presently the bowl was full to the brim.

"Look at the bottle," he said, holding it up; "it is full yet!"

I glanced at Satan, and in that moment he vanished.

Then Father Adolf rose up, flushed and excited, crossed himself, and began to thunder in his great voice, "This house is bewitched and accursed!" People began to cry and shriek and crowd toward the door. "I summon this household to..."

His words were cut off short. His face became red, then purple, but he could not utter another sound.

Then I saw Satan, a transparent film, melt into the astrologer's body; then the astrologer put up his hand, and apparently in his own voice said, "Wait. Remain where you are."

All stopped where they stood.

"Bring a funnel!"

Ursula brought it, trembling and scared, and he stuck it in the bottle and took up the great bowl and began to pour the wine back, the people gazing and dazed with astonishment, for they knew the bottle was already full before he began. He emptied the whole of the bowl into the bottle, then smiled out over the room, chuckled, and said, indifferently: "It is nothing. Anybody can do it! With my powers I can even do much more."

A frightened cry burst out everywhere. "Oh, my God, he is possessed!" and there was a tumultuous rush for the door which swiftly emptied the house of all who did not belong in it except us boys and Meidling. We boys knew the secret, and would have told it if we could, but we couldn't. We were very thankful to Satan for furnishing that good help at the needful time.

**Marget was pale**, and crying; Meidling looked kind of petrified; Ursula the same; but Gottfried was the worst—he couldn't stand, he was so weak and scared. For he was of a witch family, you know, and it would be bad for him to be suspected. Agnes came loafing in, looking pious and unaware, and wanted to rub up against Ursula and be petted, but Ursula was afraid of her and shrank away from her, but pretending she was not meaning any incivility, for she knew very well it wouldn't answer to have strained relations with that kind of a cat.

But we boys took Agnes and petted her, for Satan would not have befriended her if he had not had a good opinion of her, and that was endorsement enough for us. He seemed to trust anything that hadn't the Moral Sense.

Outside, the guests, panic-stricken, scattered in every direction and fled in a pitiable state of terror; and such a tumult as they made with their running and sobbing and shrieking and shouting that soon all the village came flocking from their houses to see what had happened, and they thronged the street and shouldered and jostled one another in excitement and fright. And then Father Adolf appeared, and they fell apart in two walls like the cloven Red Sea, and presently down this lane the astrologer came, striding and mumbling, and where he passed, the lanes surged back in packed masses, and fell silent with awe, and their eyes stared and their breasts heaved, and several women fainted; and when he was gone by the crowd swarmed together and followed him at a distance, talking excitedly and asking questions and finding out the facts.

Finding out the facts and passing them on to others, with improvements—improvements which soon enlarged the bowl of wine to a barrel, and made the one bottle hold it all and yet remain empty to the last.

When the astrologer reached the market square he went straight to a juggler, fantastically dressed, who was keeping three brass balls in the air, and took them from him and faced around upon the approaching crowd and said: "This poor clown is ignorant of his art. Come forward and see an expert perform."

18

So saying, he tossed the balls up one after another and set them whirling in a slender bright oval in the air, and added another, then another and another, and soon—no one seeing whence he got them—adding, adding, adding, the oval lengthening all the time, his hands moving so swiftly that they were just a web or a blur and not distinguishable as hands; and such as counted said there were now a hundred balls in the air.

The spinning great oval reached up twenty feet in the air and was a shining and glinting and wonderful sight. Then he folded his arms and told the balls to go on spinning without his help—and they did it.

After a couple of minutes, he said, "There, that will do," and the oval broke and came crashing down, and the balls scattered abroad and rolled every whither. And wherever one of them came, the people fell back in dread, and no one would touch it. It made him laugh, and he scoffed at the people and called them cowards and old women.

Then he turned and saw the tightrope, and said foolish people were daily wasting their money to see a clumsy and ignorant varlet degrade that beautiful art; now they should see the work of a master. With that he made a spring into the air and lit firm on his feet on the rope. Then he hopped the whole length of it back and forth on one foot, with his hands clasped over his eyes; and next he began to throw somersaults, both backward and forward, and threw twenty-seven.

The people murmured, for the astrologer was old, and always before had been halting of movement and at times even lame, but he was nimble enough now and went on with his antics in the liveliest manner.

Finally he sprang lightly down and walked away, and passed up the road and around the corner and disappeared. Then that great, pale, silent, solid crowd drew a deep breath and looked into one another's faces as if they said: "Was it real? Did you see it, or was it only I—and was I dreaming?" Then they broke into a low murmur of talking, and fell apart in couples, and moved toward their homes, still talking in that awed way, with faces close together and laying a hand on an arm and making other such gestures as people make when they have been deeply impressed by something.

**We boys followed behind our fathers**, and listened, catching all we could of what they said; and when they sat down in our house and continued their talk they still had us for company. They were in a sad mood, for it was certain, they said, that disaster for the village must follow this awful visitation of witches and devils. Then my father remembered that Father Adolf had been struck dumb at the moment of his denunciation.

"They have not ventured to lay their hands upon an anointed servant of God before," he said; "and how they could have dared it this time I cannot make out, for he wore his crucifix. Isn't it so?"

"Yes," said the others, "we saw it."

"It is serious, friends, it is very serious. Always before, we had a protection. It has failed."

The others shook, as with a sort of chill, and muttered those words over.

"It has failed."

"God has forsaken us."

"It is true," said Seppi Wohlmeyer's father. "There is nowhere to look for help."

"The people will realize this," said Nikolaus's father, the judge, "and despair will take away their courage and their energies. We have indeed fallen upon evil times."

He sighed, and Wohlmeyer said, in a troubled voice: "The report of it all will go about the country, and our village will be shunned as being under the displeasure of God. The Golden Stag will know hard times."

"True, neighbor," said my father; "all of us will suffer—all in repute, many in estate. And, good God!"

"What is it?"

"That can come—to finish us!"

"Name it... um Gottes Willen!"

"The Interdict!"

It smote like a thunderclap, and they were like to swoon with the terror of it. Then the dread of this calamity roused their energies, and they stopped brooding and began to consider ways to avert it. They discussed this, that, and the other way, and talked till the afternoon was far spent, then confessed that at present they could arrive at no decision. So they parted sorrowfully, with oppressed hearts which were filled with bodings.

While they were saying their parting words I slipped out and set my course for Marget's house to see what was happening there. I met many people, but none of them greeted me. It ought to have been surprising, but it was not, for they were so distraught with fear and dread that they were not in their right minds, I think; they were white and haggard, and walked like persons in a dream, their eyes open but seeing nothing, their lips moving but uttering nothing, and worriedly clasping and unclasping their hands without knowing it.

**At Marget's it was like a funeral**. She and Wilhelm sat together on the sofa, but said nothing, and not even holding hands. Both were steeped in gloom, and Marget's eyes were red from the crying she had been doing.

She said: "I have been begging him to go, and come no more, and so save himself alive. I cannot bear to be his murderer. This house is bewitched, and no inmate will escape the fire. But he will not go, and he will be lost with the rest."

Wilhelm said he would not go; if there was danger for her, his place was by her, and there he would remain. Then she began to cry again, and it was all so mournful that I wished I had stayed away.

There was a knock, now, and Satan came in, fresh and cheery and beautiful, and brought that winy atmosphere of his and changed the whole thing. He never said a word about what had been happening, nor about the awful fears which were freezing the blood in the hearts of the community, but began to talk and rattle on about all manner of gay and pleasant things; and next about music—an artful stroke which cleared away the remnant of Marget's depression and brought her spirits and her interests broad awake. She had not heard anyone talk so well and so knowingly on that subject before, and she was so uplifted by it and so charmed that what she was feeling lit up her face and came out in her words; and Wilhelm noticed it and did not look as pleased as he ought to have done. And next Satan branched off into poetry, and recited some, and did it well, and Marget was charmed again; and again Wilhelm was not as pleased as he ought to have been, and this time Marget noticed it and was remorseful.

**I fell asleep to pleasant music** that night—the patter of rain upon the panes and the dull growling of distant thunder. Away in the night Satan came and roused me and said: "Come with me. Where shall we go?"

"Anywhere—so it is with you."

Then there was a fierce glare of sunlight, and he said, "This is China."

That was a grand surprise, and made me sort of drunk with vanity and gladness to think I had come so far—so much, much farther than anybody else in our village, including Bartel Sperling, who had such a great opinion of his travels. We buzzed around over that empire for more than half an hour, and saw the whole of it. It was wonderful, the spectacles we saw; and some were beautiful, others too horrible to think. Finally we stopped flitting and lit.

We sat upon a mountain commanding a vast landscape of mountain-range and gorge and valley and plain and river, with cities and villages slumbering in the sunlight, and a glimpse of blue sea on the farther verge. It was a tranquil and dreamy picture, beautiful to the eye and restful to the spirit. If we could only make a change like that whenever we wanted to, the world would be easier to live in than it is, for change of scene shifts the mind's burdens to the other shoulder and banishes old, shopworn wearinesses from mind and body both.

We talked together, and I had the idea of trying to reform Satan and persuade him to lead a better life. I told him about all those things he had been doing, and begged him to be more considerate and stop making people unhappy. I said I knew he did not mean any harm, but that he ought to stop and consider the possible consequences of a thing before launching it in that impulsive and random way of his; then he would not make so much trouble. He was not hurt by this plain speech; he only looked amused and surprised, and said:

"What? I do random things? Indeed, I never do. I stop and consider possible consequences? Where is the need? I know what the consequences are going to be. Always."

"Oh, Satan, then how could you do these things?"

"Well, I will tell you, and you must understand if you can. You belong to a singular race. Every man is a suffering-machine and a happiness-machine combined. The two functions work together harmoniously, with a fine and delicate precision, on the give-and-take principle. For every happiness turned out in the one department, the other stands ready to modify it with a sorrow or a pain—maybe a dozen. In most cases the man's life is about equally divided between happiness and unhappiness. When this is not the case, the unhappiness predominates— always; never the other.

"Sometimes a man's make and disposition are such that his misery-machine is able to do nearly all the business. Such a man goes through life almost ignorant of what happiness is. Everything he touches, everything he does, brings a misfortune upon him. You have seen such people? To that kind of a person life is not an advantage, is it? It is only a disaster. Sometimes for an hour's happiness a man's machinery makes him pay years of misery. Don't you know that? It happens every now and then. I will give you a case or two presently. Now the people of your village are nothing to me—you know that, don't you?"

I did not like to speak out too flatly, so I said I had suspected it.

"Well, it is true that they are nothing to me. It is not possible that they should be. The difference between them and me is abysmal, immeasurable. They have no intellect."

"No intellect?"

"Nothing that resembles it. At a future time, I will examine what man calls his mind and give you the details of that chaos, then you will see and understand. Men have nothing in common with me—there is no point of contact; they have foolish little feelings and foolish little vanities and impertinences and ambitions; their foolish little life is but a laugh, a sigh, and extinction; and they have no sense. Only the Moral Sense.

"I will show you what I mean. Here is a red spider, not so big as a pin's head. Can you imagine an elephant being interested in him—caring whether he is happy or isn't, or whether he is wealthy or poor, or whether his sweetheart returns his love or not, or whether his mother is sick or well, or whether he is looked up to in society or not, or whether his enemies will smite him or his friends desert him, or whether his hopes will suffer blight or his political ambitions fail, or whether he shall die in the bosom of his family or neglected and despised in a foreign land? These things can never be important to the elephant; they are nothing to him; he cannot shrink his sympathies to the microscopic size of them. Man is to me as the red spider is to the elephant. The elephant has nothing against the spider—he cannot get down to that remote level.

"I have nothing against man. The elephant is indifferent; I am indifferent. The elephant would not take the trouble to do the spider an ill turn; if he took the notion he might do him a good turn, if it came in his way and cost nothing. I have done men good service, but no ill turns.

"The elephant lives a century, the red spider a day; in power, intellect, and dignity the one creature is separated from the other by a distance which is simply astronomical. Yet in these, as in all qualities, man is immeasurably further below me than is the wee spider below the elephant. Man's mind clumsily and tediously and laboriously patches little trivialities together and gets a result—such as it is. My mind creates! Do you get the force of that? Creates anything it desires—and in a moment. Creates without material. Creates fluids, solids, colors—anything, everything—out of the airy nothing which is called Thought. A man imagines a silk thread, imagines a machine to make it, imagines a picture, then by weeks of labor embroiders it on canvas with the thread. I think the whole thing, and in a moment it is before you—created.

"I think a poem, music, the record of a game of chess—anything—and it is there. This is the immortal mind: Nothing is beyond its reach. Nothing can obstruct my vision; the rocks are transparent to me, and darkness is daylight. I do not need to open a book; I take the whole of its contents into my mind at a single glance, through the cover; and in a million years I could not forget a single word of it, or its place in the volume. Nothing goes on in the skull of man, bird, fish, insect, or other creature which can be hidden from me. I pierce the learned man's brain with a single glance, and the treasures which cost him threescore years to accumulate are mine; he can forget, and he does forget, but I retain.

"Now, then, I perceive by your thoughts that you are understanding me fairly well. Let us proceed. Circumstances might so fall out that the elephant could like the spider—supposing he can see it—but he could not love it. His love is for his own kind—for his equals. An angel's love is sublime, adorable, divine, beyond the imagination of man—infinitely beyond it! But it is limited to his own august order. If it fell upon one of your race for only an instant, it would consume its object to ashes. No, we cannot love men, but we can be harmlessly indifferent to them; we can also like them, sometimes. I like you and the boys, I like Father Peter, and for your sakes I am doing all these things for the villagers."

He saw that I was thinking a sarcasm, and he explained his position.

"I have wrought well for the villagers, though it does not look like it on the surface. Your race never know good fortune from ill. They are always mistaking the one for the other. It is because they cannot see into the future. What I am doing for the villagers will bear good fruit some day; in some cases to themselves; in others, to unborn generations of men. No one will ever know that I was the cause, but it will be none the less true, for all that. Among you boys, you have a game: You stand a row of bricks on end a few inches apart; you push a brick, it knocks its neighbor over, the neighbor knocks over the next brick—and so on till all the row is prostrate. That is human life. A child's first act knocks over the initial brick, and the rest will follow inexorably. If you could see into the future, as I can, you would see everything that was going to happen to that creature; for nothing can change the order of its life after the first event has determined it. That is, nothing will change it, because each act unfailingly begets an act, that act begets another, and so on to the end, and the seer can look forward down the line and see just when each act is to have birth, from cradle to grave."

"Does God order the career?"

"Foreordain it? No. The man's circumstances and environment order it. His first act determines the second and all that follow after. But suppose, for argument's sake, that the man should skip one of these acts; an apparently trifling one, for instance; suppose that it had been appointed that on a certain day, at a certain hour and minute and second and fraction of a second he should go to the well, and he didn't go. That man's career would change utterly, from that moment; thence to the grave it would be wholly different from the career which his first act as a child had arranged for him. Indeed, it might be that if he had gone to the well he would have ended his career on a throne, and that omitting to do it would set him upon a career that would lead to beggary and a pauper's grave.

"For instance: if at any time—say in boyhood—Columbus had skipped the triflingest little link in the chain of acts projected and made inevitable by his first childish act, it would have changed his whole subsequent life, and he would have become a priest and died obscure in an Italian village, and America would not have been discovered for two centuries afterward. I know this. To skip any one of the billion acts in Columbus's chain would have wholly changed his life. I have examined his billions of possible careers, and in only one of them occurs the discovery of America. You people do not suspect that all of your acts are of one size and importance, but it is true; to snatch at an appointed fly is as big with fate for you as is any other appointed act—"

"As the conquering of a continent, for instance?"

"Yes. Now, then, no man ever does drop a link—the thing has never happened! Even when he is trying to make up his mind as to whether he will do a thing or not, that itself is a link, an act, and has its proper place in his chain; and when he finally decides an act, that also was the thing which he was absolutely certain to do. You see, now, that a man will never drop a link in his chain. He cannot. If he made up his mind to try, that project would itself be an unavoidable link—a thought bound to occur to him at that precise moment, and made certain by the first act of his babyhood."

It seemed so dismal!

"He is a prisoner for life," I said sorrowfully, "and cannot get free."

"No, of himself he cannot get away from the consequences of his first childish act. But I can free him."

I looked up wistfully.

"I have changed the careers of a number of your villagers."

I tried to thank him, but found it difficult, and let it drop.

"I shall make some other changes. You know that little Lisa Brandt?"

"Oh yes, everybody does. My mother says she is so sweet and so lovely that she is not like any other child. She says she will be the pride of the village when she grows up; and its idol, too, just as she is now."

"I shall change her future."

"Make it better?" I asked.

"Yes. And I will change the future of Nikolaus."

I was glad, this time, and said, "I don't need to ask about his case; you will be sure to do generously by him."

"It is my intention."

Straight off I was building that great future of Nicky's in my imagination, and had already made a renowned general of him and hofmeister at the court, when I noticed that Satan was

28

waiting for me to get ready to listen again. I was ashamed of having exposed my cheap imaginings to him, and was expecting some sarcasms, but it did not happen. He proceeded with his subject:

"Nicky's appointed life is sixty-two years."

"That's grand!" I said.

"Lisa's, thirty-six. But, as I told you, I shall change their lives and those ages. Two minutes and a quarter from now, Nikolaus will wake out of his sleep and find the rain blowing in. It was appointed that he should turn over and go to sleep again. But I have appointed that he shall get up and close the window first. That trifle will change his career entirely. He will rise in the morning two minutes later than the chain of his life had appointed him to rise. By consequence, thenceforth nothing will ever happen to him in accordance with the details of the old chain."

He took out his watch and sat looking at it a few moments, then said: "Nikolaus has risen to close the window. His life is changed, his new career has begun. There will be consequences."

It made me feel creepy; it was uncanny.

"But for this change, certain things would happen twelve days from now. For instance, Nikolaus would save Lisa from drowning. He would arrive on the scene at exactly the right moment—four minutes past ten, the long-ago appointed instant of time—and the water would be shoal, the achievement easy and certain. But he will arrive some seconds too late, now; Lisa will have struggled into deeper water. He will do his best, but both will drown."

"Oh, Satan! Oh, dear Satan!" I cried, with the tears rising in my eyes. "Save them! Don't let it happen. I can't bear to lose Nikolaus, he is my loving playmate and friend; and think of Lisa's poor mother!"

I clung to him and begged and pleaded, but he was not

moved. He made me sit down again, and told me I must hear him out.

"I have changed Nikolaus's life, and this has changed Lisa's. If I had not done this, Nikolaus would save Lisa, then he would catch cold from his drenching; one of your race's fantastic and desolating scarlet fevers would follow, with pathetic after-effects; for forty-six years he would lie in his bed a paralytic log, deaf, dumb, blind, and praying night and day for the blessed relief of death. Shall I change his life back?"

"Oh no! Oh, not for the world! In charity and pity leave it as it is."

"It is best so. I could not have changed any other link in his life and done him so good a service. He had a billion possible careers, but not one of them was worth living; they were charged full with miseries and disasters. But for my intervention he would do his brave deed twelve days from now—a deed begun and ended in six minutes—and get for all reward those forty-six years of sorrow and suffering I told you of. It is one of the cases I was thinking of a while ago when I said that sometimes an act which brings the actor an hour's happiness and self-satisfaction is paid for—or punished—by years of suffering."

I wondered what poor little Lisa's early death would save her from.

He answered the thought:

"From ten years of pain and slow recovery from an accident, and then from nineteen years' pollution, shame, depravity, crime, ending with death at the hands of the executioner. Twelve days hence she will die; her mother would save her life if she could. Am I not kinder than her mother?"

"Yes... oh, indeed yes; and wiser."

"Father Peter's case is coming on presently. He will be acquitted, through unassailable proofs of his innocence."

"Why, Satan, how can that be? Do you really think it?"

"Indeed, I know it. His good name will be restored, and the rest of his life will be happy."

"I can believe it. To restore his good name will have that effect."

"His happiness will not proceed from that cause. I shall change his life that day, for his good. He will never know his good name has been restored."

In my mind—and modestly—I asked for particulars, but Satan paid no attention to my thought. Next, my mind wandered to the astrologer, and I wondered where he might be.

"In the moon," said Satan, with a fleeting sound which I believed was a chuckle. "I've got him on the cold side of it, too. He doesn't know where he is, and is not having a pleasant time; still, it is good enough for him, a good place for his star studies. I shall need him presently; then I shall bring him back and possess him again. He has a long and cruel and odious life before him, but I will change that, for I have no feeling against him and am quite willing to do him a kindness. I think I shall get him burned."

He had such strange notions of kindness! But angels are made so, and do not know any better. Their ways are not like our ways; and, besides, human beings are nothing to them; they think they are only freaks. It seems to me odd that he should put the astrologer so far away; he could have dumped him in Germany just as well, where he would be handy.

"Far away?" said Satan. "To me no place is far away; distance does not exist for me. The sun is less than a hundred million miles from here, and the light that is falling upon us has taken eight minutes to come; but I can make that flight, or any other, in a fraction of time so minute that it cannot be measured by a watch. I have but to think the journey, and it is accomplished."

I held out my hand and said, "The light lies upon it; think it into a glass of wine, Satan."

He did it. I drank the wine.

"Break the glass," he said.

I broke it.

"There—you see it is real. The villagers thought the brass balls were magic stuff and as perishable as smoke. They were afraid to touch them. You are a curious lot, your race. But come along; I have business. I will put you to bed."

Said and done. Then he was gone; but his voice came back to me through the rain and darkness saying, "Yes, tell Seppi, but no other."

It was the answer to my thought.

**Sleep would not come**. It was not because I was proud of my travels and excited about having been around the big world to China, and feeling contemptuous of Bartel Sperling, "the traveler," as he called himself, and looked down upon us others because he had been to Vienna once and was the only Eseldorf boy who had made such a journey and seen the world's wonders. At another time that would have kept me awake, but it did not affect me now. No, my mind was filled with Nikolaus, my thoughts ran upon him only, and the good days we had seen together at romps and frolics in the woods and the fields and the river in the long summer days, and skating and sliding in the winter when our parents thought we were in school. And now he was going out of this young life, and the summers and winters would come and go, and we others would rove and play as before, but his place would be vacant; we should see him no more.

Tomorrow he would not suspect, but would be as he had always been, and it would shock me to hear him laugh, and see him do lightsome and frivolous things, for to me he would be a corpse, with waxen hands and dull eyes, and I should see the shroud around his face; and next day he would not suspect, nor the next, and all the time his handful of days would be wasting swiftly away and that awful thing coming nearer and nearer, his fate closing steadily around him and no one knowing it but Seppi and me.

Twelve days—only twelve days. It was awful to think of. I noticed that in my thoughts I was not calling him by his familiar names, Nick and Nicky, but was speaking of him by his full name, and reverently, as one speaks of the dead. Also, as incident after incident of our comradeship came thronging into my mind out of the past, I noticed that they were mainly cases where I had wronged him or hurt him, and they rebuked me and reproached me, and my heart was wrung with remorse, just as it is when we remember our unkindnesses to friends who have passed beyond the veil, and we wish we could have them back again, if only for a moment, so that we could go on our knees to them and say, "Have pity, and forgive."

Once when we were nine years old, he went a long errand of nearly two miles for the fruiterer, who gave him a splendid big apple for reward, and he was flying home with it, almost beside himself with astonishment and delight, and I met him, and he let me look at the apple, not thinking of treachery, and I ran off with it, eating it as I ran, he following me and begging; and when he overtook me, I offered him the core, which was all that was left; and I laughed. Then he turned away, crying, and said he had meant to give it to his little sister. That smote me, for she was slowly getting well of a sickness, and it would have been a proud moment for him, to see her joy and surprise and have her caresses. But I was ashamed to say I was ashamed, and only said something rude and mean, to pretend I did not care, and he made no reply in words, but there was a wounded look in his face as he turned away toward his home which rose before me many times in after years, in the night, and reproached me and made me ashamed again. It had grown dim in my mind, by and by, then it disappeared; but it was back now, and not dim.

Once at school, when we were eleven, I upset my ink and

spoiled four copy-books, and was in danger of severe punishment; but I put it upon him, and he got the whipping.

And only last year I had cheated him in a trade, giving him a large fishhook which was partly broken through for three small sound ones. The first fish he caught broke the hook, but he did not know I was blamable, and he refused to take back one of the small hooks which my conscience forced me to offer him, but said, "A trade is a trade; the hook was bad, but that was not your fault."

No, I could not sleep. These little, shabby wrongs upbraided me and tortured me, and with a pain much sharper than one feels when the wrongs have been done to the living. Nikolaus was living, but no matter; he was to me as one already dead. The wind was still moaning about the eaves, the rain still pattering upon the panes.

**In the morning** I sought out Seppi and told him. It was down by the river. His lips moved, but he did not say anything. He only looked dazed and stunned, and his face turned very white. He stood like that a few moments, the tears welling into his eyes, then he turned away and I locked my arm in his, and we walked along thinking, but not speaking. We crossed the bridge and wandered through the meadows and up among the hills and the woods, and at last the talk came and flowed freely, and it was all about Nikolaus and was a recalling of the life we had lived with him. And every now and then Seppi said, as if to himself:

"Twelve days! Less than twelve days."

We said we must be with him all the time; we must have all of him we could; the days were precious now. Yet we did not go to seek him. It would be like meeting the dead, and we were afraid. We did not say it, but that was what we were feeling. And so it gave us a shock when we turned a curve and came upon Nikolaus face to face. He shouted, gaily:

"Hi-hi! What is the matter? Have you seen a ghost?"

We couldn't speak, but there was no occasion; he was willing to talk for us all, for he had just seen Satan and was in high spirits about it. Satan had told him about our trip to China, and he had begged Satan to take him on a journey, and Satan had promised. It was to be a far journey, and wonderful and beautiful; and Nikolaus had begged him to take us, too, but he said no, he would take us some day, maybe, but not now. Satan would come for him on the 13th, and Nikolaus was already counting the hours, he was so impatient.

**That was the fatal day.** We were already counting the hours, too.

We wandered many a mile, always following paths which had been our favorites from the days when we were little, and always we talked about the old times. All the blitheness was with Nikolaus; we others could not shake off our depression. Our tone toward Nikolaus was so strangely gentle and tender and yearning that he noticed it, and was pleased; and we were constantly doing him deferential little offices of courtesy, and saying, "Wait, let me do that for you," and that pleased him, too. I gave him seven fishhooks—all I had—and made him take them; and Seppi gave him his new knife and a humming-top painted red and yellow—atonements for swindles practiced upon him formerly, as I learned later, and probably no longer remembered by Nikolaus now. These things touched him, and he could not have believed that we loved him so; and his pride in it and gratefulness for it cut us to the heart, we were so undeserving of them. When we parted at last, he was radiant, and said he had never had such a happy day.

As we walked along homeward, Seppi said, "We always prized him, but never so much as now, when we are going to lose him."

Next day and every day we spent all of our spare time with Nikolaus; and also added to it time which we (and he) stole from work and other duties, and this cost the three of us some sharp scoldings, and some threats of punishment. Every morning two of us woke with a start and a shudder, saying, as the days flew along, "Only ten days left;" "only nine days left;" "only eight;" "only seven." Always it was narrowing. Always Nikolaus was gay and happy, and always puzzled because we were not. He wore his invention to the bone trying to invent ways to cheer us up, but it was only a hollow success; he could see that our jollity had no heart in it, and that the laughs we broke into came up against some obstruction or other and suffered damage and decayed into a sigh. He tried to find out what the matter was, so that he could help us out of our trouble or make it lighter by sharing it with us; so we had to tell many lies to deceive him and appease him.

But the most distressing thing of all was that he was always making plans, and often they went beyond the 13th! Whenever that happened it made us groan in spirit. All his mind was fixed upon finding some way to conquer our depression and cheer us up; and at last, when he had but three days to live, he fell upon the right idea and was jubilant over it—a boys-and-girls' frolic and dance in the woods, up there where we first met Satan, and this was to occur on the 14th. It was ghastly, for that was his funeral day. We couldn't venture to protest; it would only have brought a "Why?" which we could not answer. He wanted us to help him invite his guests, and we did it—one can refuse nothing to a dying friend. But it was dreadful, for really we were inviting them to his funeral.

It was an awful eleven days; and yet, with a lifetime stretching back between today and then, they are still a grateful memory to me, and beautiful. In effect, they were days of companionship with one's sacred dead, and I have known no comradeship that was so close or so precious. We clung to the hours and the minutes, counting them as they wasted away, and parting with them with that pain and bereavement which a miser feels who sees his hoard filched from him coin by coin by robbers and is helpless to prevent it.

**When the evening of the last day came,** we stayed out too long; Seppi and I were in fault for that; we could not bear to part with Nikolaus; so it was very late when we left him at his door. We lingered near awhile, listening; and that happened which we were fearing. His father gave him the promised punishment, and we heard his shrieks. But we listened only a moment, then hurried away, remorseful for this thing which we had caused. And sorry for the father, too; our thought being, "If he only knew—if he only knew!"

In the morning, Nikolaus did not meet us at the appointed place, so we went to his home to see what the matter was. His mother said:

"His father is out of all patience with these goings-on, and will not have any more of it. Half the time when Nick is needed he is not to be found; then it turns out that he has been gadding around with you two. His father gave him a flogging last night. It always grieved me before, and many's the time I have begged him off and saved him, but this time he appealed to me in vain, for I was out of patience myself."

"I wish you had saved him just this one time," I said, my voice trembling a little; "it would ease a pain in your heart to remember it someday."

She was ironing at the time, and her back was partly toward me. She turned about with a startled or wondering look in her face and said, "What do you mean by that?"

I was not prepared, and didn't know anything to say; so it was awkward, for she kept looking at me; but Seppi was alert and spoke up:

"Why, of course it would be pleasant to remember, for the very reason we were out so late was that Nikolaus got to telling how good you are to him, and how he never got whipped when you were by to save him; and he was so full of it, and we were so full of the interest of it, that none of us noticed how late it was getting."

"Did he say that? Did he?" and she put her apron to her eyes.

"You can ask Theodor—he will tell you the same."

"It is a dear, good lad, my Nick," she said. "I am sorry I let him get whipped; I will never do it again. To think—all the time I was sitting here last night, fretting and angry at him, he was loving me and praising me! Dear, dear, if we could only know! Then we shouldn't ever go wrong; but we are only poor, dumb beasts groping around and making mistakes. I shan't ever think of last night without a pang."

She was like all the rest; it seemed as if nobody could open a mouth, in these wretched days, without saying something that made us shiver. They were "groping around," and did not know what true, sorrowfully true things they were saying by accident.

Seppi asked if Nikolaus might go out with us.

"I am sorry," she answered, "but he can't. To punish him further, his father doesn't allow him to go out of the house today."

We had a great hope! I saw it in Seppi's eyes. We thought, "If he cannot leave the house, he cannot be drowned." Seppi asked, to make sure:

"Must he stay in all day, or only the morning?"

"All day. It's such a pity, too; it's a beautiful day, and he is so unused to being shut up. But he is busy planning his party, and maybe that is company for him. I do hope he isn't too lonesome."

Seppi saw that in her eye which emboldened him to ask if we might go up and help him pass his time.

"And welcome!" she said, right heartily. "Now I call that real friendship, when you might be abroad in the fields and the woods, having a happy time. You are good boys, I'll allow that, though you don't always find satisfactory ways of improving it. Take these cakes—for yourselves—and give him this one, from his mother."

**The first thing we noticed** when we entered Nikolaus's room was the time—a quarter to 10. Could that be correct? Only such a few minutes to live! I felt a contraction at my heart. Nikolaus jumped up and gave us a glad welcome. He was in good spirits over his plannings for his party and had not been lonesome.

"Sit down," he said, "and look at what I've been doing. And I've finished a kite that you will say is a beauty. It's drying, in the kitchen; I'll fetch it."

He had been spending his penny savings in fanciful trifles of various kinds, to go as prizes in the games, and they were marshaled with fine and showy effect upon the table. He said:

"Examine them at your leisure while I get mother to touch up the kite with her iron if it isn't dry enough yet."

Then he tripped out and went clattering downstairs, whistling.

We did not look at the things; we couldn't take any interest in anything but the clock. We sat staring at it in silence, listening to the ticking, and every time the minute-hand jumped we nodded recognition—one minute fewer to cover in the race for life or for death.

Finally Seppi drew a deep breath and said: "Two minutes to ten. Seven minutes more and he will pass the death point. Theodor, he is going to be saved! He's going to—"

"Hush! I'm on needles. Watch the clock and keep still."

Five minutes more. We were panting with the strain and the excitement. Another three minutes, and there was a footstep on the stair.

"Saved!" And we jumped up and faced the door.

The old mother entered, bringing the kite. "Isn't it a beauty?" she said. "And, dear me, how he has slaved over it—ever since daylight, I think, and only finished it awhile before you came." She stood it against the wall, and stepped back to take a view of it. "He drew the pictures his own self, and I think they are very good. The church isn't so very good, I'll have to admit, but look at the bridge—anyone can recognize the bridge in a minute. He asked me to bring it up.... Dear me! it's seven minutes past ten, and I—"

"But where is he?"

"He? Oh, he'll be here soon; he's gone out a minute."

"Gone out?"

"Yes. Just as he came downstairs, little Lisa's mother came in and said the child had wandered off somewhere, and as she was a little uneasy I told Nikolaus to never mind about his father's orders—go and look her up.... Why, how white you two do look! I do believe you are sick. Sit down; I'll fetch something. That cake has disagreed with you. It is a little heavy, but I thought—"

She disappeared without finishing her sentence, and we hurried at once to the back window and looked toward the river. There was a great crowd at the other end of the bridge, and people were flying toward that point from every direction.

"Oh, it is all over—poor Nikolaus! Why, oh, why did she let him get out of the house!"

"Come away," said Seppi, half sobbing, "come quick—we can't bear to meet her; in five minutes she will know."

But we were not to escape. She came upon us at the foot of the stairs, with her cordials in her hands, and made us come in and sit down and take the medicine. Then she watched the effect, and it did not satisfy her; so she made us wait longer, and kept upbraiding herself for giving us the unwholesome cake.

Presently the thing happened which we were dreading.

There was a sound of tramping and scraping outside, and a crowd came solemnly in, with heads uncovered, and laid the two drowned bodies on the bed.

"Oh, my God!" that poor mother cried out, and fell on her knees, and put her arms about her dead boy and began to cover the wet face with kisses. "Oh, it was I that sent him, and I have been his death. If I had obeyed, and kept him in the house, this would not have happened. And I am rightly punished; I was cruel to him last night, and him begging me, his own mother, to be his friend."

And so she went on and on, and all the women cried, and pitied her, and tried to comfort her, but she could not forgive herself and could not be comforted, and kept on saying if she had not sent him out he would be alive and well now, and she was the cause of his death.

It shows how foolish people are when they blame themselves for anything they have done. Satan knows, and he said nothing happens that your first act hasn't arranged to happen and made inevitable; and so, of your own motion you can't ever alter the scheme or do a thing that will break a link. Next we heard screams, and Frau Brandt came wildly plowing and plunging through the crowd with her dress in disorder and hair flying loose, and flung herself upon her dead child with moans and kisses and pleadings and endearments; and by and by she rose up almost exhausted with her outpourings of passionate emotion, and clenched her fist and lifted it toward the sky, and her tear-drenched face grew hard and resentful, and she said:

"For nearly two weeks I have had dreams and presentiments and warnings that death was going to strike what was most precious to me, and day and night and night and day I have groveled in the dirt before Him praying Him to have pity on my innocent child and save it from harm—and here is His answer!"

Why, He had saved it from harm—but she did not know.

She wiped the tears from her eyes and cheeks, and stood awhile gazing down at the child and caressing its face and its hair with her hands; then she spoke again in that bitter tone: "But in His hard heart is no compassion. I will never pray again."

She gathered her dead child to her bosom and strode away, the crowd falling back to let her pass, and smitten dumb by the awful words they had heard. Ah, that poor woman! It is as Satan said, we do not know good fortune from bad, and are always mistaking the one for the other. Many a time since I have heard people pray to God to spare the life of sick persons, but I have never done it.

**Both funerals took place** at the same time in our little church next day. Everybody was there, including the party guests. Satan was there, too; which was proper, for it was on account of his efforts that the funerals had happened. Nikolaus had departed this life without absolution, and a collection was taken up for masses, to get him out of purgatory. Only two-thirds of the required money was gathered, and the parents were going to try to borrow the rest, but Satan furnished it. He told us privately that there was no purgatory, but he had contributed in order that Nikolaus's parents and their friends might be saved from worry and distress. We thought it very good of him, but he said money did not cost him anything.

At the graveyard, the body of little Lisa was seized for debt by a carpenter to whom the mother owed fifty groschen for work done the year before. She had never been able to pay this, and was not able now. The carpenter took the corpse home and kept it four days in his cellar, the mother weeping and imploring about his house all the time; then he buried it in his brother's cattle-yard, without religious ceremonies. It drove the mother wild with grief and shame, and she forsook her work and went daily about the town, cursing the carpenter and blaspheming the laws of the emperor and the church, and it was pitiful to see.

Seppi asked Satan to interfere, but he said the carpenter and the rest were members of the human race and were acting quite neatly for that species of animal. He would interfere if he found a horse acting in such a way, and we must inform him when we came across that kind of horse doing that kind of human thing, so that he could stop it. We believed this was sarcasm, for of course there wasn't any such horse.

But after a few days, we found that we could not abide that poor woman's distress, so we begged Satan to examine her several possible careers, and see if he could not change her, to her profit, to a new one. He said the longest of her careers as they now stood gave her forty-two years to live, and her shortest one twenty-nine, and that both were charged with grief and hunger and cold and pain. The only improvement he could make would be to enable her to skip a certain three minutes from now; and he asked us if he should do it. This was such a short time to decide in that we went to pieces with nervous excitement, and before we could pull ourselves together and ask for particulars he said the time would be up in a few more seconds; so then we gasped out, "Do it!"

"It is done," he said; "she was going around a corner; I have turned her back; it has changed her career."

"Then what will happen, Satan?"

"It is happening now. She is having words with Fischer, the weaver. In his anger Fischer will straightway do what he would not have done but for this accident. He was present when she stood over her child's body and uttered those blasphemies."

"What will he do?"

"He is doing it now—betraying her. In three days she will go to the stake."

We could not speak; we were frozen with horror, for if we had not meddled with her career she would have been spared this

43

awful fate. Satan noticed these thoughts, and said:

"What you are thinking is strictly human-like—that is to say, foolish. The woman is advantaged. Die when she might, she would go to heaven. By this prompt death she gets twenty-nine years more of heaven than she is entitled to, and escapes twenty-nine years of misery here."

A moment before we were bitterly making up our minds that we would ask no more favors of Satan for friends of ours, for he did not seem to know any way to do a person a kindness but by killing him; but the whole aspect of the case was changed now, and we were glad of what we had done and full of happiness in the thought of it.

After a little, I began to feel troubled about Fischer, and asked, timidly, "Does this episode change Fischer's life-scheme, Satan?"

"Change it? Why, certainly. And radically. If he had not met Frau Brandt a while ago he would die next year, thirty-four years of age. Now he will live to be ninety, and have a pretty prosperous and comfortable life of it, as human lives go."

We felt a great joy and pride in what we had done for Fischer, and were expecting Satan to sympathize with this feeling; but he showed no sign, and this made us uneasy. We waited for him to speak, but he didn't; so, to assuage our solicitude we had to ask him if there was any defect in Fischer's good luck. Satan considered the question a moment, then said, with some hesitation:

"Well, the fact is, it is a delicate point. Under his several former possible life-careers he was going to heaven."

We were aghast. "Oh, Satan! and under this one—"

"There, don't be so distressed. You were sincerely trying to do him a kindness; let that comfort you."

"Oh, dear, dear, that cannot comfort us. You ought to have told us what we were doing, then we wouldn't have acted so."

But it made no impression on him. He had never felt a pain or a sorrow, and did not know what they were, in any really informing way. He had no knowledge of them except theoretically—that is to say, intellectually. And of course that is no good. One can never get any but a loose and ignorant notion of such things except by experience. We tried our best to make him comprehend the awful thing that had been done and how we were compromised by it, but he couldn't seem to get hold of it. He said he did not think it important where Fischer went to; in heaven he would not be missed, there were "plenty there."

We tried to make him see that he was missing the point entirely; that Fischer, and not other people, was the proper one to decide about the importance of it; but it all went for nothing; he said he did not care for Fischer—there were plenty more Fischers.

The next minute, Fischer went by on the other side of the way, and it made us sick and faint to see him, remembering the doom that was upon him, and we the cause of it. And how unconscious he was that anything had happened to him! You could see by his elastic step and his alert manner that he was well satisfied with himself for doing that hard turn for poor Frau Brandt. He kept glancing back over his shoulder expectantly. And, sure enough, pretty soon Frau Brandt followed after, in charge of the officers and wearing jingling chains. A mob was in her wake, jeering and shouting, "Blasphemer and heretic!" and some among them were neighbors and friends of her happier days. Some were trying to strike her, and the officers were not taking as much trouble as they might to keep them from it.

"Oh, stop them, Satan!" It was out before we remembered that he could not interrupt them for a moment without changing their whole after-lives. He puffed a little puff toward them with his lips, and they began to reel and stagger and grab at the empty air; then they broke apart and fled in every direction, shrieking, as if in intolerable pain. He had crushed a rib of each of them with that little puff. We could not help asking if their life-chart was changed.

"Yes, entirely. Some have gained years, some have lost them. Some few will profit in various ways by the change, but only that few."

We did not ask if we had brought poor Fischer's luck to any of them. We did not wish to know. We fully believed in Satan's desire to do us kindnesses, but we were losing confidence in his judgment. It was at this time that our growing anxiety to have him look over our life-charts and suggest improvements began to fade out and give place to other interests.

**For a day or two,** the whole village was a chattering turmoil over Frau Brandt's case and over the mysterious calamity that had overtaken the mob, and at her trial the place was crowded. She was easily convicted of her blasphemies, for she uttered those terrible words again and said she would not take them back. When warned that she was imperiling her life, she said they could take it in welcome, she did not want it. She would rather live with the professional devils in perdition than with these imitators in the village.

They accused her of breaking all those ribs by witchcraft, and asked her if she was not a witch?

She answered scornfully: "No. If I had that power, would any of you holy hypocrites be alive five minutes? No. I would strike you all dead. Pronounce your sentence and let me go. I am tired of your society."

So they found her guilty, and she was excommunicated and cut off from the joys of heaven and doomed to the fires of hell; then she was clothed in a coarse robe and delivered to the secular arm, and conducted to the marketplace, the bell solemnly tolling the while. We saw her chained to the stake, and saw the first film of blue smoke rise on the still air. Then her hard face softened, and she looked upon the packed crowd in front of her and said, with gentleness:

"We played together once, in long-agone days when we were innocent little creatures. For the sake of that, I forgive you."

We went away then, and did not see the fires consume her, but we heard the shrieks, although we put our fingers in our ears. When they ceased we knew she was in heaven, notwithstanding the excommunication; and we were glad of her death and not sorry that we had brought it about.

**One day, a little while after this**, Satan appeared again. We were always watching out for him, for life was never very stagnant when he was by. He came upon us at that place in the woods where we had first met him. Being boys, we wanted to be entertained; we asked him to do a show for us.

"Very well," he said; "would you like to see a history of the progress of the human race? Its development of that product which it calls civilization?"

We said we should.

So, with a thought, he turned the place into the Garden of Eden, and we saw Abel praying by his altar; then Cain came walking toward him with his club, and did not seem to see us, and would have stepped on my foot if I had not drawn it in. He spoke to his brother in a language which we did not understand; then he grew violent and threatening, and we knew what was going to happen, and turned away our heads for the moment; but we heard the crash of the blows and heard the shrieks and the groans; then there was silence, and we saw Abel lying in his blood and gasping out his life, and Cain standing over him and looking down at him, vengeful and unrepentant.

Then the vision vanished, and was followed by a long series of unknown wars, murders, and massacres. Next we had the

Flood, and the Ark tossing around in the stormy waters, with lofty mountains in the distance showing veiled and dim through the rain.

Satan said: "The progress of your race was not satisfactory. It is to have another chance now."

The scene changed, and we saw Noah overcome with wine.

Next, we had Sodom and Gomorrah, and "the attempt to discover two or three respectable persons there," as Satan described it.

Next, Lot and his daughters in the cave.

Next came the Hebraic wars, and we saw the victors massacre the survivors and their cattle, and save the young girls alive and distribute them around.

Next we had Jael; and saw her slip into the tent and drive the nail into the temple of her sleeping guest; and we were so close that when the blood gushed out it trickled in a little, red stream to our feet, and we could have stained our hands in it if we had wanted to.

Next we had Egyptian wars, Greek wars, Roman wars, hideous drenchings of the earth with blood; and we saw the treacheries of the Romans toward the Carthaginians, and the sickening spectacle of the massacre of those brave people. Also we saw Caesar invade Britain—"not that those barbarians had done him any harm, but because he wanted their land, and desired to confer the blessings of civilization upon their widows and orphans," as Satan explained.

Next, Christianity was born. Then ages of Europe passed in review before us, and we saw Christianity and Civilization march hand in hand through those ages, "leaving famine and death and desolation in their wake, and other signs of the progress of the human race," as Satan observed.

And always we had wars, and more wars, and still other wars—all over Europe, all over the world. "Sometimes in the private interest of royal families," Satan said, "sometimes to crush a weak nation; but never a war started by the aggressor for any clean purpose—there is no such war in the history of the race."

"Now," said Satan, "you have seen your progress down to the present, and you must confess that it is wonderful—in its way. We must now exhibit the future."

He showed us slaughters more terrible in their destruction of life, more devastating in their engines of war, than any we had seen.

"You perceive," he said, "that you have made continual progress. Cain did his murder with a club; the Hebrews did their murders with javelins and swords; the Greeks and Romans added protective armor and the fine arts of military organization and generalship; the Christian has added guns and gunpowder; a few centuries from now he will have so greatly improved the deadly effectiveness of his weapons of slaughter that all men will confess that without Christian civilization war must have remained a poor and trifling thing to the end of time."

Then he began to laugh in the most unfeeling way, and make fun of the human race, although he knew that what he had been saying shamed us and wounded us. No one but an angel could have acted so; but suffering is nothing to them; they do not know what it is, except by hearsay.

More than once, Seppi and I had tried in a humble and diffident way to convert him, and as he had remained silent, we had taken his silence as a sort of encouragement; necessarily, then, this talk of his was a disappointment to us, for it showed that we had made no deep impression upon him. The thought made us sad, and we knew then how the missionary must feel when he has been cherishing a glad hope and has seen it blighted. We kept our grief to ourselves, knowing that this was not the time to continue our work.`

Satan laughed his unkind laugh to a finish; then he said: "It is a remarkable progress. In five or six thousand years, five or six high civilizations have risen, flourished, commanded the wonder of the world, then faded out and disappeared; and not one of them except the latest ever invented any sweeping and adequate way to kill people. They all did their best—to kill being the chiefest ambition of the human race and the earliest incident in its history—but only the Christian civilization has scored a triumph to be proud of. Two or three centuries from now, it will be recognized that all the competent killers are Christians; then the pagan world will go to school to the Christian—not to acquire his religion, but his guns. The Turk and the Chinaman will buy those to kill missionaries and converts with."

By this time his theater was at work again, and before our eyes, nation after nation drifted by, during two or three centuries, a mighty procession, an endless procession, raging, struggling, wallowing through seas of blood, smothered in battle-smoke through which the flags glinted and the red jets from the cannon darted; and always we heard the thunder of the guns and the cries of the dying.

"And what does it amount to?" said Satan, with his evil chuckle. "Nothing at all. You gain nothing; you always come out where you went in. For a million years the race has gone on monotonously propagating itself and monotonously reperforming this dull nonsense—to what end? No wisdom can guess! Who gets a profit out of it? Nobody but a parcel of usurping little monarchs and nobilities who despise you; would feel defiled if you touched them; would shut the door in your face if you proposed to call; whom you slave for, fight for, die for, and are not ashamed of it, but proud; whose existence is a perpetual insult to you, and you are afraid to resent it; who are mendicants supported by your alms, yet assume toward you the airs of benefactor toward beggar; who address you in the language of master to slave, and are answered in the language of slave to master; who are worshiped by you with your mouth, while in your heart—if you have one—you despise yourselves for it.

"The first man was a hypocrite and a coward, qualities which have not yet failed in his line; it is the foundation upon which all civilizations have been built. Drink to their perpetuation! Drink to their augmentation! Drink to—"

Then he saw by our faces how much we were hurt, and he cut his sentence short and stopped chuckling, and his manner changed. He said, gently: "No, we will drink one another's health, and let civilization go. The wine which has flown to our hands out of space by desire is earthly, and good enough for that other toast; but throw away the glasses; we will drink this one in wine which has not visited this world before."

We obeyed, and reached up and received the new cups as they descended. They were shapely and beautiful goblets, but they were not made of any material that we were acquainted with. They seemed to be in motion, they seemed to be alive; and certainly the colors in them were in motion. They were very brilliant and sparkling, and of every tint, and they were never still, but flowed to and fro in rich tides which met and broke and flashed out dainty explosions of enchanting color. I think it was most like opals washing about in waves and flashing out their splendid fires.

But there is nothing to compare the wine with. We drank it, and felt a strange and witching ecstasy as of heaven go stealing through us, and Seppi's eyes filled and he said worshipingly:

"We shall be there someday, and then—"

He glanced furtively at Satan, and I think he hoped Satan would say, "Yes, you will be there someday," but Satan seemed to be thinking about something else, and said nothing. This made me feel ghastly, for I knew he had heard; nothing, spoken or unspoken, ever escaped him.

Poor Seppi looked distressed, and did not finish his remark.

**The goblets rose and clove their way** into the sky, a triplet of radiant sundogs, and disappeared. Why didn't they stay? It seemed a bad sign, and depressed me. Should I ever see mine again? Would Seppi ever see his? For as much as a year Satan continued these visits, but at last he came less often, and then for a long time he did not come at all. This always made me lonely and melancholy. I felt that he was losing interest in our tiny world and might at any time abandon his visits entirely.

When one day he finally came to me, I was overjoyed, but only for a little while. He had come to say goodbye, he told me, and for the last time. He had investigations and undertakings in other corners of the universe, he said, that would keep him busy for a longer period than I could wait for his return.

"And you are going away, and will not come back anymore?"

"Yes," he said. "We have comraded long together, and it has been pleasant—pleasant for both; but I must go now, and we shall not see each other anymore."

"In this life, Satan, but in another? We shall meet in another, surely?"

Then, all tranquilly and soberly, he made the strange answer, "There is no other."

A subtle influence blew upon my spirit from his, bringing with it a vague, dim, but blessed and hopeful feeling that the incredible words might be true—even must be true.

"Have you never suspected this, Theodor?"

"No. How could I? But if it can only be true—"

"It is true."

A gust of thankfulness rose in my breast, but a doubt checked it before it could issue in words, and I said, "But... but... we have seen that future life—seen it in its actuality, and so—"

"It was a vision—it had no existence."

I could hardly breathe for the great hope that was struggling in me. "A vision? A vi—"

"Life itself is only a vision, a dream."

It was electrical. By God! I had had that very thought a thousand times in my musings!

"Nothing exists; all is a dream. God, man, the world, the sun, the moon, the wilderness of stars—a dream, all a dream; they have no existence. Nothing exists save empty space—and you!"

"I!"

"And you are not you. You have no body, no blood, no bones, you are but a thought. I myself have no existence; I am but a dream—your dream, creature of your imagination. In a moment you will have realized this, then you will banish me from your visions and I shall dissolve into the nothingness out of which you made me....

"I am perishing already... I am failing... I am passing away. In a little while you will be alone in shoreless space, to wander its limitless solitudes without friend or comrade forever. For you will remain a thought, the only existent thought, and by your nature inextinguishable, indestructible. But I, your poor servant, have revealed you to yourself and set you free. Dream other dreams, and better!

"Strange that you should not have suspected years ago— centuries, ages, eons ago! For you have existed, companionless, through all the eternities. Strange, indeed, that you should not have suspected that your universe and its contents were only dreams, visions, fiction! Strange, because they are so frankly and hysterically insane—like all dreams: a God who could make good children as easily as bad, yet preferred to make bad ones; who could have made every one of them happy, yet never made a single happy one; who made them prize their bitter life, yet stingily cut it short; who gave his angels eternal happiness unearned, yet required his other children to earn it; who gave his angels painless lives, yet cursed his other children with biting miseries and maladies of mind and body; who mouths justice and invented hell—mouths mercy and invented hell—mouths Golden Rules, and forgiveness multiplied by seventy times seven, and invented hell; who mouths morals to other people and has none himself; who frowns upon crimes, yet commits them all; who created man without invitation, then tries to shuffle the responsibility for man's acts upon man, instead of honorably placing it where it belongs, upon himself; and finally, with altogether divine obtuseness, invites this poor, abused slave to worship him!

"You perceive, now, that these things are all impossible except in a dream. You perceive that they are pure and puerile insanities, the silly creations of an imagination that is not conscious of its freaks—in a word, that they are a dream, and you the maker of it. The dream-marks are all present; you should have recognized them earlier.

"It is true, that which I have revealed to you: There is no God, no universe, no human race, no earthly life, no heaven, no hell. It is all a dream—a grotesque and foolish dream. Nothing exists but you. And you are but a thought—a vagrant thought, a useless thought, a homeless thought, wandering forlorn among the empty eternities!"

He vanished, and left me appalled; for I knew, and realized, that all he had said was true.

*The preceding is an excerpt from a longer, unfinished work of this title. It contains the latter portions of the work and ends at the full work's conclusion. In it and a companion unfinished manuscript, "Schoolhouse Hill" (to be presented later in this collection), Twain dealt with the issues of what Satan represented to human beings and how he might have been a trifle misunderstood by orthodox interpreters.*

# Tom Quartz

One of my comrades was one of the gentlest spirits that ever bore its patient cross in a weary exile: grave and simple Dick Baker, pocket-miner of Dead-House Gulch. He was forty-six, gray as a rat, earnest, thoughtful, slenderly educated, slouchily dressed and clay-soiled, but his heart was finer metal than any gold his shovel ever brought to light—than any, indeed, that ever was mined or minted.

Whenever he was out of luck and a little down-hearted, he would fall to mourning over the loss of a wonderful cat he used to own (for where women and children are not, men of kindly impulses take up with pets, for they must love something). And he always spoke of the strange sagacity of that cat with the air of a man who believed in his secret heart that there was something human about it—maybe even supernatural.

I heard him talking about this animal once. He said:

**Gentlemen, I used to have a cat here,** by the name of Tom

Quartz, which you'd a took an interest in I reckon—most anybody would. I had him here eight year—and he was the remarkablest cat I ever see. He was a large gray one of the Tom specie, an' he had more hard, natchral sense than any man in this camp—'n' a power of dignity—he wouldn't let the Gov'ner of Californy be familiar with him.

He never ketched a rat in his life—'peared to be above it. He never cared for nothing but mining. He knowed more about mining, that cat did, than any man I ever, ever see. You couldn't tell him noth'n 'bout placer diggin's, 'n' as for pocket mining, why he was just born for it.

He would dig out after me an' Jim when we went over the hills prospect'n', and he would trot along behind us for as much as five mile, if we went so fur. An' he had the best judgment about mining ground—why you never see anything like it. When we went to work, he'd scatter a glance around, 'n' if he didn't think much of the indications, he would give a look as much as to say, "Well, I'll have to get you to excuse me," 'n' without another word, he'd hyste his nose into the air 'n' shove for home.

But if the ground suited him, he would lay low 'n' keep dark till the first pan was washed, 'n' then he would sidle up 'n' take a look, an' if there was about six or seven grains of gold he was satisfied—he didn't want no better prospect 'n' that—'n' then he would lay down on our coats and snore like a steamboat till we'd struck the pocket, an' then get up 'n' superintend. He was nearly lightnin' on superintending.

Well, bye an' bye, up comes this yer quartz excitement. Everybody was into it—everybody was pick'n' 'n' blast'n' instead of shovelin' dirt on the hillside—everybody was put'n' down a shaft instead of scrapin' the surface. Noth'n' would do Jim, but we must tackle the ledges, too, 'n' so we did.

We commenced put'n' down a shaft, 'n' Tom Quartz, he begin to wonder what in the Dickens it was all about. He hadn't ever seen any mining like that before, 'n' he was all upset, as you may say—he couldn't come to a right understanding of it no way—it was too many for him. He was down on it, too, you bet you—he was down on it powerful—'n' always appeared to consider it the cussedest foolishness out. But that cat, you know, was always agin newfangled arrangements—somehow he never could abide 'em. You know how it is with old habits.

But by an' by, Tom Quartz begin to git sort of reconciled a little, though he never could altogether understand that eternal sinkin' of a shaft an' never pannin' out anything. At last he got to comin' down in the shaft, hisself, to try to cipher it out. An' when he'd git the blues, 'n' feel kind o'scruffy, 'n' aggravated 'n' disgusted—knowin' as he did, that the bills was runnin' up all the time an' we warn't makin' a cent—he would curl up on a gunny sack in the corner an' go to sleep.

Well, one day when the shaft was down about eight foot, the rock got so hard that we had to put in a blast—the first blast 'n' we'd ever done since Tom Quartz was born. An' then we lit the fuse 'n' clumb out 'n' got off 'bout fifty yards—'n' forgot 'n' left Tom Quartz sound asleep on the gunny sack.

In 'bout a minute, we seen a puff of smoke bust up out of the hole, 'n' then everything let go with an awful crash, 'n' about four million ton of rocks 'n' dirt 'n' smoke 'n; splinters shot up 'bout a mile an' a half into the air, an' by George, right in the dead centre of it was old Tom Quartz a goin' end over end, an' a snortin' an' a sneez'n', an' a clawin' an' a reachin' for things like all possessed.

But it warn't no use, you know, it warn't no use. An' that was the last we see of him for about two minutes 'n' a half. An' then all of a sudden it begin to rain rocks and rubbage, an' directly he come down ker-whop about ten foot off f'm where we stood Well, I reckon he was p'raps the orneriest lookin' beast you ever see. One ear was sot back on his neck, 'n' his tail was stove up, 'n' his eye-winkers was swinged off, 'n' he was all blacked up with powder an' smoke, an' all sloppy with mud 'n' slush f'm one end to the other.

Well sir, it warn't no use to try to apologize—we couldn't say a word. He took a sort of a disgusted look at hisself, 'n' then he looked at us—an' it was just exactly the same as if he had said, "Gents, may be you think it's smart to take advantage of a cat that 'ain't had no experience of quartz minin', but I think different"—an' then he turned on his heel 'n' marched off home without ever saying another word.

That was jest his style. An' maybe you won't believe it, but after that you never see a cat so prejudiced agin quartz mining as what he was. An' by an' bye, when he did get to goin' down in the shaft agin, you'd 'a been astonished at his sagacity. The minute we'd tetch off a blast 'n' the fuse'd begin to sizzle, he'd give a look as much as to say: "Well, I'll have to git you to excuse me," an' it was surpris'n' the way he'd shin out of that hole 'n' go f'r a tree. Sagacity? It ain't no name for it. 'Twas inspiration!"

**I said, "Well, Mr. Baker**, his prejudice against quartz-mining was remarkable, considering how he came by it. Couldn't you ever cure him of it?"

"Cure him! No! When Tom Quartz was sot once, he was always sot—and you might a blowed him up as much as three million times 'n' you'd never a broken him of his cussed prejudice agin quartz mining."

The affection and the pride that lit up Baker's face when he delivered this tribute to the firmness of his humble friend of other days, will always be a vivid memory with me.

*"Tom Quartz" is an excerpt from Mark Twain's 1872 book,* Roughing It.

# The Petrified Man

A petrified man was found some time ago in the mountains south of Gravelly Ford. Every limb and feature of the stony mummy was perfect, not even excepting the left leg, which has evidently been a wooden one during the lifetime of the owner—which lifetime, by the way, came to a close about a century ago, in the opinion of a savan who has examined the defunct.

The body was in a sitting posture, and leaning against a huge mass of croppings; the attitude was pensive, the right thumb resting against the side of the nose; the left thumb partially supported the chin, the fore-finger pressing the inner corner of the left eye and drawing it partly open; the right eye was closed, and the fingers of the right hand spread apart.

This strange freak of nature created a profound sensation in the vicinity, and our informant states that by request, Justice Sewell or Sowell, of Humboldt City, at once proceeded to the spot and held an inquest on the body. The verdict of the jury was that "deceased came to his death from protracted exposure," etc.

The people of the neighborhood volunteered to bury the poor unfortunate, and were even anxious to do so; but it was discovered, when they attempted to remove him, that the water which had dripped upon him for ages from the crag above, had coursed down his back and deposited a limestone sediment under him which had glued him to the bed rock upon which he sat, as with a cement of adamant, and Judge S. refused to allow the charitable citizens to blast him from his position.

The opinion expressed by his Honor that such a course would be little less than sacrilege, was eminently just and proper. Everybody goes to see the stone man, as many as three hundred having visited the hardened creature during the past five or six weeks.

*Mark Twain wrote "The Petrified Man" as a short, satirical piece for the* Virginia City Territorial Enterprise, *where it appeared on Oct. 4, 1862.*

# A Ghost's Tale

I took a large room, far up Broadway, in a huge old building whose upper stories had been wholly unoccupied for years until I came. The place had long been given up to dust and cobwebs, to solitude and silence. I seemed groping among the tombs and invading the privacy of the dead, that first night I climbed up to my quarters. For the first time in my life a superstitious dread came over me; and as I turned a dark angle of the stairway and an invisible cobweb swung its slazy woof in my face and clung there, I shuddered as one who had encountered a phantom.

I was glad enough when I reached my room and locked out the mold and the darkness. A cheery fire was burning in the grate, and I sat down before it with a comforting sense of relief. For two hours I sat there, thinking of bygone times; recalling old scenes, and summoning half- forgotten faces out of the mists of the past; listening, in fancy, to voices that long ago grew silent for all time, and to once familiar songs that nobody sings now. And as my reverie softened down to a sadder and sadder pathos, the shrieking of the winds outside softened to a wail, the angry beating of the rain against the panes diminished to a tranquil patter, and one by one the noises in the street subsided, until the hurrying footsteps of the last belated straggler died away in the distance and left no sound behind.

The fire had burned low. A sense of loneliness crept over me. I arose and undressed, moving on tiptoe about the room, doing stealthily what I had to do, as if I were environed by sleeping enemies whose slumbers it would be fatal to break. I covered up in bed, and lay listening to the rain and wind and the faint creaking of distant shutters, till they lulled me to sleep.

I slept profoundly, but how long I do not know. All at once I found myself awake, and filled with a shuddering expectancy. All was still. All but my own heart—I could hear it beat. Presently the bedclothes began to slip away slowly toward the foot of the bed, as if someone were pulling them! I could not stir; I could not speak. Still the blankets slipped deliberately away, till my breast was uncovered. Then, with a great effort, I seized them and drew them over my head. I waited, listened, waited. Once more that steady pull began, and once more I lay torpid a century of dragging seconds till my breast was naked again. At last I roused my energies and snatched the covers back to their place and held them with a strong grip. I waited. By and by I felt a faint tug, and took a fresh grip. The tug strengthened to a steady strain—it grew stronger and stronger. My hold parted, and for the third time the blankets slid away. I groaned. An answering groan came from the foot of the bed! Beaded drops of sweat stood upon my forehead. I was more dead than alive. Presently I heard a heavy footstep in my room—the step of an elephant, it seemed to me— it was not like anything human. But it was moving from me— there was relief in that. I heard it approach the door—pass out without moving bolt or lock—and wander away among the dismal corridors, straining the floors and joists till they creaked again as it passed—and then silence reigned once more.

When my excitement had calmed, I said to myself, "This is a dream—simply a hideous dream." And so I lay thinking it over until I convinced myself that it was a dream, and then a comforting laugh relaxed my lips and I was happy again. I got up and struck a light; and when I found that the locks and bolts were just as I had left them, another soothing laugh welled in my heart and rippled from my lips. I took my pipe and lit it, and was just sitting down before the fire, when down went the pipe out of my nerveless fingers, the blood forsook my cheeks, and my placid breathing was cut short with a gasp! In the ashes on the hearth, side by side with my own bare footprint, was another, so vast that in comparison mine was but an infant's! Then I *had* had a visitor, and the elephant tread was explained.

I put out the light and returned to bed, palsied with fear. I lay a long time, peering into the darkness, and listening. Then I heard a grating noise overhead, like the dragging of a heavy body across the floor; then the throwing down of the body, and the shaking of my windows in response to the concussion. In distant parts of the building I heard the muffled slamming of doors. I heard, at intervals, stealthy footsteps creeping in and out among the corridors, and up and down the stairs. Sometimes these noises approached my door, hesitated, and went away again. I heard the clanking of chains faintly, in remote passages, and listened while the clanking grew nearer—while it wearily climbed the stairways, marking each move by the loose surplus of chain that fell with an accented rattle upon each succeeding step as the goblin that bore it advanced. I heard muttered sentences; half-uttered screams that seemed smothered violently; and the swish of invisible garments, the rush of invisible wings. Then I became conscious that my chamber was invaded—that I was not alone. I heard sighs and breathings about my bed, and mysterious whisperings. Three little spheres of soft phosphorescent light appeared on the ceiling directly over my head, clung and glowed there a moment, and then dropped —two of them upon my face and one upon the pillow. They, spattered, liquidly, and felt warm. Intuition told me they had— turned to gouts of blood as they fell—I needed no light to satisfy myself of that. Then I saw pallid faces, dimly luminous, and white uplifted hands, floating bodiless in the air—floating a moment and then disappearing. The whispering ceased, and the voices and the sounds, and a solemn stillness followed. I waited and listened. I felt that I must have light or die. I was weak with fear. I slowly raised myself toward a sitting posture, and my face came in contact with a clammy hand! All strength went from me apparently, and I fell back like a stricken invalid. Then I heard the rustle of a garment; it seemed to pass to the door and go out.

When everything was still once more, I crept out of bed, sick and feeble, and lit the gas with a hand that trembled as if it were aged with a hundred years. The light brought some little cheer to my spirits. I sat down and fell into a dreamy contemplation of that great footprint in the ashes. By and by its outlines began to waver and grow dim. I glanced up and the broad gas-flame was slowly wilting away. In the same moment I heard that elephantine tread again. I noted its approach, nearer and nearer, along the musty halls, and dimmer and dimmer the light waned.

The tread reached my very door and paused—the light had dwindled to a sickly blue, and all things about me lay in a spectral twilight. The door did not open, and yet I felt a faint gust of air fan my cheek, and presently was conscious of a huge, cloudy presence before me. I watched it with fascinated eyes. A pale glow stole over the Thing; gradually its cloudy folds took shape—an arm appeared, then legs, then a body, and last a great sad face looked out of the vapor. Stripped of its filmy housings, naked, muscular and comely, the majestic Cardiff Giant loomed above me!

All my misery vanished—for a child might know that no harm could come with that benignant countenance. My cheerful spirits returned at once, and in sympathy with them the gas flamed up brightly again. Never a lonely outcast was so glad to welcome company as I was to greet the friendly giant. I said:

"Why, is it nobody but you? Do you know, I have been scared to death for the last two or three hours? I am most honestly glad to see you. I wish I had a chair—Here, here, don't try to sit down in that thing—"

But it was too late. He was in it before I could stop him and down he went—I never saw a chair shivered so in my life.

"Stop, stop, you'll ruin ev—"

Too late again. There was another crash, and another chair was resolved into its original elements.

"Confound it, haven't you got any judgment at all? Do you want to ruin all the furniture on the place? Here, here, you petrified fool—"

But it was no use. Before I could arrest him, he had sat down on the bed, and it was a melancholy ruin.

"Now what sort of a way is that to do? First you come lumbering about the place bringing a legion of vagabond goblins along with you to worry me to death, and then when I overlook an indelicacy of costume which would not be tolerated anywhere by cultivated people except in a respectable theater, and not even there if the nudity were of your sex, you repay me by wrecking all the furniture you can find to sit down on. And why will you? You damage yourself as much as you do me. You have broken off the end of your spinal column, and littered up the floor with chips of your hams till the place looks like a marble yard. You ought to be ashamed of yourself—you are big enough to know better."

"Well, I will not break any more furniture. But what am I to do? I have not had a chance to sit down for a century." And the tears came into his eyes.

"Poor devil," I said, "I should not have been so harsh with you. And you are an orphan, too, no doubt. But sit down on the floor here—nothing else can stand your weight—and besides, we cannot be sociable with you away up there above me; I want you down where I can perch on this high counting-house stool and gossip with you face to face."

So he sat down on the floor and lit a pipe which I gave him, threw one of my red blankets over his shoulders, inverted my sitz-bath on his head, helmet fashion, and made himself picturesque and comfortable. Then he crossed his ankles, while I renewed the fire, and exposed the flat, honeycombed bottoms of his prodigious feet to the grateful warmth.

"What is the matter with the bottom of your feet and the back of your legs, that they are gouged up so?"

"Infernal chilblains—I caught them clear up to the back of my head, roosting out there under Newell's farm. But I love the place; I love it as one loves his old home. There is no peace for me like the peace I feel when I am there."

We talked along for half an hour, and then I noticed that he looked tired, and spoke of it.

"Tired?" he said. "Well, I should think so. And now I will tell you all about it, since you have treated me so well. I am the spirit of the Petrified Man that lies across the street there in the museum. I am the ghost of the Cardiff Giant. I can have no rest, no peace, till they have given that poor body burial again. Now what was the most natural thing for me to do, to make men satisfy this wish? Terrify them into it! haunt the place where the body lay! So I haunted the museum night after night. I even got other spirits to help me. But it did no good, for nobody ever came to the museum at midnight. Then it occurred to me to come over the way and haunt this place a little. I felt that if I ever got a hearing I must succeed, for I had the most efficient company that perdition could furnish. Night after night we have shivered around through these mildewed halls, dragging chains, groaning, whispering, tramping up and down stairs, till, to tell you the truth, I am almost worn out. But when I saw a light in your room tonight I roused my energies again and went at it with a deal of the old freshness. But I am tired out—entirely fagged out. Give me, I beseech you, give me some hope!" I lit off my perch in a burst of excitement, and exclaimed:

"This transcends everything! everything that ever did occur! Why you poor blundering old fossil, you have had all your trouble for nothing—you have been haunting a plaster cast of yourself—the real Cardiff Giant is in Albany!—[A fact. The original fraud was ingeniously and fraudfully duplicated, and exhibited in New York as the "only genuine" Cardiff Giant (to the unspeakable disgust of the owners of the real colossus) at the very same time that the latter was drawing crowds at a museum is Albany,]—Confound it, don't you know your own remains?"

I never saw such an eloquent look of shame, of pitiable humiliation, overspread a countenance before.

The Petrified Man rose slowly to his feet, and said:

"Honestly, is that true?"

"As true as I am sitting here."

He took the pipe from his mouth and laid it on the mantel,

then stood irresolute a moment (unconsciously, from old habit, thrusting his hands where his pantaloons pockets should have been, and meditatively dropping his chin on his breast); and finally said:

"Well, I never felt so absurd before. The Petrified Man has sold everybody else, and now the mean fraud has ended by selling its own ghost! My son, if there is any charity left in your heart for a poor friendless phantom like me, don't let this get out. Think how you would feel if you had made such an ass of yourself."

I heard his stately tramp die away, step by step down the stairs and out into the deserted street, and felt sorry that he was gone, poor fellow—and sorrier still that he had carried off my red blanket and my bathtub.

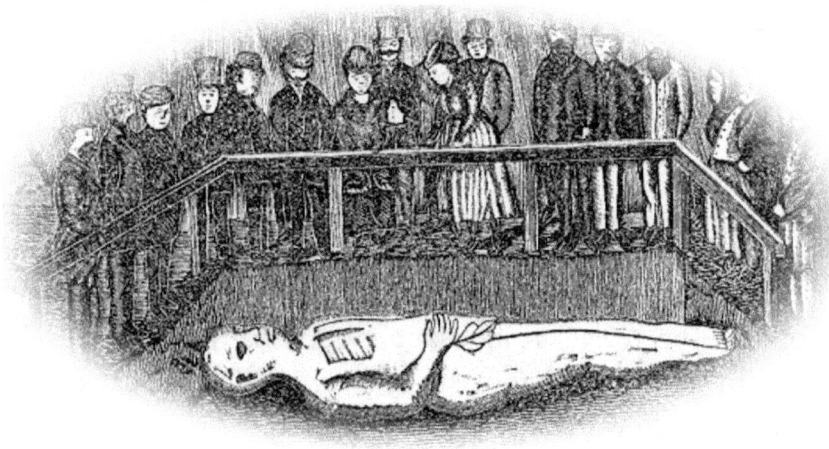

*"A Ghost's Tale,"* also known as *"A Ghost Story,"* by *Mark Twain, was first published in 1870. It followed the "discovery" the previous year of a 10-foot-tall petrified man in Cardiff, New York. The entire thing turned out to be a hoax, which Twain spoofed in this story.*

*"Get your facts first, and you can distort them as much as you please."*

Quoted by Rudyard Kipling
in *From Sea to Sea*

"*I am an old man and have known a great many troubles, but most of them never happened.*"

Attributed to Twain by the *Washington Post*,
September 11, 1910

# More Ghosts...

Are we to be scared to death every time we venture into the street? May we be allowed to go quietly about our business, or are we to be assailed at every corner by fearful apparitions?

As we were plodding home at the ghostly hour last night, thinking about the haunted house humbug, we were suddenly riveted to the pavement in a paroxysm of terror by that blue and yellow phantom who watches over the destinies of the shooting gallery, this side of the International [Hotel, in Virginia City].

Seen in daylight, placidly reclining against his board in the doorway, with his blue coat, and his yellow pants, and his high boots, and his fancy hat, just lifted from his head, he is rather an engaging youth than otherwise; but at dead of night, when he pops out his pallid face at you by candle light, and stares vacantly upon you with his uplifted hat and the eternal civility of his changeless brow, and the ghostliness of his general appearance heightened by that gravestone inscription over his stomach, "today shooting for chickens here," you are apt to think of spectres starting up from behind tombstones, and you weaken accordingly—the cold chills creep over you—your hair stands on end—you reverse your front, and with all possible alacrity, you change your base.

*"More Ghosts" appears in a scrapbook kept by Mark Twain's brother, Orion Clemens. It is referred to there as a New Year's Day column published in the* Territorial Enterprise, *with the likely year of publication being 1863.*

# MARK TWAIN

"Don't part with your illusions. When they are gone
you may still exist, but you have ceased to live."

Pudd'nhead Wilson's New Calendar

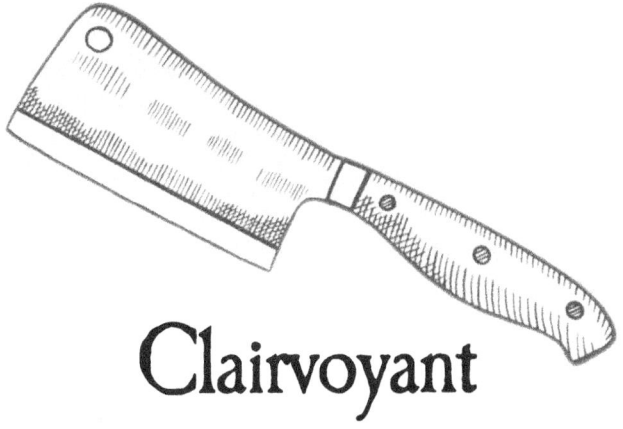

# Clairvoyant

W hen I was a boy, there came to our village of Hannibal, on the Mississippi, a young Englishman named John H. Day, and went to work in the shop of old Mr. Stevens the jeweler, on Main Street. He excited the usual two or three days' curiosity due to a newcomer in such a place; and after that, as he seemed to prefer to keep to himself, the people bothered themselves no more about him, and he was left to his own devices. It was not difficult to give him his way in this, for he was taciturn, absorbed, and therefore uncompanionable and unattractive. As for looks, he was well enough, though there was nothing striking about him except his eyes, which, when in repose, suggested smouldering fires, and, when the man was stirred, surprised one by their exceeding brilliancy.

Mr. Day slept, cooked for himself, and ate, in the back part of the jewelry shop, and he was not seen outside the place oftener than once in twenty-four hours. He seemed to be nearly always at work, days, nights and Sundays. By and by, one noted this curious thing: He would accost a citizen, go to his house once, apparently study him an hour, then drop the acquaintanceship.

You must understand that there were no castes in our society, and the jeweler's journeyman was as good as anybody and could go anywhere. At the end of a year, he had in this way made and discarded the acquaintanceship of pretty much everybody. So here was a man who might be said to know all the town; and yet if anyone were spoken to about him, the reply would have to be, "Well, I have met him—once—but I am not acquainted with him; I don't know him."

It was odd—Mr. Day really knew everybody, after a fashion, and yet had wrought so quietly and gradually, that the town's impression was that he didn't know anybody and didn't wish to.

He seemed to have but one object in view in contriving his brief acquaintanceships; and that was, to get an opportunity to examine people's ears to see if they were threatened with deafness. He did not claim that he could cure deafness, or do anything for it at all; he only claimed that if a person had the seeds of future deafness in him, he could discover the fact. The physicians said that this was nonsense; nevertheless, as Mr. Day did not charge anything for his examinations, the people were all willing to let him inspect their ears.

He had no disposition to keep his theory a secret; but while his explanations of it sounded plausible to the general public, they only confirmed the physicians in their conviction that there was nothing in it. In time, the irreverent came to speak of Day as the "Earbug," and he of course got the reputation of being a monomaniac—if "reputation" is not too large a word to apply to a person who was so little talked about.

By and by, I was apprenticed to the jeweler, and was placed under the tuition of his journeyman. Day was kind to me, and gentle; but during the first week or two, he did not speak to me, except in the way of business, although I was with him all day and slept in the same room with him every night. I quickly grew to be fond of my silent comrade, and often stayed about him, evenings, when I could have been out at play. He would work diligently at something or other until I went to bed at ten. Then, as the stillness of the night came on and I seemed to be sleeping (which I wasn't), he would presently tilt himself back in his chair and close his eyes—and then the strong interest of the evening began, for me. Smiles would flash across his face; then the signs of sharp mental pain; then furies of passion. This stirring panorama of emotions would continue for hours, sometimes, and move me, excite me, exhaust me like a stage-play. Now and then, he would glance at the clock, mutter the time and the day of the month, and say something like this: "People who think they know him would say the thing is incredible." Then he would take a fat notebook out of his breast pocket and write something in it.

I marveled at these things, but took it out in marveling; I believed that observing them clandestinely was dishonorable enough without gossiping about them.

**One summer night**, about midnight, I was watching him through my half-closed lids, waiting for him to begin—for he had been reading all the evening, to my disappointment and discontent. Now he put down his book, and for a moment appeared to be doing something with his hands, I could not see what; then he settled himself back in his chair, closed his eyes peacefully, and the next moment sprang out of his seat with his face lit with horror and snatched me from the bed, stood me on my feet, and said:

"Run! Don't stop to dress! Young Ratcliff, the crazy one, is going to murder his mother. Don't tell anybody I said it."

Before I knew what I was about, I was flying up the deserted street in my shirt; and before I had had time to come to myself and realize what a fool I was to rush after one lunatic at the say-so of another, I had covered the two hundred yards that lay between our shop and the Ratcliff homestead, and was thundering at the ancient knocker of the side door with all my might.

Then I came to myself, and felt foolish enough; I turned and looked toward the hut in a corner of the yard where young Ratcliff was kept in confinement; and sure enough, here came young Ratcliff flying across the yard in the moonlight, as naked as I was, and I saw the flash of a butcher knife which he was flourishing in his hand.

I shouted "Help!" and "Murder!" and then fled away, still shouting these cries.

When I got back to the shop, Day was not there; but in the course of half an hour he came in, and for the first time was talkative. He said a crowd gathered and captured the lunatic after he was inside the house and climbing the stairs toward his mother's room. He said Mrs. Ratcliff ought to know that I had saved her life, but he would take it as a great favor if I would keep carefully secret the fact of his own connection with the matter. I said I would, and it seemed to please him; and from that time forward, he began to talk with me more or less every day, and I became his one intimate friend.

We talked a good deal that night, and at last I asked him why he hadn't gone to give the alarm himself instead of sending me, but he did not reply; and by and by, when I ventured to ask him how he had divined that a man two hundred yards away was about to murder his mother, he was silent again; so I made up my mind that I would not push him too closely with questions thenceforward, at least until his manner should invite the venture.

**Almost every day, now**, my curiosity was laid on the rack. For instance, we would be sitting at work, and I would chance to mention some man or woman; whereupon Day would take up the person as a preacher would a text, and proceed in the placidest way to delineate his character in the most elaborate, searching and detailed way—and in nine cases out of ten, his delineation would contain one and sometimes a couple of the most absurd blunders, though otherwise perfect. I would point these out to him, but it never made any difference, he said he was right, and stuck calmly to his position.

Then I would say, "Do you know this man personally?"

And he would answer, in all cases, "No, not what you would call personally; I have met him once, for an hour."

And when I retorted, "Why, I've known him all my life," he would simply say, as sufficient answer, "No matter; I know him as he is, you merely know him as he seems to be."

On one occasion, something brought up the name of G—, who had killed B— four years before, in a quarrel over some birds, the gentlemen being out shooting together at the time. Straightway, Mr. Day began to paint G—'s character, according to his custom; and it was beautiful to hear him; you couldn't help saying to yourself all the time, "How true that is; how well he does it; how perfectly he knows this man, inside and out." But all at once, as usual, he spoilt it all, by remarking upon G—'s remorse on account of the homicide.

"Remorse!" I said. "What an idea that is. Why, the thing that G—is mainly hated for, in this town, is that he can be so perpetually and unchangeably cheerful, day in and day out, with that thing in his memory."

Day looked at me gravely and said: "I tell you the man has never had one good, full, restful, peaceful hour in all these four years. He thinks of that crime with every breath he draws, and all his days are days of torture."

I said I didn't believe it and couldn't believe it.

Day said: "He has wanted to commit suicide, this long time."

I said that that statement would make the public laugh if they could hear it.

"No matter. He is his mother's idol, and is resolved to live while she lives; but he is also resolved to release himself when she dies. You will see; he will kill himself when she is taken away, and people will think grief for her loss moved him to it. She has been very sick for a week or two, now. If she should die, then you will see."

She did die, two or three days after that, and G— killed himself the same night.

**My days were full of interest**, passed, as they were, in the presence of this fascinating and awful power. Now and then came an incident which one could smile at.

One day old Mr. E—, a miserly person but of honorable reputation came into the shop and said to Mr. Day: "Here is a bill on a broken Indiana bank which you gave me last Thursday in change. I ought to have brought it back sooner, but I was called away to Palmyra."

Day gave him a good bill for it, and E— thanked him and went away. Then Day stood there with the bad bill in his hand, thinking, and presently said, as if to himself:

"There must be some mistake; I couldn't pay out a ten dollar bill and not remember it."

Then he did a thing which I had often seen him do before. He took a metal box out of his pocket, searched in it, put it back, and the next moment he said, in a surprised voice: "Why, the man is a pitiful rascal."

"What has he done?" I asked.

"He has brought me a bad bill which he knew he did not get here."

I wanted to ask how he knew; but I restrained that impulse, and merely said it was a pity the shop had to lose all that money.

"It isn't lost," said Day; "he is on his way back, now, to get his bad bill again."

A minute or two later, Mr. E— bustled in, and said he had been mistaken about getting that bill in our shop, and he couldn't see how he happened to make such a... And there he stopped. Day was looking him placidly in the face, and just there E— looked up, caught his eye, stopped speaking, turned red, re-exchanged the bills, and went away without another word, looking very crestfallen.

I was prodigiously surprised, and said so; but Day said that if he had thought a moment, he would have suspected E— in the first place.

"He was the first man in whose parlor I sat in this town. I spent an hour or two there, talking; and he had it in his mind to forge T.R. Selmes's name to a check, for he was in money difficulties at the time."

"He—forge a check! Impossible. Did he say he was going to?"

"Nonsense—of course he didn't. But he had it in his mind to do it. I made a memorandum of it at the time."

He got out his notebook, and said:

"No, it wasn't Selmes—it was Brittingham he was going to forge it on."

*Mark Twain wrote "Clairvoyant" in 1883-84.*

"*I am constructed like everybody else, and enjoy a compliment as well as any other fool, but I do like to have the other side presented. And there is another side. I have a wicked side. Estimable friends who know all about it would tell you and take a certain delight in telling you things that I have done, and things further that I have not repented. The real life that I live, and the real life that I suppose all of you live, is a life of interior sin. That is what makes life valuable and pleasant. To lead a life of undiscovered sin! That is true joy.*"

Speech to the Society of American Authors,
November 15, 1900

# Among the Spirits

There was a séance in town a few nights since. As I was making for it, in company with the reporter of an evening paper, he said he had seen a gambler named Gus Graham shot down in a town in Illinois years ago by a mob, and as he was probably the only person in San Francisco who knew of the circumstance, he thought he would "give the spirits Graham to chaw on awhile." (This young creature is a Democrat, and speaks with the native strength and inelegance of his tribe.)

In the course of the show, he wrote his old pal's name on a slip of paper, and folded it up tightly and put it in a hat which was passed around, and which already had about 500 similar documents in it. The pile was dumped on the table, and the medium began to take them up one by one and lay them aside, asking, "Is this spirit present? Or this? Or this?"

About one in fifty would rap, and the person who sent up

the name would rise in his place and question the defunct. At last a spirit seized the medium's hand and wrote "Gus Graham" backward. Then the medium went skirmishing through the papers for the corresponding name. And that old sport knew his card by the back! When the medium came to it, after picking up fifty others, he rapped!

A committeeman unfolded the paper, and it was the right one. I sent for it and got it. It was all right. However, I suppose all Democrats are on sociable terms with the devil. The young man got up and asked:

"Did you die in '51? '52? '53? '54?"

Ghost: "Rap, rap, rap."

"Did you die of cholera? Diarrhea? Dysentery? Dog bite? Smallpox? Violent death?"

"Rap, rap, rap."

"Were you hanged? Drowned? Stabbed? Shot?"

"Rap, rap, rap."

"Did you die in Mississippi? Kentucky? New York? Sandwich Islands? Texas? Illinois?"

"Rap, rap, rap."

"In Adams County? Madison? Randolph?"

"Rap, rap, rap."

It was no use trying to catch the departed gambler. He knew his hand, and played it like a major.

**About this time**, a couple of Germans stepped forward: an elderly man and a spry young fellow, cocked and primed for a sensation. They wrote some names. Then young Ollendorff said something which sounded like, "*Ist ein geist hieraus?*" (Bursts of laughter from the audience.)

Three raps, signifying that there was a *geist hieraus*.

"*Vollen sie schriehen?*" (More laughter.)

Three raps.

"*Finzig stollen, linsowfterowlickterhairowfterfrowleineru hackfolder-ol?*"

Incredible as it may seem, the spirit cheerfully answered "Yes" to that astonishing proposition.

The audience grew more and more boisterously mirthful with every fresh question, and they were informed that the performance could not go on in the midst of so much levity. They became quiet.

The German ghost didn't appear to know anything at all—couldn't answer the simplest questions. Young Ollendorff finally stated some numbers, and tried to get at the time of the spirit's death; it appeared to be considerably mixed as to whether it died in 1811 or 1812, which was reasonable enough, as it had been so long ago. At last it wrote "12."

Tableau! Young Ollendorff sprang to his feet in a state of consuming excitement. He exclaimed:

"Laties und shentlemen! I write de name fon a man vot lifs! Speerit-rabbing dells me he ties in yahr eighteen hoondred und dwelf, but he yoos as live und hefty as—"

The Medium: "Sit down, sir!"

Ollendorff: "But I vant to—"

Medium: "You are not here to make speeches, sir. Sit down!" (Mr. O. had squared himself for an oration.)

Mr. O.: "But de speerit cheat! Dere is no such speerit." (All this time, applause and laughter by turns from the audience.)

Medium: "Take your seat, sir, and I will explain this matter."

And she explained. And in that explanation she let off a blast which was so terrific that I half expected to see young Ollendorff shot up through the roof. She said he had come up there with fraud and deceit and cheating in his heart, and a kindred spirit had come from the land of shadows to commune with him! She was terribly bitter. She said in substance, though not in words, that perdition was full of just such fellows as Ollendorff, and they were ready on the slightest pretext to rush in and assume anybody's name, and rap and write and lie and swindle with a perfect looseness whenever they could rope in a living affinity like poor Ollendorff to communicate with! (Great applause and laughter.)

Ollendorff stood his ground with good pluck, and was going to open his batteries again, when a storm of cries arose all over the house, "Get down! Go on! Clear out! Speak on! We'll hear you! Climb down from that platform! Stay where you are! Vamose! Stick to your post! Say your say!"

The medium rose up and said if Ollendorff remained, she would not. She recognized no one's right to come there and insult her by practicing a deception upon her, and attempting to bring ridicule upon so solemn a thing as her religious belief. The audience then became quiet, and the subjugated Ollendorff retired from the platform.

**The other German raised a spirit**, questioned it at some length in his own language, and said the answers were correct. The medium claimed to be entirely unacquainted with the German language.

Just then a gentleman called me to the edge of the platform and asked me if I were a Spiritualist.

I said I was not.

He asked me if I were prejudiced.

I said, not more than any other unbeliever; but I could not believe in a thing which I could not understand, and I had not seen anything yet that I could by any possibility cipher out. He said, then, that he didn't think I was the cause of the diffidence shown by the spirits, but he knew there was an antagonistic influence around that table somewhere; he had noticed it from the first. There was a painful negative current passing to his sensitive organization from that direction constantly. I told him I guessed it was that other fellow; and I said, "Blame a man who was all the time shedding these infernal negative currents!"

This appeared to satisfy the mind of the inquiring fanatic, and he sat down.

I had a very dear friend, who, I had heard, had gone to the spirit-land, or perdition, or some of those places, and I desired to know something concerning him. There was something so awful, though, about talking with living, sinful lips to the ghostly dead, that I could hardly bring myself to rise and speak. But at last I got tremblingly up and said with a low and trembling voice:

"Is the spirit of John Smith present?"

(You never can depend on these Smiths; you call for one, and the whole tribe will come clattering out of hell to answer you.)

"Whack! whack! whack! whack!"

Bless me! I believe all the dead and damned John Smiths between San Francisco and perdition boarded that poor little table at once! I was considerably set back—stunned, I may say. The audience urged me to go on, however, and I said:

"What did you die of?"

The Smiths answered to every disease and casualty that men can die of.

"Where did you die?"

They answered "Yes" to every locality I could name while my geography held out.

"Are you happy where you are?"

There was a vigorous and unanimous "No!" from the late Smiths.

"Is it warm there?"

An educated Smith seized the medium's hand and wrote:

"It's no name for it."

"Did you leave any Smiths in that place when you came

away?"

"Dead loads of them!"

I fancied I heard the shadowy Smiths chuckle at this feeble joke—the rare joke that there could be live loads of Smiths where all are dead.

"How many Smiths are present?"

"Eighteen millions—the procession now reaches from here to the other side of China."

"Then there are many Smiths in the kingdom of the lost?"

"The Prince Apollyon calls all newcomers 'Smith' on general principles; and continues to do so until he is corrected, if he chances to be mistaken."

"What do lost spirits call their dread abode?"

"They call it the Smithsonian Institute."

**I got hold of the right Smith at last**—the particular Smith I was after—my dear, lost, lamented friend—and learned that he died a violent death. I feared as much. He said his wife talked him to death. Poor wretch!

By and by, up started another Smith. A gentleman in the audience said that this was his Smith. So he questioned him, and this Smith said he, too, died by violence. He had been a good deal tangled in his religious belief, and was a sort of a cross between a Universalist and a Unitarian; has got straightened out and changed his opinions since he left here; said he was perfectly happy.

We proceeded to question this talkative and frolicsome old parson. Among spirits I judge he is the gayest of the gay. He said he had no tangible body; a bullet could pass through him and never make a hole; rain could pass through him as through vapor, and not discommode him in the least (so I suppose he don't know enough to come in when it rains—or don't care enough).

Says heaven and hell are simply mental conditions; spirits in the former have happy and contented minds, and those in the latter are torn by remorse of conscience.

Says as far as he is concerned, he is all right—he is happy; would not say whether he was a very good or a very bad man on earth (the shrewd old waterproof nonentity! I asked the question so that I might average my own chances for his luck in the other world, but he saw my drift).

Says he has an occupation there—puts in his time teaching and being taught; says there are spheres—grades of perfection— he is making very good progress—has been promoted a sphere or so since his matriculation (I said mentally, "Go slow, old man, go slow, you have got all eternity before you," and he replied not).

He don't know how many spheres there are (but I suppose there must be millions, because if a man goes galloping through them at the rate this old Universalist is doing, he will get through an infinitude of them by the time he has been there as long as old Sesostris and those ancient mummies; and there is no estimating how high he will get in even the infancy of eternity—I am afraid the old man is scouring along rather too fast for the style of his surroundings, and the length of time he has got on his hands).

Says spirits cannot feel heat or cold (which militates somewhat against all my notions of orthodox damnation—fire and brimstone).

Says spirits commune with each other by thought—they have no language.

Says the distinctions of sex are preserved there, and so forth and so on.

**The old parson wrote and talked for an hour**, and showed by his quick, shrewd, intelligent replies, that he had not been sitting up nights in the other world for nothing; he had been prying into everything worth knowing, and finding out everything he possibly could—as he said himself. When he did not understand a thing, he hunted up a spirit who could explain it, consequently he is pretty thoroughly posted. And for his accommodating conduct and his uniform courtesy to me, I sincerely hope he will continue to progress at his present velocity until he lands on the very roof of the highest sphere of all, and thus achieves perfection.

*Mark Twain wrote this satirical story about a séance in 1866.*

# Lake of Death

Mono Lake lies in a lifeless, treeless, hideous desert, eight thousand feet above the level of the sea, and is guarded by mountains 2,000 feet higher, whose summits are always clothed in clouds.

Mono, it is sometimes called, and sometimes the "Dead Sea of California." It is one of the strangest freaks of Nature to be found in any land, but it is hardly ever mentioned in print and very seldom visited, because it lies away off the usual routes of travel and besides is so difficult to get at that only men content to endure the roughest life will consent to take upon themselves the discomforts of such a trip.

This solemn, silent, sailless sea—this lonely tenant of the loneliest spot on earth—is little graced with the picturesque. It is an unpretending expanse of grayish water, about a hundred miles in circumference, with two islands in its centre, mere upheavals of rent and scorched and blistered lava, snowed over with gray banks and drifts of pumice-stone and ashes, the winding sheet of the dead volcano, whose vast crater the lake has seized upon and occupied.

A man cannot drink the water of Mono Lake, for it is nearly pure lye.

There are no fish in Mono Lake—no frogs, no snakes, no polliwogs—nothing, in fact, that goes to make life desirable. Millions of wild ducks and seagulls swim about the surface, but no living thing exists under the surface except a white feathery sort of worm, one half an inch long, which looks like a bit of white thread frayed out at the sides. If you dip up a gallon of water, you will get about 15,000 of these. They give to the water a sort of grayish-white appearance.

Then there is a fly, which looks something like our house fly. These settle on the beach to eat the worms that wash ashore—and any time, you can see there a belt of flies an inch deep and six feet wide, and this belt extends clear around the lake—a belt of flies one hundred miles long. If you throw a stone among them, they swarm up so thick that they look dense, like a cloud. You can hold them under water as long as you please—they do not mind it—they are only proud of it. When you let them go, they pop up to the surface as dry as a patent office report, and walk off as unconcernedly as if they had been educated especially with a view to affording instructive entertainment to man in that particular way.

The lake is two hundred feet deep, and its sluggish waters are so strong with alkali that if you only dip the most hopelessly soiled garment into them once or twice, and wring it out, it will be found as clean as if it had been through the ablest of washerwomen's hands. While we camped there, our laundry work was easy. We tied the week's washing astern of our boat, and sailed a quarter of a mile, and the job was complete, all to the wringing out.

If we threw the water on our heads and gave them a rub or so, the white lather would pile up three inches high. This water is not good for bruised places and abrasions of the skin.

**We had a valuable dog.** He had raw places on him. He had more raw places on him than sound ones. He was the rawest dog I almost ever saw. He jumped overboard one day to get away from the flies. But it was bad judgment. In his condition, it would have been just as comfortable to jump into the fire.

The alkali water nipped him in all the raw places simultaneously, and he struck out for the shore with considerable interest. He yelped and barked and howled as he went—and by the time he got to the shore, there was no bark to him—for he had barked the bark all out of his inside, and the alkali water had cleaned the bark all off his outside, and he probably wished he had never embarked in any such enterprise.

He ran round and round in a circle, and pawed the earth and clawed the air, and threw double somersaults, sometimes backward and sometimes forward, in the most extraordinary manner. He was not a demonstrative dog, as a general thing, but rather of a grave and serious turn of mind, and I never saw him take so much interest in anything before. He finally struck out over the mountains, at a gait which we estimated at about 250 miles an hour, and he is going yet.

This was about nine years ago. We look for what is left of him along here every day.

*This story is an excerpt from* Roughing It.

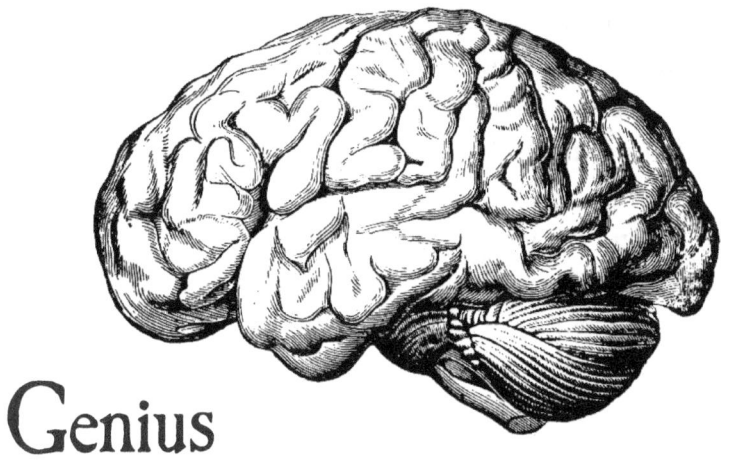

# Genius

Genius, like gold and precious stones,
is chiefly prized because of its rarity.

> Geniuses are people who dash off weird, wild,
> incomprehensible poems with astonishing facility,
> and get booming drunk and sleep in the gutter.

Genius elevates its possessor to ineffable spheres
far above the vulgar world and fills his soul
with regal contempt for the gross and sordid things of
earth.

> It is probably on account of this
> that people who have genius
> do not pay their board, as a general thing.

Geniuses are very singular.
If you see a young man who has frowsy hair
and distraught look, and affects eccentricity in dress,
you may set him down for a genius.

# MARK TWAIN

*If he sings about the degeneracy of a world*
*which courts vulgar opulence*
*and neglects brains,*
*he is undoubtedly a genius.*

*If he is too proud to accept assistance,*
*and spurns it with a lordly air*
*at the very same time*
*that he knows he can't make a living to save his life,*
*he is most certainly a genius.*

> *If he hangs on and sticks to poetry,*
> *notwithstanding sawing wood comes handier to*
> *him, he is a true genius.*

*If he throws away every opportunity in life*
*and crushes the affection and the patience of his friends*
*and then protests in sickly rhymes of his hard lot,*
*and finally persists,*
*in spite of the sound advice of persons who have got sense*
*but not any genius,*
*persists in going up some infamous back alley*
*dying in rags and dirt,*
*he is beyond all question a genius.*

> *But above all things,*
> *to deftly throw the incoherent ravings of insanity*
> *into verse*
> *and then rush off and get booming drunk,*
> *is the surest of all the different signs*
> *of genius.*

Good for Steamship
**AMERICA,**
AND CONNECTING STEAMER

**C. A. TRANSIT CO'S LINE TO NEW YORK, VIA NICARAGUA.**

Ticket No. _____ *San Francisco,* _____ *1866.*

CONTRACT to transport by SEA, NOT TRANSFERABLE, AND GOOD FOR THIS TRIP ONLY.

STEERAGE.

Baggage in excess of 50 pounds, 10 cents per pound. "BAGGAGE" as understood to mean Wearing Apparel only

For value received, on the conditions herein, hereby mutually agreed to, the Central American Transit Co. contracts to furnish to

Berth, No.

**STEERAGE** *passage from* SAN FRANCISCO *to* NEW YORK,

**On Steamers of their Line; to sail this date.**

The dangers of the Seas, Lakes, Rivers and Harbors, restraint of Governments, collision, detention, discomforts and ailments arising therefrom, Fire and Accidents to Machinery, Boiler and Vessel, of every kind, EXCEPTED.

Without accountability for the loss of any baggage, merchandise, gold, silver, or property of any kind, unless a bill of lading or receipt, signed therefor, and freight thereon is paid. Ship's regulations to be complied with. (Good for Steamships on both oceans only.)

I. W. RAYMOND, AGENT.

Berths on connecting Steamers allotted in the order of the Ticket No.

(Such passage will be furnished with a Transit ticket from ocean to ocean.) Per _____

TICKETS to be surrendered to the Purser of Steamship on the Atlantic.

❖   ❖   ❖

Mark Twain wrote "Genius" on Dec. 21, 1866, while aboard the steamship America, which had left San Francisco a week earlier bound for New York. The trip was marred by a cholera outbreak that killed 1 in every 20 passengers and left Twain ill, along with hundreds of others.

"*Our heroes are the men who do things which we recognize with regret and sometimes with a secret shame that we cannot do.*"

Mark Twain's Autobiography

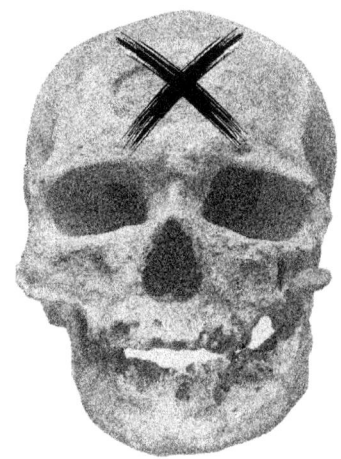

# The Cross of the Mysterious Avenger

When I, as a boy, first saw the mouth of the Missouri River, it was twenty-two or twenty-three miles above St. Louis, according to the estimate of pilots; the wear and tear of the banks have moved it down eight miles since then; and the pilots say that within five years the river will cut through and move the mouth down five miles more, which will bring it within ten miles of St. Louis.

About nightfall we passed the large and flourishing town of Alton, Illinois; and before daylight next morning the town of Louisiana, Missouri, a sleepy village in my day, but a brisk railway center now; however, all the towns out there are railway centers now. I could not clearly recognize the place. This seemed odd to me, for when I retired from the rebel army in '61, I retired upon Louisiana in good order; at least in good enough order for a person who had not yet learned how to retreat according to the rules of war, and had to trust to native genius. It seemed to me that for a first attempt at a retreat it was not badly done. I had done no advancing in all that campaign that was at all equal to it.

There was a railway bridge across the river here well sprinkled with glowing lights, and a very beautiful sight it was.

At seven in the morning, we reached Hannibal, Missouri, where my boyhood was spent. I had had a glimpse of it fifteen years ago, and another glimpse six years earlier, but both were so brief that they hardly counted. The only notion of the town that remained in my mind was the memory of it as I had known it when I first quitted it twenty-nine years ago. That picture of it was still as clear and vivid to me as a photograph. I stepped ashore with the feeling of one who returns out of a dead-and-gone generation. I had a sort of realizing sense of what the Bastille prisoners must have felt when they used to come out and look upon Paris after years of captivity, and note how curiously the familiar and the strange were mixed together before them. I saw the new houses—saw them plainly enough—but they did not affect the older picture in my mind, for through their solid bricks and mortar I saw the vanished houses, which had formerly stood there, with perfect distinctness.

**During my three days' stay in the town**, I woke up every morning with the impression that I was a boy—for in my dreams the faces were all young again, and looked as they had looked in the old times—but I went to bed a hundred years old, every night—for meantime I had been seeing those faces as they are now.

Of course I suffered some surprises, along at first, before I had become adjusted to the changed state of things. I met young ladies who did not seem to have changed at all; but they turned out to be the daughters of the young ladies I had in mind—sometimes their grand-daughters. When you are told that a stranger of fifty is a grandmother, there is nothing surprising about it; but if, on the contrary, she is a person whom you knew as a little girl, it seems impossible. You say to yourself, "How can a little girl be a grandmother?" It takes some little time to accept and realize the fact that while you have been growing old, your friends have not been standing still, in that matter.

I noticed that the greatest changes observable were with the women, not the men. I saw men whom thirty years had changed but slightly; but their wives had grown old. These were good women; it is very wearing to be good.

There was a saddler whom I wished to see; but he was gone. Dead, these many years, they said. Once or twice a day, the saddler used to go tearing down the street, putting on his coat as he went; and then everybody knew a steamboat was coming. Everybody knew, also, that John Stavely was not expecting anybody by the boat—or any freight, either; and Stavely must have known that everybody knew this, still it made no difference to him; he liked to seem to himself to be expecting a hundred thousand tons of saddles by this boat, and so he went on all his life, enjoying being faithfully on hand to receive and receipt for those saddles, in case by any miracle they should come. A malicious Quincy paper used always to refer to this town, in derision as "Stavely's Landing." Stavely was one of my earliest admirations; I envied him his rush of imaginary business, and the display he was able to make of it, before strangers, as he went flying down the street struggling with his fluttering coat.

But there was a carpenter who was my chiefest hero. He was a mighty liar, but I did not know that; I believed everything he said. He was a romantic, sentimental, melodramatic fraud, and his bearing impressed me with awe. I vividly remember the first time he took me into his confidence. He was planing a board, and every now and then he would pause and heave a deep sigh; and occasionally mutter broken sentences—confused and not intelligible—but out of their midst an ejaculation sometimes escaped which made me shiver and did me good: one was, "O God, it is his blood!" I sat on the tool chest and humbly and shudderingly admired him, for I judged he was full of crime.

At last he said in a low voice, "My little friend, can you keep a secret?"

I eagerly said I could.

"A dark and dreadful one?"

I satisfied him on that point.

"Then I will tell you some passages in my history; for oh, I MUST relieve my burdened soul, or I shall die!"

He cautioned me once more to be "as silent as the grave;" then he told me he was a "red-handed murderer." He put down his plane, held his hands out before him, contemplated them sadly, and said, "Look, with these hands I have taken the lives of thirty human beings!"

The effect which this had upon me was an inspiration to him, and he turned himself loose upon his subject with interest and energy. He left generalizing, and went into details: began with his first murder, described it, told what measures he had taken to avert suspicion; then passed to his second homicide, his third, his fourth, and so on. He had always done his murders with a bowie-knife, and he made all my hairs rise by suddenly snatching it out and showing it to me.

At the end of this first séance, I went home with six of his fearful secrets among my freightage, and found them a great help to my dreams, which had been sluggish for a while back. I sought him again and again, on my Saturday holidays; in fact I spent the summer with him—all of it which was valuable to me. His fascinations never diminished, for he threw something fresh and stirring, in the way of horror, into each successive murder. He always gave names, dates, places—everything. This by and by enabled me to note two things: that he had killed his victims in every quarter of the globe, and that these victims were always named Lynch.

The destruction of the Lynches went serenely on, Saturday after Saturday, until the original thirty had multiplied to sixty—and more to be heard from yet; then my curiosity got the better of my timidity, and I asked how it happened that these justly punished persons all bore the same name.

My hero said he had never divulged that dark secret to any living being; but felt that he could trust me, and therefore he would lay bare before me the story of his sad and blighted life.

He had loved one "too fair for earth," and she had reciprocated "with all the sweet affection of her pure and noble nature." But he had a rival, a "base hireling" named Archibald Lynch, who said the girl should be his, or he would "dye his hands in her heart's best blood." The carpenter, "innocent and happy in love's young dream," gave no weight to the threat, but led his "golden-haired darling to the altar," and there, the two were made one; there also, just as the minister's hands were stretched in blessing over their heads, the fell deed was done—with a knife—and the bride fell a corpse at her husband's feet.

And what did the husband do? He plucked forth that knife, and kneeling by the body of his lost one, swore to "consecrate his life to the extermination of all the human scum that bear the hated name of Lynch."

That was it. He had been hunting down the Lynches and slaughtering them, from that day to this—twenty years. He had always used that same consecrated knife; with it he had murdered his long array of Lynches, and with it he had left upon the forehead of each victim a peculiar mark—a cross, deeply incised.

Said he: "The cross of the Mysterious Avenger is known in Europe, in America, in China, in Siam, in the Tropics, in the Polar Seas, in the deserts of Asia, in all the earth. Wherever in the uttermost parts of the globe, a Lynch has penetrated, there has the Mysterious Cross been seen, and those who have seen it have shuddered and said, "It is his mark, he has been here." You have heard of the Mysterious Avenger—look upon him, for before you stands no less a person! But beware— breathe not a word to any soul. Be silent, and wait. Some morning, this town will flock aghast to view a gory corpse; on its brow will be seen the awful sign, and men will tremble and whisper, 'He has been here—it is the Mysterious Avenger's mark!' You will come here, but I shall have vanished; you will see me no more."

**This ass had been reading the *Jibbenainosay*** [an 1837 novel by Robert Montgomery Bird], no doubt, and had had his poor romantic head turned by it; but as I had not yet seen the book then, I took his inventions for truth, and did not suspect that he was a plagiarist.

However, we had a Lynch living in the town, and the more I reflected upon his impending doom, the more I could not sleep.

It seemed my plain duty to save him, and a still plainer and more important duty to get some sleep for myself, so at last I ventured to go to Mr. Lynch and tell him what was about to happen to him—under strict secrecy. I advised him to "fly," and certainly expected him to do it.

But he laughed at me, and he did not stop there: He led me down to the carpenter's shop, gave the carpenter a jeering and scornful lecture upon his silly pretensions, slapped his face, made him get down on his knees and beg—then went off and left me to contemplate the cheap and pitiful ruin of what, in my eyes, had so lately been a majestic and incomparable hero. The carpenter blustered, flourished his knife, and doomed this Lynch in his usual volcanic style, the size of his fateful words undiminished; but it was all wasted upon me. He was a hero to me no longer, but only a poor, foolish, exposed humbug. I was ashamed of him, and ashamed of myself. I took no further interest in him, and never went to his shop any more. He was a heavy loss to me, for he was the greatest hero I had ever known. The fellow must have had some talent; for some of his imaginary murders were so vividly and dramatically described that I remember all their details yet.

*"The Cross of the Mysterious Avenger" is an excerpt from Mark Twain's* Life of on the Mississippi, *with the introductory section taken from Chapter 53 and the section concerning the Mysterious Avenger appearing in Chapter 55. The book, published in 1883, was inspired by a trip down the river in 1880, which sparked in the author a desire to document the river as it had been during his youth.*

# Lake of Fire,
# Pillar of Flame

We bought horses and bent our way over the summer-clad mountain-terraces, toward the great volcano of Kilauea (Ke-low-way-ah). We made nearly a two days' journey of it, but that was on account of laziness.

Toward sunset on the second day, we reached an elevation of some 4,000 feet above sea level, and as we picked our careful way through billowy wastes of lava long generations ago stricken dead and cold in the climax of its tossing fury, we began to come upon signs of the near presence of the volcano—signs in the nature of ragged fissures that discharged jets of sulfurous vapor into the air, hot from the molten ocean down in the bowels of the mountain.

Shortly the crater came into view.

I have seen Vesuvius since, but it was a mere toy, a child's volcano, a soup-kettle, compared to this. Mount Vesuvius is a shapely cone 3,600 feet high; its crater an inverted cone only three hundred feet deep, and not more than a thousand feet in diameter, if as much as that; its fires meagre, modest, and docile. But here was a vast, perpendicular, walled cellar, 900 feet deep in some places, 1,300 in others, level-floored, and *ten miles in circumference!* Here was a yawning pit upon whose floor the armies of Russia could camp, and have room to spare.

Perched upon the edge of the crater, at the opposite end from where we stood, was a small lookout house—say three miles away. It assisted us, by comparison, to comprehend and appreciate the great depth of the basin—it looked like a tiny martin-box clinging at the eaves of a cathedral. After some little time spent in resting and looking and ciphering, we hurried on to the hotel.

By the path, it is half a mile from the Volcano House to the lookout house. After a hearty supper, we waited until it was thoroughly dark and then started to the crater. The first glance in that direction revealed a scene of wild beauty. There was a heavy fog over the crater, and it was splendidly illuminated by the glare from the fires below. The illumination was two miles wide and a mile high, perhaps; and if you ever, on a dark night and at a distance, beheld the light from thirty or forty blocks of distant buildings all on fire at once, reflected strongly against overhanging clouds, you can form a fair idea of what this looked like.

A colossal column of cloud towered to a great height in the

air immediately above the crater, and the outer swell of every one of its vast folds was dyed with a rich crimson luster, which was subdued to a pale rose tint in the depressions between. It glowed like a muffled torch and stretched upward to a dizzy height toward the zenith. I thought it just possible that its like had not been seen since the children of Israel wandered on their long march through the desert so many centuries ago over a path illuminated by the mysterious "pillar of fire." And I was sure that I now had a vivid conception of what the majestic "pillar of fire" was like, which almost amounted to a revelation.

Arrived at the little thatched lookout house, we rested our elbows on the railing in front and looked abroad over the wide crater and down over the sheer precipice at the seething fires beneath us. The view was a startling improvement on my daylight experience. I turned to see the effect on the balance of the company and found the reddest-faced set of men I almost ever saw. In the strong light, every countenance glowed like red-hot iron, every shoulder was suffused with crimson and shaded rearward into dingy, shapeless obscurity! The place below looked like the infernal regions and these men like half-cooled devils just come up on a furlough.

I turned my eyes upon the volcano again.

The "cellar" was tolerably well lighted up. For a mile and a half in front of us and half a mile on either side, the floor of the abyss was magnificently illuminated; beyond these limits, the mists hung down their gauzy curtains and cast a deceptive gloom over all that made the twinkling fires in the remote corners of the crater seem countless leagues removed—made them seem like the campfires of a great army far away.

Here was room for the imagination to work! You could imagine those lights the width of a continent away—and that hidden under the intervening darkness were hills, and winding rivers, and weary wastes of plain and desert—and even then the tremendous vista stretched on, and on, and on!—to the fires and far beyond! You could not compass it. It was the idea of eternity made tangible, and the longest end of it made visible to the naked eye!

The greater part of the vast floor of the desert under us was as black as ink, and apparently smooth and level; but over a mile square of it was ringed and streaked and striped with a thousand branching streams of liquid and gorgeously brilliant fire! It looked like a colossal railroad map of the State of Massachusetts done in chain lightning on a midnight sky. Imagine it. Imagine a coal-black sky shivered into a tangled network of angry fire!

Here and there were gleaming holes a hundred feet in diameter, broken in the dark crust, and in them the melted lava—the color a dazzling white just tinged with yellow—was boiling and surging furiously; and from these holes branched numberless bright torrents in many directions, like the spokes of a wheel, and kept a tolerably straight course for a while and then swept round in huge rainbow curves, or made a long succession of sharp worn fence angles, which looked precisely like the fiercest jagged lightning.

These streams met other streams, and they mingled with and crossed and recrossed each other in every conceivable direction, like skate tracks on a popular skating ground. Sometimes streams twenty or thirty feet wide flowed from the holes to some distance without dividing—and through the opera-glasses we could see that they ran down small, steep hills and were genuine cataracts of fire, white at their source, but soon cooling and turning to the richest red, grained with alternate lines of black and gold.

Every now and then, masses of the dark crust broke away and floated slowly down these streams like rafts down a river. Occasionally the molten lava flowing under the superincumbent crust broke through—split a dazzling streak, from 500 to a thousand feet long, like a sudden flash of lightning, and then acre after acre of the cold lava parted into fragments, turned up edgewise like cakes of ice when a great river breaks up, plunged downward and were swallowed in the crimson cauldron.

Then the wide expanse of the "thaw" maintained a ruddy glow for a while, but shortly cooled and became black and level again. During a "thaw," every dismembered cake was marked by a glittering white border which was superbly shaded inward by aurora borealis rays, which were a flaming yellow where they joined the white border, and from thence toward their points tapered into glowing crimson, then into a rich, pale carmine, and finally into a faint blush that held its own a moment and then dimmed and turned black.

Some of the streams preferred to mingle together in a tangle of fantastic circles, and then they looked something like the confusion of ropes one sees on a ship's deck when she has just taken in sail and dropped anchor—provided one can imagine those ropes on fire.

Through the glasses, the little fountains scattered about looked very beautiful. They boiled, and coughed, and spluttered, and discharged sprays of stringy red fire—of about the consistency of mush, for instance—from ten to fifteen feet into the air, along with a shower of brilliant white sparks—a quaint and unnatural mingling of gouts of blood and snowflakes!

We had circles and serpents and streaks of lightning all twined and wreathed and tied together, without a break throughout an area more than a mile square (that amount of ground was covered, though it was not strictly "square"), and it was with a feeling of placid exultation that we reflected that many years had elapsed since any visitor had seen such a splendid display—since any visitor had seen anything more than the now snubbed and insignificant "North" and "South" lakes in action. We had been reading old files of Hawaiian newspapers and the

"Record Book" at the Volcano House, and were posted.

I could see the North Lake lying out on the black floor away off in the outer edge of our panorama, and knitted to it by a web-work of lava streams. In its individual capacity, it looked very little more respectable than a schoolhouse on fire. True, it was about 900 feet long and two or three hundred wide, but then, under the present circumstances, it necessarily appeared rather insignificant, and besides it was so distant from us.

I forgot to say that the noise made by the bubbling lava is not great, heard as we heard it from our lofty perch. It makes three distinct sounds—a rushing, a hissing, and a coughing or puffing sound; and if you stand on the brink and close your eyes, it is no trick at all to imagine that you are sweeping down a river on a large low-pressure steamer, and that you hear the hissing of the steam about her boilers, the puffing from her escape-pipes and the churning rush of the water abaft her wheels. The smell of sulfur is strong, but not unpleasant to a sinner.

We left the lookout house at ten o'clock in a half-cooked condition, because of the heat from Pele's furnaces, and wrapping up in blankets, for the night was cold, we returned to our hotel.

**The next night was appointed** for a visit to the bottom of the crater, for we desired to traverse its floor and see the "North Lake" (of fire) which lay two miles away, toward the further wall.

After dark, half a dozen of us set out, with lanterns and native guides, and climbed down a crazy, thousand-foot pathway in a crevice fractured in the crater wall, and reached the bottom in safety.

The eruption of the previous evening had spent its force, and the floor looked black and cold; but when we ran out upon it we found it hot yet, to the feet, and it was likewise riven with crevices which revealed the underlying fires gleaming vindictively. A neighboring cauldron was threatening to

110

overflow, and this added to the dubiousness of the situation. So the native guides refused to continue the venture, and then everybody deserted except a stranger named Marlette. He said he had been in the crater a dozen times in daylight and believed he could find his way through it at night. He thought that a run of 300 yards would carry us over the hottest part of the floor and leave us our shoe-soles.

His pluck gave me backbone. We took one lantern and instructed the guides to hang the other to the roof of the lookout house to serve as a beacon for us in case we got lost, and then the party started back up the precipice, and Marlette and I made our run. We skipped over the hot floor and over the red crevices with brisk dispatch and reached the cold lava safe, but with pretty warm feet.

Then we took things leisurely and comfortably, jumping tolerably wide and probably bottomless chasms, and threading our way through picturesque lava upheavals with considerable confidence. When we got fairly away from the cauldrons of boiling fire, we seemed to be in a gloomy desert, and a suffocatingly dark one, surrounded by dim walls that seemed to tower to the sky. The only cheerful objects were the glinting stars high overhead.

**By and by, Marlette shouted, "Stop!"** I never stopped quicker in my life.

I asked what the matter was. He said we were out of the path. He said we must not try to go on till we found it again, for we were surrounded with beds of rotten lava through which we could easily break and plunge down a thousand feet.

I thought 800 would answer for me, and was about to say so when Marlette partly proved his statement by accidentally crushing through and disappearing to his arm-pits. He got out, and we hunted for the path with the lantern. He said there was only one path and that it was but vaguely defined. We could not find it.

The lava surface was all alike in the lantern light. But he was an ingenious man. He said it was not the lantern that had informed him that we were out of the path, but his feet. He had noticed a crisp grinding of fine lava needles under his feet, and some instinct reminded him that, in the path, these were all worn away.

So he put the lantern behind him, and began to search with his boots instead of his eyes. It was good sagacity. The first time his foot touched a surface that did not grind under it, he announced that the trail was found again; and after that we kept up a sharp listening for the rasping sound, and it always warned us in time.

It was a long tramp, but an exciting one. We reached the North Lake between 10 and 11 o'clock, and sat down on a huge overhanging lava shelf, tired but satisfied. The spectacle presented was worth coming double the distance to see. Under us, and stretching away before us, was a heaving sea of molten fire of seemingly limitless extent. The glare from it was so blinding that it was some time before we could bear to look upon it steadily. It was like gazing at the sun at noonday, except that the glare was not quite so white.

At unequal distances all around the shores of the lake were nearly white-hot chimneys or hollow drums of lava, four or five feet high, and up through them were bursting gorgeous sprays of lava-gouts and gem spangles, some white, some red and some golden—a ceaseless bombardment, and one that fascinated the eye with its unapproachable splendor. The more distant jets, sparkling up through an intervening gossamer veil of vapor, seemed miles away; and the further the curving ranks of fiery fountains receded, the more fairy-like and beautiful they appeared.

Now and then the surging bosom of the lake under our noses would calm down ominously and seem to be gathering strength for an enterprise; and then, all of a sudden, a red dome of lava of the bulk of an ordinary dwelling would heave itself aloft like an escaping balloon, then burst asunder, and out of its heart would flit a pale-green film of vapor, and float upward and vanish in the darkness—a released soul soaring homeward from captivity with the damned, no doubt.

The crashing plunge of the ruined dome into the lake again would send a world of seething billows lashing against the shores and shaking the foundations of our perch. By and by, a loosened mass of the hanging shelf we sat on tumbled into the lake, jarring the surroundings like an earthquake and delivering a suggestion that may have been intended for a hint, and may not.

We did not wait to see.

We got lost again on our way back, and were more than an hour hunting for the path. We were where we could see the beacon lantern at the lookout house at the time, but thought it was a star and paid no attention to it. We reached the hotel at two o'clock in the morning, pretty well tuckered out.

*"Lake of Fire, Pillar of Flame" (editor's title) is an excerpt from Mark Twain's* Roughing It, *in which he recounts his journey to the Sandwich Islands, aka Hawai'i. Twain's background as a reporter is on full display in this piece, in which he provides a stunning and detailed description of Kilauea.*

# Ghost Life on the Mississippi

The recent death of an old Saint Louis and New Orleans pilot has brought the following strange story to light. I shall not attempt, by any word of my own, to secure the reader's belief in it, but I will merely relate the simple facts in the case, as they fell from the lips of a dying man, and leave him to form his own opinion. Fictitious names, however, will be used throughout the narrative, in accordance with the wishes of certain actors in the mysterious drama who are still living.

Joseph Millard, the pilot referred to, was a master of his profession, a good man, and a truthful man; and this tale, coming from his lips, while in a perfectly sound state of mind, and stretched upon his death-bed, leaves but a small field for the cavilings of the incredulous. Until that hour, the whole thing had been kept a profound secret by himself and the other witnesses of the horrible affair.

And now for the facts.

A number of years ago, a Saint Louis and New Orleans packet, which I will call the "Boreas," was on her way up the river, and at about 10 o'clock at night, the sky, which had before been clear, suddenly became overcast, and snow commenced falling soon afterwards. The boat was near the head of Dog Tooth Bend at the time. The Captain stepped out of the "Texas," and said to the pilot on watch:

"Well, I reckon Goose Island wouldn't be a very safe place for the Boreas tonight, Mr. Jones. So, if it keeps on snowing at this rate, I reckon you had better bring her to at the first wood-pile you come across near the head of Dog Tooth or Buffalo Island."

The little narrow bend around Goose Island is called the "Grave-Yard," because of the numerous wrecks of steamboats that have found a tomb in it. Besides these obstructions, a great many large snags stood directly in the way at the time I speak of, and the narrow channel being very "shoal" also, the best of piloting was necessary in order to "run" Goose Island in safety, even in daylight.

Mr. Jones passed the woodyards in silence, and held his way up the river through the driving rain; for that very day he had declared that Goose Island "had no terrors for him, on any kind of night," and had been laughed at by several other pilots, who jestingly called him the "King of Pilots." He was still angry and sullen, and occasionally, as he thought of the jest, he would grate his teeth and mutter that "he would show them that he was the king of pilots in reality."

At about half past eleven, the other pilot came up, having

been called too soon, through a mistake on the part of the watchman, and noticing that the boat was approaching the foot of Goose Island , he said: "Why, Jones, surely you are not going to run this place on such a night as this?"

"I'll take her through, if the Devil seizes me for it in five minutes afterwards!"

And through those hidden dangers—and shrouded in that Egyptian darkness—the steamer plowed her way, watched by an unerring eye and guided by a master hand, whose nerves trembled not for a single instant! And snags and wrecks remained untouched.

"Now, who is king of pilots!"

And those were the last words of William Jones, pilot.

Then he gave up the wheel and left the pilot house, and when the 4 o'clock watch was called, he could not be found. There was blood upon the "nosing" of the starboard guard, and a fireman said, the next day, that a man fell from the boiler deck in the night, and he thought his head struck that place, but that the watchman only laughed at him when he mentioned it, and said he had a fertile imagination.

**When the Boreas arrived at Saint Louis,** she was sold, and lay idle the balance of the summer, and fall, and finally left for New Orleans in the dead of winter, with an entirely new set of officers—Joe Millard and Ben. Reubens, pilots.

One cold, raw night, as the boat was approaching Goose Island, snow commenced falling, and it soon became almost too dark to run. This reminded Joe of the almost forgotten Jones; and he determined to try and get the boat up into the little bend as far as the "Shingle Pile," and lay up till morning, as he preferred having the balance of Goose Island in daylight.

He had just gained the foot of the bend when the snow commenced falling so densely that he could see nothing at all—

not even the trees on the shore at his side. He stopped the engines, of course.

At that moment he felt conscious that he was not alone—that someone was in the pilot house with him—although he had bolted the door on the inside, to keep it from blowing open, and that was the only mode of ingress! Yes, he was sure he could distinguish the dim outline of a human figure standing on the opposite side of the wheel.

A moment after, he heard the bell lines pulled—heard the handles strike the frame as they fell back to their places, and then the faint tinkle of the answering bells came up from below. In an instant, the wheel was jerked out of his hands, and a sudden gleam of light from a crack in the stovepipe revealed the ghastly features of William Jones, with a great piece of skin, ragged and bloody, torn loose from his forehead and dangling and flapping over his left eye—the other eye dead and fixed and lusterless—hair wet and disordered, and the whole body bent and shapeless, like that of a drowned man, and apparently rigid as marble, except the hands and arms, which seemed alone endued with life and motion!

Joseph Millard's blood curdled in his veins, and he trembled in every limb at the horrid vision. And yet he was a brave man, and held no superstitious notions. He would have left the accursed place, but he seemed bound with bands of iron. He tried to call for help, but his tongue refused its office; he caught the sound of the watchman's heavy tramp on the hurricane deck—would no signal draw his attention? But the trial was vain—he could neither move nor speak—and aid and comfort almost in a whisper's reach of him. Then the footsteps died away, and the desperate man was left alone with his fearful company.

Riveted to the spot, he listened to the clashing engines and the moaning of the frosty wind, while that ghostly pilot steered the vessel through darkness such as no human eye could penetrate. Millard expected every moment to hear the timbers crashing against wreck or snag, but he was deceived. Through every danger that infested the way, the dead man steered in safety, turning the wheel from one side to the other calmly and quietly as if it had been noonday.

**It seemed to Millard** as if an age had passed over his head when he heard something fall on the floor with a slight clatter on the other side of the wheel; he did not know what it was—he only shuddered, and wondered what it meant. Soon after, by the faint light from the crack in the stovepipe, he saw his ghostly comrade moving silently towards the door—saw him lean against it for a moment, open it, and disappear.

Millard mustered strength enough to stop the engines, and at the same moment, he heard the voice of his partner at the door. He stepped back to open it, and found that it was still bolted on the inside!

Poor Millard was now utterly confounded. He felt qualified to swear that he had seen the shape—no matter what it was—man or ghost or devil—go out at that very door—and yet it was still bolted! And so securely too that he hardly had strength enough left to unfasten it. But when the feat was at last accomplished, he sank down, exhausted, and trembling from head to foot like a man with the palsy.

"Why how is this, Joe?—out in such a snowstorm, when one can't see the chimneys, let alone the derricks and jackstaff! You're beating Jones himself, Joe. Where are we, man? Where are we?"

"God only knows! Land her, Ben, for Heaven's sake, if you can ever find the shore."

During a momentary lull in the storm, Ben felt his way to shore, and rounded to under Philadelphia Point. And then he proceeded to question Joe.

"Swear that you will never mention the matter during my

life, and I will tell you what I have seen this night; but on no other terms will I open my lips—for if the story should get abroad, Joseph Millard would become the laughingstock of the whole river, Ben."

Reubens wondered much at Millard's strange conduct; his curiosity was raised, however, and he took the oath. And quaking and shuddering, his comrade told the fearful tale.

Reubens was silent for a moment, after Millard had finished.

"You spoke of something that fell and rattled on the floor, Joe... What do you suppose it was?"

"It startled me when it fell, but I have no idea what it was, Ben."

"Well, I'll go after a lantern, and we'll soon find out."

"What! and leave me here by myself! I wouldn't stay here alone five minutes for a dozen steamboats."

So they both went, and soon returned with a light. Near the footboard, on the starboard side of the wheel, they saw a glittering object, which proved to be a silver watch, lying open, with the crystal detached and broken in half. The break seemed recent. Neatly engraved, on the back of the watch, were these words.

"WILLIAM JONES—PRESENTED BY HIS FATHER."

*"Ghost Life in the Mississippi" was written by Twain c. 1861.*

# The Aged Pilot Man

*On the Erie Canal, it was,*
*All on a summer's day,*
*I sailed forth with my parents*
*Far away to Albany.*

> *From out the clouds at noon that day*
> *There came a dreadful storm,*
> *That piled the billows high about,*
> *And filled us with alarm.*

*A man came rushing from a house,*
*Saying, "Snub up your boat I pray,*

*Snub up your boat, snub up, alas,*
*Snub up while yet you may."*

> *Our captain cast one glance astern,*
> *Then forward glanced he,*
> *And said, "My wife and little ones*
> *I never more shall see."*

*Said Dollinger the pilot man,*
*In noble words, but few,*
*"Fear not, but lean on Dollinger,*
*And he will fetch you through."*

> *The boat drove on, the frightened mules*
> *Tore through the rain and wind,*
> *And bravely still, in danger's post,*
> *The whip-boy strode behind.*

*"Come 'board, come 'board," the captain cried,*
*"Nor tempt so wild a storm;"*
*But still the raging mules advanced,*
*And still the boy strode on.*

> *Then said the captain to us all,*
> *"Alas, 'tis plain to me,*
> *The greater danger is not there,*
> *But here upon the sea.*

*So let us strive, while life remains,*
*To save all souls on board,*
*And then if die at last we must,*

# DARK TWAIN

*Let... I cannot speak the word!"*

> *Said Dollinger the pilot man,*
> *Tow'ring above the crew,*
> *"Fear not, but trust in Dollinger,*
> *And he will fetch you through."*

*"Low bridge! low bridge!" all heads went down,*
*The laboring bark sped on;*
*A mill we passed, we passed church,*
*Hamlets, and fields of corn;*
*And all the world came out to see,*
*And chased along the shore*
*Crying, "Alas, alas, the sheeted rain,*
*The wind, the tempest's roar!*
*Alas, the gallant ship and crew,*
*Can nothing help them more?"*

> *And from our deck sad eyes looked out*
> *Across the stormy scene:*
> *The tossing wake of billows aft,*
> *The bending forests green,*
> *The chickens sheltered under carts*
> *In lee of barn the cows,*
> *The scurrying swine with straw in mouth,*
> *The wild spray from our bows!*

*"She balances!*
*She wavers!*
*Now let her go about!*
*If she misses stays and broaches to,*

We're all"—then with a shout,
"Huray! huray!
Avast! belay!
Take in more sail!
Lord, what a gale!
Ho, boy, haul taut on the hind mule's tail!"
"Ho! lighten ship! ho! man the pump!
Ho, hostler, heave the lead!

    "A quarter-three!—'tis shoaling fast!
    Three feet large!—t-h-r-e-e feet!—
    Three feet scant!" I cried in fright
    "Oh, is there no retreat?"

Said Dollinger, the pilot man,
As on the vessel flew,
"Fear not, but trust in Dollinger,
And he will fetch you through."

    A panic struck the bravest hearts,
    The boldest cheek turned pale;
    For plain to all, this shoaling said
    A leak had burst the ditch's bed!
    And, straight as bolt from crossbow sped,
    Our ship swept on, with shoaling lead,
    Before the fearful gale!

"Sever the tow-line! Cripple the mules!"
Too late! There comes a shock!
Another length, and the fated craft
Would have swum in the saving lock!

# DARK TWAIN

Then gathered together the shipwrecked crew
And took one last embrace,
While sorrowful tears from despairing eyes
Ran down each hopeless face;
And some did think of their little ones
Whom they never more might see,
And others of waiting wives at home,
And mothers that grieved would be.

But of all the children of misery there
On that poor sinking frame,
But one spake words of hope and faith,
And I worshipped as they came:
Said Dollinger the pilot man,
(O brave heart, strong and true!)
"Fear not, but trust in Dollinger,
For he will fetch you through."

Lo! scarce the words have passed his lips
The dauntless prophet say'th,
When every soul about him seeth
A wonder crown his faith!

And count ye all, both great and small,
As numbered with the dead:
For mariner for forty year,
On Erie, boy and man,
I never yet saw such a storm, Or one't with it began!"

So overboard a keg of nails
And anvils three we threw,

*Likewise four bales of gunny-sacks,*
*Two hundred pounds of glue,*
*Two sacks of corn, four ditto wheat,*
*A box of books, a cow,*
*A violin, Lord Byron's works,*
*A rip-saw and a sow.*


*A curve! a curve! the dangers grow!*
*"Labbord!—stabbord!—s-t-e-a-d-y!—so! —*
*Hard-a-port, Dol!—hellum-a-lee!*
*Haw the head mule!—the aft one gee!*
*Luff!—bring her to the wind!"*


*For straight a farmer brought a plank,*
*(Mysteriously inspired)*
*And laying it unto the ship,*
*In silent awe retired.*


*Then every sufferer stood amazed*
*That pilot man before;*
*A moment stood. Then wondering turned,*
*And speechless walked ashore.*

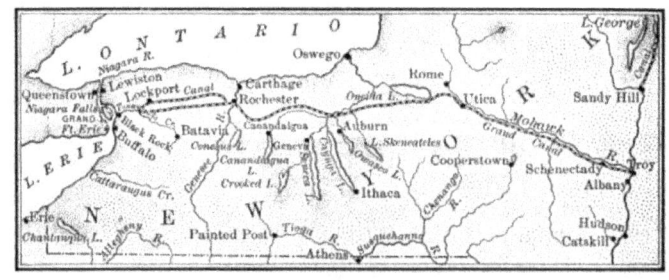

Twain included "The Aged Pilot Man" in Roughing It.

# A Human Bloodhound

*The story of Harbison*

My father... was always more interested in reasoning out the origin of a curious thing than he was in playing and fussing with the thing itself. But to others the particulars in Harbison's case were the most interesting part. It was so with me, and that was natural, I being only a boy and not a philosopher; and it was so with the Corpse and also with his brother the lawyer—his elder brother, I mean—Edward; for Alfred, the other one, as I have already indicated, was too sick a man in those days to care for earthly things of any kind.

If anyone in the village could be said to be intimate with Harbison, it was the Corpse; and next to him, Johnson. These two knew all about Harbison from his own lips; he talked with them pretty freely, although he was so reserved with the rest of the community. In turn they talked freely together about

Harbison almost every day; and of course, situated as I was, I heard it all.

And so, in the course of time, I came to know as much about that human freak as there was to know. It gave him a tremendous interest in my eyes, and I used to stare at him with a fascinated gaze and an imagination surcharged with uncanny fancies as he passed by. The bigness of him, his breadth of shoulder, his slow and stately tread, his head bent in thought, his gloomy mien, the absence of the usual signs of age—these things, assisted by his story, made him an impressive figure—and the three purple birthmark stripes across his face gave him the air of looking through a grating and supplied a touch of weirdness to the general effect which properly rounded it out and perfected it.

**He was five or six years old** before he found out that he was not as other children were. He was playing near a deserted house in a deserted field one day with some small comrades, in the summer gloaming, when a small creature raced past them and ran into the house.

The startled children wondered what it was.

He said it was a little cat.

They said no, it might be a little dog, and it might be a little rabbit, it was too dark to tell. He said they were stupid—come, and he would show them the cat. So they entered the house and stood within the ruined door, but would venture no further, for the place was dark. He said, "I told you so—there she is, over there."

"Where?"

"In the corner."

"Do you see her?"

"No."

"Then how do you know?"

"Why, can't I smell her? Can't you?"

They laughed and said he was a little fool; and they made so much fun of him that he was ashamed, and went and brought the cat, to establish his case.

The children told the wonderful thing at home, and everybody came and tested him, and he was soon a much sought lion. This was pleasant enough for a time, but it presently became a distress and a bother; not to himself alone, but to his mother as well.

He grew ashamed of being different from other children, and of being called a "dog-boy," and the matter was a distress to his mother because she lived a secluded life and neither paid nor received visits, and did not wish to know anyone. Exhibitions of the boy's strange gift were stopped entirely, and by and by, they ceased from being called for. After that, the young widow's peace was not disturbed again, and in time the lad's specialty dropped out of the people's talk and became a forgotten thing.

**In his age**, Harbison did not make a secret of his gift, but it was not easy to get him to make idle exhibitions of it for the satisfaction of curiosity-mongers. He allowed Johnson and the Corpse to test him whenever they chose, in private, and so of course I had plenty of chances to be a witness.

There was a strong feeling in the town against the Corpse on account of the new religion which he pretended to be getting up, and when the manuscript of his extravagant "Account of the Creation" was stolen, it was Harbison who hunted the thief down and got it back. I was to blame for the theft, and was well scared when I missed the MS., for I had been often warned to put it away when I was called from my copying, but this time I didn't do it because I was only going across the street and expected to be back in a moment.

But there was a street fight, and it lasted as much as ten minutes, and that was what made the trouble. I had left Johnson and the Corpse chatting in the front room, and of course they were a sufficient protection for the back one. Would have been, but for the fight. I was back from the fight a little before they were, and when I found the place empty and both doors standing open, I was frightened. And cause enough, too. A glance into the back room realized that to me. My superiors arrived just then, and I told them what had happened, and I was almost crying. Of course the Corpse comforted me and said it wasn't any great matter, he could write it again and do it better this time—which was a lie, it made him sick and pale to think of that vast loss, but he was a good heart and couldn't bear to see anybody suffer if a lie could help him out any.

To make matters as bad as possible, Harbison was out of town and not expected back for a week, otherwise the thing would not have been so serious. But at this moment, when I was feeling my worst, Harbison stepped in. It was a great relief to us all. Harbison named the fifteen or twenty citizens who had been in the front room in the course of the day, then he went into the back room and said only one person had been in there besides me.

He named poor old deacon West!

That was a thunder-clap out of a clear sky, for if there was a man in the town with a more honorable record than the deacon, he had not been discovered yet. I went along with Harbison, but Johnson and the Corpse didn't wish to go, and stayed behind.

The deacon was confused, and ostensibly indignant, but Harbison walked by him and into a bedroom, and went to the bed and said, "It's about this bed somewhere; will you search, deacon, or must I? Spare me that."

So the deacon apologized, and got it out from between the ticks. He said he had done wrong, but not from a selfish motive; he had heard that it was a wicked book and would do harm if published, and he wanted to save the people from moral injury by destroying it; but he was willing to confess that he had done wrong, and he begged that for the sake of his previous good name we would not tell his sin. We promised, and that was the end of it.

**When Harbison was tracking anything,** you would not know it by the look of him, for he walked erect and did not need to stoop down to get the scent. He knew the scent of every person in the town, and could go along the empty streets at midnight and name all the people who had gone about them during the day.

Also, he not only knew an old scent from a new one, but he could name the age in hours. He would say "Mr. Black passed here about four hours ago, and stepped on the track made by Mr. White about twenty hours ago." And if you went and inquired, you would find he was right.

He couldn't ever be alone! The streets were crowded with the scent-spectres of men and women and dogs and cats and children, for him, when they were empty for you and you couldn't see a living thing. It was like crowding your way through swarms of ghosts when you walked by night with him, and although it was dead, still you seemed to hear them rustle. It was very interesting and unpleasant, and I always liked it. When he found that I didn't talk and he could trust me, he took me along for company many a time—particularly after I had the luck to do him the good turn mentioned in a previous chapter. He mainly walked at night, and late; he liked to know who had been around during the day, but he didn't want their physical company.

He could keep secrets himself. The time that Jack Collins disappeared and everybody thought he was drowned, Harbison knew he was hiding in the town all the while; for he came out disguised and took exercise on dark nights and Harbison ran across his scent, and we followed it to his hiding place and had a talk with him. We went there more than once, but didn't betray him.

Harbison could go and walk through the church on a Sunday afternoon and name every person who had attended church and Sunday school there in the morning. No dog had any advantage of him; with the wind in his favor, he could detect a stranger or any animal a measured distance of—I don't remember how many yards, but I know he could beat any of our hunting dogs on distance. He couldn't name the stranger, but he could name the animal without seeing it. I saw him stand the leeward of a decaying and offensive dead horse and "point" a covey of partridges that were behind some bushes twenty yards to windward of it. I smelt the horse myself, but not the birds. Our hunters had doubts about the birds, but Harbison was right, as it turned out. He said that there were 500 smells present—of earth, grass, water, bees, bugs, butterflies, snakes, toads, numberless wild flowers and all manner of things, including the strenuous horse—but that each had its own peculiar and individual scent and projected it through the horse's fragrance distinct, undefiled, and easily recognizable.

His sense of smell may be likened to the visual capacity of the most powerful microscope. Such a microscope makes large and clear a myriad of things that are wholly invisible to the naked eye, and Harbison's gift made smellable to him a myriad of things which to us are destitute of smell. To him, rocks, sand, bricks— in fact everything—had a smell; a smell of its own; and he could go in the dark into a room which he had never been in before and by his nose locate every object in it and come out and name each of them and its place—always pretending to do it by sight. He could go on naming and locating the things until the listener was tired—which would happen before he could name all of them, of course, if there happened to be a thousand.

He said that no two cats smelt alike, nor no two bricks, nor no two nails, nor apples, nor pieces of paper, nor men, nor elephants, nor fleas, nor flies, nor coins, nor anything you could mention in the universe. He said no two faces, nor hands, nor apples, nor peas, nor grains of sand, nor any other two things were ever of exactly the same form and dimensions, and that this law of nature was rigidly carried out in the matter of smells. He said that all the air was thick with smells, and that none of them was to him or to the finest dog unpleasant; and that it was the foolish prejudice of our training that made carrion unpleasant to us—it was not unpleasant to any savage.

His sense of smell would have been eyes for him if he had lost his sight. Wherever he was—even in the densest fog—he knew where every big and little object around about him was located, and the nature of it; and could name it and go straight to it and lay his hand upon it. By his talent he could tell when it was going to rain or snow, without having to go outside and consult the wind or the clouds.

His smell-memory was miraculous, and enduring. He said he did not think it possible for him to ever forget the smell of a friend; certainly not of an enemy. He said Ulysses' aged dog did not recognize his long-exiled master by his face and form, but by his smell.

You could blindfold Harbison and bring fifty books from a library and deliver them to him one at a time as fast as he could take them and lay them down; and then you could carry them back and make a list of them as a help to your memory, scatter them here and there and yonder among the shelves, and send for him to come and find them. He would make his way through the house, easily following your track with his bandage on, and pass along the shelves and touch the fifty chosen books and no others. All done by niceness of sight, he pretended.

**Lost children were a specialty with Harbison**. A child of his acquaintance could not lose itself, winter or summer, on ice or sand or rocks or ground, where he couldn't find it. He was nonplussed only once. That was the time that Clark's little boy wandered away. Harbison walked the whole circuit of the yard, and said little Billy was in the house somewhere—he hadn't left the yard. The parents knew better, and were frightened; they believed Harbison had lost his discriminating sight. They said they had seen Billy playing outside the fence. Harbison went the rounds again, and said Billy was still on the premises; he said he knew the track that Billy's shoe would leave, and it wasn't there; there was no small track but a stranger's.

"Show me where he was playing, outside."

They took him to the place, but Harbison said, "Billy hasn't been here—it's the stranger." Then he had an idea, and said, "How thoughtless you are—he has new shoes on, hasn't he? Why didn't you say so?"

That was what had made the trouble. They swiftly followed the new shoes into the woods, and tracked them around a wide and erratic course; and when night came on, papa and the others retired from the hunt and sat down in the deeps of the forest to wait—for they had confidence in Harbison's capacities—but mamma held Harbison's hand and plowed through the briers and over the tree-roots and dead logs with him, for mothers can't wait; and toward midnight she had her desire and her reward, for they found the child curled up asleep on the ground, with his hands and face stained with the purple blood of blackberries, these signs being clearly visible to Harbison's nose.

**It was Harbison that saved Henry Blake** once, when he was in a bad scrape. He was a loafer and a thief, but that was believed to be the worst of him; but one winter's night, screams were heard in the widow Aldrich's house, and Blake came flying out at the door and was caught. The widow was found lying on the floor of her bedroom upstairs, covered with wounds and gasping her last.

She died without speaking.

Blake declared that he was not guilty of the murder. He said he had often robbed the widow's cellar of eatables, and that he was down there on the like errand when he heard the screams and tried to make his escape undetected. He had taken a few potatoes, and they were still in his overcoat pockets—they could search. Which they did, and found nothing else; nothing else except sixteen dollars in paper money. That was a bad detail, for two reasons: in the first place, it was too much money for Blake to honestly possess at one time, and in the second place he had concealed it in the lining of his hat. He explained that he had stolen it from a stranger, but as he confessed that he couldn't produce the stranger, the explanation went for nothing.

By this time all the town had gathered, and the cry "lynch him, lynch him!" went up in a general chorus. A rope was brought and an end of it thrown over the limb of a tree; a tar-barrel was fired, and as the flame and smoke rose and the glare lit up the angry faces of the people and the cringing form of the noosed and beseeching poor outcast, Harbison came bursting through the crowd and seized Blake's end of the rope just as the executioners had begun to haul down upon the other.

He said, "This man didn't do it; I'll find you the right one."

The statement was doubted.

"Come with me," Harbison said, "and bring him along, if you like; you needn't let him out of your hands till I've shown you."

The crowd followed him to the house and upstairs, with lights, and he said: "There—lift the blind, and you will see that the window is up."

They found it was true, but said, "What of it?"

"Well, the man came in there, over the shed, and he went out that way, again."

"But how can you prove it?"

"By finding the man. Come with me, and I will do it."

"Is it your smell that you are depending on?"

"Yes."

"All right, then. That is satisfactory. Who is the man?"

"I don't know; it's a stranger."

There were murmurs, and something was said about a bird in the hand being worth several in the bush, and Blake began to plead again; but Harbison said, "You shall come with me, Blake. I will take care of you."

He was able to do it; that was recognized. The procession moved. Harbison walked around the house, picked up the track, and started off at a brisk pace, down the lane, into the road, over a rail fence, through a stubble-field, and onward to the river, then out on the ice and straight toward the further shore through a thaw-mist which was rapidly thickening into a fog...

*What became of Harbison after that would never be known. Twain's unfinished manuscript breaks off here, leaving both his fate and that of the stranger he was tracking a mystery, an ironic and unsettling "end" to a story that, until that point, had emphasized the certitude that nearly always accompanied Harbison's gift.*

# A Curious
# Pleasure Excursion

We have received the following advertisement, but, inasmuch as it concerns a matter of deep and general interest, we feel fully justified in inserting it in our reading-columns. We are confident that our conduct in this regard needs only explanation, not apology.

—Ed., *N. Y. Herald.*

MARK TWAIN

## ADVERTISEMENT

This is to inform the public that, in connection with Mr. Barnum, I have leased the comet for a term, of years; and I desire also to solicit the public patronage in favor of a beneficial enterprise which we have in view.

We propose to fit up comfortable, and even luxurious, accommodations in the comet for as many persons as will honor us with their patronage, and make an extended excursion among the heavenly bodies. We shall prepare 1,000,000 state-rooms in the tail of the comet (with hot and cold water, gas, looking-glass, parachute, umbrella, etc., in each), and shall construct more if we meet with a sufficiently generous encouragement. We shall have billiard rooms, card rooms, music rooms, bowling alleys and many spacious theaters and free libraries; and on the main deck we propose to have a driving park, with upward of 100,000 miles of roadway in it. We shall publish daily newspapers also.

**Departure of the comet:** The comet will leave New York at 10 p.m.. on the 20th inst., and therefore it will be desirable that the passengers be on board by 8 at the latest, to avoid confusion in getting under way. It is not known whether passports will be necessary or not, but it is deemed best that passengers provide them, and so guard against all contingencies.

No dogs will be allowed on board. This rule has been made in deference to the existing state of feeling regarding these animals, and will be strictly adhered to.

The safety of the passengers will in all ways be jealously looked to. A substantial iron railing will be put up all around the comet, and no one will be allowed to go to the edge and look over unless accompanied by either my partner or myself.

**The Postal Service** will be of the completest character. Of course the telegraph, and the telegraph only, will be employed;

consequently, friends occupying state-rooms 20,000,000 and even 30,000,000 miles apart will be able to send a message and receive a reply inside of eleven days. Night messages will be half-rate. The whole of this vast postal system will be under the personal superintendence of Mr. Hale of Maine.

Meals served at all hours. Meals served in staterooms charged extra.

**Hostility is not apprehended** from any great planet, but we have thought it best to err on the safe side, and therefore have provided a proper number of mortars, siege guns, and boarding pikes. History shows that small, isolated communities, such as the people of remote islands, are prone to be hostile to strangers, and so the same may be the case with the inhabitants of stars of the tenth or twentieth magnitude.

We shall in no case wantonly offend the people of any star, but shall treat all alike with urbanity and kindliness, never conducting ourselves toward an asteroid after a fashion which we could not venture to assume toward Jupiter or Saturn. I repeat that we shall not wantonly offend any star; but at the same time, we shall promptly resent any injury that may be done us, or any insolence offered us, by parties or governments residing in any star in the firmament. Although averse to the shedding of blood, we shall still hold this course rigidly and fearlessly, not only toward single stars, but toward constellations.

We shall hope to leave a good impression of America behind us in every nation we visit, from Venus to Uranus. And, at all events, if we cannot inspire love we shall at least compel respect for our country wherever we go.

**We shall take with us**, free of charge, a great force of missionaries, and shed the true light upon all the celestial orbs which, physically aglow, are yet morally in darkness. Sunday schools will be established wherever practicable. Compulsory education will also be introduced.

The comet will visit Mars first, and proceed to Mercury, Jupiter, Venus, and Saturn. Parties connected with the government of the District of Columbia and with the former city government of New York, who may desire to inspect the rings, will be allowed time and every facility. Every star of prominent magnitude will be visited, and time allowed for excursions to points of interest inland.

The Dog Star has been stricken from the program. Much time will be spent in the Great Bear, and, indeed, in every constellation of importance. So, also, with the Sun and Moon and the Milky Pay, otherwise the Gulf Stream of the Skies.

**Clothing suitable for wear in the sun** should be provided. Our program has been so arranged that we shall seldom go more than 100,000,000 of miles at a time without stopping at some star. This will necessarily make the stoppages frequent and preserve the interest of the tourist. Baggage checked through to any point on the route. Parties desiring to make only a part of the proposed tour, and thus save expense, may stop over at any star they choose and wait for the return voyage.

After visiting all the most celebrated stars and constellations in our system and personally, inspecting the remotest sparks that even the most powerful telescope can now detect in the firmament, we shall proceed with good heart upon A STUPENDOUS VOYAGE of discovery among the countless whirling worlds that make turmoil in the mighty wastes of space that stretch their solemn solitudes, their unimaginable vastness billions upon billions of miles away beyond the farthest verge of telescopic vision, till by comparison the little sparkling vault we used to gaze at on Earth shall seem like a remembered phosphorescent flash of spangles which some tropical voyager's prow stirred into life for a single instant, and which ten thousand miles of phosphorescent seas and tedious lapse of time had since diminished to an incident utterly trivial in his recollection.

Children occupying seats at the first table will be charged full fare. FIRST-CLASS FARE from the Earth to Uranus, including visits to the Sun and Moon and all the principal planets on the route, will be charged at the low rate of $2 for every 50,000,000 miles of actual travel. A great reduction will be made where parties wish to make the round trip.

**This comet is new** and in thorough repair and is now on her first voyage. She is confessedly the fastest on the line. She makes 20,000,000 miles a day, with her present facilities; but, with a picked American crew and good weather, we are confident we can get 40,000,000 out of her. Still, we shall never push her to a dangerous speed, and we shall rigidly prohibit racing with other comets.

Passengers desiring to diverge at any point or return will be transferred to other comets. We make close connections at all principal points with all reliable lines. Safety can be depended upon. It is not to be denied that the heavens are infested with OLD RAMSHACKLE COMETS that have not been inspected or overhauled in 10,000 years, and which ought long ago to have been destroyed or turned into hail-barges, but with these we have no connection whatever. Steerage passengers not allowed abaft the main hatch.

**Complimentary round-trip tickets** have been tendered to General Butler, Mr. Shepherd, Mr. Richardson, and other eminent gentlemen, whose public services have entitled them to the rest and relaxation of a voyage of this kind. Parties desiring to make the round trip will have extra accommodation.

The entire voyage will be completed, and the passengers

landed in New York again, on the 14th of December, 1991. This is, at least, forty years quicker than any other comet can do it in. Nearly all the back-pay members contemplate making the round trip with us in case their constituents will allow them a holiday. Every harmless amusement will be allowed on board, but no pools permitted on the run of the comet—no gambling of any kind.

All fixed stars will be respected by us, but such stars as seem, to need fixing we shall fix. If it makes trouble, we shall be sorry, but firm.

Mr. Coggia having leased his comet to us, she will no longer be called by his name, but by my partner's. N. B.— Passengers by paying double fare will be entitled to a share in all the new stars, suns, moons, comets, meteors, and magazines of thunder and lightning we may discover.

**Patent-medicine people** will take notice that WE CARRY BULLETIN BOARDS and a paintbrush along for use in the constellations, and are open to terms. Cremationists are reminded that we are going straight to—some hot place—and are open to terms. To other parties, our enterprise is a pleasure excursion, but individually, we mean business. We shall fly our comet for all it is worth.

FOR FURTHER PARTICULARS, or for freight or passage, apply on board, or to my partner, but not to me, since I do not take charge of the comet until she is under way. It is necessary, at a time like this, that my mind should not be burdened with small business details.

Mark Twain

*This tongue-in-cheek "advertisement" was published at the time of the "Comet Scare" in the summer of 1874, in which Coggia's Comet generated a good deal of excitement (and some trepidation) at its approach. Twain took the opportunity to poke fun at all the commotion, creating a mock invitation to "passengers" who might wish to take a ride on the comet. His inclusion of P.T. Barnum as a partner was a tip-off that the whole thing was nothing more than an exaggerated put-on, but one can't help but see a modern parallel in the "space tourism" industry. The comet was discovered by its namesake at Marseille, France, on April 17, 1874.*

"I would renew my youth and talk and talk and talk, and have the times I used to have when I was in the dear old Sagebrush State, the time of my life. The spirit is willing, but the flesh will not stand the long journey."

Letter from Twain printed in the *San Francisco Call*, May 30, 1905

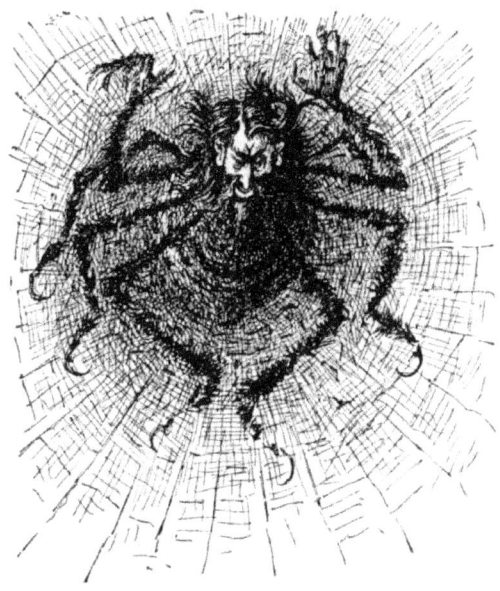

# Rise of the Tarantulas

We were approaching the end of our long journey. It was the morning of the twentieth day. At noon we would reach Carson City, the capital of Nevada Territory. We were not glad, but sorry. It had been a fine pleasure trip; we had fed fat on wonders every day; we were now well accustomed to stage life, and very fond of it; so the idea of coming to a standstill and settling down to a humdrum existence in a village was not agreeable, but, on the contrary, depressing.

Visibly our new home was a desert, walled in by barren, snowclad mountains. There was not a tree in sight. There was no vegetation but the endless sagebrush and greasewood. All nature was gray with it. We were plowing through great deeps of powdery alkali dust that rose in thick clouds and floated across the plain like smoke from a burning house. We were coated with it like millers; so were the coach, the mules, the mailbags, the driver—we and the sagebrush and the other scenery were all one monotonous color.

Long trains of freight wagons in the distance enveloped in ascending masses of dust suggested pictures of prairies on fire. These teams and their masters were the only life we saw. Otherwise, we moved in the midst of solitude, silence and desolation. Every twenty steps, we passed the skeleton of some dead beast of burden, with its dust-coated skin stretched tightly over its empty ribs. Frequently a solemn raven sat upon the skull or the hips and contemplated the passing coach with meditative serenity.

By and by, Carson City was pointed out to us. It nestled in the edge of a great plain and was a sufficient number of miles away to look like an assemblage of mere white spots in the shadow of a grim range of mountains overlooking it, whose summits seemed lifted clear out of companionship and consciousness of earthly things.

We arrived, disembarked, and the stage went on. It was a "wooden" town; its population 2,000 souls. The main street consisted of four or five blocks of little white frame stores which were too high to sit down on, but not too high for various other purposes; in fact, hardly high enough. They were packed close together, side by side, as if room were scarce in that mighty plain. The sidewalk was of boards that were more or less loose and inclined to rattle when walked upon.

In the middle of the town, opposite the stores, was the "plaza" which is native to all towns beyond the Rocky Mountains—a large, unfenced, level vacancy, with a liberty pole in it, and very useful as a place for public auctions, horse trades, and mass meetings, and likewise for teamsters to camp in. Two other sides of the plaza were faced by stores, offices and stables. The rest of Carson City was pretty scattering.

We were introduced to several citizens, at the stage office and on the way up to the governor's from the hotel—among others, to a Mr. Harris, who was on horseback; he began to say something, but interrupted himself with the remark: "I'll have to get you to excuse me a minute; yonder is the witness that swore I helped to rob the California coach—a piece of impertinent intermeddling, sir, for I am not even acquainted with the man."

Then he rode over and began to rebuke the stranger with a six-shooter, and the stranger began to explain with another. When the pistols were emptied, the stranger resumed his work (mending a whiplash), and Mr. Harris rode by with a polite nod, homeward bound, with a bullet through one of his lungs, and several in his hips; and from them issued little rivulets of blood that coursed down the horse's sides and made the animal look quite picturesque. I never saw Harris shoot a man after that, but it recalled to mind that first day in Carson.

**This was all we saw that day**, for it was 2 o'clock, now, and according to custom the daily "Washoe Zephyr" set in; a soaring dust-drift about the size of the United States set up edgewise came with it, and the capital of Nevada Territory disappeared from view. Still, there were sights to be seen which were not wholly uninteresting to newcomers; for the vast dust cloud was thickly freckled with things strange to the upper air—things living and dead, that flitted hither and thither, going and coming, appearing and disappearing among the rolling billows of dust— hats, chickens and parasols sailing in the remote heavens; blankets, tin signs, sagebrush and shingles a shade lower; doormats and buffalo robes lower still; shovels and coal scuttles on the next grade; glass doors, cats and little children on the next; disrupted lumber yards, light buggies and wheelbarrows on the next; and down only thirty or forty feet above ground was a scurrying storm of emigrating roofs and vacant lots.

It was something to see that much. I could have seen more, if I could have kept the dust out of my eyes.

But seriously, a Washoe wind is by no means a trifling matter. It blows flimsy houses down, lifts shingle roofs occasionally, rolls up tin ones like sheet music, now and then blows a stagecoach over and spills the passengers; and tradition says the reason there are so many bald people there, is that the wind blows the hair off their heads while they are looking skyward after their hats. Carson streets seldom look inactive on summer afternoons, because there are so many citizens skipping around their escaping hats, like chambermaids trying to head off a spider.

The "Washoe Zephyr" (Washoe is a pet nickname for Nevada) is a peculiarly Scriptural wind, in that no man knoweth "whence it cometh." That is to say, where it originates. It comes right over the mountains from the west, but when one crosses the ridge, he does not find any of it on the other side! It probably

is manufactured on the mountaintop for the occasion, and starts from there.

It is a pretty regular wind, in the summertime. Its office hours are from 2 in the afternoon till 2 the next morning; and anybody venturing abroad during those twelve hours needs to allow for the wind or he will bring up a mile or two to leeward of the point he is aiming at. And yet, the first complaint a Washoe visitor to San Francisco makes, is that the sea winds blow so, there! There is a good deal of human nature in that.

**We found the state palace** of the Governor of Nevada Territory to consist of a white frame one-story house with two small rooms in it and a stanchion supported shed in front—for grandeur—it compelled the respect of the citizen and inspired the Indians with awe. The newly arrived Chief and Associate Justices of the Territory, and other machinery of the government, were domiciled with less splendor. They were boarding around privately, and had their offices in their bedrooms.

The Secretary and I took quarters in the "ranch" of a worthy French lady by the name of Bridget O'Flannigan, a camp follower of His Excellency the Governor. She had known him in his prosperity as commander-in-chief of the Metropolitan Police of New York, and she would not desert him in his adversity as Governor of Nevada. Our room was on the lower floor, facing the plaza, and when we had got our bed, a small table, two chairs, the government fire-proof safe, and the Unabridged Dictionary into it, there was still room enough left for a visitor—maybe two, but not without straining the walls.

But the walls could stand it—at least the partitions could, for they consisted simply of one thickness of white "cotton domestic" stretched from corner to corner of the room. This was the rule in Carson—any other kind of partition was the rare exception. And if you stood in a dark room and your neighbors in

149

the next had lights, the shadows on your canvas told queer secrets sometimes! Very often these partitions were made of old flour sacks basted together; and then the difference between the common herd and the aristocracy was that the common herd had unornamented sacks, while the walls of the aristocrat were overpowering with rudimental fresco—i.e., red and blue mill brands on the flour sacks.

Occasionally, also, the better classes embellished their canvas by pasting pictures from Harper's Weekly on them. In many cases, too, the wealthy and the cultured rose to spittoons and other evidences of a sumptuous and luxurious taste. (Washoe people take a joke so hard that I must explain that the above description was only the rule; there were many honorable exceptions in Carson—plastered ceilings and houses that had considerable furniture in them.)

We had a carpet and a genuine queensware washbowl. Consequently we were hated without reserve by the other tenants of the O'Flannigan "ranch." When we added a painted oil-cloth window curtain, we simply took our lives into our own hands. To prevent bloodshed, I removed upstairs and took up quarters with the untitled plebeians in one of the fourteen white pine cot-bedsteads that stood in two long ranks in the one sole room of which the second story consisted.

**It was a jolly company**, the fourteen. They were principally voluntary camp followers of the governor, who had joined his retinue by their own election at New York and San Francisco and came along, feeling that, in the scuffle for little Territorial crumbs and offices, they could not make their condition more precarious than it was—and might reasonably expect to make it better. They were popularly known as the "Irish Brigade," though there were only four or five Irishmen among all the governor's retainers. His good-natured Excellency was much annoyed at the gossip his henchmen created—especially when there arose a rumor that they were paid assassins of his, brought along to quietly reduce the Democratic vote when desirable!

Mrs. O'Flannigan was boarding and lodging them at ten dollars a week apiece, and they were cheerfully giving their notes for it. They were perfectly satisfied, but Bridget presently found that notes that could not be discounted were but a feeble constitution for a Carson boarding house. So she began to harry the governor to find employment for the "Brigade." Her importunities and theirs together drove him to a gentle desperation at last, and he finally summoned the Brigade to the presence. Then, said he:

"Gentlemen, I have planned a lucrative and useful service for you—a service which will provide you with recreation amid noble landscapes, and afford you never-ceasing opportunities for enriching your minds by observation and study. I want you to survey a railroad from Carson City westward to a certain point! When the legislature meets, I will have the necessary bill passed and the remuneration arranged."

"What, a railroad over the Sierra Nevada Mountains?"

"Well, then, survey it eastward to a certain point!"

He converted them into surveyors, chain-bearers and so on, and turned them loose in the desert. It was "recreation" with a vengeance! Recreation on foot, lugging chains through sand and sagebrush, under a sultry sun and among cattle bones, coyotes and tarantulas. "Romantic adventure" could go no further.

They surveyed very slowly, very deliberately, very carefully. They returned every night during the first week, dusty, footsore, tired, and hungry, but very jolly. They brought in great store of prodigious hairy spiders—tarantulas—and imprisoned them in covered tumblers upstairs in the "ranch." After the first week, they had to camp on the field, for they were getting well eastward. They made a good many inquiries as to the location of that indefinite "certain point," but got no information. At last, to a peculiarly urgent inquiry of "How far eastward?" Gov. Nye telegraphed back:

"To the Atlantic Ocean, blast you!—and then bridge it and go on!"

This brought back the dusty toilers, who sent in a report and ceased from their labors. The governor was always comfortable about it; he said Mrs. O'Flannigan would hold him for the Brigade's board anyhow, and he intended to get what entertainment he could out of the boys; he said, with his old-time pleasant twinkle, that he meant to survey them into Utah and then telegraph Brigham to hang them for trespass!

**The surveyors brought back** more tarantulas with them, and so we had quite a menagerie arranged along the shelves of the room. Some of these spiders could straddle over a common saucer with their hairy, muscular legs, and when their feelings were hurt, or their dignity offended, they were the wickedest-looking desperadoes the animal world can furnish. If their glass prison-houses were touched ever so lightly they were up and spoiling for a fight in a minute. Starchy? Proud? Indeed, they would take up a straw and pick their teeth like a member of Congress.

There was, as usual, a furious "zephyr" blowing the first night of the Brigade's return, and about midnight the roof of an adjoining stable blew off, and a corner of it came crashing through the side of our ranch. There was a simultaneous awakening, and a tumultuous muster of the Brigade in the dark, and a general tumbling and sprawling over each other in the narrow aisle between the bed rows. In the midst of the turmoil, Bob H— sprung up out of a sound sleep, and knocked down a shelf with his head. Instantly he shouted:

"Turn out, boys—the tarantulas is loose!"

No warning ever sounded so dreadful. Nobody tried, any longer, to leave the room, lest he might step on a tarantula. Every man groped for a trunk or a bed, and jumped on it. Then followed the strangest silence—a silence of grisly suspense it was, too—waiting, expectancy, fear. It was as dark as pitch, and one had to imagine the spectacle of those fourteen scant-clad men roosting gingerly on trunks and beds, for not a thing could be seen.

Then came occasional little interruptions of the silence, and one could recognize a man and tell his locality by his voice, or locate any other sound a sufferer made by his gropings or changes of position. The occasional voices were not given to much speaking—you simply heard a gentle ejaculation of "Ow!" followed by a solid thump, and you knew the gentleman had felt a hairy blanket or something touch his bare skin and had skipped from a bed to the floor.

Another silence.

Presently you would hear a gasping voice say: "Su-su-something's crawling up the back of my neck!"

Every now and then, you could hear a little subdued scramble and a sorrowful "O Lord!" and then you knew that somebody was getting away from something he took for a tarantula, and not losing any time about it, either.

Directly a voice in the corner rang out wild and clear: "I've got him! I've got him!" [Pause, and probable change of circumstances.] "No, he's got me! Oh, ain't they never going to fetch a lantern!"

The lantern came at that moment, in the hands of Mrs. O'Flannigan, whose anxiety to know the amount of damage done by the assaulting roof had not prevented her waiting a judicious interval, after getting out of bed and lighting up, to see if the wind was done, now, upstairs, or had a larger contract.

**The landscape presented** when the lantern flashed into the room was picturesque, and might have been funny to some people, but was not to us. Although we were perched so strangely upon boxes, trunks and beds, and so strangely attired, too, we were too earnestly distressed and too genuinely miserable to see any fun about it, and there was not the semblance of a smile anywhere visible.

I know I am not capable of suffering more than I did during those few minutes of suspense in the dark, surrounded by those creeping, bloody-minded tarantulas. I had skipped from bed to bed and from box to box in a cold agony, and every time I touched anything that was furzy I fancied I felt the fangs. I had rather go to war than live that episode over again.

**Nobody was hurt**. The man who thought a tarantula had "got him" was mistaken—only a crack in a box had caught his finger. Not one of those escaped tarantulas was ever seen again. There were ten or twelve of them. We took candles and hunted the place high and low for them, but with no success.

Did we go back to bed then? We did nothing of the kind. Money could not have persuaded us to do it. We sat up the rest of the night playing cribbage and keeping a sharp lookout for the enemy.

*"Rise of the Tarantulas" (editor's title) is a story excerpted from Twain's* Roughing It.

"*Medicine has its office, it does its share and does it well; but without hope back of it, its forces are crippled and only the physician's verdict can create that hope when the facts refuse to create it.*"

Letter to Dr. W. W. Baldwin, c. 1903

# Bad Medicine

A long outside of the front fence ran the country road; dusty in the summertime, and a good place for snakes— they liked to lie in it and sun themselves; when they were rattlesnakes or puff adders, we killed them; when they were black snakes, or racers, or belonged to the fabled "hoop" breed, we fled, without shame; when they were "house snakes" or "garters" we carried them home and put them in Aunt Patsy's work basket for a surprise; for she was prejudiced against snakes, and always when she took the basket in her lap and they began to climb out of it, it disordered her mind.

She never could seem to get used to them; her opportunities went for nothing. And she was always cold toward bats, too, and could not bear them; and yet I think a bat is as friendly a bird as there is. My mother was Aunt Patsy's sister, and had the same wild superstitions. A bat is beautifully soft and silky; I do not know any creature that is pleasanter to the touch, or is more grateful for caressings, if offered in the right spirit.

I know all about these coleoptera, because our great cave, three miles below Hannibal, was multitudinously stocked with them, and often I brought them home to amuse my mother with. It was easy to manage if it was a school day, because then I had ostensibly been to school and hadn't any bats. She was not a suspicious person, but full of trust and confidence; and when I said "There's something in my coat pocket for you," she would put her hand in. But she always took it out again, herself; I didn't have to tell her. It was remarkable, the way she couldn't learn to like private bats. The more experience she had, the more she could not change her views.

I think she was never in the cave in her life; but everybody else went there. Many excursion parties came from considerable distances up and down the river to visit the cave. It was miles in extent, and was a tangled wilderness of narrow and lofty clefts and passages. It was an easy place to get lost in; anybody could do it—including the bats. I got lost in it myself, along with a lady, and our last candle burned down to almost nothing before we glimpsed the search party's lights winding about in the distance.

"Injun Joe" got lost in there once, and would have starved to death if the bats had run short. But there was no chance of that; there were myriads of them. He told me all his story. In the book called "Tom Sawyer," I starved him entirely to death in the cave, but that was in the interest of art; it never happened.

"General" Gaines, who was our first town drunkard before Jimmy Finn got the place, was lost in there for the space of a week, and finally pushed his handkerchief out of a hole in a hilltop near Saverton, several miles down the river from the cave's mouth, and somebody saw it and dug him out. There is nothing the matter with his statistics except the handkerchief. I knew him for years, and he hadn't any. But it could have been his nose. That would attract attention.

The cave was an uncanny place, for it contained a corpse— the corpse of a young girl of fourteen. It was in a glass cylinder enclosed in a copper one which was suspended from a rail which bridged a narrow passage. The body was preserved in alcohol, and it was said that loafers and rowdies used to drag it up by the hair and look at the dead face.

**The girl was the daughter** of a St. Louis surgeon of extraordinary ability and wide celebrity. He was an eccentric man, and did many strange things. He put the poor thing in that forlorn place himself.

He was a physician as well as a surgeon; and sometimes in cases where medicines failed to save, he developed other resources. He fell out, once, with a family whose physician he was, and after that they ceased to employ him. But a time came when he was once more called. The lady of the house was very ill, and had been given up by her doctors. He came into the room and stopped, and stood still, and looked around upon the scene; he had his great slouch hat on, and a quarter of an acre of gingerbread under his arm, and while he looked meditatively about, he broke hunks from his cake, munched them, and let the crumbs dribble down his breast to the floor.

The lady lay pale and still, with her eyes closed; about the bed, in the solemn hush, were grouped the family softly sobbing, some standing, some kneeling. Presently the doctor began to take up the medicine bottles and sniff at them contemptuously and throw them out of the open window. When they were all gone, he ranged up to the bed, laid his slab of gingerbread on the dying woman's breast, and said roughly:

"What are you idiots sniveling about? There's nothing the matter with this humbug. Put out your tongue!"

159

The sobbings stopped, and the angry mourners changed their attitudes and began to upbraid the doctor for his cruel behavior in this chamber of death; but he interrupted them with an explosion of profane abuse, and said:

"A pack of snuffling fat-wits, do you think you can teach me my business? I tell you there is nothing the matter with the woman—nothing the matter but laziness. What she wants is a beefsteak and a washtub. With her damned society training, she—"

Then the dying woman rose up in bed, and the light of battle was in her eye. She poured out upon the doctor her whole insulted mind—just a volcanic eruption, accompanied by thunder and lightning, whirlwinds and earthquakes, pumice stone and ashes. It brought the reaction which he was after, and she got well. This was the lamented Dr. McDowell, whose name was so great and so honored in the Mississippi Valley a decade before the Civil War.

**Beyond the road** where the snakes sunned themselves was a dense young thicket, and through it a dim-lighted path led a quarter of a mile; then out of the dimness one emerged abruptly upon a level great prairie which was covered with wild strawberry plants, vividly starred with prairie pinks, and walled in on all sides by forests. The strawberries were fragrant and fine, and in the season we were generally there in the crisp freshness of the early morning, while the dew-beads still sparkled upon the grass and the woods were ringing with the first songs of the birds.

Down the forest slopes to the left were the swings. They were made of bark stripped from hickory saplings. When they became dry, they were dangerous. They usually broke when a child was forty feet in the air, and this was why so many bones had to be mended every year. I had no ill luck myself, but none of my cousins escaped. There were eight of them, and at one time and another they broke fourteen arms among them. But it cost next to nothing, for the doctor worked by the year—$25 for the whole family.

I remember two of the Florida doctors, Chowning and Meredith. They not only tended an entire family for $25 a year, but furnished the medicines themselves. Good measure, too. Only the largest persons could hold a whole dose. Castor oil was the principal beverage. The dose was half a dipperful, with half a dipperful of New Orleans molasses added to help it down and make it taste good, which it never did.

The next standby was calomel; the next, rhubarb; and the next, jalap. Then they bled the patient, and put mustard plasters on him. It was a dreadful system, and yet the death-rate was not heavy. The calomel was nearly sure to salivate the patient and cost him some of his teeth. There were no dentists. When teeth became touched with decay or were otherwise ailing, the doctor knew of but one thing to do: He fetched his tongs and dragged them out. If the jaw remained, it was not his fault.

**Doctors were not called**, in cases of ordinary illness; the family's grandmother attended to those. Every old woman was a doctor, and gathered her own medicines in the woods, and knew how to compound doses that would stir the vitals of a cast-iron dog. And then there was the "Indian doctor," a remnant of his tribe, deeply read in the mysteries of nature and the secret properties of herbs; and most backwoodsmen had high faith in his powers and could tell of wonderful cures achieved by him.

In Mauritius, away off yonder in the solitudes of the Indian Ocean, there is a person who answers to our Indian doctor of the old times. He has had no teaching as a doctor, yet there is one disease which he is master of and can cure, and the doctors can't. They send for him when they have a case. It is a child's disease of a strange and deadly sort, and he cures it with a herb medicine which he makes, himself, from a prescription which has come down to him from his father and grandfather. He will not let anyone see it. He keeps the secret of its components to himself, and it is feared that he will die without divulging it; then there will be consternation in Mauritius. I was told these things by the people there, in 1896 .

We had the "faith-doctor," too, in those early days—a woman. Her specialty was toothache. She was a farmer's old wife, and lived five miles from Hannibal. She would lay her hand on the patient's jaw and say "Believe!" and the cure was prompt. Mrs. Utterback. I remember her very well. Twice I rode out there behind my mother, horseback, and saw the cure performed. My mother was the patient.

Dr. Meredith removed to Hannibal, by and by, and was our family physician there, and saved my life several times. Still, he was a good man and meant well. Let it go.

I was always told that I was a sickly and precarious and tiresome and uncertain child, and lived mainly on allopathic medicines during the first seven years of my life. I asked my mother about this, in her old age—she was in her eighty-eighth year—and said:

"I suppose that during all that time you were uneasy about me?"

"Yes, the whole time."

"Afraid I wouldn't live?"

After a reflective pause—ostensibly to think out the facts:

"No—afraid you would."

*"Bad Medicine" (editor's title) is excerpted from Twain's* My Autobiography, *1897.*

# An Old West Hanging

I saw a man hanged the other day. John Melanie, of France. He was the first man ever hanged in this city (or country either), where the first twenty-six graves in the cemetery were those of men who died by shots and stabs.

I never had witnessed an execution before, and did not believe I could be present at this one without turning away my head at the last moment. But I did not know what fascination there was about the thing, then. I only went because I thought I ought to have a lesson, and because I believed that if ever it would be possible to see a man hanged, and derive satisfaction from the spectacle, this was the time. For John Melanie was no common murderer—else he would have gone free. He was a heartless assassin. A year ago, he secreted himself under the house of a woman of the town who lived alone, and in the dead watches of the night, he entered her room, knocked her senseless with a billet of wood as she slept, and then strangled her with his fingers. He carried off all her money, her watches, and every article of her wearing apparel, and the next day, with quiet effrontery, put some crepe on his arm and walked in her funeral procession.

Afterward, he secreted himself under the bed of another woman of the town, and in the middle of the night was crawling out with a slung-shot in one hand and a butcher knife in the other, when the woman discovered him, alarmed the neighborhood with her screams, and he retreated from the house. Melanie sold dresses and jewelry here and there until some of the articles were identified as belonging to the murdered courtesan. He was arrested and then his later intended victim recognized him.

After he was tried and condemned to death, he used to curse and swear at all who approached him; and he once grossly insulted some young Sisters of Charity who came to minister kindly to his wants. The morning of the execution, he joked with the barber, and told him not to cut his throat—he wanted the distinction of being hanged.

This is the man I wanted to see hung. I joined the appointed physicians, so that I might be admitted within the charmed circle and be close to Melanie. Now I never more shall be surprised at anything. That assassin got out of the closed carriage, and the first thing his eye fell upon was that awful gallows towering above a great sea of human heads, out yonder on the hillside and his cheek never blanched, and never a muscle quivered! He strode firmly away, and skipped gaily up the steps of the gallows like a happy girl. He looked around upon the people, calmly; he examined the gallows with a critical eye, and with the pleased curiosity of a man who sees for the first time a wonder he has often heard of. He swallowed frequently, but there was no evidence of trepidation about him—and not the slightest air of braggadocio whatever. He prayed with the priest, and then drew out an abusive manuscript and read from it in a clear, strong voice, without a quaver in it. It was a broad, thin sheet of paper, and he held it apart in front of him as he stood. If ever his hand trembled in even the slightest degree, it never quivered that paper. I watched him at that sickening moment when the sheriff was fitting the noose about his neck, and pushing the knot this way and that to get it nicely adjusted to the hollow under his ear—and if they had been measuring Melanie for a shirt, he could not have been more perfectly serene.

I never saw anything like that before. My own suspense was almost unbearable—my blood was leaping through my veins, and my thoughts were crowding and trampling upon each other. Twenty moments to live—fifteen to live—ten to live—five—three—heaven and earth, how the time galloped! And yet that man stood there unmoved though he knew that the sheriff was reaching deliberately for the drop while the black cap descended over his quiet face—then down through the hole in the scaffold the strap-bound figure shot like a dart! A dreadful shiver started at the shoulders, violently convulsed the whole body all the way down, and died away with a tense drawing of the toes downward, like a doubled fist—and all was over!

I saw it all. I took exact note of every detail, even to Melanie's considerately helping to fix the leather strap that bound his legs together and his quiet removal of his slippers—and I never wish to see it again. I can see that stiff, straight corpse hanging there yet, with its black pillowcased head turned rigidly to one side, and the purple streaks creeping through the hands and driving the fleshy hue of life before them. Ugh!

# MARK TWAIN

*"An Old West Hanging" (editor's title) is a newspaper article penned by Mark Twain in 1868 for the* Chicago Republican. *Twain happened to be in Virginia City for a series of lectures at the time of the hanging. Some 4,000 spectators turned out for the execution of Villain (his real name; Twain's account included a variant form), who had been convicted of murdering "harlot with a heart of gold" Julia Bulette. This piece provides a glimpse into Twain's style as a journalist covering a very real event, as opposed to producing fanciful "quaints" such as "The Petrified Man" and "Bloody Massacre at Empire City."*

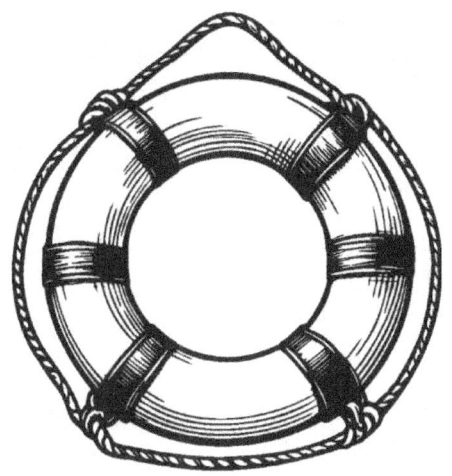

# The Death of Prose

I always had taken an interest in young people who wanted to become poets. I remember I was particularly interested in one budding poet when I was a reporter. His name was Butter.

One day he came to me and said, disconsolately, that he was going to commit suicide—he was tired of life, not being able to express his thoughts in poetic form. Butter asked me what I thought of the idea.

I said I would; that it was a good idea. "You can do me a friendly turn. You go off in a private place and do it there, and I'll get it all. You do it, and I'll do as much for you sometime."

At first, he determined to drown himself. Drowning is so nice and clean, and writes up so well in a newspaper.

But things ne'er do go smoothly in weddings, suicides, or courtships. Only there at the edge of the water, where Butter was to end himself, lay a life-preserver—a big round canvas one, which would float after the scrap-iron was soaked out of it.

Butter wouldn't kill himself with the life-preserver in sight, and so I had an idea. I took it to a pawnshop, and soaked it for a revolver. The pawnbroker didn't think much of the exchange, but when I explained the situation, he acquiesced.

We went up on top of a high building, and this is what happened to the poet:

He put the revolver to his forehead and blew a tunnel straight through his head. The tunnel was about the size of your finger. You could look right through it. The job was complete; there was nothing in it.

Well, after that, that man never could write prose, but he could write poetry. He could write it after he had blown his brains out. There is lots of that talent all over the country, but the trouble is they don't develop it.

*"The Death of Prose" (editor's title) is an excerpt from Twain's speech "On Poetry, Veracity, and Suicide," delivered at a Manhattan Dickens Fellowship dinner in New York City on February 7, 1906.*

# The Fable
# of the Yellow Terror

Along, long time ago, the Butterflies held a vast territory which was flowery and fragrant and beautiful. The Butterflies were of many kinds, but all the kinds were richly clothed, and all had a fine and cultivated taste in colors and were highly trained in etiquette, and deportment and in the other graces and accomplishments which make the charm of life in an advanced and elegant civilization.

There was not another civilization among the animals that approached that of the Butterflies. They were very proud of it, insufferably proud of it, and always anxious to spread it around the planet and cram it down other people's throats and improve them.

They had an idea that they were the only people that knew the true way to be happy and how to lam happiness into other people and make them good. So they sent missionaries to all the pagan insects to teach them how to be tranquil and unafraid on a deathbed, and then sent trader-bugs to make them long for the deathbed, and then followed up the trader-bugs with diplomat-bugs and undertaker-bugs to perfect the blessings of the conferred civilization and furnish the deathbed, and charge for the funeral.

There was hardly a single Butterfly of all the millions that did not boast of this civilization with his mouth, and laugh at it in private. For truly it was a whitewashed hum-bug, and few there were that prayed for it. Except with the mouth.

The Butterflies had what is called a cinch on a great and profitable art. This was the art of making honey. Also a cinch on another great and profitable art. This was the art of killing. For in those days the Butterfly had a sting. He not only had a sting, but he was the only bird in the world that had studied out how to use it scientifically and devastatingly. It made him Boss. There was not a weak and ignorant nation that could stand against him. Multitudes were nothing to him—nothing at all. If they had a property he wanted, he went there and took it, and gave them his civilization in the place of it, and was pleased with himself, and praised his Maker for being always on his side, which was quite true, and for giving him such a chance to be noble and do good.

His whole time was taken up in shoving his civilization and his honey. His whole ambition was to widen and ever widen the market for his honey, and get richer and richer and richer and holier and holier and holier all the time.

At last, he had covered all the ground but one. That was the vast empire of the Bees. He tried to get in there, but was warned away. He kept trying, but the Bees kept discouraging him.

Courteously, but firmly.

The Bees were a simple and peaceable folk, poor and hard-working and honest, and they did not want any civilization. They begged to be let alone; they held out against all persuasions. They wanted no honey, and said so. They did not know how to make it themselves, and did not wish to learn.

They still held out. Courteously and kindly, but firmly.

**At last the Butterflies were tired of this**. They said that a nation that had a chance to get civilization and buy honey and didn't take it was a block in the way of progress and enlightenment and the yearning desires of God, and must be made to accept the boon and bless the booner; so they set about working up a moral-plated pretext, and soon they found a good one, and advertised it.

They said that those fat and diligent and contented Bees, munching grass and cabbage, ignorant of honey, ignorant of civilization and rapacity and treachery and robbery and murder and prayer and one thing and another, and joying in their eventless life and in the sumptuous beauty of their golden jackets, were a Yellow Peril.

It took.

It went like wildfire.

It was a splendid phrase.

It didn't seem to have any meaning, as applied to a faraway and unoffending mighty multitude that hadn't a desire in the world but to stay by themselves and be let alone, but that did not signify: A Yellow Peril is a Yellow Peril, and a shuddery and awful thing to think of, and has to be crushed, mashed, obliterated, whether there is any such thing or not.

So each of the different tribes of Butterflies sent in a two-hundred-dollar missionary with the private purpose of getting him massacred and collecting a million dollars cash damages on him, along with a couple of provinces and such other things as might be lying around; and when the Bees resisted, civilization had its chance! When it got through, there wasn't a Bee that wasn't bruised and battered and sore, and most humble and apologetic and submissive.

The enlightened world of Butterflydom rejoiced and gave thanks. And properly; for wasn't the Yellow Peril over and done with, for good and all?

It looked so. Then there was a great peace, and a holy tranquility, and the Finger of God was visible in it all, as usual. When a paying job is finished and rounded up, he is a cross-eyed shortsighted person indeed who can't find the Finger of God in it.

**Things went on handsomely**. And handsomer and handsomer all the time. The Bees began to like honey and buy it. And they liked it better and better, and bought more and more of it, and civilization was happy to the marrow. One clever tribe of Bees even began to learn how to make honey itself—which made civilization proud, and it said, "They are rising out of their darkness—we have lifted them up—how noble we are, and how good."

Next that tribe wanted to learn the other great art, the sacred monopoly of the loftiest of civilizations—the art of how to kill and cripple and mutilate, scientifically. And they did learn it, and with astonishing quickness and brilliancy. Whereupon civilization rejoiced yet more, and was prouder of its nobleness and beneficence than ever.

For a time.

Then there was an episode. This progressive tribe of Bees had picked up another specialty of all high civilizations, ancient and modern—land-grabbing; and presently, while working this specialty it came into collision with a vast tribe of Butterflies who were likewise out grabbing territory, and a fight resulted. The Bees showed that they had learned to be remarkably prompt and handy with their stings, those little weapons which had been so harmless until education taught them what God had intended the weapons for.

There was a market for wise observations, now, and a grave gray Grasshopper supplied it. He said to a prominent Butterfly:

"You have taught one tribe of Bees how to use its sting, it will teach its brother-tribe. The two together will be able to banish all the Butterflies someday, and keep them out; for they are uncountable in numbers and will be unconquerable when educated. Also, you have given the Bees the honey appetite— forced it upon them—and now the frenzy of it will never leave them. Also, you have taught the brilliant tribe how to make it, and you will see results. They will make as prime an article of honey as any Butterfly can turn out; they will make it cheaper than any Butterfly can make it; they are here on the spot, you are the other side of the world, transportation will cost them nothing—you can't compete. They will get this vast market, and starve you out, and make you stay at home, where they used to beg you to stay, and you wouldn't listen.

"That will happen, no matter how this present scuffle may turn out. Whether Bee or Butterfly win, it is all the same, the Butterfly will have lost the market. There are five hundred million Bees; it is not likely that you can whip them without combining, and there is nothing in your history to indicate that your tribes can combine, even when conferring enlightenment and annexing swag are the prize. Yet if you do not subdue them now, before they get well trained and civilized, they may break over the frontiers someday and go land-grabbing in Europe, to do honor to your teaching.

"It may be that you will lose your stings and your honey-art by and by, from lack of practice, and be and remain merely elegant and ornamental. Maybe you ought to have let the Yellow Peril alone, as long as there wasn't any. Yet you ought to be proud, for in creating a something out of a nothing, you have done what was never done before, save by the Creator of all things."

The Butterfly gave thanks, coldly, and the Grasshopper asked for his passports.

❖  ❖  ❖

*"The Fable of the Yellow Terror" dates from c. 1904.*

# Bloody Massacre
# At Empire City

From Abram Curry, who arrived here yesterday afternoon from Carson, we have learned the following particulars concerning a bloody massacre which was committed in Ormsby County night before last. It seems that during the past six months a man named P. Hopkins, or Philip Hopkins, has been residing with his family in the old log house just at the edge of the great pine forest which lies between Empire City and Dutch Nick's.

The family consisted of nine children—five girls and four boys—the oldest of the group, Mary, being nineteen years old, and the youngest, Tommy, about a year and a half. Twice in the past two months Mrs. Hopkins, while visiting in Carson, expressed fears concerning the sanity of her husband, remarking that of late he had been subject to fits of violence, and that during the prevalence of one of these he had threatened to take her life.

It was Mrs. Hopkins' misfortune to be given to exaggeration, however, and but little attention was paid to what she said. About 10 o'clock on Monday evening, Hopkins dashed into Carson on horseback, with his throat cut from ear to ear, and bearing in his hand a reeking scalp from which the warm, smoking blood was still dripping, and fell in a dying condition in front of the Magnolia Saloon. Hopkins expired in the course of five minutes, without speaking. The long red hair of the scalp he bore marked it as that of Mrs. Hopkins.

A number of citizens, headed by Sheriff Gasherie, mounted at once and rode down to Hopkins' house, where a ghastly scene met their gaze. The scalpless corpse of Mrs. Hopkins lay across the threshold, with her head split open and her right hand almost severed from the wrist. Near her lay the ax with which the murderous deed had been committed. In one of the bedrooms six of the children were found, one in bed and the others scattered about the floor.

They were all dead.

Their brains had evidently been dashed out with a club, and every mark about them seemed to have been made with a blunt instrument. The children must have struggled hard for their lives, as articles of clothing and broken furniture were strewn about the room in the utmost confusion. Julia and Emma, aged respectively fourteen and seventeen, were found in the kitchen, bruised and insensible, but it is thought their recovery is possible.

The eldest girl, Mary, must have taken refuge, in her terror, in the garret, as her body was found there, frightfully mutilated, and the knife with which her wounds had been inflicted still sticking in her side.

The two girls, Julia and Emma, who had recovered sufficiently to be able to talk yesterday morning, state that their father knocked them down with a billet of wood and stamped on them. They think they were the first attacked. They further state that Hopkins had shown evidence of derangement all day, but had exhibited no violence. He flew into a passion and attempted to murder them because they advised him to go to bed and compose his mind.

Curry says Hopkins was about forty-two years of age, and a native of Western Pennsylvania; he was always affable and polite, and until very recently we had never heard of his ill-treating his family. He had been a heavy owner in the best mines of Virginia and Gold Hill, but when the San Francisco papers exposed the game of cooking dividends in order to bolster up our stocks he grew afraid and sold out, and invested to an immense amount in the Spring Valley Water Company of San Francisco. He was advised to do this by a relative of his, one of the editors of the *San Francisco Bulletin*, who had suffered pecuniarily by the dividend-cooking system as applied to the Daney Mining Company recently.

Hopkins had not long ceased to own in the various claims on the Comstock lead, however, when several dividends were cooked on his newly acquired property, their water totally dried up, and Spring Valley stock went down to nothing. It is presumed that this misfortune drove him mad and resulted in his killing himself and the greater portion of his family.

The newspapers of San Francisco permitted this water company to go on borrowing money and cooking dividends, under cover of which cunning financiers crept out of the tottering concern, leaving the crash to come upon poor and unsuspecting stockholders, without offering to expose the villainy at work.

We hope the fearful massacre detailed above may prove the saddest result of their silence.

## Twain's exposition...

[I intended this article as] a fine satire upon the financial expedients of "cooking dividends," a thing which became shamefully frequent on the Pacific Coast for a while.

Once more, in my self-complacent simplicity, I felt that the time had arrived for me to rise up and be a reformer. I put this reformatory satire in the shape of a fearful "Massacre at Empire City." The San Francisco papers were making a great outcry about the iniquity of the Daney Silver-Mining Company, whose directors had declared a "cooked" or false dividend, for the purpose of increasing the value of their stock, so that they could sell out at a comfortable figure, and then scramble from under the tumbling concern. And while abusing the Daney, those papers did not forget to urge the public to get rid of all their silver stocks and invest in sound and safe San Francisco stocks, such as the

Spring Valley Water Company, etc.

But right at this unfortunate juncture, behold the Spring Valley cooked a dividend too! And so, under the insidious mask of an invented "bloody massacre," I stole upon the public unawares with my scathing satire upon the dividend-cooking system. In about half a column of imaginary human carnage, I told how a citizen had murdered his wife and nine children, and then committed suicide. And I said slyly, at the bottom, that the sudden madness of which this melancholy massacre was the result had been brought about by his having allowed himself to be persuaded by the California papers to sell his sound and lucrative Nevada silver stocks, and buy into Spring Valley just in time to get cooked along with that company's fancy dividend, and sink every cent he had in the world.

Ah, it was a deep, deep satire, and most ingeniously contrived. But I made the horrible details so carefully and conscientiously interesting that the public devoured them greedily, and wholly overlooked the following distinctly stated facts, to wit:

- The murderer was perfectly well known to every creature in the land as a bachelor, and consequently he could not murder his wife and nine children.

- He murdered them "in his splendid dressed-stone mansion just in the edge of the great pine forest between Empire City and Dutch Nick's," when even the very pickled oysters that came on our tables knew that there was not a "dressed-stone mansion" in all Nevada Territory; also that, so far from there being a "great pine forest between Empire City and Dutch Nick's," there wasn't a solitary tree within fifteen miles of either place.

- And, finally, it was patent and notorious that Empire City and Dutch Nick's were one and the same place, and contained only six houses anyhow, and consequently there could be no forest between them.

And on top of all these absurdities I stated that this diabolical murderer, after inflicting a wound upon himself that the reader ought to have seen would kill an elephant in the twinkling of an eye, jumped on his horse and rode four miles, waving his wife's reeking scalp in the air, and thus performing, entered Carson City with tremendous éclat, and dropped dead in front of the chief saloon, the envy and admiration of all beholders.

Well, in all my life I never saw anything like the sensation that little satire created. It was the talk of the town, it was the talk of the territory. Most of the citizens dropped gently into it at breakfast, and they never finished their meal. There was something about those minutely faithful details that was a sufficing substitute for food. Few people that were able to read took food that morning. Dan and I (Dan was my reportorial associate) took our seats on either side of our customary table in the "Eagle Restaurant," and, as I unfolded the shred they used to call a napkin in that establishment, I saw at the next table two stalwart innocents with that sort of vegetable dandruff sprinkled about their clothing which was the sign and evidence that they were in from the Truckee with a load of hay.

The one facing me had the morning paper folded to a long, narrow strip, and I knew, without any telling, that that strip represented the column that contained my pleasant financial satire. From the way he was excitedly mumbling, I saw that the heedless son of a hay-mow was skipping with all his might, in order to get to the bloody details as quickly as possible; and so he was missing the guide-boards I had set up to warn him that the whole thing was a fraud.

Presently, his eyes spread wide open, just as his jaws swung asunder to take in a potato approaching it on a fork; the potato halted, the face lit up redly, and the whole man was on fire with excitement. Then he broke into a disjointed checking off of the particulars—his potato cooling in midair meantime, and his mouth making a reach for it occasionally, but always bringing up suddenly against a new and still more direful performance of my hero. At last he looked his stunned and rigid comrade impressively in the face, and said, with an expression of concentrated awe: "Jim, he b'iled his baby, and he took the old 'oman's skelp. Cuss'd if I want any breakfast!"

And he laid his lingering potato reverently down, and he and his friend departed from the restaurant empty but satisfied.

He never got down to where the satire part of it began. Nobody ever did. They found the thrilling particulars sufficient. To drop in with a poor little moral at the end of such a gorgeous massacre was like following the expiring sun with a candle and hope to attract the world's attention to it.

The idea that anybody could ever take my massacre for a genuine occurrence never once suggested itself to me, hedged about as it was by all those telltale absurdities and impossibilities concerning the "great pine forest," the "dressed-stone mansion," etc.

But I found out then, and never have forgotten since, that we never read the dull explanatory surroundings of marvelously exciting things when we have no occasion to suppose that some irresponsible scribbler is trying to defraud us; we skip all that, and hasten to revel in the blood-curdling particulars and be happy.

❖ ❖ ❖

*"Bloody Massacre at Empire City," appeared as a news story in the* Virginia City Territorial Enterprise *on*

*Ocober. 28, 1863. It was written as satire, but several other newspapers picked it up and printed it as fact. The exposition is found in* Sketches New and Old, *published in 1882.*

# Jim Blaine and

# His Grandfather's Ram

Every now and then, in these days, the boys used to tell me I ought to get one Jim Blaine to tell me the stirring story of his grandfather's old ram—but they always added that I must not mention the matter unless Jim was drunk at the time—just comfortably and sociably drunk. They kept this up until my curiosity was on the rack to hear the story.

I got to haunting Blaine; but it was of no use. The boys always found fault with his condition: He was often moderately but never satisfactorily drunk. I never watched a man's condition with such absorbing interest, such anxious solicitude; I never so pined to see a man uncompromisingly drunk before.

At last, one evening, I hurried to his cabin, for I learned that this time his situation was such that even the most fastidious could find no fault with it—he was tranquilly, serenely, symmetrically drunk—not a hiccup to mar his voice, not a cloud upon his brain thick enough to obscure his memory. As I entered, he was sitting upon an empty powder-keg, with a clay pipe in one hand and the other raised to command silence. His face was round, red, and very serious; his throat was bare and his hair tumbled; in general appearance and costume he was a stalwart miner of the period. On the pine table stood a candle, and its dim light revealed "the boys" sitting here and there on bunks, candle-boxes, powder-kegs, etc. They said:

"Sh—! Don't speak—he's going to commence."

I found a seat at once, and Blaine said:

"I don't reckon them times will ever come again. There never was a more bullier old ram than what he was. Grandfather fetched him from Illinois—got him of a man by the name of Yates—Bill Yates—maybe you might have heard of him; his father was a deacon—Baptist—and he was a rustler, too; a man had to get up ruther early to get the start of old Thankful Yates; it was him that put the Greens up to jining teams with my grandfather when he moved West.

"Seth Green was prob'ly the pick of the flock; he married a Wilkerson—Sarah Wilkerson—good cretur, she was—one of the likeliest heifers that was ever raised in old Stoddard, everybody said that knowed her. She could heft a bar'l of flour as easy as I can flirt a flapjack. And spin? Don't mention it! Independent? Humph! When Sile Hawkins come a browsing around her, she let him know that for all his tin he couldn't trot in harness alongside of her. You see, Sile Hawkins was—no, it warn't Sile Hawkins, after all—it was a galoot by the name of Filkins—I disremember his first name; but he was a stump—come into pra'r meeting drunk, one night, hooraying for Nixon,

184

becuz he thought it was a primary; and old deacon Ferguson up and scooted him through the window, and he lit on old Miss Jefferson's head, poor old filly.

"She was a good soul—had a glass eye and used to lend it to old Miss Wagner, that hadn't any, to receive company in; it  warn't big enough, and when Miss Wagner warn't noticing, it would get twisted around in the socket, and look up, maybe, or out to one side, and every which way, while t'other one was looking as straight ahead as a spyglass. Grown people didn't mind it, but it most always made the children cry, it was so sort of scary. She tried packing it in raw cotton, but it wouldn't work, somehow—the cotton would get loose and stick out and look so kind of awful that the children couldn't stand it no way. She was always dropping it out, and turning up her old dead-light on the company empty, and making them oncomfortable, becuz she never could tell when it hopped out, being blind on that side, you see.

"So somebody would have to hunch her and say, 'Your game eye has fetched loose, Miss Wagner dear'—and then all of them would have to sit and wait till she jammed it in again—wrong side before, as a general thing, and green as a bird's egg, being a bashful cretur and easy sot back before company. But being wrong side before warn't much difference, anyway, becuz her own eye was sky-blue and the glass one was yaller on the front side, so whichever way she turned it, it didn't match nohow.

"Old Miss Wagner was considerable on the borrow, she was. When she had a quilting, or Dorcas S'iety at her house, she gen'ally borrowed Miss Higgins's wooden leg to stump around on; it was considerable shorter than her other pin, but much she minded that. She said she couldn't abide crutches when she had company, becuz they were so slow; said when she had company and things had to be done, she wanted to get up and hump herself.

"She was as bald as a jug, and so she used to borrow Miss Jacops's wig—Miss Jacops was the coffin-peddler's wife—a ratty old buzzard, he was, that used to go roosting around where people was sick, waiting for 'em; and there that old rip would sit all day, in the shade, on a coffin that he judged would fit the can'idate; and if it was a slow customer and kind of uncertain, he'd fetch his rations and a blanket along and sleep in the coffin nights. He was anchored out that way, in frosty weather, for about three weeks, once, before old Robbins's place, waiting for him; and after that, for as much as two years, Jacops was not on speaking terms with the old man, on account of his disapp'inting him. He got one of his feet froze, and lost money, too, becuz old Robbins took a favorable turn and got well.

"The next time Robbins got sick, Jacops tried to make up with him, and varnished up the same old coffin and fetched it along; but old Robbins was too many for him; he had him in, and 'peared to be powerful weak; he bought the coffin for ten dollars, and Jacops was to pay it back and twenty-five more besides if Robbins didn't like the coffin after he'd tried it. And then Robbins died, and at the funeral he bursted off the lid and riz up in his shroud and told the parson to let up on the performances, becuz he could not stand such a coffin as that.

"You see, he had been in a trance once before, when he was young, and he took the chances on another, cal'lating that if he made the trip it was money in his pocket, and if he missed fire he couldn't lose a cent. And by George, he sued Jacops for the rhino and got jedgment; and he set up the coffin in his back parlor and said he 'lowed to take his time, now.

"It was always an aggravation to Jacops, the way that miserable old thing acted. He moved back to Indiany pretty soon—went to Wellsville—Wellsville was the place the Hogadorns was from. Mighty fine family. Old Maryland stock.

"Old Squire Hogadorn could carry around more mixed licker, and cuss better than most any man I ever see. His second wife was the widder Billings—she that was Becky Martin; her dam was deacon Dunlap's first wife. Her oldest child, Maria, married a missionary and died in grace—et up by the savages. They et him, too, poor feller—biled him. It warn't the custom, so they say, but waiting for a customer, they explained to friends of his'n that went down there to bring away his things, that they'd tried missionaries every other way and never could get any good out of 'em—and so it annoyed all his relations to find out that that man's life was fooled away just out of a dern'd experiment, so to speak.

"But mind you, there ain't anything ever reely lost; everything that people can't understand and don't see the reason of does good if you only hold on and give it a fair shake; Prov'dence don't fire no blank ca'tridges, boys. That there missionary's substance, unbeknowns to himself, actu'ly converted every last one of them heathens that took a chance at the barbacue. Nothing ever fetched them but that. Don't tell me it was an accident that he was biled. There ain't no such a thing as an accident.

"When my uncle Lem was leaning up agin a scaffolding once, sick, or drunk, or suthin, an Irishman with a hod full of bricks fell on him out of the third story and broke the old man's back in two places. People said it was an accident. Much accident there was about that. He didn't know what he was there for, but he was there for a good object. If he hadn't been there, the Irishman would have been killed. Nobody can ever make me believe

187

anything different from that.

"Uncle Lem's dog was there. Why didn't the Irishman fall on the dog? Becuz the dog would a seen him a coming and stood from under. That's the reason the dog warn't appinted. A dog can't be depended on to carry out a special providence. Mark my words it was a put-up thing. Accidents don't happen, boys. Uncle Lem's dog—I wish you could a seen that dog. He was a reglar shepherd—or ruther he was part bull and part shepherd—splendid animal; belonged to parson Hagar before uncle Lem got him.

"Parson Hagar belonged to the Western Reserve Hagars; prime family; his mother was a Watson; one of his sisters married a Wheeler; they settled in Morgan County, and he got nipped by the machinery in a carpet factory and went through in less than a quarter of a minute; his widder bought the piece of carpet that had his remains wove in, and people come a hundred mile to 'tend the funeral. There was fourteen yards in the piece. She wouldn't let them roll him up, but planted him just so—full length. The church was middling small where they preached the funeral, and they had to let one end of the coffin stick out of the window. They didn't bury him—they planted one end, and let him stand up, same as a monument. And they nailed a sign on it and put—put on—put on it—sacred to—the m-e-m-o-r-y—of fourteen y-a-r-d-s—of three-ply—car...pet—containing all that was—m-o-r-t-a-l—of—of— W-i-l-l-i-a-m—W-h-e—"

**Jim Blaine had been growing gradually drowsy** and drowsier—his head nodded, once, twice, three times—dropped peacefully upon his breast, and he fell tranquilly asleep. The tears were running down the boys' cheeks—they were suffocating with suppressed laughter—and had been from the start, though I had never noticed it. I perceived that I was "sold."

I learned then that Jim Blaine's peculiarity was that whenever he reached a certain stage of intoxication, no human power could keep him from setting out, with impressive unction, to tell about a wonderful adventure which he had once had with his grandfather's old ram—and the mention of the ram in the first sentence was as far as any man had ever heard him get, concerning it. He always maundered off, interminably, from one thing to another, till his whisky got the best of him and he fell asleep.

What the thing was that happened to him and his grandfather's old ram is a dark mystery to this day, for nobody has ever yet found out.

*"Jim Blaine and his Grandfather's Ram," appeared in Chapter 13 of Twain's book* Roughing It.

"Yes, the wee creatures that inhabit the bodies of us germs, and feed upon us, and rot us with disease. Ah, what could they have been created for? They give us pain, they make our lives miserable, they murder us—and where is the use of it all, where the wisdom? Our birth is a mystery, our little life is a mystery and a trouble, we pass and are seen no more; all is mystery, mystery, mystery; we know not whence we came, nor why, we know not whither we go, nor why we go. ... It suggests the possibility, and substantially the certainty, that man is himself a microbe, and his globe a blood-corpuscle drifting with its shining brethren of the Milky Way down a vein of the Master and Maker of all things, Whose body, mayhap, glimpsed partwise from the earth by night, and receding and lost to view in the measureless remotenesses of Space—is what men name the Universe."

Three Thousand Years Among the Microbes
1905

# The Great Dark

### Statement by Mrs. Edwards

We were in no way prepared for this dreadful thing. We were a happy family, we had been happy from the beginning; we did not know what trouble was, we were not thinking of it nor expecting it.

My husband was thirty-five years old, and seemed ten years younger, for he was one of those fortunate people who by nature are overcharged with breezy spirits and vigorous health, and from whom cares and troubles slide off without making any impression. He was my ideal, and indeed my idol. In my eyes, he was everything that a man ought to be, and in spirit and body beautiful. We were married when I was a girl of 16, and we now had two children, comely and dear little creatures: Jessie, 8 years old, and Bessie, 6.

The house had been in a pleasant turmoil all day, this 19th of March, for it was Jessie's birthday. Henry (my husband) had romped with the children till I was afraid he would tire them out and unfit them for their party in the evening, which was to be a children's fancy dress dance; and so I was glad when at last in the edge of the evening he took them to our bedroom to show them the grandest of all the presents, the microscope.

I allowed them fifteen minutes for this show. I would put the children into their costumes, then, and have them ready to receive their great flock of little friends and the accompanying parents. Henry would then be free to jot down in shorthand (he was a past-master in that art) an essay which he was to read at the social club the next night. I would show the children to him in their smart costumes when the party should be over and the goodnight kisses due.

I left the three in a state of great excitement over the microscope, and at the end of the fifteen minutes I returned for the children. They and their papa were examining the wonders of a drop of water through a powerful lens. I delivered the children to a maid and they went away.

Henry said, "I will take forty winks and then go to work. But I will make a new experiment with the drop of water first. Won't you please strengthen the drop with the merest touch of Scotch whisky and stir up the animals?"

Then he threw himself on the sofa and, before I could speak, he uttered a snore. That came of romping the whole day. In reaching for the whisky decanter, I knocked off the one that contained brandy, and it broke. The noise stopped the snore. I stooped and gathered up the broken glass hurriedly in a towel, and when I rose to put it out of the way, he was gone.

I dipped a broomstraw in the Scotch whisky and let a wee drop fall upon the glass slide where the water drop was, then I crossed to the glass door to tell him it was ready. But he had lit the gas and was at his table writing. It was the rule of the house not to disturb him when he was at work, so I went about my affairs in the picture gallery, which was our house's ballroom.

## Statement by Mr. Edwards

We were experimenting with the microscope. And pretty ignorantly. Among the little glass slides in the box we found one labeled "section of a fly's eye." In its centre was faintly visible a dot. We put it under a low-power lens, and it showed up like a fragment of honeycomb. We put it under a stronger lens, and it became a window sash. We put it under the most powerful lens of all, then there was room in the field for only one pane of the several hundred. We were childishly delighted and astonished at the magnifying capacities of that lens, and said, "Now we can find out if there really are living animals in a drop of water, as the books say."

We brought some stale water from a puddle in the carriage house, where some rotten hay lay soaking, sucked up a dropperful, and allowed a tear of it to fall on a glass slide. Then we worked the screws and brought the lens down until it almost touched the water; then shut an eye and peered eagerly down through the barrel.

A disappointment—nothing showed.

Then we worked the screws again and made the lens touch the water.

Another disappointment—nothing visible.

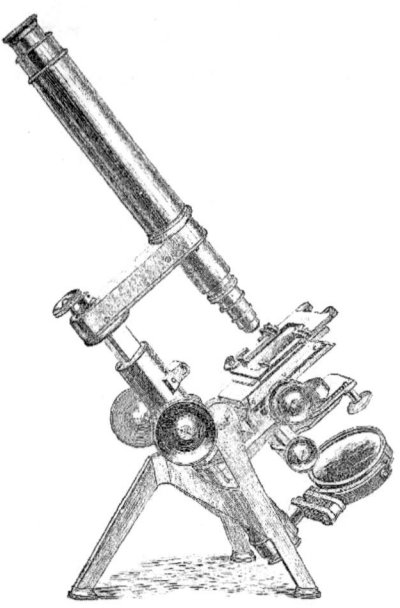

Once more we worked the screws and projected the lens hard against the glass slide itself. Then we saw the animals! Not frequently, but now and then. For a time there would be a great empty blank; then a monster would enter one horizon of this great white sea made so splendidly luminous by the reflector and go plowing across and disappear beyond the opposite horizon. Others would come and go at intervals and disappear.

The lens was pressing against the glass slide; therefore how could those bulky creatures crowd through between and not get stuck? Yet they swam with perfect freedom; it was plain that they had all the room and all the water that they needed. Then how unimaginably little they must be! Moreover, that wide circular sea which they were traversing was only a small part of our drop of stale water; it was not as big as the head of a pin; whereas the entire drop, flattened out on the glass, was as big around as a child's finger-ring. If we could have gotten the whole drop under the lens, we could have seen those gruesome fishes swim leagues and leagues before they dwindled out of sight at the further shore!

I threw myself on the sofa profoundly impressed by what I had seen, and oppressed with thinkings. An ocean in a drop of water—and unknown, uncharted, unexplored by man! By man, who gives all his time to the Africas and the poles, with this unsearched marvelous world right at his elbow. Then the Superintendent of Dreams appeared at my side, and we talked it over. He was willing to provide a ship and crew, but said, "It will be like any other voyage of the sort—not altogether a holiday excursion."

"That is all right; it is not an objection."

"You and your crew will be much diminished, as to size, but you need not trouble about that, as you will not be aware of it. Your ship itself, stuck upon the point of a needle, would not be discoverable except through a microscope of very high power."

"I do not mind these things. Get a crew of whalers. It will be well to have men who will know what to do in case we have trouble with those creatures."

"Better still if you avoid them."

"I shall avoid them if I can, for they have done me no harm, and I would not wantonly hurt any creature, but I shan't run from them. They have an ugly look, but I thank God I am not afraid of the ugliest that ever plowed a drop of water."

"You think so now, with your 5 feet 8, but it will be a different matter when the mote that floats in a sunbeam is Mont Blanc compared to you."

"It is no matter; you have seen me face dangers before—"

"Finish with your orders—the night is slipping away."

"Very well, then. Provide me a naturalist to tell me the names of the creatures we see; and let the ship be a comfortable one and perfectly appointed and provisioned, for I take my family with me."

**Half a minute later** (as it seemed to me), a hoarse voice broke on my ear: "Topsails all—let go the lee brace—sheet home the stuns'l boom—hearty, now, and all together!"

I turned out, washed the sleep out of my eyes with a dash of cold water, and stepped out of my cabin, leaving Alice quietly sleeping in her berth. It was a blustering night and dark, and the air was thick with a driving mist out of which the tall masts and bellying clouds of sail towered spectrally, faintly flecked here and there aloft by the smothered signal lanterns. The ship was heaving and wallowing in the heavy seas, and it was hard to keep one's footing on the moist deck. Everything was dimmed to obliteration, almost; the only thing sharply defined was the foamy mane of white water, sprinkled with phosphorescent sparks, which broke away from the lee bow. Men were within twenty steps of me, but I could not make out their figures; I only knew they were there by their voices.

I heard the quartermaster report to the second mate, "Eight bells, sir."

"Very well. Make it so."

Then I heard the muffled sound of the distant bell, followed by a far-off cry: "Eight bells and a cloudy morning—anchor watch turn out!"

I saw the glow of a match photograph a pipe and part of a face against a solid bank of darkness, and groped my way thither and found the second mate.

"What of the weather, mate?"

"I don't see that it's any better, sir, than it was the first day out, ten days ago; if anything it's worse—thicker and blacker, I mean. You remember the spitting snow flurries we had that night?"

"Yes."

"Well, we've had them again tonight. And hail and sleet besides, b'George! And here it comes again."

We stepped into the sheltering lee of the galley, and stood there listening to the lashing of the hail along the deck and the singing of the wind in the cordage.

The mate said, "I've been at sea thirty years, man and boy, but for a level ten-day stretch of unholy weather this bangs anything I ever struck, north of the Horn—if we are north of it. For I'm blest if I know where we are. Do you?"

It was an embarrassing question. I had been asked it very confidentially by my captain, long ago, and had been able to state that I didn't know; and had been discreet enough not to go into any particulars; but this was the first time that any officer of the ship had approached me with the matter.

I said, "Well, no, I'm not a sailor, but I am surprised to hear you say you don't know where we are."

He was caught. It was his turn to be embarrassed. First he began to hedge, and vaguely let on that perhaps he did know, after all; but he made a lame fist of it, and presently gave it up and concluded to be frank and take me into his confidence.

"I'm going to be honest with you, sir—and don't give me away." He put his mouth close to my ear and sheltered it against the howling wind with his hand to keep from having to shout, and said impressively, "Not only I don't know where we are, sir, but by God, the captain himself don't know!

"No, sir, he don't know where he is; lets on to, but he don't. I mean, he lets on to the crew, and his daughters, and young Phillips the purser, and of course to you and your family, but here lately he don't let on any more to the chief mate and me. And worried? I tell you he's worried plumb to his vitals."

"I must say I don't much like the look of this, Mr. Turner."

"Well, don't let on, sir; keep it to yourself. Maybe it'll come out all right; hope it will. But you look at the facts. Just look at the facts. We sail north, see? North-and-by-east-half-east, to be exact. Noon the fourth day out, heading for Sable Island—ought to see it, weather rather thin for this voyage. Don't see it. Think the dead reckoning ain't right, maybe. We bang straight along, all the afternoon. No Sable Island. Damned if we didn't run straight over it! It warn't there. What do you think of that?"

"Dear me, it is awful—awful—if true."

"If true. Well, it is true. True as anything that ever was, I take my oath on it. And then Greenland. We three banked our hopes on Greenland. Night before last we couldn't sleep for uneasiness; just anxiety, you know, to see if Greenland was going to be there. By the dead reckoning she was due to be in sight along anywhere from five to seven in the morning, if clear enough. But we stayed on deck all night. Of course, two of us had no business there, and had to scuttle out of the way whenever a man came along, or they would have been suspicious. But five o'clock came, seven o'clock, eight o'clock, ten o'clock, and at last twelve—and then the captain groaned and gave in! He knew well enough that if there had been any Greenland left, we'd have knocked a corner off of it long before that."

"This is appalling!"

"You may hunt out a bigger word than that and it won't cover it, sir. And Lord, to see the captain, gray as ashes, sweating and worrying over his chart all day yesterday and all day today, and spreading his compasses here and spreading them there, and getting suspicious of his chronometer, and damning the dead-reckoning—just suffering death and taxes, you know, and me and the chief mate helping and suffering, and that purser and the captain's oldest girl spooning and cackling around, just in heaven! I'm a poor man, sir, but if I could buy out half of each of 'em's ignorance and put it together and make it a whole, blamed if I wouldn't put up my last nickel to do it, you hear me. Now—"

A wild gust of wind drowned the rest of his remark and smothered us in a fierce flurry of snow and sleet. He darted away and disappeared in the gloom, but first I heard his voice hoarsely shouting, "Turn out, all hands, shorten sail!"

There was a rush of feet along the deck, and then the gale brought the dimmed sound of far-off commands: "Mizzen foretop halyards there—all clue-garnets heave and away—now then, with a will—sheet home!"

And then the plaintive notes that told that the men were handling the kites:

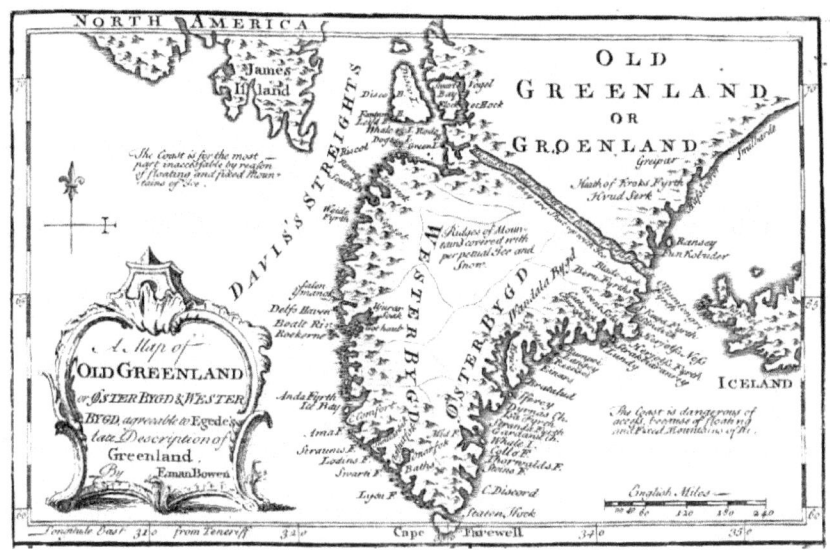

*If you get there, before I do—*
*Hi-ho-o-o, roll a man down;*
*If you get there before I do,*
*O, give a man time to roll a man down!*

By and by, all was still again. Meantime I had shifted to the other side of the galley to get out of the storm, and there Mr. Turner presently found me.

"That's a specimen," said he. "I've never struck any such weather anywheres. You are bowling along on a wind that's as steady as a sermon, and just as likely to last, and before you can say 'Jack Robinson,' the wind whips around from weather to lee, and if you don't jump for it you'll have your canvas blown out of the cat-heads and sailing for heaven in rags and tatters. I've never seen anything to begin with it. But then I've never been in the middle of Greenland before—in a ship—middle of where it used to be, I mean. Would it worry you if I was to tell you something, sir?"

"Why, no, I think not. What is it?"

"Let me take a turn up and down, first, to see if anybody's in earshot." When he came back he said, "What should you think if you was to see a whale with hairy spider-legs to it as long as the foretogallant backstay and as big around as the mainmast?"

I recognized the creature; I had seen it in the microscope. But I didn't say so. I said, "I should think I had a little touch of the jimjams."

"The very thing I thought, so help me! It was the third day out, at a quarter to five in the morning. I was out astraddle of the bowsprit in the drizzle, bending on a scuttle-butt, for I don't trust that kind of a job to a common sailor, when all of a sudden that creature plunged up out of the sea the way a porpoise does, not a hundred yards away—I saw 250 feet of him and his fringes—and then he turned in the air like a triumphal arch, shedding Niagaras of water, and plunged head first under the sea with an awful swash of sound, and by that time we were close aboard him and in another ten yards we'd have hit him. It was my belief that he tried to hit us, but by the mercy of God he was out of practice. The lookout on the foc'sle was the only man around, and thankful I was, or there could have been a mutiny. He was asleep on the binnacle—they always sleep on the binnacle, it's the best place to see from—and it woke him up and he said, 'Good land, what's that, sir?' and I said, 'It's nothing, but it might have been, for any good a stump like you is for a lookout.' I was pretty far gone, and said I was sick, and made him help me onto the foc'sle; and then I went straight off and took the pledge;

for I had been going it pretty high for a week before we sailed, and I made up my mind that I'd rather go dry the rest of my life than see the like of that thing again."

"Well, I'm glad it was only the jimjams." (Jitters)

"Wait a minute, I ain't done. Of course I didn't enter it on the log—"

"Of course not—"

"For a man in his right mind don't put nightmares in the log. He only puts the word 'pledge' in, and takes credit for it if anybody inquires; and knows it will please the captain, and hopes it'll get to the owners. Well, two days later the chief mate took the pledge!"

"You don't mean it!"

"Sure as I'm standing here. I saw the word on the book. I didn't say anything, but I felt encouraged. Now then, listen to this: day before yesterday I'm dumm'd if the captain didn't take the pledge!"

"Oh, come!"

"It's a true bill—I take my oath. There was the word. Then we begun to put this and that together, and next we began to look at each other kind of significant and willing, you know; and of course giving the captain the preceedence, for it wouldn't become us to begin, and we nothing but mates. And so yesterday, sure enough, out comes the captain—and we called his hand. Said he was out astern in a snow-flurry about dawn, and saw a creature shaped like a wood-louse and as big as a turreted monitor, go racing by and tearing up the foam, in chase of a fat animal the size of an elephant and creased like a caterpillar—and saw it dive after it and disappear; and so he begun to prepare his soul for the pledge and break it to his entrails."

"It's terrible!"

"The pledge? You bet your bottom dollar. If I—"

"No, I don't mean the pledge; I mean it is terrible to be lost at sea among such strange, uncanny brutes."

"Yes, there's something in that, too, I don't deny it. Well, the thing that the mate saw was like one of these big long lubberly canal boats, and it was ripping along like the Empire Express; and the look of it gave him the cold shivers, and so he begun to arrange his earthly affairs and go for the pledge."

"Turner, it is dreadful—dreadful. Still, good has been done; for these pledges—"

"Oh, they're off!"

"Off?"

"Cert'nly. Can't be jimjams; couldn't all three of us have them at once, it ain't likely. What do you want with a pledge when there ain't any occasion for it? There he goes!"

He was gone like a shot, and the night swallowed him up. Now all of a sudden, with the wind still blowing hard, the seas went down and the deck became as level as a billiard table! Were all the laws of Nature suspended? It made my flesh creep; it was like being in a haunted ship. Pretty soon the mate came back panting, and sank down on a cable-tier, and said, "Oh, this is an awful life; I don't think we can stand it long. There's too many horribles in it. Let me pant a little, I'm in a kind of a collapse."

"What's the trouble?"

"Drop down by me, sir—I mustn't shout. There—now you're all right." Then he said sorrowfully, "I reckon we've got to take it again."

"Take what?"

"The pledge."

"Why?"

"Did you see that thing go by?"

"What thing?"

"A man."

"No. What of it?"

"This is four times that I've seen it; and the mate has seen it, and so has the captain. Haven't you ever seen it?"

"I suppose not. Is there anything extraordinary about it?"

"Extra-ordinary? Well, I should say!"

"How is it extraordinary?"

He said in an awed voice that was almost like a groan, "Like this, for instance: You put your hand on him, and he ain't there."

"What do you mean, Turner?"

"It's as true as I'm sitting here, I wish I may never stir. The captain's getting morbid and religious over it, and says he wouldn't give a damn for ship and crew if that thing stays aboard."

"You curdle my blood. What is the man like? Isn't it just one of the crew, that you glimpse and lose in the dark?"

"You take note of this: It wears a broad slouch hat and a long cloak. Is that a whaler outfit, I'll ask you? A minute ago I was as close to him as I am to you; and I made a grab for him, and what did I get? A handful of air, that's all. There warn't a sign of him left."

"I do hope the pledge will dispose of it. It must be a work of the imagination, or the crew would have seen it."

"We're afraid they have. There was a deal of whispering going on last night in the middle watch. The captain dealt out grog, and got their minds on something else; but he is mighty uneasy, because of course he don't want you or your family to hear about that man, and would take my scalp if he knew what I'm doing now; and besides, if such a thing got a start with the crew, there'd be a mutiny, sure."

"I'll keep quiet, of course; still, I think it must be an output of imaginations overstrung by the strange fishes you think you saw; and I am hoping that the pledge—"

"I want to take it now. And I will."

"I'm witness to it. Now come to my parlor and I'll give you a cup of hot coffee and—"

"Oh, my goodness, there it is again! It's gone... Lord, it takes a body's breath... It's the jimjams I've got—I know it for sure. I want the coffee; it'll do me good. If you could help me a little, sir—I feel as weak as Sabbath grog."

**We groped along the sleety deck** to my door and entered, and there in the bright glare of the lamps sat (as I was half expecting) the man of the long cloak and the slouch hat, on the sofa—my friend the Superintendent of Dreams.

I was annoyed, for a moment, for of course I expected Turner to make a jump at him, get nothing, and be at once in a more miserable state than he already was. I reached for my cabin door and closed it, so that Alice might not hear the scuffle and get a fright. But there wasn't any. Turner went on talking, and took no notice of the Superintendent. I gave the Superintendent a grateful look; and it was an honest one, for this thing of making himself visible and scaring people could do harm.

"Lord, it's good to be in the light, sir," said Turner, rustling comfortably in his yellow oilskins, "it lifts a person's spirits right up. I've noticed that these cussed jimjam blatherskites ain't as apt to show up in the light as they are in the dark, except when you've got the trouble in your attic pretty bad."

Meantime we were dusting the snow off each other with towels.

"You're mighty well fixed here, sir: chairs and carpets and rugs and tables and lamps and books and everything lovely, and so warm and comfortable and homey; and the roomiest parlor I ever struck in a ship, too. Land, hear the wind, don't she sing! And not a sign of motion!—rip goes the sleet again!—ugly, you bet!— and here? Why here it's only just the more cozier on account of it. Dern that jimjam, if I had him in here once, I bet you I'd sweat him. Because I don't mind saying that I don't grab at him as earnest as I want to, outside there, and ain't as disappointed as I ought to be when I don't get him; but here in the light I ain't afraid of no jimjam."

It made the Superintendent of Dreams smile a smile that was full of pious satisfaction to hear him. I poured a steaming cup of coffee and handed it to Turner and told him to sit where he pleased and make himself comfortable and at home; and before I could interfere he had sat down in the Superintendent of Dreams' lap!—no, sat down through him. It cost me a gasp, but only that, nothing more.

The Superintendent of Dreams' head was larger than Turner's, and surrounded it, and was a transparent spirit-head fronted with a transparent spirit-face; and this latter smiled at me as much as to say give myself no uneasiness, it is all right. Turner was smiling comfort and contentment at me at the same time, and the double result was very curious, but I could tell the smiles apart without trouble. The Superintendent of Dreams' body enclosed Turner's, but I could see Turner through it, just as one sees objects through thin smoke. It was interesting and pretty. Turner tasted his coffee and set the cup down in front of him with a hearty:

"Now I call that prime! 'George, it makes me feel the way old Cap'n Jimmy Starkweather did, I reckon, the first time he tasted grog after he'd been off his allowance three years. The way of it was this. It was there in Fairhaven by New Bedford, away back in the old early whaling days before I was born; but I heard about it the first day I was born, and it was a ripe old tale then, because they keep only the one fleet of yarns in commission down New Bedford-way, and don't ever restock and don't ever repair. And I came near hearing it in old Cap'n Jimmy's own presence once, when I was ten years old and he was ninety-two; but I didn't, because the man that asked Cap'n Jimmy to tell about it got crippled, and the thing didn't materialize. It was Cap'n Jimmy that crippled him. Land, I thought I sh'd die! The very recollection of it—"

The very recollection of it so powerfully affected him that it shut off his speech and he put his head back and spread his jaws and laughed himself purple in the face. And while he was doing it, the Superintendent of Dreams emptied the coffee into the slop bowl and set the cup back where it was before.

When the explosion had spent itself, Turner swabbed his face with his handkerchief and said, "There! That laugh has scoured me out and done me good; I hain't had such another one—well, not since I struck this ship, now that's sure. I'll whet up and start over."

He took up his cup, glanced into it, and it was curious to observe the two faces that were framed in the front of his head. Turner's was long and distressed; the Superintendent of Dreams' was wide, and broken out of all shape with a convulsion of silent laughter. After a little, Turner said in a troubled way—"I'm dumm'd if I recollect drinking that."

I didn't say anything, though I knew he must be expecting me to say something. He continued to gaze into the cup a while, then looked up wistfully and said:

"Of course I must have drunk it, but I'm blest if I can recollect whether I did or not. Lemme see. First you poured it out, then I set down and put it before me here; next I took a sup and said it was good, and set it down and begun about old Cap'n Jimmy—and then—and then—" He was silent a moment, then said, "It's as far as I can get. It beats me. I reckon that after that I was so kind of full of my story that I didn't notice whether I—" He stopped again, and there was something almost pathetic about the appealing way in which he added, "But I did drink it, didn't I? You see me do it—didn't you?"

I hadn't the heart to say no.

"Why, yes, I think I did. I wasn't noticing particularly, but it seems to me that I saw you drink it—in fact, I am about certain of it."

I was glad I told the lie; it did him so much good, and so lightened his spirits, poor old fellow.

"Of course I done it! I'm such a fool. As a general thing, I wouldn't care, and I wouldn't bother anything about it; but when there's jimjams around the least little thing makes a person suspicious, you know. If you don't mind, sir—thanks, ever so much."

**The Superintendent of Dreams** separated himself and moved along the sofa a foot or two away from Turner. I was glad of that; it looked like a truce. Turner swallowed his cup of coffee; I poured another; he began to sip it, the pleasant influence worked a change, and soon he was a rational man again, and comfortable. Now a sea came aboard, hit our deck house a stunning thump, and went hissing and seething aft.

"Oh, that's the ticket," said Turner, "the dummdest weather that ever I went pleasure excursioning in. And how did it get aboard? You answer me that: There ain't any motion to the ship. These mysteriousnesses—well, they just give me the cold shudders. And that reminds me. Do you mind my calling your attention to another peculiar thing or two—on conditions as before—solid secrecy, you know?"

"I'll keep it to myself. Go on."

"The Gulf Stream's gone to the devil!"

"What do you mean?"

"It's the fact, I wish I may never die. From the day we sailed till now, the water's been the same temperature right along, I'll take my oath. The Gulf Stream don't exist anymore; she's gone to the devil."

"It's incredible, Turner! You make me gasp."

"Gasp away, if you want to; if things go on so, you ain't going to forget how for want of practice. It's the wooliest voyage, take it by and large—why, look here! You are a landsman, and there's no telling what a landsman can't overlook if he tries. For instance, have you noticed that the nights and days are exactly alike, and you can't tell one from t'other except by keeping tally?"

"Why, yes, I have noticed it in a sort of indifferent general way, but—"

"Have you kept a tally, sir?"

"No, it didn't occur to me to do it."

"I thought so. Now you know, you couldn't keep it in your head, because you and your family are free to sleep as much as you like, and as it's always dark, you sleep a good deal, and you are pretty irregular, naturally. You've all been a little seasick from the start—tea and toast in your own parlor here—no regular time—order it as each of you pleases. You see? You don't go down to meals—they would keep tally for you. So you've lost your reckoning. I noticed it an hour ago."

"How?"

"Well, you spoke of tonight. It ain't tonight at all; it's just noon, now."

"The fact is, I don't believe I have often thought of its being day, since we left. I've got into the habit of considering it night all the time; it's the same with my wife and the children."

"There it is, you see. Mr. Edwards, it's perfectly awful; now ain't it, when you come to look at it? Always night—and such dismal nights, too. It's like being up at the pole in the wintertime. And I'll ask you to notice another thing: this sky is as empty as my sou'wester there."

"Empty?"

"Yes, sir. I know it. You can't get up a day, in a Christian country, that's so solid black the sun can't make a blurry glow of some kind in the sky at high noon—now can you?"

"No, you can't."

"Have you ever seen a suspicion of any such a glow in this sky?"

"Now that you mention it, I haven't."

He dropped his voice and said impressively, "Because there ain't any sun. She's gone where the Gulf Stream twineth."

"Turner! Don't talk like that."

"It's confidential, or I wouldn't. And the moon. She's at the full—by the almanac she is. Why don't she make a blur? Because there ain't any moon. And moreover—you might rake this on-completed sky a hundred year with a dragnet and you'd never scoop a star! Why? Because there ain't any. Now then, what is your opinion about all this?"

"Turner, it's so gruesome and creepy that I don't like to think about it—and I haven't any. What is yours?"

He said, dismally, "That the world has come to an end. Look at it yourself. Just look at the facts. Put them together and add them up, and what have you got? No Sable Island; no Greenland; no Gulf Stream; no day, no proper night; weather that don't jibe with any sample known to the Bureau; animals that would start a panic in any menagerie, chart no more use than a horse blanket, and the heavenly bodies gone to hell! And on top of it all, that jimjam that I've put my hand on more than once and he warn't there—I'll swear it. The ship's bewitched. You don't believe in the jim, and I've sort of lost faith myself, here in the bright light; but if this cup of coffee was to—"

The cup began to glide slowly away, along the table. The hand that moved it was not visible to him. He rose slowly to his feet and stood trembling as if with an ague, his teeth knocking together and his glassy eyes staring at the cup. It slid on and on, noiseless; then it rose in the air, gradually reversed itself, poured its contents down the Superintendent's throat—I saw the dark stream trickling its way down through his hazy breast—then it returned to the table, and without sound of contact, rested there. The mate continued to stare at it for as much as a minute; then he drew a deep breath, took up his sou'wester, and without looking to the right or the left, walked slowly out of the room like one in a trance, muttering, "I've got them—I've had the proof."

I said, reproachfully, "Superintendent, why do you do that?"

"Do what?"

"Play these tricks."

"What harm is it?"

"Harm? It could make that poor devil jump overboard."

"No, he's not as far gone as that."

"For a while he was. He is a good fellow, and it was a pity to scare him so. However there are other matters that I am more concerned about just now."

"Can I help?"

"Why yes, you can; and I don't know anyone else that can."

"Very well, go on."

"By the dead-reckoning we have come twenty-three hundred miles."

"The actual distance is twenty-three-fifty."

"Straight as a dart in the one direction—mainly."

"Apparently."

"Why do you say apparently? Haven't we come straight?"

"Go on with the rest. What were you going to say?"

"This. Doesn't it strike you that this is a pretty large drop of water?"

"No. It is about the usual size—six thousand miles across."

"Six thousand miles!"

"Yes."

"Twice as far as from New York to Liverpool?"

"Yes."

"I must say it is more of a voyage than I counted on. And we are not a great deal more than halfway across, yet. When shall we get in?"

"It will be some time yet."

"That is not very definite. Two weeks?"

"More than that."

I was getting a little uneasy.

"But how much more? A week?"

"All of that. More, perhaps."

"Why don't you tell me? A month more, do you think?"

"I am afraid so. Possibly two—possibly longer, even."

I was getting seriously disturbed by now.

"Why, we are sure to run out of provisions and water."

"No you'll not. I've looked out for that. It is what you are loaded with."

"Is that so? How does that come?"

"Because the ship is chartered for a voyage of discovery. Ostensibly she goes to England, takes aboard some scientists, then sails for the South Pole."

"I see. You are deep."

"I understand my business."

I turned the matter over in my mind a moment, then said, "It is more of a voyage than I was expecting, but I am not of a worrying disposition, so I do not care, so long as we are not going to suffer hunger and thirst."

"Make yourself easy, as to that. Let the trip last as long as it may, you will not run short of food and water, I go bail for that."

"All right, then. Now explain this riddle to me: Why is it always night?"

"That is easy. All of the drop of water is outside the luminous circle of the microscope except one thin and delicate rim of it. We are in the shadow; consequently in the dark."

"In the shadow of what?"

"Of the brazen end of the lens-holder."

"How can it cover such a spread with its shadow?"

"Because it is several thousand miles in diameter. For dimensions, that is nothing. The glass slide which it is pressing against, and which forms the bottom of the ocean we are sailing upon, is thirty thousand miles long, and the length of the microscope barrel is a hundred and twenty thousand. Now then, if—"

"You make me dizzy. I—"

"If you should thrust that glass slide through what you call the 'great' globe, 11,000 miles of it would stand out on each side—it would be like impaling an orange on a table-knife. And so—"

"It gives me the headache. Are these the fictitious proportions which we and our surroundings and belongings have acquired by being reduced to microscopic objects?"

"They are the proportions, yes—but they are not fictitious. You do not notice that you yourself are in any way diminished in size, do you?"

"No, I am my usual size, so far as I can see."

"The same with the men, the ship and everything?"

"Yes—all natural."

"Very good; nothing but the laws and conditions have undergone a change. You came from a small and very insignificant world. The one you are in now is proportioned according to microscopic standards—that is to say, it is inconceivably stupendous and imposing."

It was food for thought. There was something overpowering in the situation, something sublime. It took me a while to shake off the spell and drag myself back to speech.

Presently I said, "I am content; I do not regret the voyage—far from it. I would not change places with any man in that cramped little world. But tell me: Is it always going to be dark?"

"Not if you ever come into the luminous circle under the lens. Indeed you will not find that dark!"

"If we ever. What do you mean by that? We are making

steady good time; we are cutting across this sea on a straight course."

"Apparently."

"There is no apparently about it."

"You might be going around in a small and not rapidly widening circle."

"Nothing of the kind. Look at the telltale compass over your head."

"I see it."

"We changed to this easterly course to satisfy—well, to satisfy everybody but me. It is a pretense of aiming for England—in a drop of water! Have you noticed that needle before?"

"Yes, a number of times."

"Today, for instance?"

"Yes—often."

"Has it varied a jot?"

"Not a jot."

"Hasn't it always kept the place appointed for it—from the start?"

"Yes, always."

"Very well. First we sailed a northerly course; then tilted easterly; and now it is more so. How is that going around in a circle?"

He was silent. I put it at him again. He answered with lazy indifference, "I merely threw out the suggestion."

"All right, then; cornered; let it stand at that. Whenever you happen to think of an argument in support of it, I shall be glad to hear about it."

He did not like that very well, and muttered something about my being a trifle airy. I retorted a little sharply, and followed it up by finding fault with him again for playing tricks on Turner. He said Turner called him a blatherskite. I said, "No matter; you let him alone, from this out. And moreover, stop appearing to people—stop it entirely."

His face darkened. He said, "I would advise you to moderate your manner. I am not used to it, and I am not pleased with it."

The rest of my temper went then. I said, angrily, "You may like it or not, just as you choose. And moreover, if my style doesn't suit you, you can end the dream as soon as you please—right now, if you like."

He looked me steadily in the eye for a moment, then said, with deliberation, "The dream? Are you quite sure it is a dream?"

It took my breath away.

"What do you mean? Isn't it a dream?"

He looked at me in that same way again; and it made my blood chilly this time. Then he said, "You have spent your whole life in this ship. And this is real life. Your other life was the dream!"

It was as if he had hit me, it stunned me so. Still looking at me, his lip curled itself into a mocking smile, and he wasted away like a mist and disappeared.

**I sat a long time,** thinking uncomfortable thoughts.

We are strangely made. We think we are wonderful creatures. Part of the time we think that, at any rate. And during that interval, we consider with pride our mental equipment, with its penetration, its power of analysis, its ability to reason out clear conclusions from confused facts, and all the lordly rest of it; and then comes a rational interval and disenchants us. Disenchants us and lays us bare to ourselves, and we see that intellectually we are really no great things; that we seldom really know the thing we think we know; that our best-built certainties are but sand houses and subject to damage from any wind of doubt that blows.

So little a time before, I knew that this voyage was a dream, and nothing more; a wee little puff or two of doubt had blown against that certainty, unhelped by fact or argument, and already it was dissolving away. It seemed an incredible thing, and it hurt my pride of intellect, but it had to be confessed.

When I came to consider it, these ten days had been such intense realities! So intense that by comparison the life I had lived before them seemed distant, indistinct, slipping away and fading out in a far perspective—exactly as a dream does when you sit at breakfast trying to call back its details. I grew steadily more and more nervous and uncomfortable—and a little frightened, though I would not quite acknowledge this to myself. Then came this disturbing thought: If this transformation goes on, how am I going to conceal it from my wife? Suppose she should say to me, "Henry, there is something the matter with you, you are acting strangely; something is on your mind that you are concealing from me; tell me about it, let me help you," what answer could I make?

I was bound to act strangely if this went on—bound to bury myself in deeps of troubled thought; I should not be able to help it. She had a swift eye to notice, where her heart was concerned, and a sharp intuition, and I was an impotent poor thing in her hands when I had things to hide and she had struck the trail.

I have no large amount of fortitude, staying power. When there is a fate before me I cannot rest easy until I know what it is. I am not able to wait. I want to know, right away. So, I would call Alice, now, and take the consequences. If she drove me into a corner, and I found I could not escape, I would act according to my custom—come out and tell her the truth. She had a better head than mine, and a surer instinct in grouping facts and getting their meaning out of them. If I was drifting into dangerous waters now, she would be sure to detect it and as sure to set me right and save me. I would call her, and keep out of the corner if I could; if I couldn't, why—I couldn't, that is all.

**She came, refreshed with sleep**, and looking her best self: that is to say, looking like a girl of nineteen, not a matron of twenty-five; she wore a becoming wrapper, or tea gown, or whatever it is called, and it was trimmed with ribbons and limp stuff—lace, I suppose; and she had her hair balled up and nailed to its place with a four-pronged tortoise-shell comb.

She brought a basket of pink and gray crewels with her, for she was crocheting a jacket—for the cat, probably, judging by the size of it. She sat down on the sofa and set the basket on the table, expecting to have a chance to get to work by and by; not right away, because a kitten was curled up in it asleep, fitting its circle snugly, and the repose of the children's kittens was a sacred thing and not to be disturbed.

She said, "I noticed that there was no motion—it was what waked me, I think—and I got up to enjoy it, it is such a rare thing."

"Yes, rare enough, dear: We do have the most unaccountably strange weather."

"Do you think so, Henry? Does it seem strange weather to you?"

She looked so earnest and innocent that I was rather startled, and a little in doubt as to what to say. Any sane person could see that it was perfectly devilish weather and crazy beyond imagination, and so how could she feel uncertain about it?

"Well, Alice, I may be putting it too strong, but I don't think so; I think a person may call our weather by any hard name he pleases and be justified."

"Perhaps you are right, Henry. I have heard the sailors talk the same way about it, but I did not think that that meant much, they speak so extravagantly about everything. You are not always extravagant in your speech—often you are, but not always—and so it surprised me a little to hear you." Then she added tranquilly and musingly, "I don't remember any different weather."

It was not quite definite.

"You mean on this voyage, Alice."

"Yes, of course. Naturally. I haven't made any other."

She was softly stroking the kitten—and apparently in her right mind. I said cautiously, and with seeming indifference, "You mean you haven't made any other this year. But the time we went to Europe—well, that was very different weather."

"The time we went to Europe, Henry?"

"Certainly, certainly—when Jessie was a year old."

She stopped stroking the kitty, and looked at me inquiringly. "I don't understand you, Henry."

She was not a joker, and she was always truthful. Her remark blew another wind of doubt upon my wasting sand-edifice of certainty. Had I only dreamed that we went to Europe? It seemed a good idea to put this thought into words.

"Come, Alice, the first thing you know you will be imagining that we went to Europe in a dream."

She smiled, and said, "Don't let me spoil it, Henry, if it is pleasant to you to think we went. I will consider that we did go, and that I have forgotten it."

"But Alice dear, we did go!"

"But Henry dear, we didn't go!"

She had a good head and a good memory, and she was always truthful. My head had been injured by a fall when I was a boy, and the physicians had said at the time that there could be ill effects from it someday. A cold wave struck me now; perhaps the effects had come. I was losing confidence in the European trip. However, I thought I would make another try.

"Alice, I will give you a detail or two; then maybe you will remember."

"A detail or two from the dream?"

"I am not at all sure that it was a dream; and five minutes ago I was sure that it wasn't. It was seven years ago. We went over in the Batavia. Do you remember the Batavia?"

"I don't, Henry."

"Captain Moreland. Don't you remember him?"

"To me he is a myth, Henry."

"Well, it beats anything. We lived two or three months in London, then six weeks in a private hotel in George Street, Edinburgh—Veitch's. Come!"

"It sounds pleasant, but I have never heard of these things before, Henry."

"And Doctor John Brown, of Rab and His Friends—you were ill, and he came every day; and when you were well again he still came every day and took us all around while he paid his visits, and we waited in his carriage while he prescribed for his patients. And he was so dear and lovely. You must remember all that, Alice."

"None of it, dear; it is only a dream."

"Why, Alice, have you ever had a dream that remained as distinct as that, and which you could remember so long?"

"So long? It is more than likely that you dreamed it last night."

"No indeed! It has been in my memory seven years."

"Seven years in a dream, yes—it is the way of dreams. They put seven years into two minutes, without any trouble. Isn't it so?"

I had to acknowledge that it was.

"It seems almost as if it couldn't have been a dream, Alice; it seems as if you ought to remember it."

"Wait! It begins to come back to me." She sat thinking a while, nodding her head with satisfaction from time to time. At last she said, joyfully, "I remember almost the whole of it, now."

"Good!"

"I am glad I got it back. Ordinarily I remember my dreams very well; but for some reason this one—"

"This one, Alice? Do you really consider it a dream, yet?"

"I don't consider anything about it, Henry, I know it; I know it positively."

The conviction stole through me that she must be right, since she felt so sure. Indeed I almost knew she was. I was privately becoming ashamed of myself now, for mistaking a clever illusion for a fact. So I gave it up, then, and said I would let it stand as a dream. Then I added, "It puzzles me; even now it seems almost as distinct as the microscope."

"Which microscope?"

"Well, Alice, there's only the one."

"Very well, which one is that?"

"Bother it all, the one we examined this ocean in, the other day."

"Where?"

"Why, at home of course."

"What home?"

"Alice, it's provoking. Why, our home. In Springport."

"Dreaming again. I've never heard of it."

That was stupefying. There was no need of further beating about the bush; I threw caution aside, and came out frankly.

"Alice, what do you call the life we are leading in this ship? Isn't it a dream?"

She looked at me in a puzzled way and said, "A dream, Henry? Why should I think that?"

"Oh, dear me, I don't know! I thought I did, but I don't. Alice, haven't we ever had a home? Don't you remember one?"

"Why, yes—three. That is, dream homes, not real ones. I have never regarded them as realities."

"Describe them."

She did it, and in detail; also our life in them. Pleasant enough homes, and easily recognizable by me. I could also recognize an average of two out of seven of the episodes and incidents which she threw in. Then I described the home and the life which (as it appeared to me) we had so recently left. She recognized it—but only as a dream home. She remembered nothing about the microscope and the children's party. I was in a corner; but it was not the one which I had arranged for.

"Alice, if those were dream homes, how long have you been in this ship? You say this is the only voyage you have ever made."

"I don't know. I don't remember. It is the only voyage we have made—unless breaking it to pick up this crew of strangers in place of the friendly dear men and officers we had sailed with so many years makes two voyages of it. How I do miss them: Captain Hall, and Williams the sail-maker, and Storrs the chief mate, and—" She choked up, and the tears began to trickle down her cheeks. Soon she had her handkerchief out and was sobbing.

I realized that I remembered those people perfectly well. Damnation! I said to myself, are we real creatures in a real world, all of a sudden, and have we been feeding on dreams in an imaginary one since nobody knows when—or how is it? My head was swimming.

"Alice! Answer me this. Do you know the Superintendent of Dreams?"

"Certainly."

"Have you seen him often?"

"Not often, but several times."

"When did you see him first?"

"The time that Robert the captain's boy was eaten."

"Eaten?"

"Yes. Surely you haven't forgotten that?"

"But I have, though. I never heard of it before." (I spoke the truth. For the moment I could not recall the incident.)

Her face was full of reproach.

"I am sorry, if that is so. He was always good to you. If you are jesting, I do not think it is in good taste."

"Now don't treat me like that, Alice, I don't deserve it. I am not jesting, I am in earnest. I mean the boy's memory no offence, but although I remember him I do not remember the circumstance—I swear it. Who ate him?"

"Do not be irreverent, Henry, it is out of place. It was not a who, at all."

"What then—a which?"

"Yes."

"What kind of a which?"

"A spider-squid. Now you remember it I hope."

"Indeed and deed and double-deed I don't, Alice, and it is the real truth. Tell me about it, please."

"I suppose you see now, Henry, what your memory is worth. You can remember dream trips to Europe well enough, but things in real life—even the most memorable and horrible things—pass out of your memory in twelve years. There is something the matter with your mind."

It was very curious. How could I have forgotten that tragedy? It must have happened; she was never mistaken in her facts, and she never spoke with positiveness of a thing which she was in any degree uncertain about. And this tragedy—twelve years ago—

"Alice, how long have we been in this ship?"

"Now how can I know, Henry? It goes too far back. Always, for all I know. The earliest thing I can call to mind was papa's death by the sun heat and mamma's suicide the same day. I was four years old, then. Surely you must remember that, Henry."

"Yes... Yes. But it is so dim. Tell me about it—refresh my memory."

"Why, you must remember that we were in the edge of a great white glare once for a little while: a day, or maybe two days... only a little while, I think, but I remember it, because it was the only time I was ever out of the dark, and there was a great

221

deal of talk of it for long afterwards. Why, Henry, you must remember a wonderful thing like that."

"Wait. Let me think." Gradually, detail by detail, the whole thing came back to me; and with it the boy's adventure with the spider-squid; and then I recalled a dozen other incidents, which Alice verified as incidents of our ship life, and said I had set them forth correctly.

It was a puzzling thing—my freaks of memory; Alice's, too. By testing, it was presently manifest that the vacancies in my ship life memories were only apparent, not real; a few words by way of reminder enabled me to fill them up, in almost all cases, and give them clarity and vividness. What had caused these temporary lapses? Didn't these very lapses indicate that the ship life was a dream, and not real?

It made Alice laugh.

I did not see anything foolish in it, or anything to laugh at, and I told her so. And I reminded her that her own memory was as bad as mine, since many and many a conspicuous episode of our land life was gone from her, even so striking an incident as the water-drop exploration with the microscope—It made her shout.

I was wounded; and said that if I could not be treated with respect I would spare her the burden of my presence and conversation. She stopped laughing, at once, and threw her arms about my neck. She said she would not have hurt me for the world, but she supposed I was joking; it was quite natural to think I was not in earnest in talking gravely about this and that and the other dream-phantom as if it were a reality.

"But Alice, I was in earnest, and I *am* in earnest. Look at it— examine it. If the land life was a dream life, how is it that you remember so much of it exactly as I remember it?"

She was amused again, inside—I could feel the quiver; but there was no exterior expression of it, for she did not want to

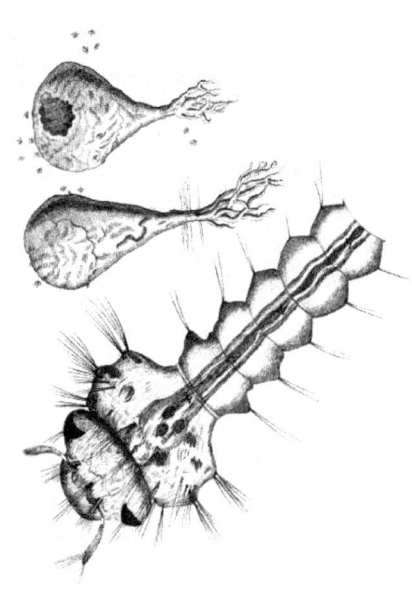

hurt me again.

"Dear heart, throw the whole matter aside! Stop puzzling over it; it isn't worth it. It is perfectly simple. It is true that I remember a little of that dream life just as you remember it, but that is an accident; the rest of it—and by far the largest part—does not correspond with your recollections. And how could it? People can't be expected to remember each other's dreams, but only their own. You have put me into your land dreams a thousand times, but I didn't always know I was there; so how could I remember it? Also I have put you into my land dreams a thousand times when you didn't know it—and the natural result is that when I name the circumstances you don't always recall them.

"But how different it is with this real life, this genuine life in the ship! Our recollections of it are just alike. You have been forgetting episodes of it today—I don't know why; it has surprised me and puzzled me—but the lapse was only temporary; your memory soon rallied again. Now it hasn't rallied in the case of land dreams of mine—in most cases it hasn't. And it's not going to, Henry. You can be sure of that."

She stopped and tilted her head up in a thinking attitude and began to unconsciously tap her teeth with the ivory knob of a crochet needle. Presently she said, "I think I know what is the matter. I have been neglecting you for ten days while I have been grieving for our old shipmates and pretending to be seasick so that I might indulge myself with solitude; and here is the result— you haven't been taking exercise enough."

I was glad to have a reason—any reason that would excuse my memory—and I accepted this one, and made confession. There was no truth in the confession, but I was already getting handy with these evasions. I was a little sorry for this, for she had always trusted my word, and I had honored this trust by telling her the truth many a time when it was a sharp sacrifice to me to do it.

She looked me over with gentle reproach in her eye, and said, "Henry, how can you be so naughty? I watch you so faithfully and make you take such good care of your health that you owe me the grace to do my office for me when for any fair reason I am for a while not on guard. When have you boxed with George last?"

What an idea it was! It was a good place to make a mistake, and I came near to doing it. It was on my tongue's end to say that I had never boxed with anyone; and as for boxing with a man-servant... and so on; but I kept back my remark, and in place of it tried to look like a person who didn't know what to say. It was easy to do, and I probably did it very well.

"You do not say anything, Henry. I think it is because you have a good reason. When have you fenced with him? Henry, you are avoiding my eye. Look up. Tell me the truth: have you fenced with him a single time in the last ten days?"

So far as I was aware I knew nothing about foils, and had never handled them; so I was able to answer: "I will be frank with you, Alice—I haven't."

"I suspected it. Now, Henry, what can you say?"

I was getting some of my wits back, now, and was not altogether unprepared, this time.

"Well, Alice, there hasn't been much fencing weather, and when there was any, I—well, I was lazy, and that is the shameful truth."

"There's a chance now, anyway, and you mustn't waste it. Take off your coat and things."

She rang for George, then she got up and raised the sofa seat and began to fish out boxing gloves, and foils and masks from the locker under it, softly scolding me all the while. George put his head in, noted the preparations, then entered and put himself in boxing trim.

**George was gloved and skipping** about in an imaginary fight, and Alice told me to get to work with him. She took pencil and paper and got ready to keep game. I stepped forward to position—then a curious thing happened: I seemed to remember a thousand boxing bouts with George, the whole boxing art came flooding in upon me, and I knew just what to do! I was a prey to no indecisions, I had no trouble. We fought six rounds, I held my own all through, and I finally knocked George out. I was not astonished; it seemed a familiar experience. Alice showed no surprise, George showed none; apparently it was an old story to them.

The same thing happened with the fencing. I suddenly knew that I was an experienced old fencer; I expected to get the victory, and when I got it, it seemed but a repetition of something which had happened numberless times before.

We decided to go down to the main saloon and take a regular meal in the regular way—the evening meal. Alice went away to dress. Just as I had finished dressing, the children came romping in, warmly and prettily clad, and nestled up to me, one on each side, on the sofa, and began to chatter. Not about a former home; no, not a word of that, but only about this ship home and its concerns and its people.

They cared for no other home, real or unreal, and wanted no better one. They were innocent witnesses and free from prejudice.

When we went below, we found the roomy saloon well-lighted and brightly and prettily furnished, and a very comfortable and inviting place altogether. Everything seemed substantial and genuine, there was nothing to suggest that it might be a work of the imagination.

The talk and the feeding went along in a natural way, I could find nothing unusual about it anywhere. The captain was pale, and had a jaded and harassed look, and was subject to little fits of absence of mind; and these things could be said of the mate, also, but this was all natural enough, considering the grisly time they had been having, and certainly there was nothing about it to suggest that they were dream creatures or that their troubles were unreal.

The stranger at my side was about 45 years old, and he had the half-subdued, half-resigned look of a man who had been under a burden of trouble a long time. He was tall and thin; he had a bushy black head, and black eyes which burned when he was interested, but were dull and expressionless when his thoughts were far away—and that happened every time he dropped out of the conversation. He forgot to eat, then, his hands became idle, his dull eye fixed itself upon his plate or upon vacancy, and now and then he would draw a heavy sigh out of the depths of his breast.

These three were exceptions; the others were chatty and cheerful, and they were like a pleasant little family party together.

The captain and the mate managed to seem comfortable enough until Phillips raised the subject of the day's run, the position of the ship, distance out, and so on; then they became irritable, and sharp of speech, and were unkinder to the young fellow than the case seemed to call for. His sweetheart was distressed to see him so treated before all the company, and she spoke up bravely in his defense and reproached her father for making an offence out of so harmless a thing. This only brought her into trouble, and procured for her so rude a retort that she was consumed with shame, and left the table crying.

The pleasure was all gone, now; everybody felt personally affronted and wantonly abused. Conversation ceased, and an uncomfortable silence fell upon the company; through it one could hear the wailing of the wind and the dull tramp of the sailors and the muffled words of command overhead, and this made the silence all the more dismal.

The dinner was a failure. While it was still unfinished the company began to break up and slip out, one after another; and presently none was left but me.

**I sat long, sipping black coffee** and smoking. And thinking; groping about in my dimming land-past. An incident of my American life would rise upon me, vague at first, then grow more distinct and articulate, then sharp and clear; then in a moment it was gone, and in its place was a dull and distant image of some long-past episode whose theatre was this ship—and then it would develop, and clarify, and become strong and real. It was fascinating, enchanting, this spying among the elusive mysteries of my bewitched memory, and I went up to my parlor and continued it, with the help of punch and pipe, hour after hour, as long as I could keep awake. With this curious result: that the main incidents of both my lives were now recovered, but only those of one of them persistently gathered strength and vividness—our life in the ship! Those of our land life were good enough, plain enough, but in minuteness of detail they fell perceptibly short of those others; and in matters of feeling—joy, grief, physical pain, physical pleasure—immeasurably short!

Some mellow notes floated to my ear, muffled by the moaning wind—six bells in the morning watch. So late! I went to bed. When I woke in the middle of the so-called day the first thing I thought of was my night's experience.

Already my land life had faded a little—but not the other.

*This is a condensed version of a story fragment written by Twain in 1898. He left it untitled and unfinished ("The Great Dark" was applied to it later), but he made detailed notes as to how he planned to finish it. The beginning of a "Book II," not included here, included a harrowing encounter with a giant squid and the disappearance of the Edwardses' two children, who are later rescued. The manuscript broke off following an unsuccessful mutiny—the third such attempt by the crew—and a stirring speech from the captain.*

*Twain's notes on the rest of the story indicated that he planned to extend the story some ten or fifteen years. He planned to have the sea dry up when the ship reached the reflected light of the microscope. The Edwards children were to have been taken prisoner by another ship, and Henry was to have undertaken a trek over the now-dry seabed with the captain in order to rescue them. In the end, however, he would find only their mummified bodies. The story was to have concluded with Henry awaking from his dream as Alice comes in with the children to say goodnight.*

*"The Impartial Friend: Death, the only immortal who treats us all alike, whose pity and whose peace and whose refuge are for all—the soiled and the pure, the rich and the poor, the loved and the unloved."*

Three Thousand Years Among the Microbes
1905

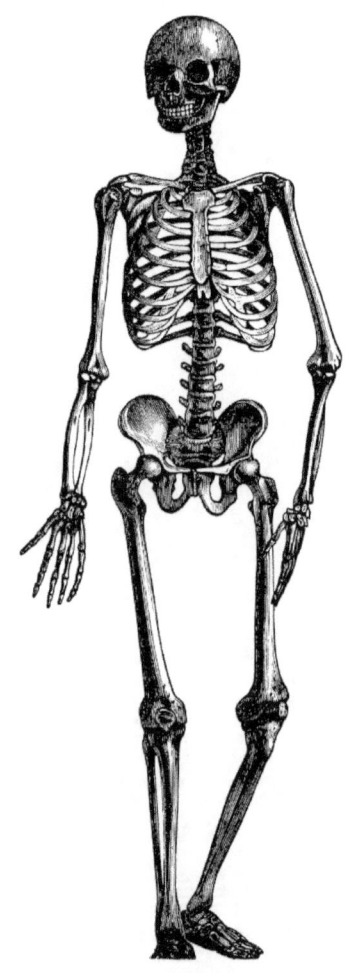

# A Curious Dream

Night before last, I had a singular dream. I seemed to be sitting on a doorstep (in no particular city perhaps) ruminating, and the time of night appeared to be about 12 or 1 o'clock. The weather was balmy and delicious. There was no human sound in the air, not even a footstep. There was no sound of any kind to emphasize the dead stillness, except the occasional hollow barking of a dog in the distance and the fainter answer of a further dog.

Presently, up the street, I heard a bony clack-clacking, and guessed it was the castanets of a serenading party. In a minute more, a tall skeleton, hooded, and half-clad in a tattered and moldy shroud, whose shreds were flapping about the ribby latticework of its person, swung by me with a stately stride and disappeared in the gray gloom of the starlight. It had a broken and worm-eaten coffin on its shoulder and a bundle of something in its hand. I knew what the clack-clacking was then; it was this party's joints working together, and his elbows knocking against his sides as he walked.

I may say I was surprised. Before I could collect my thoughts and enter upon any speculations as to what this apparition might portend, I heard another one coming, for I recognized his clack-clack. He had two-thirds of a coffin on his shoulder, and some foot- and headboards under his arm. I mightily wanted to peer under his hood and speak to him, but when he turned and smiled upon me with his cavernous sockets and his projecting grin as he went by, I thought I would not detain him.

He was hardly gone when I heard the clacking again, and another one issued from the shadowy half-light. This one was bending under a heavy gravestone, and dragging a shabby coffin after him by a string. When he got to me, he gave me a steady look for a moment or two, and then rounded to and backed up to me, saying:

"Ease this down for a fellow, will you?"

I eased the gravestone down till it rested on the ground, and in doing so noticed that it bore the name of "John Baxter Copmanhurst," with "May, 1839," as the date of his death. Deceased sat wearily down by me, and wiped his os frontis with his major maxillary—chiefly from former habit I judged, for I could not see that he brought away any perspiration.

"It is too bad, too bad," said he, drawing the remnant of the shroud about him and leaning his jaw pensively on his hand. Then he put his left foot up on his knee and fell to scratching his anklebone absently with a rusty nail which he got out of his coffin.

"What is too bad, friend?"

"Oh, everything, everything. I almost wish I never had died."

"You surprise me. Why do you say this? Has anything gone wrong? What is the matter?"

"Matter! Look at this shroud-rags. Look at this gravestone, all battered up. Look at that disgraceful old coffin. All a man's property going to ruin and destruction before his eyes, and ask him if anything is wrong? Fire and brimstone!"

"Calm yourself, calm yourself," I said. "It is too bad—it is certainly too bad, but then I had not supposed that you would much mind such matters situated as you are."

"Well, my dear sir, I do mind them. My pride is hurt, and my comfort is impaired—destroyed, I might say. I will state my case—I will put it to you in such a way that you can comprehend it, if you will let me," said the poor skeleton, tilting the hood of his shroud back, as if he were clearing for action, and thus unconsciously giving himself a jaunty and festive air very much at variance with the grave character of his position in life—so to speak—and in prominent contrast with his distressful mood.

"Proceed," said I.

"I reside in the shameful old graveyard a block or two above you here, in this street—there, now, I just expected that cartilage would let go—third rib from the bottom, friend, hitch the end of it to my spine with a string, if you have got such a thing about you, though a bit of silver wire is a deal pleasanter, and more durable and becoming, if one keeps it polished—to think of shredding out and going to pieces in this way, just on account of the indifference and neglect of one's posterity!"

And the poor ghost grated his teeth in a way that gave me a wrench and a shiver, for the effect is mightily increased by the absence of muffling flesh and cuticle.

"I reside in that old graveyard, and have for these thirty years; and I tell you things are changed since I first laid this old tired frame there, and turned over, and stretched out for a long sleep,

233

with a delicious sense upon me of being done with bother, and grief, and anxiety, and doubt, and fear, forever and ever, and listening with comfortable and increasing satisfaction to the sexton's work, from the startling clatter of his first spadeful on my coffin till it dulled away to the faint patting that shaped the roof of my new home—delicious! My! I wish you could try it tonight!"

And out of my reverie deceased fetched me a rattling slap with a bony hand.

"Yes, sir, thirty years ago I laid me down there, and was happy. For it was out in the country then—out in the breezy, flowery, grand old woods, and the lazy winds gossiped with the leaves, and the squirrels capered over us and around us, and the creeping things visited us, and the birds filled the tranquil solitude with music. Ah, it was worth ten years of a man's life to be dead then! Everything was pleasant. I was in a good neighborhood, for all the dead people that lived near me belonged to the best families in the city.

"Our posterity appeared to think the world of us. They kept our graves in the very best condition; the fences were always in faultless repair; headboards were kept painted or whitewashed, and were replaced with new ones as soon as they began to look rusty or decayed; monuments were kept upright, railings intact and bright; the rose bushes and shrubbery trimmed, trained, and free from blemish; the walks clean and smooth and graveled.

"But that day is gone by. Our descendants have forgotten us. My grandson lives in a stately house built with money made by these old hands of mine, and I sleep in a neglected grave with invading vermin that gnaw my shroud to build them nests withal! I and friends that lie with me founded and secured the prosperity of this fine city, and the stately bantling of our loves leaves us to rot in a dilapidated cemetery which neighbors curse and strangers scoff at.

"See the difference between the old time and this, for instance: Our graves are all caved in now; our headboards have rotted away and tumbled down; our railings reel this way and that, with one foot in the air, after a fashion of unseemly levity; our monuments lean wearily, and our gravestones bow their heads, discouraged; there be no adornments any more—no roses, nor shrubs, nor graveled walks, nor anything that is a comfort to the eye; and even the paintless old board fence that did make a show of holding us sacred from companionship with beasts and the defilement of heedless feet, has tottered till it overhangs the street, and only advertises the presence of our dismal resting place and invites yet more derision to it.

"And now we cannot hide our poverty and tatters in the friendly woods, for the city has stretched its withering arms abroad and taken us in, and all that remains of the cheer of our old home is the cluster of lugubrious forest trees that stand, bored and weary of a city life, with their feet in our coffins, looking into the hazy distance and wishing they were there. I tell you, it is disgraceful!

"You begin to comprehend—you begin to see how it is. While our descendants are living sumptuously on our money, right around us in the city, we have to fight hard to keep skull and bones together. Bless you, there isn't a grave in our cemetery that doesn't leak. Not one. Every time it rains in the night, we have to climb out and roost in the trees, and sometimes we are wakened suddenly by the chilly water trickling down the back of our necks. Then I tell you there is a general heaving up of old graves and kicking over of old monuments, and scampering of old skeletons for the trees! Bless me, if you had gone along there some such nights after twelve you might have seen as many as fifteen of us roosting on one limb, with our joints rattling drearily and the wind wheezing through our ribs! Many a time we have perched there for three or four dreary hours, and then come down, stiff and chilled through and drowsy, and borrowed each other's skulls to bail out our graves with—if you will glance up in my mouth now as I tilt my head back, you can see that my headpiece is half full of old dry sediment. How top-heavy and stupid it makes me sometimes!

"Yes, sir, many a time, if you had happened to come along just before the dawn, you'd have caught us bailing out the graves and hanging our shrouds on the fence to dry. Why, I had an elegant shroud stolen from there one morning—think a party by the name of Smith took it, that resides in a plebeian graveyard over yonder—I think so because the first time I ever saw him he hadn't anything on but a check shirt, and the last time I saw him, which was at a social gathering in the new cemetery, he was the best-dressed corpse in the company—and it is a significant fact that he left when he saw me.

"And presently an old woman from here missed her coffin— she generally took it with her when she went anywhere, because she was liable to take cold and bring on the spasmodic rheumatism that originally killed her if she exposed herself to the night air much. She was named Hotchkiss—Anna Matilda Hotchkiss—you might know her? She has two upper front teeth, is tall, but a good deal inclined to stoop, one rib on the left side gone, has one shred of rusty hair hanging from the left side of her head, and one little tuft just above and a little forward of her right ear, has her underjaw wired on one side where it had worked loose, small bone of left forearm gone—lost in a fight, has a kind of swagger in her gait and a 'gallus' way of going with: her arms akimbo and her nostrils in the air has been pretty free and easy, and is all damaged and battered up till she looks like a queensware crate in ruins. Maybe you have met her?"

"God forbid!" I involuntarily ejaculated, for somehow I was not looking for that form of question, and it caught me a little off my guard. But I hastened to make amends for my rudeness, and say, "I simply meant I had not had the honor, for I would not deliberately speak discourteously of a friend of yours. You were saying that you were robbed, and it was a shame, too, but it appears by what is left of the shroud you have on that it was a costly one in its day. How did..."

A most ghastly expression began to develop among the decayed features and shriveled integuments of my guest's face, and I was beginning to grow uneasy and distressed, when he told me he was only working up a deep, sly smile, with a wink in it, to suggest that about the time he acquired his present garment a ghost in a neighboring cemetery missed one. This reassured me, but I begged him to confine himself to speech thenceforth, because his facial expression was uncertain. Even with the most elaborate care, it was liable to miss fire. Smiling should especially be avoided. What he might honestly consider a shining success was likely to strike me in a very different light. I said I liked to see a skeleton cheerful, even decorously playful, but I did not think smiling was a skeleton's best hold.

"Yes, friend," said the poor skeleton, "the facts are just as I have given them to you. Two of these old graveyards—the one that I resided in and one further along—have been deliberately neglected by our descendants of today until there is no occupying them any longer. Aside from the osteological discomfort of it—and that is no light matter this rainy weather—the present state of things is ruinous to property. We have got to move or be content to see our effects wasted away and utterly destroyed.

"Now, you will hardly believe it, but it is true, nevertheless, that there isn't a single coffin in good repair among all my acquaintance—now that is an absolute fact. I do not refer to low people who come in a pine box mounted on an express wagon, but I am talking about your high-toned, silver-mounted burial case, your monumental sort, that travel under black plumes at the head of a procession and have choice of cemetery lots. I mean folks like the Jarvises, and the Bledsoes and Burlings, and such. They are all about ruined. The most substantial people in our set, they were. And now look at them: utterly used up and poverty-stricken. One of the Bledsoes actually traded his monument to a late barkeeper for some fresh shavings to put under his head.

"I tell you it speaks volumes, for there is nothing a corpse takes so much pride in as his monument. He loves to read the inscription. He comes after a while to believe what it says himself, and then you may see him sitting on the fence night after night enjoying it. Epitaphs are cheap, and they do a poor chap a world of good after he is dead, especially if he had hard luck while he was alive. I wish they were used more.

"Now I don't complain, but confidentially I do think it was a little shabby in my descendants to give me nothing but this old slab of a gravestone, and all the more that there isn't a compliment on it. It used to have 'GONE TO HIS JUST REWARD' on it, and I was proud when I first saw it, but by and by I noticed that whenever an old friend of mine came along, he would hook his chin on the railing and pull a long face and read along down till he came to that, and then he would chuckle to himself and walk off, looking satisfied and comfortable. So I scratched it off to get rid of those fools.

"But a dead man always takes a deal of pride in his monument. Yonder goes half a dozen of the Jarvises now, with the family monument along. And Smithers and some hired specters went by with his a while ago. Hello, Higgins, goodbye, old friend! That's Meredith Higgins—died in '44—belongs to our set in the cemetery. Fine old family. I am on the most familiar terms with him; he didn't hear me was the reason he didn't answer me. And I am sorry, too, because I would have liked to introduce you. You would admire him. He is the most disjointed, sway-backed, and generally distorted old skeleton you ever saw, but he is full of fun. When he laughs, it sounds like rasping two stones together, and he always starts it off with a cheery screech like raking a nail across a windowpane.

"Hey, Jones! That is old Columbus Jones. Shroud cost four hundred dollars; entire trousseau, including monument, twenty-seven hundred. This was in the spring of '26. It was enormous style for those days. Dead people came all the way from the Alleghanies to see his things—the party that occupied the grave next to mine remembers it well.

"Now do you see that individual going along with a piece of a headboard under his arm, one leg bone below his knee gone, and not a thing in the world on? That is Barstow Dalhousie, and next to Columbus Jones he was the most sumptuously outfitted person that ever entered our cemetery.

"We are all leaving. We cannot tolerate the treatment we are receiving at the hands of our descendants. They open new cemeteries, but they leave us to our ignominy. They mend the streets, but they never mend anything that is about us or belongs to us. Look at that coffin of mine! Yet I tell you in its day it was a piece of furniture that would have attracted attention in any drawing room in this city. You may have it if you want it. I can't afford to repair it. Put a new bottom in her, and part of a new top, and a bit of fresh lining along the left side, and you'll find her about as comfortable as any receptacle of her species you ever tried. No thanks no, don't mention it. You have been civil to me, and I would give you all the property I have got before I would seem ungrateful.

"Now this winding-sheet is a kind of a sweet thing in its way, if you would like to—No? Well, just as you say, but I wished to be fair and liberal there's nothing mean about me. Goodbye, friend, I must be going. I may have a good way to go tonight, don't know. I only know one thing for certain, and that is that I am on the emigrant trail now, and I'll never sleep in that crazy old cemetery again. I will travel till I find respectable quarters, if I have to hoof it to New Jersey. All the boys are going. It was decided in public conclave, last night, to emigrate, and by the time the sun rises there won't be a bone left in our old habitations. Such cemeteries may suit my surviving friends, but they do not suit the remains that have the honor to make these remarks.

"My opinion is the general opinion. If you doubt it, go and see how the departing ghosts upset things before they started. They were almost riotous in their demonstrations of distaste. Hello, here are some of the Bledsoes, and if you will give me a lift with this tombstone, I guess I will join company and jog along with them—mighty respectable old family, the Bledsoes, and used to always come out in six-horse hearses and all that sort of thing fifty years ago when I walked these streets in daylight. Goodbye, friend."

And with his gravestone on his shoulder, he joined the grisly procession, dragging his damaged coffin after him, for notwithstanding he pressed it upon me so earnestly, I utterly refused his hospitality. I suppose that for as much as two hours these sad outcasts went clacking by, laden with their dismal effects, and all that time I sat pitying them. One or two of the youngest and least dilapidated among them inquired about midnight trains on the railways, but the rest seemed unacquainted with that mode of travel, and merely asked about common public roads to various towns and cities, some of which are not on the map now, and vanished from it and from the earth as much as thirty years ago, and some few of them never had existed anywhere but on maps, and private ones in real estate agencies at that. And they asked about the condition of the cemeteries in these towns and cities, and about the reputation the citizens bore as to reverence for the dead.

This whole matter interested me deeply, and likewise compelled my sympathy for these homeless ones.

And it all seeming real, and I not knowing it was a dream, I mentioned to one shrouded wanderer an idea that had entered my head to publish an account of this curious and very sorrowful exodus, but said also that I could not describe it truthfully, and just as it occurred, without seeming to trifle with a grave subject and exhibit an irreverence for the dead that would shock and distress their surviving friends. But this bland and stately remnant of a former citizen leaned him far over my gate and whispered in my ear, and said:

"Do not let that disturb you. The community that can stand such graveyards as those we are emigrating from can stand anything a body can say about the neglected and forsaken dead that lie in them."

At that very moment a cock crowed, and the weird procession vanished and left not a shred or a bone behind.

I awoke, and found myself lying with my head out of the bed and "sagging" downward considerably—a position favorable to dreaming dreams with morals in them, maybe, but not poetry.

Note: The reader is assured that if the cemeteries in his town are kept in good order, this Dream is not leveled at his town at all, but is leveled particularly and venomously at the next town.

*"A Curious Dream," was published in 1882 as part of Twain's collection* Sketches New and Old, *which also included his first successful short story, "The Notorious Jumping Frog of Calaveras County." This story was adapted into a short drama film, released in 1907 by the Vitagraph Company of America.*

"*Let us endeavor so to live that when we come to die even the undertaker will be sorry.*"

Puddn'head Wilson's Calendar

# The Undertaker's Chat

"Now that corpse," said the undertaker, patting the folded hands of deceased approvingly, "was a brick—very way you took him he was a brick. He was so real accommodating, and so modest-like and simple in his last moments. Friends wanted metallic burial case—nothing else would do. I couldn't get it. There warn't going to be time. Anybody could see that.

"Corpse said, 'Never mind. Shake him up some kind of a box he could stretch out in comfortable, he warn't particular 'bout the general style of it.' Said he went more on room than style, anyway in a last final container.

"Friends wanted a silver door plate on the coffin, signifying who he was and wher' he was from. Now you know a fellow couldn't roust out such a gaily thing as that in a little country-town like this. What did corpse say?

"Corpse said, 'Whitewash his old canoe and dob his address and general destination onto it with a blacking-brush and a stencil-plate, 'long with a verse from some likely hymn or other, and paint him for the tomb, and mark him C.O.D., and just let him flicker.' He warn't distressed any more than you be—on the contrary, just as ca'm and collected as a hearse-horse; said he judged that wher' he was going to a body would find it considerable better to attract attention by a picturesque moral character than a natty burial-case with a swell door plate on it.

"Splendid man, he was. I'd druther do for a corpse like that 'n any I've tackled in seven year. There's some satisfaction in buryin' a man like that. You feel that what you're doing is appreciated. Lord bless you, so's he got planted before he sp'iled, he was perfectly satisfied; said his relations meant well, perfectly well, but all them preparations was bound to delay the thing more or less, and he didn't wish to be kept layin' around. You never see such a clear head as what he had, and so ca'm and so cool. Jist a hunk of brains, that is what he was. Perfectly awful. It was a ripping distance from one end of that man's head to t'other. Often and over again he's had brain-fever a-raging in one place, and the rest of the pile didn't know anything about it.

"Well, the relations they wanted a big funeral, but corpse said he was down on flummery—didn't want any procession—fill the hearse full of mourners, and get out a stern line and tow him behind. He was the most down on style of any remains I ever struck. A beautiful, simpleminded creature is was what he was, you can depend on that. He was just set on having things the way he wanted them, and he took a solid comfort in laying his little plans. He had me measure him and take a whole raft of directions; then he had the minister stand up behind along box with a tablecloth over it, to represent the coffin, and read his funeral sermon, saying 'Angcore, angcore!' at the good places, and making him scratch out every bit of brag about him, and all the hifalutin; and then he made them trot out the choir, so's he could help them pick out the tunes for the occasion, and he got them to sing 'Pop Goes the Weasel,' because he'd always liked that tune when he was downhearted, and solemn music made him sad. And when they sung that with tears in their eyes (because they all loved him), and his relations grieving around, he just laid there, as happy as a bug, and trying to beat time and showing all over how much he enjoyed it; and presently, he got worked up and excited, and tried to join in, for, mind you, he was pretty proud of his abilities in the singing line; but the first time he opened his mouth and was just going to spread himself, his breath took a walk.

"I never see a man snuffed out so sudden. Ah, it was a great loss—a powerful loss to this poor little one-horse town. Well, well, well, I hain't got time to be palavering along here—got to nail on the lid and mosey along with him; and if you'll just give me a lift, we'll skeet him into the hearse and meander along. Relations bound to have it so—don't pay no attention to dying injunctions, minute a corpse's gone; but, if I had my way, if I didn't respect his last wishes and tow him behind the hearse, I'll be cuss'd. I consider that whatever a corpse wants done for his comfort is little enough matter, and a man hain't got no right to deceive him or take advantage of him; and whatever a corpse trusts me to do I'm a-going to do, you know, even if it's to stuff him and paint him yaller and keep him for a keepsake—you hear me!"

He cracked his whip and went lumbering away with his ancient ruin of a hearse, and I continued my walk with a valuable lesson learned—that a healthy and wholesome cheerfulness is not necessarily impossible to any occupation. The lesson is likely to be lasting, for it will take many months to obliterate the memory of the remarks and circumstances that impressed it.

*"The Undertaker's Chat" first appeared on October 23, 1870 in the* Chicago Tribune *under the title "A Reminiscence of the Back Settlements."*

# The Spirited Widow

The Judge's account

I was sitting here in this old pulpit, holding court, and we were trying a big, wicked-looking Spanish desperado for killing the husband of a bright, pretty Mexican woman. It was a lazy summer day, and an awfully long one, and the witnesses were tedious. None of us took any interest in the trial except that nervous, uneasy devil of a Mexican woman. [She] had loved her husband with all her might, and now she had boiled it all down into hate, and stood here spitting it at that Spaniard with her eyes; and I tell you she would stir me up, too, with a little of her summer lightning, occasionally.

Well, I had my coat off and my heels up, lolling and sweating, and smoking one of those cabbage cigars the San Francisco people used to think were good enough for us in those times; and the lawyers they all had their coats off, and were smoking and whittling, and the witnesses the same, and so was the prisoner.

Well, the fact is, there warn't any interest in a murder trial then, because the fellow was always brought in "not guilty," the jury expecting him to do as much for them some time; and, although the evidence was straight and square against this Spaniard, we knew we could not convict him without seeming to be rather high-handed and sort of reflecting on every gentleman in the community; for there warn't any carriages and liveries then, and so the only "style" there was, was to keep your private graveyard.

But that woman seemed to have her heart set on hanging that Spaniard; and you'd ought to have seen how she would glare on him a minute, and then look up at me in her pleading way, and then turn and for the next five minutes search the jury's faces, and by and by drop her face in her hands for just a little while as if she was most ready to give up; but out she'd come again directly, and be as live and anxious as ever.

But when the jury announced the verdict—not guilty—and I told the prisoner he was acquitted and free to go, that woman rose up till she appeared to be as tall and grand as a seventy-four-gun ship, and says she: "Judge, do I understand you to say that this man is not guilty that murdered my husband without any cause before my own eyes and my little children's, and that all has been done to him that ever justice and the law can do?"

"The same," says I.

And then what do you reckon she did? Why, she turned on that smirking Spanish fool like a wildcat, and out with a "navy" and shot him dead in open court!

**That was spirited**, I am willing to admit.

"Wasn't it, though?" said the judge admiringly.

"I wouldn't have missed it for anything. I adjourned court right on the spot, and we put on our coats and went out and took up a collection for her and her cubs, and sent them over the mountains to their friends. Ah, she was a spirited wench!"

*"The Spirited Widow," was published in 1882 as part of his collection* Sketches New and Old *under the title "The Judge's 'Spirited Woman'."*

"Life was not a valuable gift, but death was. Life was a fever-dream made up of joys embittered by sorrows, pleasure poisoned by pain; a dream that was a nightmare-confusion of spasmodic and fleeting delights, ecstasies, exultations, happinesses, interspersed with long-drawn miseries, griefs, perils, horrors, disappointments, defeats, humiliations, and despairs—the heaviest curse devisable by divine ingenuity; but death was sweet, death was gentle, death was kind; death healed the bruised spirit and the broken heart, and gave them rest and forgetfulness; death was man's best friend; when man could endure life no longer, death came and set him free."

Letters from the Earth

# Ode to Stephen Dowling Bots, Dec'd

*And did young Stephen sicken,*
*And did young Stephen die?*
*And did the sad hearts thicken,*
*And did the mourners cry?*

> *No; such was not the fate of*
> *Young Stephen Dowling Bots;*
> *Though sad hearts round him thickened,*
> *'Twas not from sickness' shots.*

*No whooping cough did rack his frame,*
*Nor measles drear, with spots;*
*Not these impaired the sacred name*

*Of Stephen Dowling Bots.*

> *Despised love struck not with woe*
> *That head of curly knots,*
> *Nor stomach troubles laid him low,*
> *Young Stephen Dowling Bots.*

*O no. Then list with tearful eye,*
*Whilst I his fate do tell.*
*His soul did from this cold world fly,*
*By falling down a well.*

> *They got him out and emptied him;*
> *Alas it was too late;*
> *His spirit was gone for to sport aloft*
> *In the realms of the good and great.*

"Ode to Stephen Dowling Bots, Dec'd," is an excerpt from Twain's The Adventures of Huckleberry Finn, attributed to the fictional Emmaline Grangerford—based on Julia A. Moore, his contemporary and the writer of notoriously bad poems.

# The Spanish Mine

The Spanish mine: This comprises 100 feet of the great Comstock lead, and is situated in the midst of the Ophir claims. We visited it yesterday, in company with Mr. Kingman, assistant superintendent, and our impression is that stout-legged people with an affinity to darkness, may spend an hour or so there very comfortably. A confused sense of being buried alive, and a vague consciousness of stony dampness, and huge timbers, and tortuous caverns, and bottomless holes with endless ropes hanging down into them, and narrow ladders climbing in a short twilight through the colossal lattice work and suddenly perishing in midnight, and workmen poking about in the gloom with twinkling candles—is all, or nearly all that remains to us of our experience in the Spanish mine.

Yet, for the information of those who may wish to go down

and see how things are conducted in the realms beyond the jurisdiction of daylight, we are willing to tell a portion of what we know about it.

Entering the Spanish tunnel on A Street, you grope along by candlelight for 250 feet—but you need not count your steps— keep on going until you come to a horse. This horse works a whim used for hoisting ore from the infernal regions below, and from long service in the dark, his coat has turned to a beautiful black color.

You are now upon the confines of the ledge, and from this point, several drifts branch out to different portions of the mine. Without stopping to admire these gloomy grottoes, you descend a ladder and halt upon a landing, where you are fenced in with an open-work labyrinth of timbers some eighteen inches square, extending in front of you and behind you, and far away above you and below you, until they are lost in darkness.

These timbers are framed in squares or "stations," five feet each way, one above another, and so neatly put together that there is not room for the insertion of a knife-blade where they intersect. You are apt to wonder where the forest around you came from, and how they managed to get it into that hole, and what sums of money it must have cost, and so forth and so on, and you wind up with a confused notion that the man who designed it all had a shining talent for sawmills on a large scale. He could build the framework beautifully at any rate. Whereupon, you desist from further speculation, and waltz down a very narrow winding staircase, and the further you squirm down it, the dizzier you get and the more those open timber squares seem to whiz by you, until you feel as if you are falling through a well-ventilated shot tower with the windows all open.

Finally, after you have gone down 94 feet, you touch bottom again and find yourself in the midst of the sawmill yet, with the regular accomplishments of workmen, and windlasses, and glimmering candles and cetera, as usual. Now you can stoop and dodge about under the "stations," and get your clothes dirty, and drip hot candle grease all over your hands, and find out how they take those timbers and commence at the top of the mine, and build them together like mighty window sashes all the way down to the bottom of it; and if, after coming down that tipsy staircase, you can by any possibility make out to understand it, then you can render the information useful above ground by building the third story of your house to suit you first, and continuing its erection wrong end foremost until you wind up with the cellar.

You will also find out that, at this depth, the lead is 46 feet wide, with its sides walled and weatherboarded as compactly and substantially as those of a jail. And here and there, in little recesses, the walls of the lead are laid bare, showing the blue silver lines traced upon the white quartz, after the fashion of variegated marble—this, in places, you know, while others, where the ore is richer, the blue predominates and the white is scarcely perceptible.

From these various recesses, a swarm of workmen are constantly conveying wheelbarrow loads of quartz to the windlasses, of all shades of value, from that worth $75 to that worth $3,000 per ton—and if you should chance to be in better luck than we were, you may happen to stumble on a small specimen worth a dollar and a half a pound. Such things have occurred in the Spanish mine before now.

However, as we were saying, you are now 170 feet under the ground, and you can move about and see how the ore is quarried and moved from one place to another, and how systematically the great mine is arranged and worked altogether—and you may get into a bucket, if you please, and extend your visit to the confines of purgatory (so to speak), if you feel anxious to do so; but as this would afford you nothing more than a glance at the bottom of a drain shaft, you could better employ your time and talents in climbing that corkscrew and seeking daylight again.

And before leaving the mouth of the tunnel, you would do well to visit the office of Mr. Beckwith, the superintendent, where you can see a small cabinet of specimens from the mine which has been pronounced by scientific travelers to be one of the richest collections of the kind in the world.

*"The Spanish Mine"* was published in October 1862 in the Virginia City Territorial Enterprise, *but survives only as reprinted in the* Butte Recorder *of Oroville, California the following month. It's an example of Twain's work as a reporter describing a very real horror to the average citizen (especially a claustrophobic one) that was nonetheless a daily reality for miners on the Comstock. The sketch at the beginning of the chapter shows some of a typical mine's design, as described by Twain.*

# Death in the Desert

At 8 in the morning, we reached the remnant and ruin of what had been the important military station of "Camp Floyd," some 45 or 50 miles from Salt Lake City. At 4 p.m., we had doubled our distance and were 90 or 100 miles from Salt Lake.

And now we entered upon one of that species of deserts whose concentrated hideousness shames the diffused and diluted horrors of Sahara—an "*alkali*" desert. For 68 miles, there was but one break in it. I do not remember that this was really a break; indeed it seems to me that it was nothing but a watering depot *in the midst* of the stretch of 68 miles. If my memory serves me, there was no well or spring at this place, but the water was hauled there by mule and ox teams from the further side of the desert. There was a stage station there. It was 45 miles from the beginning of the desert, and 23 from the end of it.

We plowed and dragged and groped along, the whole live-long night, and at the end of this uncomfortable 12 hours, we finished the 45-mile part of the desert and got to the stage station where the imported water was.

The sun was just rising. It was easy enough to cross a desert in the night while we were asleep; and it was pleasant to reflect, in the morning, that we in actual person *had* encountered an absolute desert and could always speak knowingly of deserts in presence of the ignorant thenceforward. And it was pleasant also to reflect that this was not an obscure, back country desert, but a very celebrated one, the metropolis itself, as you may say. All this was very well and very comfortable and satisfactory—but now we were to cross a desert in *daylight*. This was fine—novel— romantic—dramatically adventurous—*this*, indeed, was worth living for, worth traveling for! We would write home all about it.

This enthusiasm, this stern thirst for adventure, wilted under the sultry August sun and did not last above one hour. One poor little hour—and then we were ashamed that we had "gushed" so. The poetry was all in the anticipation—there is none in the reality. Imagine a vast, waveless ocean stricken dead and turned to ashes; imagine this solemn waste tufted with ash-dusted sage bushes; imagine the lifeless silence and solitude that belong to such a place; imagine a coach, creeping like a bug through the midst of this shoreless level, and sending up tumbled volumes of dust as if it were a bug that went by steam; imagine this aching monotony of toiling and plowing kept up hour after hour, and the shore still as far away as ever, apparently; imagine team, driver, coach and passengers so deeply coated with ashes that they are all one colorless color; imagine ash-drifts roosting above moustaches and eyebrows like snow accumulations on boughs and bushes. This is the reality of it.

The sun beats down with dead, blistering, relentless malignity; the perspiration is welling from every pore in man and beast, but scarcely a sign of it finds its way to the surface—it is absorbed before it gets there; there is not the faintest breath of air stirring; there is not a merciful shred of cloud in all the brilliant firmament; there is not a living creature visible in *any* direction whither one searches the blank level that stretches its monotonous miles on every hand; there is not a sound—not a sigh—not a whisper—not a buzz, or a whir of wings, or distant pipe of bird—not even a sob from the lost souls that doubtless people that are dead air. And so the occasional sneezing of the resting mules, and the champing of the bits, grate harshly on the grim stillness, not dissipating the spell but accenting it and making one feel more lonesome and forsaken than before.

The mules, under violent swearing, coaxing and whip-cracking, would make at stated intervals a "spurt," and drag the coach a hundred or may be 200 yards, stirring up a billowy cloud of dust that rolled back, enveloping the vehicle to the wheel-tops or higher, and making it seem afloat in a fog. Then a rest followed, with the usual sneezing and bit-champing. Then another "spurt" of a hundred yards and another rest at the end of it. All day long, we kept this up, without water for the mules and without ever changing the team. At least we kept it up 10 hours, which, I take it, is a day, and a pretty honest one, in an alkali desert. It was from 4 in the morning till 2 in the afternoon. And it was so hot! And so close! And our water canteens went dry in the middle of the day, and we got so thirsty! It was so stupid and tiresome and dull! And the tedious hours did lag and drag and limp along with such a cruel deliberation! It was so trying to give one's watch a good long undisturbed spell and then take it out and find that it had been fooling away the time and not trying to get ahead any! The alkali dust cut through our lips, it persecuted our eyes, it ate through the delicate membranes and made our noses bleed and *kept* them bleeding—and truly and seriously the romance all faded far away and disappeared, and left the desert trip nothing but a harsh reality—a thirsty, sweltering, longing, hateful reality!

Two miles and a quarter an hour for 10 hours—that was what we accomplished. It was hard to bring the comprehension away down to such a snail-pace as that, when we had been used to making 8 and 10 miles an hour. When we reached the station on the farther verge of the desert, we were glad, for the first time, that the dictionary was along, because we never could have found language to tell how glad we were, in any sort of dictionary but an unabridged one with pictures in it. But there could not have been found in a whole library of dictionaries language sufficient to tell how tired those mules were after their 23- mile pull. To try to give the reader an idea of how *thirsty* they were, would be to "gild refined gold or paint the lily."

Somehow, now that it is there, the quotation does not seem to fit—but no matter, let it stay, anyhow. I think it is a graceful and attractive thing, and therefore have tried time and time again to work it in where it *would* fit, but could not succeed. These efforts have kept my mind distracted and ill at ease, and made my narrative seem broken and disjointed in places. Under these circumstances it seems to me best to leave it in, as above, since this will afford at least a temporary respite from the wear and tear of trying to "lead up" to this really apt and beautiful quotation.

**On the morning of the sixteenth day** out from St. Joseph, we arrived at the entrance of Rocky Canyon, 250 miles from Salt Lake.

On the seventeenth day, we passed the highest mountain peaks we had yet seen, and although the day was very warm the night that followed upon its heels was wintry cold and blankets were next to useless.

On the eighteenth day, we encountered the eastward-bound telegraph-constructors at Reese river station and sent a message to his Excellency Governor Nye at Carson City (distant 156 miles).

On the nineteenth day, we crossed the Great American Desert—40 memorable miles of bottomless sand, into which the coach wheels sunk from 6 inches to a foot. We worked our passage most of the way across. That is to say, we got out and walked. It was a dreary pull and a long and thirsty one, for we had no water. From one extremity of this desert to the other, the road was white with the bones of oxen and horses. It would hardly be an exaggeration to say that we could have walked the 40 miles and set our feet on a bone at every step!

The desert was one prodigious graveyard. And the log-chains, wagon tyres, and rotting wrecks of vehicles were almost as thick as the bones. I think we saw log-chains enough rusting there in the desert, to reach across any State in the Union. Do not these relics suggest something of an idea of the fearful suffering and privation the early emigrants to California endured?

**At the border of the desert** lies Carson Lake, or the "Sink" of the Carson, a shallow, melancholy sheet of water some 80 or a hundred miles in circumference. Carson river empties into it and is lost—sinks mysteriously into the earth and never appears in the light of the sun again—for the lake has no outlet whatever.

There are several rivers in Nevada, and they all have this mysterious fate. They end in various lakes or "sinks," and that is the last of them. Carson Lake, Humboldt Lake, Walker Lake, Mono Lake are all great sheets of water without any visible outlet. Water is always flowing into them; none is ever seen to flow out of them, and yet they remain always level full, neither receding nor overflowing. What they do with their surplus is only known to the Creator.

On the western verge of the desert, we halted a moment at Ragtown. It consisted of one log house and is not set down on the map.

❖  ❖  ❖

*"Death in the Desert" (editor's title) is an account of Mark Twain's crossing of two terrifying deserts, the alkali flats west of Salt Lake City in Utah, and the Forty-Mile Desert in Nevada. This selection combines much of Chapter 18 and a section of Chapter 20 from* Roughing It.

# The Enchanted Sea

Scattered about the world's oceans at enormous distances apart are spots and patches where no compass has any value. When the compass enters one of these bewitched domains, it goes insane and whirls this way and that and settles nowhere, and is scared and distressed, and cannot be comforted. The sailor must steer by sun, moon and stars when they show, and by guess when they don't, till he gets past that enchanted region.

The worst of these spots and the largest one is in the midst of the vast ocean solitudes that lie between the Cape of Good Hope and the South Pole. It is 500 miles in diameter, and is circular in shape; four-fifths of this diameter is lashed and tossed and torn by eternal storms, is smothered in clouds and fog, and swept by fierce concentric currents; but in the centre, there is a circular area a hundred miles across, in whose outer part the storms and the currents die down; and in the centre of this centre there is still a final circular area about 50 miles across where there are but the faintest suggestions of currents, no winds, no whisper of wandering zephyr, even, but everywhere the silence and peace and solemnity of a calm which is eternal.

There is a bronzed and gray sailor on board this ship who has had experience of that strange place, and the other night, after midnight, I went forward to the forecastle and got him to tell me about it. The hint came from the purser, who said it was a curious and interesting story. I kept it in my memory as well as I could, and wrote it down next day—in my own language, for I could not remember his, of course. He said that the outer great circle where the currents are—as already described by me—is known among sailors as the Devil's Race Track, and that they call the central calm Everlasting Sunday.

Here is his account:

**We got into that place by a judgment**—judgment on the captain of the ship. It was this way. We were becalmed, away down south, dead summer time, middle of December, 1853. The vessel was a brig, and a fairly good sailor; name, Mabel Thorpe; loaded with provisions and blasting powder for the new gold mines in Australia; Elliot Cable master, a rough man and hard-hearted, but he was master, and that is the truth. When he laid down the law, there wasn't pluck enough in the whole ship to take objections to it.

Now to go back a little.

About two months before, when we were lying at the dock the day we sailed, a lovely big beautiful dog came aboard, and went racing around with his nose down hunting for somebody that had been there—his owner, I reckon—and the crew caught him and shut him up below, and we sailed in an hour. He was a darling, that dog. He was full of play, and fun, and affection and good nature, the dearest and sweetest disposition that ever was.

Inside of two days, he was the pet of the whole crew. We bedded him like the aristocracy, and there wasn't a man but would divide his dinner with him, and he was ever so loving and grateful. And smart, too; smart and willing. He elected of his own notion to stand watch and watch with us. He was in the larboard watch, and he would turn out at eight bells without anybody having to tell him it was "Yo-ho, the larboard watch!" And he would tug at the ropes and help make sail or take it in, and seemed to know all about it, just like any old veteran. The crew were proud of him— well, of course they would be.

And so, as I was saying, we got becalmed when we were out about two months. It was warm that night, and still and drowsy and lazy; and the sails hung idle, and the deck-watch and the lookout and everybody else was sound asleep, including the dog, for it was his trick below and he had turned in at midnight. Well, along about an hour after midnight, there was a tremendous scratching and barking at the captain's door, and he jumped out of his bunk, and that dog was just wild with excitement, and rushed off, and just as good as told the captain to come along and come quick. You see, the ship was afire down in the hold, and he had discovered it. Down the captain plunged, and the dog rushed off, waking up the others.

Dear, dear, it was the closest fit! The fire was crowding a pile of the powder-kegs close, and in another minute or two, it would have had them, and we should have been blown into the sky. The captain snatched the pile of kegs out of reach in half a second, and we were safe, because the bulk of the powder was away up forward. And by this time we all came tearing down—white?— oh, white as ghosts when we saw what a close shave we had had. Well, then we started in and began to hug the dog. And wasn't he a proud dog? And happy? Why, if he had had speech, he couldn't have expressed it any better.

The captain snarled at us and said: "You may well hug him,

you worthless hounds! He saved my life, not you, you lazy rips. I've never cared for dogs before, but next time I hear people talking against them, I'll put in a word for this one, anyway."

Overboard went that little batch of powder kegs, and then we flew around getting food and water and compass and sextant and chart and things for the boat; and the dog helped, just like anybody else. He did a grown man's work carrying things to the boat, and then went dancing around superintending whilst we launched her. Bright? Oh, you can't think how bright he was, and intelligent.

When everybody was in the boat but the captain, and the flames were soaring up and lighting the whole ocean, he tied the dog to the foot of the mainmast and then got in himself and took the tiller and said, "All ready. Give way!"

We were all struck dumb, for a second, then all shouted at once, "Oh, captain! Going to leave the dog?"

He roared out in a fury, "Didn't you hear the order? Give way!"

Well, the tears began to run down our faces; and we said, "Why, he saved our lives—we can't leave him. Please, captain! Please let him come."

"What, in this little tub of a boat? You don't know what you are talking about. He'd be more in the way than a family of children; and he can eat as much as a family of children, too. Now, men, you know me"—and he pulled an old pepper-box revolver and pointed it—"give way!"

Well, it was pitiful, the way that poor dog acted. At first he was dancing and capering and barking, happy and proud and gay; but when he saw us going away, he stopped and stood still, gazing; it seemed as if he was trying to believe it, and couldn't. And dear, dear, how noble and handsome he was, in that red glare. He was a huge big St. Bernard, with that gentle good face and that soft loving eye that they've got.

Well, pretty soon, when he saw that he was left, he seemed to go kind of crazy; and he rose on his hind legs in the strong light, and strained and lunged and tugged at his rope, and begged and moaned and yelped—why it was as plain as if he was saying, "Oh, don't leave me, please don't leave me, I haven't done any harm." And then presently the fire swept down on him and swallowed him up, and he sent up two or three awful shrieks, and it was all over. And the men sat there crying like children.

And deep down in our hearts we believed a judgment would come on the captain for this. And it did; as you will see.

**We were in the Indian Ocean** when we lost the ship—about 500 miles south of Port Natal, and about the same distance east by south from Cape Town, South Africa. The captain set his course by the stars and struck north, because he believed we were a little south of the track of ships bound for either Natal or Australia. A smart breeze sprung up, and we went along at a good rate. In about four hours, day broke, and the first thing that showed up on the westward sea-line was the hazy top-hamper of a ship! She was eastward-bound, and making straight across our course. We raised a cheer, and altered our course to go and meet her. And there wasn't as much heart in the cheer as you might expect, for the thing we were thinking about was that our poor dog had been done to death for no use; if he had been allowed to come with us, he wouldn't have cost us any inconvenience, and no food that we couldn't spare.

The captain had an idea that he was born lucky, and he said something to the mate about it now; he said running across this ship here was pure luck—nobody else could have had such luck. Well, it certainly did look so; but at the same time we said to ourselves, how about this ship's luck that's coming? Our idea was that our captain would bring bad luck to her, and trouble to himself and us, too, on account of the way he treated the dog that saved our lives. And that is what happened, as I have said before.

In about an hour we were aboard that ship; and it happened that we knew her, and knew her crew, too; for she was sister to our ship and belonged to the same house, and was loaded at the same dock with us, and with the same kind of cargo—provisions for the new mines almost altogether, and a few other odds and ends of mining supplies, like candles and powder and fuse, and such things.

By name she was the Adelaide. She had left port a week or ten days ahead of us, but we could outsail her on a wind. Her captain had been dead about a month, now—died of a sickness of some kind—and Mrs. Moseley, his young widow, was broken-hearted, and cried pretty much all the time, and was in terror lest something should happen to her little girl, and then she would be desolate indeed. Two of the Adelaide's crew had died of the sickness, also; so that left mate, second mate and five men aboard. When we joined, that made it seventeen men, one woman and a child.

Our captain took command straight away, and began to give orders, without a by-your-leave to anybody—for that was his style. It wasn't the right way to go about it, and it made bad blood.

The captain allotted the watches and the ship continued on her course for Australia. The wind freshened, the sky grew dark, and inside of an hour, there was a terrific gale blowing. We stripped the ship and she drove helpless before it, straight south-east. And so, night and day and day and night for 18 days we drove, and never got a sight of the sun or the moon or the stars in all that time—hundreds and hundreds and hundreds of miles we wallowed through the wild seas, with never a notion of where we were but what we got from the dead reckoning.

For the last two or three days the captain had got to looking pretty white; and by this time he was just ghastly. Then we found out the reason, from the mates: the captain judged that we must be south of Kerguelan's Land, and maybe nearly halfway between that and the Antarctic Circle. Well, that news turned the rest of us white; for if it was true, we were getting into the neighborhood of the Devil's Race Track!

As that cold dark eighteenth day shut down, everybody was on deck, off-watch and all; and everybody silent; as a rule, nobody saying anything to his neighbor; nobody interested in any but the one thing—the compass. The captain stood over the forward one, watching it and never saying anything; the officers and crew crowded around the after one, watching it and never saying anything.

The night shut down black as ink; the wind screamed through the naked rigging; gusts of hail, snow, sleet followed each other right along—a wild night, and bitter cold, and the ship reeling and pitching and tumbling in a most awful way.

You couldn't see a thing; you couldn't see your hand before your face—everything was blotted out; everything except three or four faces bending over the compass light, and showing in the blackness like ghost faces that hadn't any bodies.

Then all of a sudden there was a burst of groans and curses, and the faces disappeared and others took their places. You see, the thing everybody was expecting had happened: The compass was gone crazy, and we were in the whirl and suck of the Devil's Race Track. Most of us kept the deck all night. Some slept, but it was not much good—just naps and nightmares, and wakings-up with a jerk, in a cold sweat.

When the day came, you could hardly tell it, it so little differed from the night. All the day long it was the same; you could hear the sea birds piping, but you couldn't see them— except now and then, you would get a dim glimpse of a great white albatross sailing by like a ghost.

We had nine days and nights like this—always the roaring gale and the wild sea and blustering squalls of snow and hail and sleet and the piping of the gulls and the flitting of the dim albatross; and then on the tenth morning, the gale began to slacken and the seas to go down and the squalls to get wider apart and less furious, and the blackness to soften up and shred away, and the sea birds to thin out; and about noon, we drifted out of the lofty wall of gloom and clouds into a calm sea and the open day and deep, deep stillness. The sweep of that black wall described an enormous circle; and it was so high that the furthest side of it still stood boldly up above the sea, though it was 50 miles away. We were in a trap; and that trap was the Everlasting Sunday.

**There was no need to say it**; everybody knew it. And everybody shuddered, too, and was in a cold despair. For a week, we drifted little by little around the cloud-wall, and further and further away from it; and when we seemed to have gotten 10 or 15 miles from it, we appeared to have stopped dead still. We threw empty bottles overboard and watched them. There was really no motion—at any rate in any one direction. Sometimes a bottle would stay where we threw it; sometimes after the end of an hour we could see that it had moved five or six yards ahead or as many aft.

The stillness was horrible; and the absence of life. There was not a bird or a creature of any kind in sight, the slick surface of the water was never broken by a fin, never a breath of wind fanned the dead air, and there was not a sound of any kind, even the faintest—the silence of death was everywhere. We showed no life ourselves, but sat apart, each by himself, and brooded and brooded, and scarcely ever moved. In that profound inertness, that universal paralysis of life and energy, as far as sentient beings went, there was one thing that was brimming with it, booming with it, crazy with it; and that was the compass. It whirled and whizzed this way and that, and never rested—never for a moment. It acted like a frightened thing, a thing in frantic fear for its life. And so we got afraid of it, and could not bear to look at its distress and its helpless struggles; for we came to believe that it had a soul and that it was in hell.

We never had any more weather—forever that bright sky overhead, with never a shred of cloud in it; not a flake of snow, nor drop of sleet or anything; just a dead still frosty cold, with a glistening white rime coating the decks and spars and rigging— a ship made of sparkling frostwork, she seemed. And as the days dragged on and on and on, we grew weary as death of this changeless sky, and watched the vague lightnings playing in the distant cloud-wall with a sort of envy and longing.

Try to escape? Why, none of us wanted to try. What could be the use? Of course, the captain tried; it would be just like him. He manned one of the boats and started. He disappeared in the cloud-wall for a while; got lost in it, of course—compass no use—and came near getting swamped by the heavy seas. He was not in there long; the currents soon swept him back into the Everlasting Sunday. Our ship was pretty far away, but still in sight; so he came aboard, and never said a word. His spirit was broken, too, you see, like ours; so after that he moped around again, like the rest—and prayed for death, I reckon. We all did.

One morning, when we had been in there seven months and gradually getting further and further toward the middle, an inch at a time, there was a sudden stir and excitement—the first we had known for so long that it seemed strange and new and unnatural—like something we hadn't ever experienced before; it was like corpses getting excited—corpses that had been dead many years and had forgotten the feel of it and didn't understand it. A sailor came flying along the deck blubbering and shouting, "A ship! A ship!"

The dull people sitting moping and dreaming here and there and yonder looked up at him in a kind of a drowse, and not pleasantly; for his racket and activity pained their heads and distressed them; and their brains were so blunted and sodden that at first his words couldn't find their way into their understandings, all practice in talk having ceased so long ago. But of course, we did understand, presently, and then we woke up and got wildly excited, as I was telling you.

Away off yonder, we made out a ship, sure enough; and as the daylight brightened, we made out another; and then another, and still another and another and another—a whole fleet, scattered around, a mile or so apart. We were full of amazement. When did they come, and how did they get there in that sudden way, and so many of them? We were full of joy; for maybe here was rescue for us. If they came in there on purpose, they must know the trick of how to get out again.

Well, everything was bustle and hurry, now. We got out our boats, and I pulled stroke in the chief mate's. I was twenty-three-and-a-half years old, and big and strong and an experienced sailor. We hoisted a flag, first, in the mizzen halliards—union down, of course—and left the young widow and the little girl standing under it crying for happiness when we pulled away in the frosty bright morning.

It was as much as 12 miles to the nearest ship, but we made it in three hours—without a sail, of course, there being no wind. When half of the ship's hull showed above the water, we began to wave signals, but didn't get any answer; and about this time we began to make out that she looked pretty old and crazy. The nearer we got, the crazier she looked, and there was no sign of life or movement about her.

We began to suspect the truth—and pretty soon we knew it, and our spirits fell. Why, she was just a naked old wreck, as you may say, a mouldy old skeleton, with her yards hanging every which way, and here and there a rotten rag of sailcloth drooping from the clews. As we passed under her stern, there was her name, in letters so dulled you could hardly spell them out.

The Horatio Nelson!

I gasped for breath. I knew the ship. When I was a boy of ten, my uncle Robert sailed in her as chief mate; and from that day to this she had never more been heard of—13 years.

You will know beforehand what we found: barring the frosty litter of decaying wreckage that strewed the deck, just the counterpart of our own ship, as you might say—men lying here and there and yonder, and two or three sitting, with elbow on knee and hand under chin—just as natural! No, not men—leathery shriveled-up effigies of them. Dead these dozen years. It was what we had been seeing for seven months; we would come to be like these, by and by. It was our fate foreshadowed; that is what we thought.

I found my uncle; I knew him by his watch chain. I was young, he had always been kind to me, and it made me cry a little to see him looking like that. That, and that I might be like him soon. I have the watch and chain yet, if you care to look at them. The watch had stopped at 12 minutes to 4—whether in the day or in the night I don't know; but he was dead when it ran down—that was all it could tell.

The ship's log left off where we had stopped ours—three days after the entry into the Everlasting Sunday. It told the same monotonous things that ours did, and in nearly the same words; and the blank that followed was more eloquent than the words that went before, in this case as in our own, for it meant despair. By the log, the Horatio Nelson had entered the Everlasting Sunday on the 2d of June, 1840.

We visited ship after ship, and found these dreary scenes always repeated. And always the logs ceased the third or fourth day after the ship got into this death-trap except in a single case. Where one day is exactly like another, why record them? What is there to record? The world continues to exist, but History has come to an end.

The Horatio Nelson was the latest ship there but one—a whaler from New England. She had been there six years. One English ship which had been there 33 years—the Eurydice—was overcrowded with men and women. She had 260 of these leathery corpses on board—convicts for Australia and their guards, no doubt, for down below were more than 200 sets of chains. A Spanish ship had been there 60 years; but the oldest one of all, and in almost the best repair, was a British man-of-war, the Royal Brunswick. She perished with all on board the first voyage she ever made, the old histories say—and the old ballads, too—but here she was; and here she had been, since November 10th, 1740—113 years, you see.

Clean, dry, frosty weather seems to be a good preserver of some things—clothes, for instance. At a little distance, you might have thought some of the men in this ship were still alive, they looked so natural in their funny old uniforms. And the admiral was one—old Admiral Sir John Thurlow; he was a middy in the time of Marlborough's wars, as I have read in the histories. He had his big cocked hat on, and his big epaulettes, like as if he was gotten up for Madam Tussaud's; and his coat was all over gold lace; and it was real gold, too, for it was not tarnished. He was sitting on a gun carriage, with his head leant back against the gun in a sick and weary way; and there was a rusty old leather portfolio in his lap and a pen and an empty inkstand handy. He looked fine and noble—the very type of the old fighting British admiral, the men that made England the monarch of the seas.

By a common impulse, and without orders, we formed up in front of him and uncovered in salute. Then Captain Cable stepped up to take the portfolio, but in his awkwardness, he gave a little touch to the admiral's elbow, and he fell over on the deck. Dear me, he struck as lightly and as noiseless as if he had been only a suit of clothes stuffed with wool; and a faint little cloud of leathery dust rose up from him, and we judged he had gone to pieces inside.

We uncovered again and carried him very reverently to his own cabin and laid him to rest.

*"The Enchanted Sea-Wilderness" is a discarded portion of* Following the Equator, *Twain's account of his tour around the world in 1895 and 1896. It was inspired by his observation of spots in the South Pacific where the compass "loses its head and whirls this way and that; then you give up and steer by the sun, wind, stars, moon or a guess, and trust to luck to save you till you get by that insane region."*

"There was never yet an uninteresting life. Such a thing is an impossibility. Inside of the dullest exterior there is a drama, a comedy, and a tragedy.."

The Refuge of the Derelicts

# Schoolhouse Hill

It was not much short of fifty years ago—and a frosty morning. Up the naked long slant of Schoolhouse Hill the boys and girls of Petersburg village were struggling from various directions against the fierce wind, and making slow and difficult progress. The wind was not the only hindrance, nor the worst; the slope was steel-clad in frozen snow, and the foothold offered was far from trustworthy.

Every now and then, a boy who had almost gained the schoolhouse stepped out with too much confidence, thinking himself safe, lost his footing, struck upon his back and went skimming down the hill behind his freed sled, the straggling schoolmates scrambling out of his way and applauding as he sailed by; and in a few seconds he was at the bottom with all his work to do over again. But this was fun; fun for the boy, fun for the witnesses, fun all around; for boys and girls are ignorant and do not know trouble when they see it.

Sid Sawyer, the good boy, the model boy, the cautious boy, did not lose his footing. He brought no sled, he chose his steps with care, and he arrived in safety. Tom Sawyer brought his sled and he, also, arrived without adventure, for Huck Finn was along to help, although he was not a member of the school in these days; he merely came in order to be with Tom until school "took in."

Henry Bascom arrived safely, too—Henry Bascom the new boy of last year, whose papa was a slave trader and rich; a mean boy, he was, and proud of his clothes, and he had a play-slaughterhouse at home, with all the equipment, in little, of a regular slaughterhouse, and in it he slaughtered puppies and kittens exactly as beeves were done to death down at the "Point;" and he was this year's school-bully, and was dreaded and flattered by the timid and the weak and disliked by everybody. He arrived safely because his slave-boy, Jake, helped him up the hill and drew his sled for him; and it wasn't a homemade sled but a "store" sled, and was painted, and had iron-tired runners, and came from St. Louis, and was the only store-sled in the village.

All the twenty-five or thirty boys and girls arrived at last, red and panting, and still cold, notwithstanding their yarn comforters and mufflers and mittens; and the girls flocked into the little schoolhouse and the boys packed themselves together in the shelter of its lee.

**It was noticed now** that a new boy was present, and this was a matter of extraordinary interest, for a new boy in the village was a rarer sight than a new comet in the sky. He was apparently about fifteen; his clothes were neat and tasty above the common, he had a good and winning face, and he was surpassingly handsome—handsome beyond imagination! His eyes were deep and rich and beautiful, and there was a modesty and dignity and grace and graciousness and charm about him which some of the boys, with a pleased surprise, recognized at once as familiar—they had encountered it in books about fairy-tale princes and that sort. They stared at him with a trying backwoods frankness, but he was tranquil and did not seem troubled by it.

After looking him over, Henry Bascom pushed forward in front of the others and began in an insolent tone to question him:

"Who are you? What's your name?"

The boy slowly shook his head, as if meaning by that that he did not understand.

"Do you hear? Answer up!"

Another slow shake.

"Answer up, I tell you, or I'll make you!"

Tom Sawyer said, "That's no way, Henry Bascom—it's against the rules. If you want your fuss, and can't wait till recess, which is regular, go at it right and fair; put a chip on your shoulder and dare him to knock it off."

"All right; he's got to fight, and fight now, whether he answers or not; and I'm not particular about how it's got at." He put a flake of ice on his shoulder and said, "There—knock it off if you dare!"

The boy looked inquiringly from face to face, and Tom stepped up and answered by signs. He touched the boy's right hand, then flipped off the ice with his own, put it back in its place, and indicated that that was what the boy must do. The lad smiled, put out his hand, and touched the ice with his finger. Bascom launched a blow at his face which seemed to miss; the energy of it made Bascom slip on the ice, and he departed on his back for the bottom of the hill, with cordial laughter and mock applause from the boys to cheer his way.

The bell began to ring, and the little crowd swarmed into the schoolhouse and hurried to their places. The stranger found a seat apart, and was at once a target for the wondering eyes and eager whisperings of the girls. School now "began." Archibald Ferguson, the old Scotch schoolmaster, rapped upon his desk with his ruler, rose upon his dais and stood, with his hands together, and said "Let us pray."

After the prayer, there was a hymn, then the buzz of study began, and the multiplication class was called up. It recited, up to "twelve times twelve;" then the arithmetic class followed and exposed its slates to much censure and little commendation; next came the grammar class of parsing parrots, who knew everything about grammar except how to utilize its rules in common speech.

"Spelling class!" The schoolmaster's wandering eye now fell upon the new boy, and he countermanded that order. "Hm—a stranger? Who is it? What is your name, my boy?"

The lad rose and bowed, and said—

"Pardon, monsieur—*je ne comprends pas.*"

Ferguson looked astonished and pleased, and said, in French—

"Ah, French—how pleasant! It is the first time I have heard that tongue in many years. I am the only person in this village who speaks it. You are very welcome; I shall be glad to renew my practice. You speak no English?"

"Not a word, sir."

"You must try to learn it."

"Gladly, sir."

"It is your purpose to attend my school regularly?"

"If I may have the privilege, sir."

"That is well. Take English only, for the present. The grammar has about thirty rules. It will be necessary to learn them by heart."

"I already know them, sir, but I do not know what the words mean."

"What is it you say? You know the rules of the grammar, and yet don't know English? How can that be? When did you learn them?"

"I heard your grammar class recite the rules before entering upon the rest of their lesson."

The teacher looked over his glasses at the boy a while, in a puzzled way, then said, "If you know no English words, how did you know it was a grammar lesson?"

"From similarities to the French—like the word 'grammar' itself."

"True! You have a headpiece! You will soon get the rules by heart."

"I know them by heart, sir."

"Impossible! You are speaking extravagantly; you do not know what you are saying."

The boy bowed respectfully, resumed his upright position, and said nothing.

The teacher felt rebuked, and said gently, "I should not have spoken so, and am sorry. Overlook it, my boy; recite me a rule of grammar—as well as you can—never mind the mistakes."

The boy began with the first rule and went along with his task quite simply and comfortably, dropping rule after rule unmutilated from his lips, while the teacher and the school sat with parted lips and suspended breath, listening in mute wonder. At the finish, the boy bowed again, and stood, waiting. Ferguson sat silent a moment or two in his great chair, then said—"On your honor—those rules were wholly unknown to you when you came into this house?"

"Yes, sir."

"Upon my word I believe you, on the veracity that is written in your face. No... I don't... I can't. It is beyond the reach of belief. A memory like that—an ear for pronunciation like that, is of course im... why, *no* one in the earth has such a memory as that!"

The boy bowed and said nothing. Again the old Scot felt rebuked, and said, "Of course I don't mean... I don't really mean... er... tell me: if you could *prove* in some way that you have never until now... for instance, if you could repeat other things which you have heard here. Will you try?"

With engaging simplicity and serenity, and with apparently no intention of being funny, the boy began on the arithmetic lesson, and faithfully put into his report everything the teacher had said and everything the pupils had said, and imitated the voices and style of all concerned, as follows:

"Well, I give you my word it's enough to drive a man back to the land of his fathers, and make him hide his head in the charitable heather and never more give out that *he* can teach the race! Five slates—five of the chiefest intelligences in the school—and look at them! Scots wha hae wi' Wallace bled—Harry Slater! *Yes, sir.* Since when, is it, that 17, and 45, and 68 and 21 make 155, ye unspeakable creature? *I—I—if you please, sir, Sally Fitch hunched me and I reckon it made me make a figure 9 when I was intending to make a—* There's not a 9 in the sum, you blockhead!—and ye'll get a black mark for the lie you've told; a foolish lie, ill wrought and clumsy in the invention; you have no talent—stick to the truth. Becky Thatcher! *Yes, sir, please.* Make the curtsy over again, and do it better. *Yes, sir.* Lower, still! *Yes, sir.* Very good. Now I'll just ask you how you make out that 58 from 156 leaves 43? *If you please, sir, I subtracted the 8 from the 6, which leaves—which leaves—I think it leaves 3—and then—* Peace! ye banks and braes o' bonny Doon but it's a rare answer and a credit to my patient teaching! Jack Stillson! *Yes, sir.* Straighten up, and don't d-r-a-w-l like that—it's a fatigue to hear ye! And what *have* you been setting down here: If a horse travel 96 feet in 4 seconds and two-tenths of a second, how much will a barrel of mackerel cost when potatoes are 22 cents a bushel? Answer—eleven dollars and forty-six cents. You incurable ass, don't you see that ye've mixed three questions into one? The gauds and vanities o' learning! Oh, here's a hand, my trusty fere, and gie's a hand o' thine, and we'll— out of my sight, ye maundering idiot!—"

The show was become unendurable. The boy had forgotten not a word, nor a tone, nor a look, nor a gesture, nor any shade or trifle of detail—he was letter-perfect, and the house could shut its eyes anywhere in the performance and know which individual was being imitated. The boy's deep gravity and sincerity made the exhibition more and more trying the longer he went on. For a time, in decorous, disciplined and heroic silence, house and teacher sat bursting to laugh, with the tears running down, the regulations requiring noiseless propriety and solemnity; but when the stranger recited the answer to the triple sum and then put his hands together and raised his despairing eyes toward heaven in exact imitation of Mr. Ferguson's manner, the teacher's face broke up; and with that concession the house let go with a crash and laughed its fill thenceforth. But the boy went tranquilly on and on, unheeding the screams and throes and explosions, clear to the finish; then made his bow and straightened up and stood, bland and waiting.

It took some time to quiet the school; then Mr. Ferguson said, "It is the most extraordinary thing I have seen in my life. In this world there is not another talent like yours, lad; be grateful for it, and for the noble modesty with which you bear about such a treasure. How long would you be able to keep in your memory the things which you have been uttering?"

"I cannot forget anything that I see or hear, sir."

"At all?"

"No, sir."

"It seems incredible—just impossible. Let me experiment a little—for the pure joy of it. Take my English-French dictionary and sit down and study it while I go on with the school's exercises. Shall you be disturbed by us?"

"No, sir."

He took the dictionary and began to skim the pages swiftly, one after another. Evidently he dwelt upon no page, but merely gave it a lick from top to bottom with his eye and turned it over. The schoolwork rambled on after a fashion, but it consisted of blunders, mainly, for the fascinated eyes and minds of school and teacher were oftener on the young stranger than elsewhere. At the end of twenty minutes, the boy laid the book down.

Mr. Ferguson noticed this, and said, with a touch of disappointment in his tone, "I am sorry. I saw that it did not interest you."

The boy rose and said, "Oh, sir, on the contrary!" This in French; then in English, "I have now the words of your language, but the forms not—perhaps, how you call?—the pronunciation also."

"You have the words? How many of the words do you know?"

"All, sir."

"No—no—there are 645 octavo pages. You couldn't have examined a tenth of them in this short time. A page in two seconds? It is impossible."

The boy bowed respectfully, and said nothing.

"There. I am in fault again. I shall learn of you—courtesy. Give me the book. Begin. Recite—recite!"

It was another miracle. The boy poured out, in a rushing stream, the words, the definitions, the accompanying illustrative phrases and sentences, the signs indicating the parts of speech—everything; he skipped nothing, he put in all the details, and he even got the pronunciations substantially right, since it was a pronouncing-dictionary. Teacher and school sat in a soundless and motionless spell of awe and admiration, unconscious of the flight of time, unconscious of everything but the beautiful stranger and his stupendous performance.

After a long while the juggler interrupted his recitation to say—in rather cumbrous and booky English, "It is of necessity—what you call 'of course,' n'est-ce pas?—that I now am enabled to apply the machinery of the rules of the grammar, since the meanings of the words which constitute them were become my possession." Here he stopped, quoted the violated rule, corrected his sentence, then went on: "And it is of course that I now understand the languages—language—appropriated to the lesson of arithmetic—yet not all, the dictionary being in the offensive. As for example, to-wit, 'Scots wha hae wi' Wallace bled, Sally Fitch *hunched* me, ye banks and braes o' bonny Doon, oh here's a hand my trusty fere and gie's a hand o' thine.' Some of these words are by mischance omitted from the dictionary, and thereby results confusion. Without knowledge of the signification of *hunched*, one is ignorant of the nature of the explanation preferred by the mademoiselle Thatcher; and if one shall not know what a Doon is, and whether it is a financial bank or other that is involved, one is still yet again at a loss."

Silence.

The master roused himself as if from a dream, and lifted his hands and said, "It is not a parrot—it *thinks!* Boy, ye are a marvel! With listening an hour and studying half as long, you have learned the English language. You are the only person in America that knows all its words. Let it rest, where it is—the construction will come of itself. Take up the Latin, now, and the Greek, and shorthand writing, and the mathematics. Here are the books. You shall have thirty minutes to each. Then your education will be complete. But tell me! How do you manage these things? What is your method? You do not read the page, you only skim it down with your eye, as one wipes a column of sums from a slate. You understand my English?"

"Yes, master, perfectly. I have no method, meaning I have no mystery. I see what is on the page, that is all."

"But you see it at a glance."

"But is not the particulars of the page—" He stopped to apply the rule and correct the sentence: "*are* not the particulars of the page the same as the particulars of the school? I see all the pupils at once; do I not know, then, how each is dressed, and his attitude and expression, and the color of his eyes and hair, and the length of his nose, and if his shoes are tied or not? Why shall I glance twice?"

Margaret Stover, over in the corner, drew her untied shoe back out of sight.

"Ah, well, I have seen no one else who could individualize a thousand details with one sweep of the two eyes. Maybe the eyes of the admirable creature the dragonfly can do it, but that is another matter: He has twelve thousand, and so the haul he makes with his multitudinous glance is a thing within reason and comprehension. Get at your Latin, lad." Then with a sigh, "We will proceed with our poor dull ploddings."

The boy took up the book and began to turn the pages, much as if he were carefully counting them. The school glanced with an evil joy at Henry Bascom, and was pleased to note that he was not happy. He was the only Latin pupil in the school, and his pride in this distinction was a thing through which his mates were made to endure much suffering.

The school droned and buzzed along, with the bulk of its mind and its interest not on its work but fixed in envy and discouragement upon the new scholar. At the end of half an hour it saw him lay down his Latin book and take up the Greek; it glanced contentedly at Henry Bascom, and a satisfied murmur dribbled down the benches. In turn the Greek and the mathematics were mastered, then "The New Short-Hand

Method, called Phonography" was taken up. But the phonographic study was short-lived—it lasted but a minute and twenty seconds; then the boy played with several other books.

The master noticed this, and by and by said, "So soon done with the Phonography?"

"It is only a set of compact and simple *principles*, sir. They are applicable with ease and certainty—like the principles of the mathematics. Also, the examples assist; innumerable combinations of English words are given, and the vowels eliminated. It is admirable, this system, for precision and clarity; one could write Greek and Latin with it, making word-combinations with the vowels excised, and still be understood."

"Your English is improving by leaps and bounds, my boy."

"Yes, sir. I have been reading these English books. They have furnished me the forms of the language—the moulds in which it is cast—the idioms."

"I am past wondering! I think there is no miracle that a mind like this cannot do. Pray go to the blackboard and let me see what Greek may look like in phonographic word-combinations with the vowel-signs left out. I will read some passages."

The boy took the chalk, and the trial began. The master read very slowly; then a little faster; then faster still; then as fast as he could. The boy kept up, without apparent difficulty. Then the master threw in Latin sentences, English sentences, French ones, and now and then a hardy problem from Euclid to be ciphered out. The boy was competent, all the while.

"It is amazing, my child, amazing—stupefying! Do me one more miracle, and I strike my flag. Here is a page of columns of figures. Add them up. I have seen the famous lightning-calculator do it in three minutes and a quarter, and I know the answer. I will hold the watch. Beat him!"

The boy glanced at the page, made his bow and said,—

"The total is 4,865,493 if the blurred twenty-third figure in the fifth column is a 9; if it is a 7, the total is less by 2."

"Right, and he is beaten by incredible odds; but you hadn't time to even see the blurred figure, let alone note its place. Wait till I find it—the twenty-third, did you say? Here it is, but I can't tell which it is: It may be a 9, it may be a 7. But no matter, one of your answers is right, according to which name we give the figure. Dear me, can my watch be right? It is long past the noon recess, and everybody has forgotten his dinner. In my thirty years of school-teaching experience, this has not happened before. Truly it is a day of miracles. Children, we dull moles are in no condition to further plod and grub after the excitements and bewilderments of this intellectual conflagration—school is dismissed. My wonderful scholar, tell me your name."

The school crowded forward in a body to devour the stranger at close quarters with their envying eyes; all except Bascom, who remained apart and sulked.

"Quarante-quatre, sir. Forty-four."

"Why—why—that is only a number, you know, not a name."

The boy bowed. The master dropped the subject.

"When did you arrive in our town?"

"Last night, sir."

"Have you friends or relatives among us?"

"No, sir, none. Mr. Hotchkiss allows me to lodge in his house."

"You will find the Hotchkisses good people, excellent people. Had you introductions to them?"

"No, sir."

"You see I am curious; but we are all that, in this monotonous little place, and we mean no harm. How did you make them understand what you wanted?"

"Through my signs and their compassion. It was cold, and I

was a stranger."

"Good. Good and well stated, without waste of words. It describes the Hotchkisses; it's a whole biography. Whence did you come—and how?"

Forty-four bowed.

The master said, affably, "It was another indiscretion—you will not remember it against —no, I mean you will forget it, in consid— what I am trying to say is, that you will overlook it— that is it, overlook it. I am glad you are come, grateful that you are come."

"I thank you—thank you deeply, sir."

"My official character requires that I precede you in leaving this house, therefore I do it. This is an apology. Adieu."

"Adieu, my master."

The school made way, and the old gentleman marched out between the ranks with a grave dignity proper to his official state.

**The girls went vivaciously** chattering away, eager to get home and tell of the wonders they had seen; but outside of the schoolhouse the boys grouped themselves together and waited; silent, expectant, and nervous. They paid but little attention to the bitter weather, they were apparently under the spell of a more absorbing interest.

Henry Bascom stood apart from the others, in the neighborhood of the door. The new boy had not come out, yet. Tom Sawyer had halted him to give him a warning.

"Look out for him. He'll be waiting. The bully, I mean: Hen Bascom. He's treacherous and low down."

"Waiting?"

"Yes. For you."

"What for?"

"To lick you—whip you."

"On what account?"

"Why, he's the bully this year, and you're a fresh."

"Is that a reason?"

"Plenty, yes. He's got to take your measure, and do it today—he knows that."

"It's a custom, then?"

"Yes. He's got to fight you, whether he wants to or not. But he *wants* to. You've knocked his Latin layout galley-west."

"Galley west? *Je ne*—"

"It's just a word, you know. Means you've knocked his props from under him."

"Knocked his props from under him?"

"Yes—trumped his ace."

"Trumped his—"

"Ace. That's it—pulled his leg."

"I assure you this is an error. I have not pulled his leg."

"But you don't understand. Don't you see? You've graveled him, and he's disgruntled."

The new boy's face expressed his despair. Tom reflected a moment, then his eye lighted with hope, and he said, with confidence, "Now you'll get the idea. You see, he held the age on Latin—just a lone hand, don't you know, and it made him Grand Turk and Whoopjamboreehoo of the whole school, and he went in procession all by himself, like Parker's hog. Well, you've walked up to the captain's office with *your* Latin, now, and pulled in high, low, jack and the game, and it's taken the curl out of his tail. There—that's the idea."

The new boy hesitated, passed his hand over his forehead, and began, haltingly, "It is still a little vague. It was but a poor dictionary—that French-English—and over-rich in omissions. Do you perhaps mean that he is jealous?"

"Score *one!* That's it. Jealous—the very word. Now then, there'll be a ring, and you'll fight. Can you box? do you know the trick of it?"

"No."

"I'll show you. You'll learn in two minutes and less; it don't *begin* with grammar for difficulties. Put up your fists—so. Now then, hit me... You notice how I turned that off with my left? Again... See?—turned it with my right. Dance around; caper—like this. Now I'm coming for you—look sharp... That's the ticket—I didn't arrive. Once more... Good! You're all right. Come on. It's a cold day for Henry."

**They stepped outside, now**. As they walked past Bascom, he suddenly thrust out his foot, to trip Forty-four. But the foot was no obstruction, it did not interrupt Forty-four's stride. Necessarily, then, Bascom was himself tripped. He fell heavily, and everybody laughed privately.

He got up, all a-quiver with passion, and cried out, "Off with your coat, Know-it-all—you're going to fight or eat dirt, one or t'other. Form a ring, fellows!"

He threw off his coat. The ring was formed.

"May I keep my coat on? Do the rules allow it?"

"Don't!" said Tom; "it's a disadvantage. Pull it off."

"Keep it on, you wax doll, if you want to," said Henry, "it won't do you any good either way. Time!"

Forty-four took position, with his fists up, and stood without moving, while the lithe and active Bascom danced about him, danced up toward him, feinted with his right, feinted with his left, danced away again, danced forward again—and so-on and so-on, Tom and others putting in frequent warnings for Forty-four: "Look out for him—look *o-u-t!*"

At last, Forty-four opened his guard for an instant, and in that instant Henry plunged, and let drive with all his force; but Forty-four stepped lightly aside, and Henry's impulse and a slip on the ice carried him to the ground. He got up lame but eager, and began his dance again; he presently lunged again, hit vacancy and got another fall.

After that, he respected the slippery ground, and lunged no more, and danced cautiously; he fought with energy, interest and smart judgment, and delivered a sparkling rain of blows, but none of them got home—some were dodged by a sideward tilt of the head, the others were neatly warded. He was getting winded with his violent exercise, but the other boy was still fresh, for he had done no dancing, he had struck no blows, and had had no exercise of consequence.

Henry stopped to rest and pant, and Forty-four said, "Let us not go on with it. What good can come of it?"

The boys murmured dissent; this was an election for Bully; they were personally interested, they had hopes, and their hopes were getting the color of certainties.

Henry said, "You'll stay where you are, Miss Nancy. You don't leave this ground till I know who wears the belt."

"Ah, but you already know—or ought to; therefore, where is the use of going on? You have not struck me, and I have no wish to strike you."

"Oh, you haven't, haven't you? How kind! Keep your benevolences to yourself till somebody asks you for them. Time!"

The new boy began to strike out, now; and every time he struck, Henry went down. Five times. There was great excitement among the boys. They recognized that they were going to lose a tyrant and perhaps get a protector in his place. In their happiness they lost their fears and began to shout:

"Give it him, Forty-four! Let him have it! Land him again! Another one! Give it him good!"

Henry was pluck. He went down time after time, but got patiently up and went at his work again, and did not give up until his strength was all gone.

Then he said, "The belt's yours, but I'll get even with you, yet, girly. You see if I don't." Then he looked around upon the crowd, and called eight of them by name, ending with Huck Finn, and said: "You're spotted, you see. I heard you. Tomorrow I'll begin on you, and I'll lam the daylights out of you."

For the first time, a flash of temper showed in the new boy's eye. It was only a flash; it was gone in a moment; then he said, without passion, "I will not allow that."

"You won't allow it! Who's asking you? Who cares what you allow and what you don't allow? To show you how much I care, I'll begin on them *now*."

"I cannot have it. You must not be foolish. I have spared you, till now; I have struck you only lightly. If you touch one of the boys, I will hit you *hard*."

But Henry's temper was beyond his control. He jumped at the nearest boy on his black-list, but he did not reach him; he went down under a sounding slap from the flat of the new boy's hand, and lay motionless where he fell.

"I saw it! I saw that!" This shout was from Henry's father, the slave trader—an unloved man, but respected for his muscle and his temper. He came running from his sleigh, with his whip in his hand and raised to strike. The boys fell back out of his way, and as he reached Forty-four, he brought down the whip with an angry "I'll learn you!"

Forty-four dodged deftly out of its course and seized the trader's wrist with his right hand. There was a sound of crackling bones and a groan, and the trader staggered away, saying—

"Name of God, my wrist is crushed!"

Henry's mamma arrived from the sleigh, now and broke into frenzies of lamentation over her collapsed son and her crippled husband, while the schoolboys looked on, dazed, and rather frightened at the woman's spectacular distress, but fascinated with the show and glad to be there and see it. It absorbed their attention so entirely that when Mrs. Bascom presently turned and demanded the extradition of Forty-four so that she might square accounts with him they found that he had disappeared without their having noticed it.

**Within an hour afterward**, people began to drop in at the Hotchkiss house; ostensibly to make a friendly call, really to get sight of the miraculous boy. The news they brought soon made the Hotchkisses proud of their prize and glad that they had caught him. Mr. Hotchkiss's pride and joy were frank and simple;

every new marvel that any comer added to the list of his lodger's great deeds made him a prouder and happier man than he was before, he being a person substantially without jealousies and by nature addicted to admirations.

Indeed he was a broad man in many ways; hospitable to new facts and always seeking them; to new ideas, and always examining them; to new opinions and always adopting them; a man ready to meet any novelty halfway and give it a friendly trial. He changed his principles with the moon, his politics with the weather, and his religion with his shirt. He was recognized as being limitlessly good-hearted, quite fairly above the village average intellectually, a diligent and enthusiastic seeker after truth, and a sincere believer in his newest belief, but a man who had missed his vocation—he should have been a weathervane. He was tall and handsome and courteous, with winning ways, and expressive eyes, and had a white head which looked twenty years older than the rest of him.

His good Presbyterian wife was as steady as an anvil. She was not a creature of change. When she gave shelter to an opinion, she did not make a transient guest of it, but a permanency. She was fond and proud of her husband, and believed he would have been great if he had had a proper chance—if he had lived in a metropolis, instead of a village; if his merits had been exposed to the world instead of being hidden under a bushel. She was patient with his excursions after the truth. She expected him to be saved—thought she knew that that would happen, in fact. It could only be as a Presbyterian, of course, but that would come—come of a certainty. All the signs indicated it. He had often been a Presbyterian; he was periodically a Presbyterian, and she had noticed with comfort that his period was almost astronomically regular. She could take the almanac and calculate its return with nearly as much confidence as other astronomers calculated an eclipse. His

Mohammedan period, his Methodist period, his Buddhist period, his Baptist period, his Parsi period, his Roman Catholic period, his Atheistic period—these were all similarly regular, but she cared nothing for that. She knew there was a patient and compassionate Providence watching over him that would see to it that he died in his Presbyterian period. The latest thing in religions was the Fox-girl Rochester rappings; so he was a Spiritualist for the present.

Hannah Hotchkiss exulted in the wonders brought by the visitors, and the more they brought the happier she was in the possession of that boy; but she was very human in her makeup, and she felt a little aggravated over the fact that the news had to come from the outside; that these people should know these things about her lodger before she knew them herself; that she must sit and do the wondering and exclaiming when in all fairness she ought to be doing the telling and they the applauding; that they should be able to contribute all the marvels and she none.

Finally, the widow Dawson remarked upon the circumstance that all the information was being furnished from the one side, and added, "Didn't he do anything out of the common here, sister Hotchkiss—last night or this morning?" ("Sister" in the Methodist, or Presbyterian, or Baptist, or Campbellite church—nothing more. A common form, in those days.)

Hannah was ashamed of her poverty. The only thing she was able to offer was colorless compared with the matters which she had been listening to.

"Well, no, I can't say that he did—unless you consider that we couldn't understand his language but *did* understand his signs about as easy as if they had been talk. We were astonished at it, and spoke of it afterwards."

Her young niece, Annie Fleming, spoke up and said, "Why, auntie, that wasn't all. The dog doesn't allow a stranger to come to the door at night, but he didn't bark at the boy; he acted as if he was ever so glad to see him. You said, yourself, that that never happened with a stranger before."

"It's true, as sure as I live; it had passed out of my mind, child."

She was happier, now.

Then her husband made a contribution: "I call to mind, now, that just as we stepped into his room to show him its arrangements I knocked my elbow against the wardrobe and the candle fell and went out, and—"

"Certainly!" exclaimed Hannah, "and the next moment he had struck a match and was lighting—"

"Not the stub I had dropped," cried Hotchkiss, "but a whole candle! Now the marvel is that there was only one whole candle in the room—"

"And it was clear on the *other side* of the room," interrupted Hannah, "and moreover only just the end of it was showing, where it lay on the top of the bookcase, and he had noticed it with that lightning eye of his—"

"Of course, of course!" exclaimed the company, with admiration.

"—and gone right to it in the dark without disturbing a chair. Why, sister Dawson, a *cat* couldn't have done it any quicker or better or surer! Just think of it!"

A chorus of rewarding astonishment broke out which made Hannah's whole constitution throb with pleasure; and when sister Dawson laid her hand impressively upon Hannah's hand, and then walled her eyes toward the ceiling, as much as to say, "it's beyond words, beyond words!" the pleasure rose to ecstasy.

"Wait!" said Mr. Hotchkiss, breaking out with the kind of

laugh which in the back settlements gives notice that something humorous is coming, "I can tell you a wonder that beats that to pieces—beats anything and everything that has been told about him up to date. He paid four weeks' board in advance—cash down! Petersburg can believe the rest, but you'll never catch it taking *that* statement at par."

The joke had immense success; the laugh was hearty all around.

Then Hotchkiss issued another notifying laugh, and added, "And there's another wonder on top of that; I tell you a little at a time, so as not to overstrain you. He didn't pay in wildcat at twenty-five discount, but in a currency you've forgotten the look of—minted gold! Four yellow eagle-birds—and here they are, if you don't believe me."

This was too grand and fine to be humorous; it was impressive, almost awe-inspiring. The gold pieces were passed from hand to hand and contemplated in mute reverence. Aunt Rachel, elderly slave woman, was passing cracked nuts and cider.

She offered a contribution, now:

"Now, den, dat' splain it! I uz a wonderin' 'bout dat cannel. You is right, Miss Hannah, dey uz only one in de room, en she uz on top er de bookcase. Well, she dah *yit*—she hain't been tetched."

"Not been touched?"

"No, m'am; she hain't been tetched. A ornery po' yaller taller cannel, ain't she?"

"Of course."

"Yes'm. I mould' dat cannel myself. Kin we 'ford *wax* cannels—half a dollar a pound?"

"Wax! The idea!"

"Dat new cannel's *wax!*"

"Oh, come!"

"Fo' Gawd she is. White as Miss Guthrie's store-teeth."

A delicate flattery-shot, neatly put. The widow Guthrie, 56 and dressed for 25, was pleased, and exhibited a girlish embarrassment that was very pretty. She was excusably vain of her false teeth, the only ones in the town; a costly luxury, and a fine and showy contrast with the prevailing mouth-equipment of both old and young—the kind of sharp contrast which white-washed palings make with a charred stump-fence.

Everybody wanted to see the wax candle; Annie Fleming was hurried away to fetch it, and aunt Rachel resumed.

**Her tongue was hung in the middle** and was easier to start than to stop. It would have gone on wagging, now, but that the wax candle had long ago been waiting for exhibition. Annie Fleming sat with it in her hand, with one ear drinking in aunt Rachel's fairy-tales, and the other one listening for the click of the gate-latch; for she had lost her tender little inexperienced heart to the new boy without suspecting it; awake and asleep, she had been dreaming of his beautiful face ever since she had had her first glimpse of it and she was longing to see it again and feel that enchanting and mysterious ecstasy which it had inspired in her before.

She was a dear and sweet and pretty and guileless creature, she was just turned eighteen, she did not know she was in love, she only knew that she worshiped—worshiped as the fire-worshipers worship the sun, content to see his face and feel his warmth, unworthy of a nearer intimacy, unequal to it, unfitted for it, and not requiring it or aspiring to it. Why didn't he come? Why had he not come to dinner? The hours were so slow, the day so tedious; the longest she had known in her eighteen years. All were growing more and more impatient for his coming, but their impatience was pale beside hers; and besides, they could express it, and did, but she could not have that relief, she must hide her secret, she must put on the lie of indifference and act it the best she could.

The candle was passed from hand to hand, now, and its material admired and verified; then Annie carried it away.

It was well past midafternoon, and the days were short. Annie and her aunt were to sup and spend the night with sister Guthrie on the hill, a good mile distant. What should be done? Was it worthwhile to wait longer for the boy? The company were reluctant to go without seeing him; sister Guthrie hoped she might have the distinction of his presence in her house with the niece and the aunt, and would like to wait a little longer and invite him; so it was agreed to hold on a while.

Annie returned, now, and there was disappointment in her face and a pain at her heart, though no one detected the one nor suspected the other. She said, "Aunty, he has been here, and is gone again."

"Then he must have come the back way. It's *too* bad. But are you sure? How do you know?"

"Because he has changed his clothes."

"Are there clothes there?"

"Yes; and not the ones he had this morning, nor the ones he wore last night."

"Can we see them?"

"Can't we see them?"

"Do let us go and look at them!"

Everybody wanted to see the clothes, everybody begged. So, sentries were posted to look out for the boy's approach and give notice—Annie to watch the front door and Rachel the back one—and the rest went up to Forty-four's chamber. The clothes were there, new and handsome. The coat lay spread upon the bed. Mrs. Hotchkiss took it by the skirts and held it up to display it: a flood of gold and silver coin began to pour out of the inverted pockets; the woman stood aghast and helpless; the coin piled higher and higher on the floor.

"Put it down!" shouted her husband; "drop it, can't you!"

But she was paralyzed; he snatched the coat and threw it on the bed, and the flood ceased. "Now we are in a fine fix; he can come at any moment and catch us; and we'll have to explain, if we can, how we happen to be here. Quick, all you accessories after the fact and before it—turn to; we must gather it up and put it back."

So all those chief citizens got down on their hands and knees and scrambled all around and everywhere for the coins, raking under the bed and the sofa and the wardrobe for estrays, a most undignified spectacle. The work was presently finished, but that did not restore happiness, for there was a new trouble, now: After the coat's pockets had been stuffed, there was still half a peck of coin left. It was a shameful predicament.

Nobody could get command of his wits for a moment or two; then sister Dawson made a suggestion: "No real harm is done, when you come to look at it. It is natural that we should have some curiosity about the belongings of such a wonderful stranger, and if we try to satisfy it, not meaning any harm or disrespect—"

"Right," interrupted Miss Pomeroy, the school m'am; "he's only a boy, and he wouldn't mind, and he wouldn't think it anything odd if people as old as we are should take a little liberty which he mightn't like in younger folks."

"And besides," said Judge Taylor the magistrate, "he hasn't suffered any loss, and isn't going to suffer any. Let us put the whole of the money in his table drawer and close it, and lock the room door; and when he comes, we will all tell him just how it was, and apologize. It will come out all right; I think we don't need to worry."

It was agreed that this was probably as good a plan as could be contrived in the difficult circumstances of the case; so the company took all the comfort from it they could, and were glad to get out of the place and clear for their homes without waiting longer for the boy, in case he shouldn't arrive before they got their wraps on. They said Hotchkiss could do the explaining and apologizing, and depend upon them to endorse and stand by all his statements.

"And besides," said Mrs. Wheelright, "how do we know it is real money? He may be a juggler out of India; in that case the drawer is empty, or full of sawdust by this time."

"I am afraid it's not going to happen," said Hotchkiss; "the money was rather heavy for sawdust. The thing that mainly interests me is, that I shan't sleep very well with that pile of money in the house—I shan't sleep at all if you people are going to tell about it, and so I'll ask you to keep the secret until morning; then I will make the boy send it to the bank, and you may talk as freely as you please, then."

Annie put on her things and she and her aunt departed with the rest. Darkness was approaching; the lodger was not come. What could the matter be? Mrs. Hotchkiss said he was probably coasting with his schoolmates and paying no attention to more important things—boy-like. Rachel was told to keep his supper warm and let him take his own time about coming for it; "boys will be boys, and late by nature, nights and mornings; let them be boys while they can, it's the best of life and the shortest."

It had turned warm, and clouds were gathering fast, with a promise of snow—a promise which would be kept.

As Doctor Wheelright, the stately old First-Family Virginian and imposing Thinker of the village was going out at the front door, he unloaded a Thought. It seemed to weigh a good part of a ton, and it impressed everybody: "It is my opinion—after much and careful reflection, sir—that the indications warrant the conjecture that in several ways this youth is an extraordinary person."

That verdict would go around. After such an endorsement, from such a source, the village would think twice before it ventured to think small potatoes of that boy.

**As the darkness closed down** an hour later, what is to this day called the Great Storm began. It was in reality a Blizzard, but that expressive word had not then been invented. It was this storm's mission to bury the farms and villages of a long narrow strip of country for ten days, and do it as compactly and as thoroughly as the mud and ashes had buried Pompeii nearly eighteen centuries before.

The Great Storm began its work modestly, deceptively. It made no display—there was no wind and no noise; whoever was abroad and crossed the lamp-glares flung from uncurtained windows noticed that the snow came straight down, and that it laid its delicate white carpet softly, smoothly, artistically, thickening the substance swiftly and equably; the passenger noticed also that this snow was of an unusual sort, it not coming in an airy cloud of great feathery flakes, but in a fog of white dust-forms—mere powder; just powder; the strangest snow imaginable.

By 8 in the evening this snow-fog had become so dense that lamp-glares four steps away were not visible, and without the help of artificial light a passenger could see no object till he was near enough to touch it with his hand. Whosoever was abroad now was practically doomed, unless he could soon stumble upon somebody's house. Orientation was impossible; to be abroad was to be lost. A man could not leave his own door, walk ten steps and find his way back again.

The wind rose, now, and began to sing through this ghastly fog; momently it rose higher and higher, soon its singing had developed into roaring, howling, shrieking. It gathered up the snow from the ground and drove it in massy walls ahead of it and distributed it here and there across streets and open lots and against houses, in drifts fifteen feet deep.

There were disasters, of course. Very few people were still out, but those few were necessarily in bad case. If they faced the wind, it caked their faces instantly with a thick mask of powder which closed their eyes in blindness and stopped their nostrils and their breath, and they fell where they were; if they tried to move with the wind, they soon plunged into a drift and the oncoming wall of snow buried them. Even in that little village, twenty-eight persons perished that night, some because they had heard cries of distress and went out to help, but got lost within sixty seconds, and then, seeking their own doors, went in the wrong direction and found their graves in five minutes.

**At 8, just as the wind began to softly moan** and whimper and wheeze, Mr. Hotchkiss laid his spiritualistic book down, snuffed the candle, threw an extra log on the fire, then parted his coattails and stood with his back to the blaze and began to turn over in his mind some of the information which he had been gathering about the manners and customs and industries of the spirit land, and to repeat and try to admire some of the poetry which Byron had sent thence through the rapping-mediums.

He did not know that there was a storm outside. He had been absorbed in his book for an hour and a half. Aunt Rachel appeared, now, with an armful of wood, which she flung in the box and said, "Well, seh, it's de wust I ever see; and Jeff say de same."

"Worst what?"

"Storm, seh."

"Is there a storm?"

"My! didn't you know it, seh?"

"No."

"Why, it's de beatenes' storm—tain't like nothin' you ever see, Marse Oliver—so fine—like ashes a-blowin'; why, you can't see no distance scasely. Me en Jeff was at de prar meetin', en come back a little bit ago, en come mighty near miss'n de house; en when we look out, jist dis minute it's a heap wuss'n ever. Jeff he uz a sayin'—" She glanced around; an expression of fright came into her face, and she exclaimed, "Why, I reckoned of cose he uz here—en he ain't!"

"Who?"

"Young Marse Fawty-fo'."

"Oh, he's playing somewhere; he'll be along presently."

"You hain't seen him, seh?"

"No."

"O, my Gawd!"

She fled away, and in five minutes was back again, sobbing and panting.

"He ain't in his room, his supper ain't tetched, he ain't

anywhers; I been all over de house. O, Marse Oliver de chile's lost, we ain't never gwyne to see him no mo'.'"

"Oh, nonsense, you needn't be afraid—boys don't mind a storm."

Uncle Jeff arrived at this moment, and said, "But Marse Oliver dis ain't no common storm. Has you been to look at it?"

"No."

Hotchkiss was alarmed, at last, and ran with the others to the front door and snatched it open. The wind piped a high note, and they disappeared in a world of snow which was discharged at them as if from steam-shovels.

"Shut it, shut it!" gasped the master.

It was done.

A blast of wind came that rocked the house. There was a faint and choking cry outside. Hotchkiss blenched, and said, "What can we do? It's death to go out there. But we must do something—it may be the boy."

"Wait, Marse Oliver, I'll fetch a clo'es line, en Jeff he—" She was gone, and in a moment brought it and began to tie an end around uncle Jeff's waist. "Now, den, out wid you! me en Marse Oliver'll hole on to de yuther end."

Jeff was ready; the door was opened for the plunge, and the plunge was made; but in the same instant a suffocating assault of snow closed the eyes and took away the breath of the master and Rachel and they sank gasping to the floor and the line escaped from their hands. They threw themselves on their faces, with their feet toward the door; their breath returned, and Rachel moaned, "He's gone, now!"

By the light from the hall lamp over the door, she caught a dim vision of the new boy, coming from toward the dining room, and said "Thank de good Gawd for dat much—how ever did he find de back gate?"

The boy came through against the wind and shut the front

306

door. The master and Rachel rose out of their smother of snow, and the former said, in words broken by sobs, "I'm so grateful! I never expected to see you again."

By this time, Rachel's sobs and groans and lamentations were rising above the clamors of the storm, and the boy asked what the trouble was. Hotchkiss told him about Jeff.

"I will go and fetch him, sir. Get into the parlor, and close the door."

"You will venture out? Not a step—stay where you are! I wouldn't allow—"

The boy interrupted—not with words, but only a look—and the man and the servant passed into the parlor and closed the door. Then they heard the front door close, and stood looking at each other. The storm raged on; every now and then a gust of wind burst against the house with a force which made it quake, and in the intervals it wailed like a lost soul; the listeners tallied the gusts and the intervals, losing heart all the time, and when they had counted five of each, their hopes died.

Then they opened the parlor door—to do they didn't know what —the street door sprang open at the same moment, and two snow-figures entered: the boy carrying the unconscious old man in his arms. He delivered his burden to Rachel, shut the door, and said, "A man has found refuge in the open shed over yonder; a slender, tall, wild-looking man with thin sandy beard. He is groaning. It is not much of a shelter, that shed."

He said it indifferently, and Hotchkiss shuddered.

"Oh, it is awful, awful!" he said, "he will die."

"Why is it awful?" asked the boy.

"Why? It... it... why, of course it's awful!"

"Perhaps it is as you say; I do not know. Shall I fetch him?"

"Great guns, no! Don't dream of such a thing—one miracle of the sort is enough."

"But if you want him... Do you want him?"

"Want him? I... why, I don't want him... that isn't it... I mean, why, don't you understand? It's a pity he should die, poor fellow; but we are not in a position to..."

"I will fetch him."

"Stop, stop, are you mad! Come back!"

But the boy was gone.

"Rachel, why the devil did you let him get out? Can't you see that the lad's a rank lunatic?"

"O, Marse Oliver, gim it to me, I deserve it! I's so thankful to git my ole Jeff back I ain't got no sense en can't take notice of nothin'. I's so shamed, en O, my Gawd, I..."

"We had him, and now we've lost him again; and this time for good; and it's all your fault, for being a—"

The door fell open, a snow image plunged in upon the floor, the boy's voice called, "There he is; there's others, yet," and the door closed again.

"Oh, well," cried Hotchkiss with a note of despair, "we've got to give him up, there's no saving him. Rachel!" He was flapping the snow from the new take, with a "tidy." "Bless my soul, it's Crazy Meadows! Rouse up, Jeff! Lend a hand, both of you. Drag him to my fire."

It was done.

"Now, then, blankets, food, hot water, whisky—fly around! we'll save him, he isn't more than half dead, yet."

The three worked over Crazy Meadows half an hour, and brought him around. Meantime they had kept alert ears open, listening; but their listening was unblessed. No sounds came but the rumbling and blustering of the storm. Crazy Meadows gazed around confusedly, gradually got his bearings, recognized the faces, and said, "I am saved! Hotchkiss, it seems impossible. How did it happen?"

"A boy did it—the most marvelous boy on the planet. It was lucky you had a lantern."

"Lantern? I hadn't any lantern."

"Yes, you had. You don't know. The boy described your build and beard."

"I hadn't any lantern, I tell you. There wasn't any light around."

"Marse Oliver," said Rachel, "didn't Miss Hannah say de young marster kin see in de dark?"

"Why, certainly, now that you mention it. But how could he see through that blanket of snow? My gracious, I wish he would come! Oh, but he'll never come, poor young chap, he'll never come, never anymore."

"Marse Oliver, don't you worry, de good Lawd kin take care of him."

"In this storm, you old idiot? You don't know what you're talking about. Wait. I've got an idea! Quick! Get around the table; now then, take hold of hands. Banish all obstructive influences— you want to be particular about that; the spirits can't do anything against doubt and incredulity. Silence, now, and concentrate your minds. Poor boy, if he is dead he will come and say so."

Hotchkiss bowed his head solemnly to the table, and said in a reverent tone: "Are there any spirits present? If so, please rap three times."

After a pause, the response came: three faint raps.

It was Lord Byron's spirit. Byron was the most active poet on the other side of the grave in those days, and the hardest one for a medium to get rid of. He reeled off several rods of poetry now, of his usual spiritual pattern—rhymy and jingly and all that, but not good, for his mind had decayed since he died. At the end of three-quarters of an hour, he went away to hunt for a word that would rhyme with silver—good luck and a long riddance, Crazy Meadows said, for there wasn't any such word.

Then Napoleon came and explained Waterloo all over again and how it wasn't his fault—a thing which he was always doing

309

in the St. Helena days, and latterly around the festive rapping-table. Crazy Meadows scoffed at him, and said he didn't even get the dates right, let alone the facts; and he laughed his wild mad laugh: a reedy and raspy and horrid explosion which had long been a fright to the village and its dogs, and had brought him many a volley of stones from the children.

Shakspeare arrived and did some rather poor things, and was followed by a throng of Roman statesmen and generals whose English was the only remarkable thing about their contributions; then at last, about eleven o'clock, came some thundering raps which made the table and the company jump.

"Who is it, please?"

"Forty-four!"

"Ah, how sad! We are deeply grieved, but of course we feared it and expected it. Are you happy?"

"Happy? Certainly."

"We are so glad! It is the greatest comfort to us. Where are you?"

"In hell!"

"Do materialize! Do appear to us, if only for a moment!"

Presto! There sat the boy, in their midst! Crazy Meadows fell over backwards, but gathered himself up in silence and stood apart with heaving breast and flaming eyes, staring at the boy. Hotchkiss rubbed his hands together in gratitude and delight, and his face was transfigured with the glory-light of triumph.

"Now let the doubter doubt and the scoffer scoff if they want to, but they've had their day! Ah, Forty-four, dear Forty-four, you've done our cause a noble service."

"What cause?"

"Spiritualism."

The boy turned and looked at Crazy Meadows, whose lids at once sank down and hid his wild eyes. "Go and sleep in my bed; in the morning, it will be a dream to you."

310

Meadows drifted away like one in a trance.

"What is spiritualism, sir?"

Hotchkiss eagerly explained. The boy smiled, made no comment, and changed the subject.

"Twenty-eight have perished in your village by the storm."

"Heavens! Can that be true?"

"I saw them; they are under the snow—scattered over the town."

"*Saw* them?"

The boy took no notice of the inquiry in the emphasized word.

"Yes, twenty-eight."

"What a misfortune!"

"Is it?"

"Why, how can you ask?"

"I don't know. I could have saved them if I had known it was desirable. After you wanted that man saved, I gathered the idea that it was desirable, so I searched the town and saved the rest that were straggling—thirteen."

"How noble! And how beautiful it was to die in such a work. Oh, sainted spirit, I worship your memory!"

"Whose memory?"

"Yours; and I—"

"Do you take me for dead?"

"Dead? Of course. Aren't you?"

"Certainly not."

Hotchkiss's joy was without limit or measure. He poured it eloquently out until he was breathless; then paused, and added pathetically, "It is bad for spiritualism—yes, bad, bad—but let it go—go and welcome, God knows I'm glad to have you back, even on those costly terms! And by George, we'll celebrate! I'm a teetotaler, been a teetotaler for years... months, anyway... a month... but at a time like this..."

The kettle was still on the fire, the bottle which had revived Meadows was still at hand, and in a couple of minutes he had brewed a pair of good punches. "Anyway, good enough for a person out of practice," he said.

The boy began to sip, and said it was pleasant, and asked what it was.

"Why, bless your heart, whisky of course. Can't you tell by the smell of it? And we'll have a smoke, too. I don't smoke, haven't for years—I think it's years—because I'm president of the Anti-Smoking League. But at a time like this—" He jumped up and threw a log on the fire, punched the pile into a roaring blaze, then filled a couple of cob pipes and brought them. "There, now, ain't it cozy, ain't it comfortable? And just hear the storm! My, but she's booming! But snug here? It's no name for it!"

The boy was inspecting his pipe with interest.

"What shall I do with it, sir?"

"Do with it? Do you mean to say you don't smoke? I never saw such a boy. Next you'll say you don't break the Sabbath."

"But what is the material?"

"That? Tobacco, of course."

"Oh, I see. Sir Walter Raleigh discovered it among the Indians; I read about it in the school. Yes, I understand now."

He applied the candle and began to smoke, Hotchkiss gazing at him puzzled.

"You've read about it! Upon my word! Now that I come to think about it, you don't seem to know anything except what you've read about in that school. Why how in the world could you be born and raised in the State of Missouri and never—"

"But I wasn't. I am a foreigner."

"You don't say!—and speak just like an educated native—not even an accent. Where were you raised?"

The boy answered naïvely, "Partly in heaven, partly in hell."

Hotchkiss's glass fell from one hand, his pipe from the other, and he sat staring stupidly at the boy, and breathing short. Presently, he murmured dubiously, "I reckon the punch—out of practice, you know—maybe both of us—and—" He paused, and continued to gaze and blink; then shook his thoughts together and said, "Can't tell anything about it. It is too undeveloped for me; but it's all right, we'll make a night of it. It's my opinion, speaking as a prohibitionist...."

He stooped and picked up his glass and his pipe, and went rambling on in a broken and incoherent way while he filled them, glancing furtively at the boy now and then out of the corner of his eye and trying to settle his disturbed and startled mind and get his bearings again. But the boy was not disturbed; he smoked and sipped in peace, and quiet, and manifest contentment. He took a book out of his pocket, and began to turn the pages swiftly.

Hotchkiss sat down, stirring his new punch, and keeping a wistful and uneasy eye upon him. After a minute or two, the book was laid upon the table.

"Now I know all about it," said the boy. "It is all here: tobacco, and liquors, and such things. Champagne is placed at the head of everything; and Cuban tobacco at the head of the tobaccos."

"Oh, yes, they are the gems of the planet in those lines. Why, I don't recognize this book; did you bring it in tonight?"

"Yes."

"Where from?"

"The British Museum."

Hotchkiss began to blink again, and look uneasy.

"It is a new work," added the boy. "Published yesterday."

The blinking continued. Hotchkiss started to take a sip of punch, but reconsidered the motion; shook his head and put the glass down. Upon pretext of examining the print and the binding, he opened the book; then closed it at once and pushed it away. He had seen the Museum stamp—bearing date of the preceding day. He fussed nervously at his pipe a moment; then held it to the candle with a hand that trembled and made some of the tobacco spill out, then asked timidly—

"How did you get the book?"

"I went after it myself."

"Your... self. Mercy! When?"

"While you were stooping for your pipe and glass."

Hotchkiss moaned.

"Why do you make that noise?"

"Be—because I—I am afraid."

The boy reached out and touched the trembling hand and said gently, "There. It is gone."

The troubled look passed from the old prohibitionist's face, and he said, in a sort of soft ecstasy of relief and contentment, "It tingles all through me—all through me. De—licious! Every fibre—the root of every hair—it is enchantment! Oh magician of the magicians, talk to me—talk! tell me everything."

"Certainly, if you like."

"Now, that is lovely! First I will rout out old Rachel and we'll have a bite and be comfortable and freshen up; I am pretty sharp-set after all these hours, and I reckon you are, too."

"Wait. It is not necessary. I will order something."

Smoking dishes began to descend upon the table; it was covered in a moment.

"It's the Arabian Nights come again! And I am not scared, now. I don't know why—it was that magic touch, I think. But you didn't fetch them yourself, this time; I was noticing, and you didn't go away."

"No, I sent my servants."

"I didn't see them."

"You can if you wish."

"I'd give anything!"

The servants became visible; all the room was crowded with them. Trim and shapely little fellows they were; velvety little red fellows, with short horns on their heads and spiked tails at the other end; and those that stood, stood in metal plates, and those that sat—on chairs, in a row upon settees, and on top of the bookcase with their legs dangling—had metal plates under them—"to keep from scorching the furniture," the boy quietly explained, "these have come but this moment, and of course are hot, yet."

Hotchkiss asked, a little timidly, "Are they little devils?"

"Yes."

"Real ones?"

"Oh, yes—quite."

"They—are they safe?"

"Perfectly."

"I don't need to be afraid?"

"Oh, not at all."

"Then I won't be. I think they are charming. Do they understand English?"

"No, only French. But they could be taught it in a few minutes."

"It is wonderful. Are they—you won't mind my asking—relatives?"

"Of mine? No; sons of my father's subordinates. You are dismissed, young gentlemen, for the present."

The little fiends vanished.

"Your father is—er—"

"Satan!"

"Good land!"

**Hotchkiss sank into his chair** weak and limp, and began to pour out broken words and disjointed sentences whose meanings were not always clear but whose general idea was comprehensible. To this effect: From custom bred of his upbringing and his associations, he had often talked about Satan with a freedom which was regrettable, but it was really only talk, mere idle talk, he didn't mean anything by it; in fact there were many points about Satan's character which he greatly admired, and although he hadn't said so, publicly, it was an oversight and not intentional. But from this out he meant to open his mouth boldly, let people say what they might and think what they chose...

The boy interrupted him, gently and quietly, "I don't admire him."

Hotchkiss was hard aground, now; his mouth was open, and remained so, but no words came; he couldn't think of anything judicious to say. Presently, he ventured to throw out a feeler—cautiously, tentatively, feelingly, persuasively: "You see—well, you know—it would be only natural, if I was a devil—a good, kind, honorable devil, I mean—and my father was a good, kind, honorable devil against whom narrow and perhaps wrongful or at least exaggerated prejudices..."

"But I am not a devil," said the boy, tranquilly.

Hotchkiss was badly confused, but profoundly relieved.

"I... er... I... well, you know, I suspected as much, I—I—indeed I hadn't a doubt of it; and—although it—on the whole—oh, good land, I can't understand it, of course, but I give you my word of honor I like you all the better for it, I do indeed! I feel good, now: good, and comfortable, and in fact happy. Join me: Take something! I wish to drink your health; and—and your family's."

"With pleasure. Now eat: Refresh yourself. I will smoke, if you don't mind. I like it."

"Certainly; but eat, too; aren't you hungry?"

"No, I do not get hungry."

"Is that actually so?"

"Yes."

"Ever? Never?"

"No."

"Ah, it is a pity. You miss a great deal. Now tell me about yourself, won't you?"

"I shall be glad to do it, for I have a purpose in coming to the earth, and if you should find the matter interesting, you can be useful to me."

Then the talking and eating began, simultaneously.

"I was born before Adam's fall—"

"Wh-at!"

"It seems to surprise you. Why?"

"Because it caught me unprepared. And because it is 6,000 years ago, and you look to be only about fifteen years old."

"True, that is my age, within a fraction."

"Only fifteen, and yet—"

"Counting by our system of measurement, I mean. Not yours."

"How is that?"

"A day, with us, is as a thousand years with you."

Hotchkiss was awed. A seriousness which was near to solemnity settled upon his face. After a meditative pause he said, "Surely it cannot be that you really and not figuratively mean—"

"Yes—really, not figuratively. A minute of our time is 41⅔ years of yours. By our system of measurement, I am fifteen years old; but by yours, I am 5 million, lacking 20,000 years."

Hotchkiss was stunned. He shook his head in a hopeless way, and said, resignedly, "Go on—I can't realize it—it is astronomy to me."

"Of course you cannot realize these things, but do not be troubled; measurements of time and eternity are merely conveniences, they are not of much importance. It is about a week ago that Adam fell."

"A week?—Ah, yes, your week. It is awful—that compression of time! Go on."

"I was in heaven; I had always lived in heaven, of course; until a week ago, my father had always lived there. But I saw this little world created. I was interested; we were all interested. There is much more interest attaching to the creation of a planet than attaches to the creation of a sun, on account of the life that is going to inhabit it. I have seen many suns created—many indeed, that you are not yet acquainted with, they being so remotely situated in the deeps of space that their light will not reach here for a long time yet; but the planets—I cared the most for them; we all did; I have seen millions of them made, and the Tree planted in the Garden, and the man and the woman placed in its shade, with the animals about them. I saw your Adam and Eve only once; they were happy, then, and innocent. This could have continued forever, but for my father's conduct. I read it all in the Bible in Mr. Ferguson's school. As it turned out, Adam's happiness lasted less than a day."

"Less than one day?"

"By our reckoning, I mean; by yours, he lived nine hundred and twenty years—the bulk of it unhappily."

"I see; yes, it is true."

"It was my father's fault. Then hell was created, in order that Adam's race might have a place to go to, after death—"

"They could go to heaven, too."

"That was later. Two days ago. Through the sacrifice made for them by the son of God, the Savior."

"Is hell so new?"

"It was not needed before. No Adam in any of the millions of other planets had ever disobeyed and eaten of the forbidden fruit."

"It is strange."

"No—for the others were not tempted."

"How was that?"

"There was no tempter until my father ate of the fruit himself and became one. Then he tempted other angels, and they ate of it also; then Adam and the woman."

"How did your father come to eat of it this time?"

"I did not know at the time."

"Why didn't you?"

"Because I was away when it happened; I was away some days, and did not hear of it at all and of the disaster to my father until I got back; then I went to my father's place to speak with him of it; but his trouble was so new, and so severe, and so amazing to him that he could do nothing but grieve and lament—he could not bear to talk about the details; I merely gathered that when he made the venture it was because his idea of the nature of the fruit was a most erroneous one."

"Erroneous?"

"Quite erroneous."

"You do not know in what way it was erroneous?"

"Yes, I think I know now. He probably—in fact unquestionably—supposed that the nature of the fruit was to reveal to human beings the knowledge of good and evil—that, and nothing more; but not to Satan the great angel; he had that knowledge before. We always had it—always. Now why he was moved to taste it himself is not clear; I shall never know until he tells me. But his error was—"

"Yes, what was his error?"

"His error was in supposing that a knowledge of the difference between good and evil was all that the fruit could confer."

"Did it confer more than that?"

"Consider the passage which says man is prone to evil as the sparks to fly upward. Is that true? Is that really the nature of man?—I mean your man—the man of this planet?"

"Indeed it is—nothing could be truer."

"It is not true of the men of any other planet. It explains the mystery. My father's error stands revealed in all its nakedness. The fruit's office was not confined to conferring the mere knowledge of good and evil, it conferred also the passionate and eager and hungry disposition to do evil. Prone as sparks to fly upward; in other words, prone as water to run downhill—a powerful figure, and means that man's disposition is wholly evil, uncompromisingly evil, inveterately evil, and that he is as undisposed to do good as water is undisposed to run up hill. Ah, my father's error brought a colossal disaster upon the men of this planet. It poisoned the men of this planet—poisoned them in mind and body. I see it, plainly."

"It brought death, too."

"Yes—whatever that may be. I do not quite understand it. It seems to be a sleep. You do not seem to mind sleep. By my reading, I gather that you are not conscious of either death or sleep; that nevertheless you fear the one and do not fear the other. It is very stupid. Illogical."

Hotchkiss put down his knife and fork and explained the difference between sleep and death; and how a person was not sorry when asleep, but sorry when dead, because... because... He found it was not so easy to explain why as he had supposed it was going to be; he floundered a while, then broke down. But presently he tried again, and said that death was only a sleep, but that the objection to it was that it was so long; then he remembered that time stands still when one sleeps, and so the difference between a night and a thousand years is really no difference at all so far as the sleeper is personally affected.

However, the boy was thinking, profoundly, and heard none of it; so nothing was lost. By and by the boy said, earnestly: "The fundamental change wrought in man's nature by my father's conduct must remain—it is permanent; but a part of its burden of evil consequences can be lifted from your race, and I will undertake it. Will you help?"

He was applying in the right quarter. Lifting burdens from a whole race was a fine and large enterprise, and suited Oliver Hotchkiss's size and gifts better than any contract he had ever taken hold of yet. He gave in his adhesion with promptness and enthusiasm, and wanted the scheme charted out at once. Privately, he was immeasurably proud to be connected in business with an actual angel and son of a devil, but did what he could to keep his exultation from showing.

The boy said, "I cannot map out a definite plan yet; I must first study this race. Its poisoned condition and prominent disposition to do evil differentiate it radically from any men whom I have known before, therefore it is a new race to me and must be exhaustively studied before I shall know where and how to begin. Indefinitely speaking, our plan will be confined to ameliorating the condition of the race in some ways in this life; we are not called upon to concern ourselves with its future fate; that is in abler hands than ours."

"I hope you will begin your studies right away."

"I shall. Go to bed, and take your rest. During the rest of the night and tomorrow, I will travel about the globe and personally examine some of the nationalities, and learn languages and read the world's books in the several tongues, and tomorrow night we will talk together here. Meantime the storm has made you a prisoner. Will you have one of my servants to wait on you?"

A genuine little devil all for his own! It was a lovely idea, and swelled Hotchkiss's vanity to the bursting point. He was lavish with his thanks.

"But he won't understand what I say to him."

"He will learn in five minutes. Would you like any particular one?"

"If I could have the cunning little rascal that sat down in the fire after he got cooled off..."

There was a flash of scarlet, and the little fiend was present and smiling; and he had with him some books from the school; among them the French-English dictionary and the phonographic shorthand system.

"There. Use him night and day. He knows what he is here for. If he needs help, he will provide it. He requires no lights; take them, and go to bed; leave him to study his books. In five minutes, he will be able to talk broken English in case you want him. He will read twelve or fifteen of your books in an hour and learn shorthand besides; then he will be a capable secretary. He will be visible or invisible according to your orders. Give him a name—he has one already, and so have I, but you would not be able to pronounce either of them. Goodbye."

He vanished.

Hotchkiss stood smiling all sorts of pleasant smiles of intricate and variegated pattern at his little devil, with the idea of making him understand how welcome he was; and he said to himself, "It's a bitter climate for him, poor little rascal, the fire will go down, and he will freeze; I wish I knew how to tell him to run home and warm himself whenever he wants to."

He brought blankets and made signs to him that these were for him to wrap up in; then he began to pile wood on the fire, but the red stranger took that work promptly off his hands, and did the work like an expert—which he was. Then he sat down on the fire and began to study his book, and his new master took the candle and went away to bed, meditating a name for him. "He is a dear little devil," he said, "and must have a nice one." So he named him Edward Nicholson Hotchkiss—after a brother that was dead.

*Twain wrote "Schoolhouse Hill" set in the universe of Tom Sawyer and Huck Finn, in 1898, but he didn't finish the story. It's part of a collection that includes the "The Mysterious Stranger," another unfinished story that appears early in this volume. What follows is the editor's speculation of how the story might have ended, from the perspective of a new character, Damian Hotchkiss.*

**I, Damian Hotchkiss**, came upon this manuscript in a box that had been left in the attic of my uncle's home, the occasion being that the new owner had invited me to visit and collect his belongings, being his nearest living relative.

This was a sad condition for me, as it had come about only in consequence of his daughter having taken her own life, and his wife predeceasing him in the same manner.

The box had been left open in the center of the attic, making clear that the new master of the house had wished my attention drawn there. Inside, I found not only the manuscript, but a copy of my uncle's will, deeding the home to his brother.

I found this peculiar, to say the least, as his brother had died some years before my uncle departed this world. He clearly could not have been inheritor of the Hotchkiss estate, and it was not he who now possessed it, but a mysterious stranger with a detached yet undeniable charm and a prodigious vocabulary.

But I am getting ahead of myself somewhat in describing him...

When I discovered these documents, I went downstairs again and found this man who had inherited my uncle's home—somewhat to my chagrin, I might add, being his only living relative—and inquired, a little brusquely, what he knew about it.

"Why did you leave these papers for me to discover?" I demanded.

"I thought you might like to have them," said he.

"I might have liked to have my uncle's estate," I muttered, thinking he had not heard me, then felt ashamed when I realized he had—notwithstanding that my murmuring was true.

"That will be arranged," he said, smiling.

It was then that I noticed how young the man before me appeared. He appeared no more than a teen-aged boy, yet he spoke in such a way as to give the impression that he was much older, and indeed, a man of the world. His visage was uncommonly beautiful, and his courteous demeanor disarmed me, draining me of my former irritation.

"Thank you...," I began, but he interrupted.

"As soon as I finish Mr. Twan's story, which you discovered in the attic, as I feel obliged to do so."

I started to say it was not necessary, but he held a hand up to forestall me, and it was apparent he recognized the curiosity I had sought to conceal.

"You see," he said, "I had an appointment with your uncle that I failed to keep, on which occasion I had promised to reveal the answer to a question we had both been trying to ascertain."

"What question?"

"The reason my father partook of the tree of knowledge in the Garden. I failed to discover it on my journey, but I did so on my return."

I searched his expression for some hint that he was having a laugh at my expense, but he was not laughing and seemed sober and quite resolute—though I could not fathom why.

"We are all sons of Adam," I said, "and in Adam did we sin."

A rueful smile spread across his face. "My father's transgression occurred after my birth, so he did not—indeed could not—pass it down to me. He resented me for this, as I resented him for the transgression itself, and we have been estranged ever since."

His words made no sense to me. I had heard a legend once that Adam had lain with another wife, named Lilith, before the creation of Eve from his now-missing rib.

"I am not a son of Adam," he said flatly, having somehow read my thoughts. "Or Lilitu." He employed the name used by the Sumerians, who had imagined her a goddess—or a night demon. I knew this from a course in Myths of the World at university, and was impressed that the man who stood before me knew it as well. I was also, I must admit, a tad chagrined, for I considered this piece of knowledge (and others) proprietary—at least in regard to those who lacked the privilege of a higher education. I was duly impressed, and chastened myself for my arrogance.

Freeing my tongue, I asked him, "Then who...?" But I left the question unfinished, as a sudden foreboding had washed over me concerning the answer.

He replied nonetheless: "My father is Satan."

I took a step backward, then another, barely catching myself as I stumbled over the chair in front of my uncle's old rolltop desk. I was standing in the presence of the Antichrist! But no, he couldn't be. He was surely mocking me.

"No," he said flatly, "you mistake me for another. I hate my father and do not serve him. I serve my own interests."

"Which are..."

"To finish Mr. Twain's account, as I said. He set it aside, unfinished, when I failed to return because, as I was no longer in contact with Mr. Hotchkiss, there was no conclusion for him to write. I fear I am to blame for this. I tarried too long in my investigation, though I abandoned it in a few short moments when I realized the need to return in haste. Yet I failed to consider that, for me, a thousand years is as a day to you mortals, so when I returned, I found your uncle newly lain to rest.

"I see." I did not bother to hide the skepticism in my tone. Doubting God might be a sin, but doubting the son of Satan (or that he *was* the son of Satan) was a different matter entirely

"If you are so knowledgeable," I said, "can you explain why my uncle left this house to his deceased brother, and how you came to be in possession of it?"

"Of course I can," he said matter-of-factly, "and I am happy to do so. It is, of course, quite absurd that a dying man should leave his estate to one already dead."

Far less absurd, I thought, than claiming to be the son of Satan.

I could tell he had read my thoughts again—which gave me pause in dismissing the absurdity of his claim—but, sensing that I was now doubting my own doubt, he let the matter rest.

"In fact," he continued, "he willed his estate to your brother's namesake, a devil I left in his service during my absence."

Now the absurd had crossed over into the outlandish.

"After your uncle passed, the devil Edward returned to me and revealed what had transpired in my absence."

Just when I thought he was about to pass that information on to me, he suddenly digressed: "You are, of course, aware that your uncle was a slaveholder."

I nodded, then said defensively: "But he was a good man. He freed his servants well before he died, out of a kindness to the."

"Yes, your uncle was a good man, but he also had within him the seed of Adam's sin. He did not free his servants out of kindness, but because he no longer had need of them. My devil Edward, whom I had left in his charge, had taken over every one of their duties—and more besides. He exceeded the slaves, Jeff and Rachel, in both efficiency and thoroughness, and your uncle came to depend upon him for all things, even demanding that Edward spoon-feed him every meal.

"Your aunt despaired when she came to realize that her husband would not now become a Presbyterian, as she had always hoped, but had set his course with Edward as his compass. But more than this, she became convinced—and rightly so—that Edward had displaced her in your uncle's affections; indeed, consumed his thoughts so fully that he treated poor Hannah as no more than a ghost in her own household, and so, she chose to become one."

I told him then: "I do not believe in ghosts."

To which he asserted: "Nor do I. It was a figure of speech, a euphemism to spare you knowing the unseemly manner of her death."

I did not ask, inquiring instead: "Is that also why my cousin, Annie Fleming, took her life?"

His expression changed ever so slightly, and I thought I beheld there a hint of sadness or regret. It was there in a flash, then gone again. Or had I merely imagined it?

"No," he answered, "but I am the cause of her death as well. She had taken a great liking to me, and was despondent when I vanished and did not return. She confided in Edward that she could not live without me, and that my long absence was her undoing."

I ventured to ask, "Did you share her feelings?"

But he gave no answer, and his face was inscrutable.

It was apparent to me that he would not be forthcoming in this matter, so I steered the discussion away from Annie—and back to the mystery he had sought to resolve earlier concerning his father and the fruit of Eden. "You mentioned that that you were unable to discover, in your travels, the reason for your father's treachery, but that you did so on your return."

He nodded and said, "Quite so. The answer lay in your uncle's response to Edward. My father had witnessed this in Adam and his progeny after they partook of the forbidden fruit.

Once they had done so, they were able to make servants of other men, just as your uncle did of Edward, such that these newly enslaved souls would do their masters' bidding in whatever was asked of them. My father coveted this power and tasted of the fruit himself in order to acquire it."

I stood there staring at him, aghast. "Are you saying it was man who corrupted your father and not the other way around?"

He spread his arms wide. "I suppose you could say that," he answered. "It is something of a chicken-and-the-egg situation. There is enough blame to go around. But the irony is that my father became dependent upon the servile attentions of man (offered, I may add, in the guise of service to God), and in doing so became a slave himself—just as your uncle became entirely dependent upon, and therefore enslaved to, my devil, Edward."

I threw up my hands, then pointed at him in accusation: "This IS all your fault, then!" I shouted. "You have not escaped your father's sin at all!"

"You are right," he said simply. "Sin can be learned as well as inherited. I sought to separate myself from my father, but I did so an instant too late, for I am an exceedingly fast learner, which in this case was to my detriment. It is for this reason that I now choose to depart this world, that I may do no more damage, unintended though it may be. I only wished to conclude Mr. Twain's account in deference to his spirit, for he understood these things more fully than any mortal I have encountered.

"You will find the deed to your uncle's estate on the kitchen table, made out to you with my endorsement. Edward was good enough to serve as my witness ."

I stared at him, and as I did so, he began to shimmer, like a mirage in the distance.

"Wait," I said to forestall him. "You never did tell me your name."

"Forty-four," he said in a distant echo.

I meant to ask him the meaning of it, but I was too slow, for he was gone.

*"But who prays for Satan? Who in eighteen centuries, has had the common humanity to pray for the one sinner that needed it most, our one fellow and brother who most needed a friend yet had not a single one, the one sinner among us all who had the highest and clearest right to every Christian's daily and nightly prayers, for the plain and unassailable reason that his was the first and greatest need, he being among sinners the supremest?"*

Quoted in Autobiography with Letters by William L. Phelps

*"Life would be infinitely happier if we could only be born at the age of eighty and gradually approach eighteen."*

Quoted in Autobiography with Letters by William L. Phelps

# To the Above Old People

*Sleep! for the Sun that scores another Day*
*Against the Tale allotted You to stay,*
*Reminding You, is Risen, and now*
*Serves Notice—ah, ignore it while You stay!*

    *The chill Wind blew, and those who stood before*
    *The Tavern murmured, "Having drunk his Score,*
    *Why tarries He with empty Cup? Behold,*
    *The Wine of Youth once poured, is poured no more*

*"Come, leave the Cup, and on the Winter's Snow*
*Your Summer Garment of Enjoyment throw:*
*Your Tide of Life is ebbing fast, and it,*
*Exhausted once, for You no more shall flow."*

    *While yet the Phantom of false Youth was mine,*
    *I heard a Voice from out the Darkness whine,*
    *"O Youth, O whither gone? Return,*
    *And bathe my Age in thy reviving Wine."*

*In this subduing Draught of tender green*
*And kindly Absinth, with its wimpling Sheen*
*Of dusky half-lights, let me drown*
*The haunting Pathos of the Might-Have-Been.*

    *For every nickeled Joy, marred and brief,*
    *We pay some day its Weight in golden Grief*

*Mined from our Hearts. Ah, murmur not—*
*From this one-sided Bargain dream of no Relief!*

*The Joy of Life, that streaming through their Veins*
*Tumultuous swept, falls slack—and wanes*
*The Glory in the Eye—and one by one*
*Life's Pleasures perish and make place for Pains.*

*Whether one hide in some secluded Nook—*
*Whether at Liverpool or Sandy Hook—*
*'Tis one. Old Age will search him out—and He—*
*He—He—when ready will know where to look.*

*From Cradle unto Grave I keep a House*
*Of Entertainment where may drowse*
*Bacilli and kindred Germs—or feed—or breed*
*Their festering Species in a deep Carouse.*

*Think—in this battered Caravanserai,*
*Whose Portals open stand all Night and Day,*
*How Microbe after Microbe with his Pomp*
*Arrives unasked, and comes to stay.*

*Our ivory Teeth, confessing to the Lust*
*Of masticating, once, now own Disgust*
*Of Clay-Plug'd Cavities—full soon our Snags*
*Are emptied, and our Mouths are filled with Dust.*

*Our Gums forsake the Teeth and tender grow,*
*And fat, like over-riped Figs—we know*
*The Sign—the Riggs' Disease is ours, and we*

# DARK TWAIN

*Must list this Sorrow, add another Woe;*

*Our Lungs begin to fail and soon we Cough,*
*And chilly Streaks play up our Backs, and off*
*Our fever'd Foreheads drips an icy Sweat—*
*We scoffered before, but now we may not scoff.*

>    *Some for the Bunions that afflict us prate*
>    *Of Plasters unsurpassable, and hate*
>    *To Cut a corn—ah cut, and let the Plaster go,*
>    *Nor murmur if the Solace come too late.*

*Some for the Honours of Old Age, and some*
*Long for its Respite from the Hum*
*And Clash of sordid Strife—O Fools,*
*The Past should teach them what's to Come:*

>    *Lo, for the Honours, cold Neglect instead!*
>    *For Respite, disputatious Heirs a Bed*
>    *Of Thorns for them will furnish. Go,*
>    *Seek not Here for Peace—but Yonder—with the*
>    *Dead.*

*For whether Zal and Rustam heed this Sign,*
*And even smitten thus, will not repine,*
*Let Zal and Rustam shuffle as they may,*
*The Fine once levied they must Cash the Fine.*

>    *O Voices of the Long Ago that were so dear!*
>    *Fall'n Silent, now, for many a Mould'ring Year,*
>    *O whither are ye flown? Come back,*

*And break my heart, but bless my grieving ear.*

*Some happy Day my Voice will Silent fall,*
*And answer not when some that love it call:*
*Be glad for Me when this you note—and think*
*I've found the Voices lost, beyond the Pall.*

>*So let me grateful drain the Magic Bowl*
>*That medicines hurt Minds and on the Soul*
>*The Healing of its Peace doth lay—if then*
>*Death claim me—Welcome be his Dole!*

*SANNA, SWEDEN, September 15th.*

*Private—If you don't know what Riggs's Disease of the Teeth is, the dentist will tell you. I've had it—and it is more than interesting.*

*Mark Twain wrote "To the Above Old People" in 1899, and it was published in* McClure's Magazine *the following year.*

# *About the Editors*

**Stephen H. Provost** is a former reporter and columnist with more than 30 years of experience at daily newspapers. Over the past 11 years, he has written or co-authored more than 60 books. In addition to six novels and three novellas, he has produced an extensive collection of nonfiction works on topics ranging from Nevada's pioneer days to the history of retail in the United States. He has written more than 20 books on U.S. history in the 20th century focusing on highways, towns, and culture. Stephen is the founder and publisher of Dragon Crown Books. He lives in Carson City.

**Sharon Marie Provost** is an award-winning author who specializes in horror, thrillers, and speculative fiction. Beginning her career in late 2023, she has published a novella, two short story collections, and two collaborative collections of short stories with her husband. Her first novel, *Dark Arts: Love*

*Me Tinder*, was published in 2024. It has received acclaim for its detailed and chilling story of a serial killer who turns his victims into works of art. In 2025, her *Shadow's Gate* received the Imadjinn Award for Best Short Story Collection, and she published two collaborative novels with Stephen H. Provost: *Azrael's Assassin: Testament in Blood* and *Evermore: Dark Soulmates*. Sharon is the chief operating officer of Dragon Crown Books. She has lived in Carson City since 1987.

# Did you enjoy this book?

Recommend it to a friend. And please consider **rating it and/or leaving a brief review** at Amazon, Barnes & Noble, and Goodreads.

# *Books by*
# *Stephen H. Provost*

## Fiction

Evermore (with Sharon Marie Provost)

Azrael's Assassin (with Sharon Marie Provost)

The Memortality Saga
- Memortality
- Paralucidity

Meteor Ridge

Academy of the Lost Labyrinth
- The Talismans of Time
- Pathfinder of Destiny

The Only Dragon

Identity Break

Identity Forge

Crimson Scourge

Nightmare's Eve

Nevada Nightmare's Eve (with Sharon Marie Provost)

Christmas Nightmare's Eve (with Sharon Marie Provost)

All Hallows' Nightmare's Eve
(with Sharon Marie Provost)

Shades of Love, Vol. 1

Need

Death's Doorstep

Feathercap

Madeline the Redheaded Witch
- The Reluctant Little Witch
- Madeline's Dragon Quest

The Adventures of Mark Twain in Nevada

Waffles the Poodle Dragon

Nevada Nightmares, Vol. 1 (contributor, editor)

Nevada Nightmares, Vol. 2 (contributor, editor)

*The ACES Anthology 2023 (contributor, editor)*
*The ACES Anthology 2025 (contributor, editor)*

# Nonfiction
*Mark Twain's Nevada*
*The Comstock Chronicles*
*Virginia City Then & Now*
*The Legend of Molly Bolin*
*A Whole Different League*
*California's Historic Highways series*
> *Highway 99*
> *Highway 101*

*America's Historic Highways series*
> *America's First Highways*
> *Yesterday's Highways*
> *Highways of the South*

*Highways of the West series*
> *America's Loneliest Road*
> *Victory Road*
> *The Lincoln Highway in California*
> > *(with Gary Kinst)*
> *Sierra Highway*
> *Bonanza Highway*

*Roadside Illustrated series*
> *Happy Motoring!*
> *Signpost Up Ahead: The East*
> *Signpost Up Ahead: The West*

*The Great American Shopping Experience*
*What I Tell My Friends, Vol. 1 (with Lief Sorbye)*
*Fresno Growing Up, 2024*
*Martinsville Memories*
*The Century Cities series*
> *Cambria Century, Carson City Century*
> *Charleston Century, Danville Century*

# DARK TWAIN

*Fresno Century, Goldfield Century*
*Greensboro Century, Huntington Century*
*Roanoke Century, San Luis Obispo Century*
*The Phoenix Chronicles*
*The Osiris Testament*
*The Way of the Phoenix*
*The Gospel of the Phoenix*
*The Phoenix Principle*
*Forged in Ancient Fires*
*Messiah in the Making*
*Please Stop Saying That!*
*50 Undefeated*

# *Praise for Other Works*

"Stephen has taken a subject that has been well-covered over the years—the famous Nevada silver mining town of Virginia City—and crafted something fresh and easy-to-digest. With his knack for clever wording and journalistic eye for detail (he is a former newspaper editor/reporter), Provost provides readers with an informative but not dry book about the one-time "Richest Place on Earth's" most colorful characters and important events.

— Richard Moreno, award-winning author, historian, and journalist on **The Comstock Chronicles**

"When I saw the title, I got excited—thinking it was another Mark Twain book. I'm a huge fan of Samuel Clemens! But what really surprised me was how easily I got pulled into the story. Stephen's writing is so engaging—it felt like I was right there with him, discovering things I hadn't read in other Twain books.
His storytelling is vivid and full of detail, and it's clear he puts a lot of effort into his research. Living in Nevada, I recognized many of the places Twain visited, and now I want to go back and see them again with fresh eyes. Stephen has a gift for capturing the heart of a story and sharing pieces of history that others often miss."

— Jeadene Solberg, cofounder of Northern Nevada Ghost Hunters, on **Mark Twain's Nevada**

This entertaining book is an easy read. Each Nevada town with which Samuel Clemens had interaction or visited is briefly described, along with historic photographs, some modern ones, and brief notes about its fate. Included are directions for those wishing to visit these towns, many now ghost towns or entirely vanished.

Jim Collett, Goodreads reader, on **Mark Twain's Nevada**

"Stephen and Sharon Provost did an incredible job preserving this piece of history. Thanks to their research and storytelling, this place won't be forgotten. A hundred years from now, people will still be able to read about it—and that's something special."
— Jeadene Solberg on **Chinese Camp**

"Sharon and Stephen will pull you into this page-turner from the very beginning. **Evermore** will take you down the dark side of soulmates and the desires that exist from one life to the next. Each time making them more mad, desperate to get it right or move on again to the next life to try it all over again. Will they finally find love and conquer it, or will they die trying? Read the book. You won't be disappointed.
— Maureen, Amazon reader

"The complex idea of mixing morality and mortality is a fresh twist on the human condition. ... **Memortality** is one of those books that will incite more questions than it answers. And for fandom, that's a good thing."
— Ricky L. Brown, Amazing Stories

"Punchy and fast paced, **Memortality** reads like a graphic novel. ... (Stephen H. Provost's) style makes the trippy landscapes and mind-bending plot points more believable and adds a thrilling edge to this vivid crossover fantasy."
— Foreword Reviews

"From time travel to karma earned, these short love stories range from thought-provoking to heartbreaking."
— Blue Bookwyrm Reviewer
on **Shades of Love, Vol. 1**

"The genres in this volume span horror, fantasy, and science-fiction, and each is handled deftly. ... **Nightmare's Eve** should be on your reading list. The stories are at the intersection of nightmare and lucid dreaming, up ahead a signpost ... next stop, your reading pile. Keep the nightlight on."

— R.B. Payne, Cemetery Dance

"The story feels so close, so intimate, we as readers experience the emotions, the events, and the conflicts, in what feels like real time. Gut-wrenchingly so."

— Stephen Mark Rainey, author of *Blue Devil Island*,
on **Death's Doorstep**

"Among the greatest what-ifs ever conceived—the power to bring back loved ones! This story defies genres by taking that question to its next level. You really can't put this book down.

— Ruth Goyne, former wire desk editor at *The Tennessean*
on **Memortality**

"**Memortality** is a terrific science fiction thriller that imprints on your mind like an unforgettable snapshot."

— John Palisano, award-winning author of *Nerves*
and past president of the Horror Writers Association

"**Memortality** takes a concept we've all dreamed of and turns it into our worst nightmare."

— Michael Knost, Bram Stoker award-winning author

"Provost sticks mostly to the classics: vampires, ghosts, aliens, and even dragons. But trekking familiar terrain allows the author to subvert readers' expectations. ... Provost's poetry skillfully displays the same somber themes as the stories. ... Worthy tales that prove external forces are no more terrifying than what's inside people's heads."

— Kirkus Reviews on **Nightmare's Eve**

"Stephen H. Provost has nightmares to sell. But be wary, this is no ordinary merchant of dark dreams. These are tales and poems of every sort from a writer to watch."

— Mark Onspaugh, author of *The Faceless One* and *Deadeye Jack*, on **Nightmare's Eve**